Lost Pleasures Found

To: Charlene & Sammy,
Happy reading!
Nikki ...

Lost Pleasures Found

Vikki Vaught

Copyright © 2011 by Vikki Vaught.

Library of Congress Control Number:		2010919174
ISBN:	Hardcover	978-1-4568-4086-0
	Softcover	978-1-4568-4085-3
	Ebook	978-1-4568-4087-7

All rights reserved. No part of this book may be reproduced or transmitted in any form or by any means, electronic or mechanical, including photocopying, recording, or by any information storage and retrieval system, without permission in writing from the copyright owner.

This is a work of fiction. Names, characters, places and incidents either are the product of the author's imagination or are used fictitiously, and any resemblance to any actual persons, living or dead, events, or locales is entirely coincidental.

This book was printed in the United States of America.

To order additional copies of this book, contact:
Xlibris Corporation
1-888-795-4274
www.Xlibris.com
Orders@Xlibris.com
90337

CHAPTER 1

Late July 1814

AS MELODY GLANCED around the ballroom and observed all the couples dancing, she realized that going to one ball, soiree, or garden party after another exhausted her. She felt relieved that the season was drawing to a close. She was grateful to her aunt for inviting her to visit, and she had met many lovely people, but she missed her parents desperately. As Melody smoothed down the skirt of her shimmering pale yellow evening gown, at one of the last balls of the season, she felt exasperated by the stifling heat. She slipped out of the ballroom and went out onto the terrace to cool off. She breathed a sigh of relief as she felt the cool summer breeze blowing across the terrace. Her beautiful sherry-colored eyes landed on a myriad of gorgeous flowers in full bloom. She glanced up at the sky and noticed how brightly the stars shone that night. A noise from behind startled her, and she turned around to see the most beautiful man she had ever seen, akin to Adonis. She did not usually think of men as beautiful, but this man was absolutely gorgeous. He was quite tall, at least six feet, with very broad shoulders, and unlike most of the men she had met so far, he did not need to pad his dress coat. As she allowed her eyes to roam further, she noticed that he had a trim waistline and slim hips. He reached up and adjusted his intricately tied cravat, which had a diamond stickpin in the folds. Melody lowered her flushed cheeks in embarrassment, realizing that she had been staring at this tall, muscular man in front of her, and she did not want him to think that she was too forward. As he approached her, he straightened his deep blue superfine dress coat and gazed directly into her eyes.

"Who are you? Why have I never seen you before?" He ran his fingers through his thick red gold hair, which just brushed his collar as he continued, "I know that I shouldn't be talking to you, but you look so lovely standing here against this glorious night. You take my breath away." He shifted, and his embroidered blue waistcoat glimmered in the moonlight. "I'm Henry Montgomery, by the way, and may I ask your name?"

Melody lifted her gaze, met his startling blue eyes, and answered, "My name is Melody Canterfield-Smyth, but we haven't been formally introduced, so I shouldn't be talking to you. I need to return to the ballroom now, before my aunt realizes I'm missing. Excuse me, sir." Melody stepped around him with haste and returned to the ballroom. As she entered, she immediately felt the heat of hundreds of beeswax candles in the crystal chandeliers. Between the scent of all the candles and the heavily perfumed guests, it almost stifled her.

Henry followed her with his eyes and could not imagine that anyone could be so lovely. As she hurried through the crowd, she tucked a lock of her beautiful honey blonde hair back into the curls that cascaded down her shoulders in ringlets. He noticed how her pale iridescent skin glowed in the candlelight. As he watched, he realized that her figure was just slightly plump, but in all the right places, just the type of woman that had always attracted him. As she moved through the crowd, he saw that she was very petite, probably not more than five feet tall. She had such an air of innocence about her that it made him feel protective of her, and he would not want to do anything to damage her reputation. This was someone he definitely wanted to get to know better, so he decided to find someone who could formally introduce them. He lost sight of her as she disappeared into the crowd.

As Henry scanned the room, looking for her, he found her standing with Lady Walton and walked over so she could handle the introduction for him. He said, "Lady Walton, so good to see you tonight. Thank you for inviting me to your ball. I hope I find you in good health. Could I ask you to introduce me to your lovely companion?"

"I'm pleased you could attend this evening, my lord. I am indeed in very good health. Thank you for asking. I would be happy to introduce you. Lord Montgomery, this is Miss Melody Canterfield-Smyth from Lincolnshire. Her father is Vicar Canterfield-Smyth of Little Smythington parish. Melody, this is Lord Henry Montgomery. He is one of the Duke of Sanderford's sons," Lady Walton explained.

Melody curtsied, briefly glanced up at him and said, "It's a pleasure to meet you, my lord."

He gazed at Melody and smiled as he said, "I would be honored if you would dance with me. Is this one open?" The thought of holding her in his arms, as they waltzed, excited him. He certainly hoped she would say yes.

Melody met his gaze and said, "It just so happens that this dance is available, and it would be my pleasure to dance with you."

Henry took Melody's hand, and he immediately felt a connection to her, stronger than he had ever felt before. He walked her onto the dance floor, and they took their places. She placed her hand on his shoulder, and he put his arm around her waist as the orchestra started the early strains of the waltz. It was as if they were meant to be together as they floated across the floor. They gazed into each other's eyes, and everyone else on the dance floor disappeared because he had eyes only for her. Henry realized he was staring at Melody, and he cleared his throat as he huskily said, "You're as lovely in candlelight as you were in the moonlight. I'm glad you were free for this dance, and may I say, you dance divinely. Miss Canterfield-Smyth, I have recently returned from the war on the continent, and I'm on an extended leave from my regiment, the Second Rifle Brigade. It's too bad that the season is almost over, because I would certainly like to get to know you better. Would you be free tomorrow afternoon? I'd like to take you for a drive in my curricle."

Melody looked up at him and replied, "I'd be delighted to go for a drive with you. If you would like, you could pick me up tomorrow at four o'clock. Do you know my aunt, Lady Helton? She lives on Upper Brook Street."

"I've not had the pleasure of meeting Lady Helton, but I know where she lives and four o'clock would be perfect." When the dance ended, Henry escorted her over to Lady Walton, who was standing with another woman of middle years. Melody whispered to Henry that he would need to meet her aunt, so he could ask her permission for the drive.

As they stopped in front of the woman, Melody said, "Hello, Aunt Miriam. I would like to introduce you to Lord Montgomery. He has asked me to go driving with him tomorrow."

Lady Helton beamed as she replied, "It's a pleasure to meet you, my lord. I've met your parents on several occasions through the years. I'm sure that my niece will be in good hands on your drive tomorrow."

They stood there chatting for a while, and then Henry turned to Melody and bowed as he said, "Thank you for the dance, Miss Canterfield-Smyth, and I look forward to our drive tomorrow afternoon. If you'll excuse me, I'm due to meet some friends of mine in the card room. I shall take my leave now."

Melody watched as Henry moved through the crowd and left the ballroom. She could not get over how handsome he was. She felt an odd flutter in her stomach, something she had never experienced before.

Aunt Miriam excitedly turned to Melody and said, "I do believe you have caught his eye. He is very acceptable and appears to be very interested in you, dear. It would be wonderful if you have truly caught his eye. This would be an excellent match for you."

With an exasperated expression on her sweet face, Melody said, "It's too soon to be speaking of a match, since we have only just met, Aunt Miriam. Do you think we could leave? I'm ready to go back to your house, if that is all right with you?"

"Of course, darling, I'm ready to leave also. Just let me have my coach brought around while you go get your wrap." Melody made her way through the crowd and left the ballroom. Miriam turned to Lady Walton and asked, "How did they meet? Do you know?"

Lady Walton smiled, nodded her head, and replied, "Lord Montgomery asked me to introduce them, and since I knew you would approve, I did."

"This is a very interesting turn of events. Well, I had better hurry so we can leave. I need to get my dear girl home so she can dream of her new beau!" Aunt Miriam laughed. "Good night, Lady Walton, I'll see you tomorrow for tea, as usual."

Melody was very quiet on their way back home. Aunt Miriam asked, "You seem distracted. Is it because you are so excited over meeting Lord Montgomery? He is such an attractive young man."

Melody sighed and shifted in her seat as she said, "I wish you would not keep on about this. As I mentioned earlier, it's too soon to be talking about a match, because we've only just met. I know that you want me to meet someone and fall in love, but I believe that it takes time to form an attachment."

Miriam smiled with a knowing look as she replied, "I just want you to be happy, and there does seem to be an instant attraction between the two of you. This would be wonderful, because even though Lord Montgomery is a second son, he is still in line for the title. Just think! You could actually end up a duchess. Even if that does not happen, it would still be a very good match for you and in your first season. Oh, Melody, your parents will be so pleased."

Melody hated to see her aunt get so excited over her meeting Lord Montgomery, but she knew it would not do any good to tell her to stop dreaming about it. Aunt Miriam did this every time an attractive gentleman showed an interest in her. For the first time . . . Melody was interested. She hoped that her aunt was right about Lord Montgomery, but she would never tell her that, because then her aunt would really start dreaming of wedding bells.

The coach pulled up to their house, and the footman came down the steps and helped them out of the carriage. As they were entering the house, Melody turned to her aunt and said, "I think I'll retire for the night. I'll see you in the morning."

Aunt Miriam patted her on the arm as she said, "Good night, my sweet girl. Pleasant dreams!"

Melody climbed the stairs and made her way to her bedchamber. Millie was waiting in her room, and soon, she was in her night rail and ready for bed. She thanked Millie and sent her off. As she lay there, she started thinking about the evening. Her mind went back to her meeting with Lord Montgomery. *He was such an attractive man.* While they were dancing, she felt shivers run up and down her arms as he held her for their dance. She wondered what it would be like to have someone like him love her. *Could this be the one for her?* She had never felt so attracted to anyone as she was to Lord Montgomery. *Well, it was too soon to be thinking about love. After all, she had just met him tonight.* Soon, Melody drifted off to sleep as she dreamed of seeing Lord Montgomery the next afternoon.

The next morning, she woke up feeling refreshed and slightly giddy over the thought of seeing Lord Montgomery that afternoon. She wondered if he had thought of her, as she had been thinking of him. But Melody was very practical, so she told herself to not be so silly. This probably was just a passing fancy, and soon she would forget all about him. Besides, she had quite a few things planned for the day. She was not going to woolgather all day like some silly young girl. After all, even though this was her first season, she was twenty. She was a woman with more important things to do than daydream about someone who would probably move on to someone else anyway. Just because he was so interested last night, did not mean that he would continue to be interested.

Melody got up and went about her morning ablutions. She picked out her new day dress, which was made of white linen with a pink sash just below the bodice and a matching pink flounce at the hem. Millie helped her dress, did her hair, and soon she was ready to start her day. She was due at St. Mark's Orphanage that morning at eleven o'clock, and she looked forward to playing with all the sweet little children. She was so pleased that she found the orphanage to devote her time to, since it was such a worthwhile cause. Melody also needed to go to the bookseller to see if that new Minerva Press novel had arrived yet. She was an avid reader, and it was one of her most favorite past times. Once she started reading a good book, she would get so wrapped up in the story that she found it hard to put down.

Melody went down to the breakfast room and selected her usual toast and cherry preserves, with a nice cup of hot chocolate. She looked longingly at all the wonderful pastries, but she knew that she needed to forgo them since she was trying to slim down a bit. She felt she was a little too plump and wanted to look more like the other slender girls she had met since coming to London. So as much as she would have enjoyed the pastries, she passed them up. Melody thought again about meeting Lord Montgomery. She wondered if he liked the typical tall, slender, pale blondes that were so in fashion. If so, he could not be serious about her. After all, she was none of those things; she was very short, barely five feet tall and too round to be in fashion. *She needed to quit thinking about him. This was just wasting valuable time, but oh, he had been so handsome!* Of course, being handsome was not everything. Personality was just as important, if not more so, because good looks would fade over time.

Miriam entered the breakfast room, and as she filled her plate, she turned to Melody and asked, "Are you going to the orphanage again today? I really think you are spending too much of your time there, Melody. By the way, don't forget to go to the dressmaker to pick up your new riding habit. It should be ready today."

"Oh, goodness, Aunt Miriam, I forgot all about that. What time do I need to be there?" she asked.

"You should to be there by one o'clock and don't be late, because you'll need to be home in plenty of time to get ready for your drive with Lord Montgomery. You need to be sure you make a good impression on him this afternoon. I'm so pleased that he has shown an interest in you. He is considered to be a very well-thought-of young man," Aunt Miriam said. "He was in the army, you know, during the war with France. I'm so glad that war is finally over, and that awful Bonaparte is safely locked away on the island of Elba. It's incredibly sad that so many of our fine young men were lost in that terrible war. I just hate to see all those other young men who came back wounded, with missing limbs and eyes and such. It's just terrible. Oh, I hate war! I know you were devastated about losing your dear cousin Herbert last year, but at least we have finally defeated that nasty Bonaparte! I wonder what Lord Montgomery is going to do now that the war has ended?"

Melody smiled and said, "He mentioned this to me last night, as we were dancing. He said he was on an extended leave and would soon be going to his family in Surrey. After his leave is up, he'll be rejoining his regiment. He mentioned that he eventually plans to sell his commission, but he wants to help his men get settled back into civilian life, first. How do you know so much about Lord Montgomery?"

Melody's aunt looked knowingly at her and said, "Oh, I have my ways. I know all about his family. After all, they are very good ton. His father, the Duke of Sanderford is very prominent in the House of Lords, and their family goes back to William the Conqueror. But, of course, your family is very well respected, if not as prominent as his. Yes, indeed, this would be a very fine match for you, my girl!"

Melody stood up and turned to leave the breakfast room as she said, "Aunt, please don't get your hopes up. I'm sure that nothing will come of this. It's not as if I'm a great beauty, and I really am just a simple country girl. I don't want you to be disappointed. I'm certainly not going to get too excited about anything at this point."

A footman entered the breakfast room and politely said, "Excuse me, my lady, but there is a delivery for Miss Canterfield-Smyth."

Melody looked up in astonishment as her aunt asked, "What is it Charles? Do you know who the delivery is from?"

"It's a bouquet of yellow roses, and I believe that the livery belongs to the Duke of Sanderford, my lady. Where would you like me to put them?" asked the footman.

"Well, bring them in here, of course, so we can admire them, Charles!" Aunt Miriam said. "Oh, this is wonderful, Melody. I told you he was interested. This is so exciting. I just know this is going to be something wonderful for you."

Charles returned with the most beautiful bouquet that Melody had ever seen. With a dreamy expression on her face, as she gazed at the gorgeous flowers, she said, "Oh my, they are certainly lovely. I don't think I have ever seen such beautiful roses in my life, but I'm still not going to get my hopes up yet. Remember, I did just meet the man for the first time last night. I'm sure he does this all the time and it doesn't mean anything."

"Well, I still say it's a very good sign, and I, for one, am going to enjoy watching how this all comes about for you," she replied.

Melody said, "If I'm going to get to the orphanage in time, I need to leave right away. I'll see you this afternoon when I get back."

As Melody turned to leave the room, Aunt Miriam said, "Make sure that you take your maid with you and the footman also. Remember, you must be very careful to protect your reputation at all times. This isn't like the country where you had more freedom. You must be extremely cautious, and make sure that you don't give anyone any reason to think poorly of you."

"Yes, Aunt Miriam, I'll take them both with me, and I'll be very careful. I do know what is expected of me while in town." Melody left the breakfast room and returned to her room to get her pelisse. She then went back downstairs and left for the orphanage. It was such a fine morning she decided to walk. Soon, she was at St. Mark's; she saw her friend Susan Wilton and waved to her.

"Melody, I saw you dancing with a gorgeous man last night at Lady Walton's ball. How did you meet him? What is his name? I'm so envious!" Susan said.

Melody laughed, and replied, "His name is Lord Montgomery, and he's the second son of the Duke of Sanderford. Lady Walton introduced us last night, and then he asked me to dance, but I actually met him earlier on the terrace, before we had been formally introduced. He seems to be a very pleasant young man, and he has asked me to go driving with him this afternoon."

"Oh, Melody, how exciting! I would just die for the chance to meet someone like him. Do you think he has a friend for me?" she asked.

Melody sighed as she said, "Susan, you sound as bad as my aunt. She's already got us walking down the aisle to get married, and all because some attractive man asked me to dance and go for a drive. I'm sure that it won't amount to anything, so let's not talk about it anymore, all right?"

Susan and Melody went into the orphanage and started helping with the children. Soon she forgot all about Lord Montgomery and had a very pleasant morning playing with all the children. Before she realized it, the time had flown by, and it was time to leave. Melody and Susan hugged each other as they said good-bye, and they agreed to meet again in two days.

The bookseller was on the way to the dressmakers, so she stopped in to see if the new Minerva Press novel was in. She was delighted to find that they did have it in stock. Next, she went on to the dressmaker and picked up her new riding habit, which was deep emerald green with red piping on the sleeves and around the waist of the jacket. This was a very good color for her, because it brought out the green flecks in her eyes. Melody could hardly wait to wear it on her morning rides. She loved to ride, but she had never had much of an opportunity when she lived at home, so she was just beginning to become proficient. Lady Helton had a good stable of horses and encouraged her to ride as often as she wished. Melody had taken advantage of this and had gone riding several times during the season with some of her gentlemen callers. She noticed the time and knew that she needed to hurry, if she was going to have time to get ready for her drive with Lord Montgomery.

When she arrived back at Lady Helton's house, she hurried upstairs and changed. She picked out a sprigged muslin yellow gown, with white ribbons tied under her breasts. It was one of her favorite gowns, and she hoped Lord Montgomery would think she looked pretty in it. Millie fixed her hair, braiding a matching ribbon through it. As she was leaving her room, she glanced over at the beautiful yellow roses she had received from Lord Montgomery that morning. Again, she grew excited about seeing him. Would he look at her the same way he had looked at her last night, or would he realize she was too short and plump to be of interest to him. When Melody heard someone knocking on the front door, she thought that it must be him. The footman came to let her know that Lord Montgomery was there and that he was waiting for her in the drawing room.

Once she arrived downstairs, she stopped at the door to take a deep breath, hoping it would slow her heartbeat down. She did not want to appear too anxious, so she calmly opened the door and entered the room. Lord Montgomery was standing by the mantle and looked up as she entered. Their eyes met, and again, she felt that same sensation she had felt last night when she first saw him on the terrace. Lord Montgomery bowed to her as she curtsied and lowered her eyes.

Lord Montgomery asked, "Are you ready for our drive? I brought my new curricle, and I thought we could go to Hyde Park this afternoon, if that's agreeable with you?"

Melody looked over at Henry and said, "Good afternoon, Lord Montgomery, that sounds delightful. It's such a beautiful spring day, and for a change, there's not a cloud in the sky. I noticed that this morning on my walk."

Lord Montgomery turned to Lady Helton and said, "My lady, we'll leave for the park now. I'll return Miss Canterfield-Smyth within the hour."

Lord Montgomery offered Melody his arm, and they walked out to his curricle. He helped her up into the seat, and soon, they were off. The traffic was extremely heavy, and there were dozens of carriages all going in the same direction. Lord Montgomery had to give his full attention to driving, so they did not talk. Melody looked around and noticed all the people walking along the street. There were street vendors hawking their wares and little street urchins running up to carriages trying to earn a coin or two. She realized she would miss all the hustle and bustle of London when she returned to Little Smythington. Melody sighed deeply as she thought about leaving London. Now that she had met Lord Montgomery, she was not as anxious to go home as she had been. She surreptitiously glanced over at Lord Montgomery and thought about how much she enjoyed meeting him last night. Even though they were not talking, they were very in tune to each other, just as they were when they were dancing the night before.

Soon, they arrived at the park, and the traffic cleared out. Lord Montgomery turned to Melody and smiled, then said, "You look lovely today, even lovelier than you did last night. I haven't been able to stop thinking about you. I know we only met last night, but I'm certainly looking forward to getting to know you better. Did you have a pleasant morning?"

Melody looked at Lord Montgomery as she replied, "I've been looking forward to our drive also and, yes, I did have a very pleasant morning. I volunteer at St. Mark's Orphanage, so I spent part of my morning there. I want to thank you for the beautiful roses . . . Yellow roses are my favorite." Melody glanced around at all the other carriages with so many of the ton and felt a twinge of pride because she was with such a handsome man as Lord Montgomery. Several people were looking at them as they drove by in his curricle, and she could see envy in some of the other young women's eyes. This was the first time that anything like this had ever happened to her, and she was not sure whether she liked it or not. Mostly, she found it a bit embarrassing.

Henry smiled as he said, "The roses reminded me of your smile, all sunny and bright. I'm glad you liked them. They came from the hothouse at my parents' house."

They looked into each other's eyes and smiled. She had never felt so connected to anyone in her life. This instant attraction was puzzling to her, because it had never happened to her before. Not knowing how to handle it, she looked away.

Henry boldly gazed into her eyes as he said, "I would like to get to know you better. I know we've just met, but it feels as if I've known you much longer. Have you always lived in Lincolnshire? How much longer are you going to be in London?"

As Melody looked around at all the beautiful gardens, with a myriad of color surrounding her, she said, "I've lived in Lincolnshire my entire life, and until I came to London, I had no idea how wonderful all the entertainments could be that are available here. I had never been to an opera or a play, and I found out that I love both of them. I'm supposed to leave London in three weeks, and I'll miss it terribly. Of course, I do look forward to seeing my parents again. My lord, you told me last night that you were in the army and that you have just returned from the continent. How long have you been in the army?"

"Yes, I've just returned, and I'm so relieved that we've finally defeated Bonaparte. War is very brutal, and I lost several very close friends over there. These were men that I have been fighting and serving with, for six years. I went into the army when I was eighteen years old. It was always a dream of mine, and since I was a second son, my father bought me my commission when I finished school. I'll never regret joining the army, but I'm glad the war is finally over. I'm going to be helping my brother with some of the ducal holdings, eventually. I really want to see you as much as possible over the next few weeks before you go back to Lincolnshire. Will you allow me to see you again?" he asked.

Melody felt a tremor in her belly, and her palms were damp with perspiration. It thrilled her that he wanted to see her again. "If it pleases you, I would like to see you as often as you would like." She looked up at him and just knew, she was in love, and it scared her to death. She had heard others talking about love at first sight, but she never expected it to happen to her. *She did not want to be hurt, and she was afraid that she would be, because surely he could not return her regard so quickly, could he?* She did notice that he looked so determined and earnest when he gazed into her eyes.

The drive went by quickly and soon it was time to return home. Lord Montgomery turned his curricle around, and they headed back. When they arrived, he helped her down from his curricle, and when he touched her hand, she felt a warmth run through her entire arm. The way he was looking at her, gave her an odd feeling in the pit of her stomach—something she had never felt before. Lord Montgomery's eyes darkened and he looked so intense that it sent chills up her spine. As she reached the ground, he reluctantly let go of her hand.

He turned to her and asked, "Would it be convenient for me to pick you up tomorrow at ten o'clock? I'd like for us to go riding. Do you ride?

If you do, I'd like to do that tomorrow. I'd be happy to procure a horse for you, if you need me to."

"I've been learning to ride since I arrived in London, and I enjoy it immensely. My aunt has several horses in her stable, so I'd be pleased to go riding with you, my lord." The thought of riding with Lord Montgomery sent shivers throughout her entire body.

Henry escorted her inside, and took his leave from her and Lady Helton. Just as soon as he left, her aunt immediately started asking her questions about the time that they had spent together. As Melody removed her lace gloves, she turned to her aunt and said, "We had a delightful drive, and he has asked to see me as much as possible over the next few weeks, before I leave to go back home, and I told him that I would enjoy seeing him again."

Miriam pulled her into her arms and hugged her as she said, "How absolutely marvelous! I just knew he was interested, and now he plans to court you. I'm so pleased for you, and he is such a nice young man. Melody, this is one you don't want to let get away."

Melody nervously twisted her hands and said, "Aunt Miriam, I'm scared. This is all moving so fast. How can I be sure that my feelings are real, when everything is happening so quickly? I think he is serious in his intent, but I just worry, because it's so soon after we met. I don't want to be hurt."

Aunt Miriam patted her on the arm and said, "Melody, sometimes it only takes a moment to fall in love. That is how it happened for me with your uncle, and we had twenty-five wonderful years together, before I lost him. I've missed him everyday since his death, ten years ago. I've had opportunities to be with other men and even several marriage proposals, but there will never be anyone that can take your uncle's place in my heart. All I can tell you is that sometimes, you just have to be brave and take a chance on love. See your young man as often as possible and just let nature take its course. All right, darling? I'm sure that you'll be fine. I can tell by the way he looks at you that this is going to be an enduring attachment. I'm sure he returns your regard."

CHAPTER 2

Early August 1814

MELODY AND HENRY spent time with each other everyday over the next few weeks. Each time they were together, they got to know each other a little better. The more time they spent together, the deeper their feelings grew. Each day, they would go for a drive in the park, ride their horses, or go on a picnic. In the evening, they would see each other at some of the parties that were still being held. Even though the season was almost over, some hostesses were still entertaining.

One evening, about a week after they had met, they went out onto the terrace to walk in the gardens. As they gazed into each other's eyes, Henry could feel such a strong connection with Melody.

Henry gazed into her gorgeous sherry-colored eyes and said, "I'm so delighted that you came to the party tonight. I looked forward to seeing you this evening."

"I wanted to see you too, my lord. Isn't it a beautiful evening tonight? Just look at all the stars. Oh look, there's a shooting star! I'll have to make a wish!" Melody said.

She closed her eyes to make her wish, and Henry watched her and thought she was the most radiantly beautiful woman he had ever seen. "You're so pretty with your lovely eyes shining so brightly in the moonlight. I think we have known each other long enough to use our given names, don't you? May I call you Melody, and will you please call me Henry?"

Melody gazed into Henry's crystal blue eyes and said, "Yes, I would like that very much, Henry. I agree we have known each other long enough to use our given names."

Just hearing her say his name made him want to kiss her, so he stepped in closer, put his arms around her, and lowered his head. He felt her lips tremble, and he knew she was enjoying their kiss. As she closed her eyes, he gently stroked his lips across hers. They felt as soft as a rose petal, and he deepened the kiss, yet still keeping it gentle. Her untutored response excited him, because he sensed that this was her first kiss. He made a slight groan and lifted his lips from hers. He watched as she slowly opened her eyes and sweetly smiled at him. "I'm sorry, I shouldn't have done that, but I don't regret the kiss. Your lips looked so soft that I just couldn't resist the temptation. Melody, I hold you in very high esteem, and I have the greatest respect for you. Please forgive my forwardness." He took her hand, raised it to his lips, and he felt her hand tremble as he kissed her fingers, and desire ran through his body, stronger than he could ever remember feeling.

Melody softly whispered, "I'm not offended, and I enjoyed your kiss very much. That was the first kiss I have ever received, and I thought it was wonderful, Henry."

He felt greatly honored that she had allowed him to be the first man to touch her delectable lips. Her plump lower lip had enticed him beyond endurance, and it pleased him that no other man had experienced her soft sweet lips. He stepped back and said, "As much as I enjoyed your kiss, we need to return to the ballroom, before anyone notices us missing."

They walked back through the French doors. Both of them were feeling as if something remarkable had just happened. Henry noticed his best friend walking toward them. He turned to Melody and said, "Let me introduce you to my friend Bryan Willingham, the Earl of Weston."

Weston stopped in front of Henry and asked, "Montgomery, are you ready to leave yet? Who is this lovely young lady with you? Would you please introduce us?"

Henry smiled and said, "Hello, Weston, please let me introduce you to Miss Canterfield-Smyth. She's from Lincolnshire, and she's visiting her aunt, Lady Helton."

Weston elegantly bowed and then said, "Henry has spoken of you on several occasions, and now I understand why. You're very lovely. It's a pleasure to meet you!"

Melody curtsied and said, "Thank you, my lord. Lord Montgomery has mentioned you to me also. He speaks very highly of you, and I'm pleased to make your acquaintance."

Henry turned to Melody and raised her hand to his lips as he said, "Let me take you back to your aunt. Weston and I are leaving to go meet some of our friends. I look forward to seeing you tomorrow afternoon. I'll pick you up at four o'clock so we can take our ride in the park. Oh, here's your aunt coming now."

Lady Helton smiled at Lord Weston as she said, "Hello, Lord Weston. It's so nice to see you again. How is your mother? I haven't seen her this season."

"Thank you for asking about my mother. Her health has been poor, so she decided to remain at our country estate rather than coming to town this year," Lord Weston replied.

"Please tell her I asked about her. I've always enjoyed your mother's company. I hope she gets to feeling better soon." Lady Helton turned to Melody and said, "Melody, I'm ready to leave. We promised to stop by Lady Bradford's musicale this evening, so we need to be leaving if we are going to get there in time."

"All right, Aunt Miriam, I'm ready." Melody turned to Henry and said, "Lord Montgomery, I look forward to our ride tomorrow." Then she looked over at Lord Weston and added, "It was very nice meeting you, Lord Weston."

Melody and her aunt turned and walked away. Henry turned to Lord Weston and asked, "Is she not as lovely as I told you she was?"

Weston glanced over at Henry, then he said, "Yes, she is, and she also seems very nice, if a little shy. I can see why you're so besotted with her!"

Henry grinned as he replied, "Well, I don't know that I would call myself besotted, however I do enjoy her company greatly. Let's leave and go meet our friends at White's."

The following day, Henry picked Melody up, and they went for a ride in Hyde Park, along Rotten Row. It was obvious that their horses were biting at the bit and wanted a good run. "Why don't we have a little race to that tree over there? I'll give you a head start, all right?"

Melody agreed, and she took off before Henry even had a chance to say go. She was halfway to the tree before he got his horse turned around. Once he did, he sped after her, but there was no way he could catch her. When he caught up with her, he said, "You've really improved lately. Have you been practicing in the morning?"

Melody threw her head back and laughed as she said, "I've been riding almost every morning, and I just beat you, so what do you think of that!"

Laughter was shining in Henry's eyes as he replied, "I guess I'd better watch out, and next time, I won't give you a head start, because you don't need it." Melody merrily smiled at Henry, and they continued on their ride.

Melody's heart swelled with love for Henry, and she wished he would kiss her again as he had last evening at the party. "Henry, I'm so pleased that we have become such good friends. In many ways, I feel as if I've known you for a long time."

As their horses approached a wooded area of the park, Henry asked, "Why don't we walk a bit?" Melody agreed, and he helped her down from her horse. They held hands as they walked along the path as their horses trailed behind them. It was as if they were the only people in the world. The sunlight filtered through the trees, and Melody felt a huge sense of contentment. She glanced over at Henry, and her heart accelerated because his eyes were darkened to a deep blue, and she thought he wanted to kiss her as much as she wanted to kiss him. Henry stopped walking and pulled her into his arms as he lowered his head and softly touched his lips to hers. Sweet vibrations ran through her body, and she sighed when she felt Henry's tongue slide across her lips. As Melody gasped, he slid his tongue into her mouth. It was the most amazing feeling, and she tentatively met his tongue with her own. Henry pulled her closer and deepened the kiss. Melody wound her arms up around his neck, and as he continued to kiss her, she ran her fingers through his thick red gold curls. They were pressed closely together from chest to thigh, and she felt something hard and firm against her belly.

Henry let out a groan and said, "Melody, we had better stop. I find you extremely attractive, and your kisses are sweeter than candy, but I don't want to do anything to offend you." He let her go and stepped back, but did not release her hand.

Melody glowingly replied, "Henry, you haven't offended me. I wanted you to kiss me. Your kisses are very enticing, but you're right. We do need to stop before someone comes along and sees us." Henry helped Melody mount her horse, and they continued on their ride. He escorted Melody back to her aunt's house, and they parted with promises to meet at one o'clock the next day.

On the following day, they went on a picnic. When they arrived at Hyde Park, Henry picked out a spot next to the Serpentine, and spread out a blanket he had brought with him. He had gone to Gunter's for their luncheon. There were shaved ham sandwiches and several kinds of fruit with a jug of lemonade. Henry filled a plate for Melody and handed it to her. Then he proceeded to fill his plate with all the food that remained. They sat there eating and enjoying the lovely warm afternoon when Henry asked, "What's Lincolnshire like? I haven't been there before. Do you have any brothers or sisters?"

"No, I'm an only child. My parents had me when they were in their late thirties. They tried to have a child for a long time, so when I was born, they were overjoyed. They call me their little gift from God and have said many times that I'm a true blessing to them. You know that my father is the vicar of Little Smythington parish, and we live in a very small village where everyone knows everybody's business. I had several friends while growing up, and we would always play together. You've met Susan. We've been friends since we were small children. I have another friend who lives next door to me. He and I used to go fishing, and he taught me how to skip rocks. We were constantly together while I was growing up. Brandon has recently gotten married, and his wife is expecting their first child at Christmas. I'm looking forward to seeing them when I get home. What about you? What was it like growing up as the son of a duke?" she asked.

Henry stretched out beside her as he replied, "You already know I have an elder brother. Nelson and I were best friends growing up, which is surprising, because he's seven years older than I am. I have two sisters. Helen is seventeen, and Kathryn is thirteen. Our parents didn't spend much time with us while we were growing up. They spent most of their time in London. Nelson looked after us and made sure that we were well cared for. Sanderford Park was a great place to grow up in, with lots of trees to climb and a big lake to swim in. We had everything that money could buy, but all we really wanted was our parents' love. From what you have shared, I envy you, because it's obvious that your parents love you very much."

Melody gave Henry a sympathetic smile and said, "You're right. I realize that I'm very fortunate to have such loving parents, and not everyone is so lucky. Susan lost her father when she was about ten years old, and my father has tried to fulfill a father's role for her, which she has appreciated very much, but it's not the same as having her own father. Tell me more about your childhood."

As he absently pulled at a blade of grass, he said, "You met my friend Weston. We met when I went away to school at eleven. I went to Eton, because that's where all the men in my family have gone. I enjoyed school tremendously and had quite a few friends, but Weston was my best friend. Weston couldn't join the army because he was an only child. It disappointed him greatly that he couldn't, especially when I left to go to the continent."

Melody glanced over at Henry and said, "I enjoyed meeting your friend. It's important to have close friends. Can you tell more about being in the army? Oh, and you still haven't told me what it's like having a father who's a duke. I can't imagine what that would be like."

"I would really rather not be a duke's son, but we don't always get what we wish for. I hated being treated differently just because my father was a duke. It took me longer to make friends, because all the other fellows expected me to be all stiff and proper like my father. You already know that I went into the army when I was eighteen, so that makes me four and twenty. I've loved the army, and I don't really want to leave it. But since the war is over, I would eventually be sent to India, and I'm not so sure that I would want to go there. Once I get my men situated, I'll sell my commission. I have a small estate that my grandmother left me, so I plan to live there. The estate is in Yorkshire, and that isn't too far from where you live. That's enough about me. Why don't we eat some of those delicious strawberries?" he asked.

The strawberries were delicious, and Henry made a game out of eating them. First, he would eat one, and then he would feed one to Melody. His eyes would darken when she opened her lips to take the strawberry into her mouth, and then he would lick the strawberry juice off his fingers as he looked deeply into her eyes. Melody knew Henry desired her, and it excited her even though she did not fully understand about desire. After they finished eating, they went for a walk along the Serpentine. They watched all the little children, with their nursemaids, playing by the riverbank. Melody told him how much she enjoyed her work with the orphanage and that she would some day like to be able to help in a more significant way. They shared more about themselves, and Melody knew that she had found someone very special in Henry.

On their last outing together, before she was due to leave for Lincolnshire, Henry turned to Melody and asked, "I would like to spend more time with you. Would your parents mind if I came to visit you this fall?"

As they rode along in his curricle, she said, "Henry, I'd love for you to come for a visit. I'm sure my parents would be delighted to meet you. I've thoroughly enjoyed our time together, and I would be just as pleased if you came to see me."

"I've also enjoyed spending this time with you immensely. Even though we have only known each other for a few weeks, I've grown quite fond of you, and I look forward to continuing our friendship." Henry stopped his curricle and turned to Melody. They were hidden behind some bushes, so he took her in his arms and kissed her. He flicked his tongue across her lips, so Melody parted them, and he deepened the kiss. She tasted as sweet as he remembered, and he could go on kissing her forever. He felt his passion stirring, but he knew he needed to stop, before he went too far. He did not want to frighten Melody, so he reluctantly ended their kiss. "You have the sweetest tasting mouth! You taste just like the strawberries we ate a moment ago. I never want to let you go, but we don't want anyone to see us, so we need to stop."

Melody looked at Henry and smiled, "You already know that I enjoy your kisses, and I find them very exciting. I'm going to miss you, and I look forward to your visit. When do you think you'll be able to come?"

"I need to spend a few weeks with my family and find out how I can help my brother, but I should be able to come around the middle of September. Would that be convenient for you?" he asked.

With a radiant smile on her face, she replied, "I'm sure that would be fine. I'll let my parents know when to expect you."

They arrived back at Lady Helton's house, and Henry helped her out of his curricle. As he lowered her to the ground, he held on to her, as if he never wanted to let her go. Melody's heart was beating very fast, and her hands were shaking from the emotions she was feeling. She looked into his eyes and saw his were intensely blue and filled with what she now believed was desire. While desire was a new sensation for Melody, she nevertheless knew she desired him desperately. Slowly Henry released her and stepped back. He escorted her inside to take his leave of her aunt.

Henry turned to Melody and smiled as he said, "I'll see you soon, Melody. I'll send you a note to let you know when I shall arrive in Lincolnshire."

Melody gazed into his eyes and answered, "I'll look forward to your arrival, my lord."

Henry turned to Lady Helton and said, "I've appreciated your hospitality, and I hope to see you again." Then he turned to Melody and lifted her hand to his lips. While gazing up at her, he tenderly kissed her hand. He bowed, and then he was gone.

Aunt Miriam turned to Melody and asked, "Melody what was that all about, my dear child?"

Melody replied, "Lord Montgomery has asked if he could come and visit me at my home, and I told him that I would enjoy his visit immensely."

Melody's aunt rushed to her and gave her a hug. "Oh, this is wonderful news! I just know he is falling in love with you. You mark my word, you will soon be engaged. He would never ask if he could visit you at your home if he weren't serious about his intentions."

"I think you must be right. I know that I'm falling in love with him. While I'm pleased, I'm also very apprehensive. What if I'm wrong about how he feels? It's only been three weeks since we met! Could he possibly be in love with me in so short a time?" she asked.

Aunt Miriam looked lovingly into Melody's eyes as she replied, "Darling, it's normal to be concerned, because everything has happened so quickly.

However, sometimes love happens that way. Just relax and enjoy how you are feeling. All will be well, just you wait and see!"

Melody left for Lincolnshire the next day. The trip was long and boring, but it gave her quite a bit of time to think about Henry. She knew that she was in love with him, and while it felt marvelous, she was a little frightened. Even though she was still very young, she had plans for what she wanted to do with her life, and if Henry asked her to marry him, those plans would be difficult to achieve. *Oh well, she was getting ahead of herself anyway. It's not as if he had asked her to marry him, and he could change his mind about coming to visit anyway.* She decided that she would put it out of her mind until he wrote to her, and then she just might believe he cared.

The countryside was simply gorgeous; the leaves were just beginning to turn. While Melody loved the summer, she did enjoy all the gorgeous colors of fall. Thank goodness, the weather was cooperating; they had not had any rain during the entire trip. Even though it took five days to get to Lincolnshire, they had made good time. Millie spent most of her time doing needlework, and Melody read several books, which helped to pass the time.

When she arrived home, she was glad to see her parents. Even though she had enjoyed London tremendously, she was overjoyed to be home again. She realized she had missed them terribly. They wanted to know all about her first season and how many new friends she had made. During one of their conversations, she casually mentioned Henry and said, "He mentioned that he might come to visit. His father, the Duke of Sanderford, has property in Doncaster, which is not too terribly far away. He said that he would come to visit on his way to his father's property, if that would be all right with you. I enjoyed my time in London, and I went to so many balls, soirees, and garden parties that I actually grew tired of them. Aunt Miriam was a delightful hostess and made sure that I had plenty of activities to do. Susan got me involved with St. Mark's Orphanage, and I really enjoyed spending time with all the children. We also went to the Royal Opera House in Covent Gardens, and I found it to be divine. All the singers had incredible voices, and I was extremely impressed. I know that I'll be an opera lover for the rest of my life."

Melody's mother said, "Honey, we're so pleased that you had a wonderful time. Lord Montgomery sounds like a nice young man, and we would be happy to have him come for a visit. We missed you so much, and we're just thankful you have returned to us."

CHAPTER 3

August 1814

HENRY HAD MADE up his mind. He was in love with Melody, and when he went to visit her in Lincolnshire, he would ask her father for permission to pay his addresses. After everything he had been through with the war; he was not going to waste any more time. He already knew Melody was the woman that he wanted to spend the rest of his life with. Whenever he was around her, he became very aroused, especially when he kissed her. His desire had been so strong that he found it difficult to end their kiss, but he did not want to frighten her with his passion. After all, she was an innocent, and it was up to him to protect her. When she told him he was the first man to kiss her, well words could not describe how truly special that had made him feel. He knew they would be happy together, and he felt sure that Melody returned his regard. He could tell she did, by the way she looked at him, when she did not realize he was watching her.

Henry did wonder how his father would feel about her, since he was so high in the instep. He was not going to let anything get in his way, regardless of what his father thought. It really did not matter anyway since he had never been able to please his father, no matter how hard he tried. He had not been able to figure out why his father did not seem to like him, but it had always been that way ever since he was a young child. His father always seemed to be harder on him than his brother even though he had tried so hard to live up to his father's high expectations. Neither one of his parents seemed to have much time for him while he was growing up. Now as an adult, he refused to let what they thought matter to him anymore. If they did not like Melody, then that was just too bad, because he was determined to marry her regardless of how they felt about it. Maybe he was worrying about something that would not even happen. They did not take much interest in anything he did anyway, so they might not even care enough to say anything.

His father had talked to him about marrying Lady Penelope, but he told him that he was not interested the last time he had been home two years ago. Lady Penelope was a shrew, and he had no intention of ever marrying her, no matter what his father wanted. He just hoped that they would be nice to Melody regardless of what they felt about him. Of course, he had not spent much time with either of his parents, since he had been in the army. He had left home six years ago when his father bought his commission for him. Now that was the best thing his father had ever done for him. He really did love army life, and he knew he would miss it. Now that he was probably getting married, he would not want Melody to have to follow the drum, and since staying in the army would mean being away from her for long periods of time, he knew he would not want to do that. Henry was ready to settle down, and having Melody in his life would be very appealing.

Henry decided he would not tell his father about Melody until after they were married. He certainly did not need his father's permission to marry. Thank goodness, his maternal grandmother left him an inheritance, so he did not have to depend on his father for money. He was certainly not wealthy, but he could support Melody and any children they might have.

Henry knew his brother, Nelson, would love Melody, once he met her, because she was such a sweet person and because he would understand how much Henry loved her. He wished that Nelson's wife had lived instead of dying in childbirth along with their son. He hoped that Nelson would meet someone to love, once he got over the loss of Nora. He certainly was looking forward to spending time with Nelson. It had been two years since he was home, and he really looked forward to seeing his sisters also. He could just imagine how much they had changed.

The day before he was due to leave for Sanderford Park, Henry went to his favorite jeweler to pick out a ring for Melody. He knew exactly what he wanted it to look like. As he looked over the selection of rings the jeweler had to offer, he spied a gorgeous square cut emerald with baguette diamonds on each side and immediately knew he had found the ring for her. After he paid for the ring, he returned to Sanderford House for a quiet evening before his trip home the next day.

The next morning, while he was packing up his belongings, he decided to stop by to see Weston, on his way out of town.

Henry found him at White's. Weston was reading a newspaper when he looked up and saw Henry. "Hello, Montgomery, where have you been keeping yourself? I haven't seen much of you in the last few weeks. Have you been too busy with your new love to have time for your friends?"

Henry walked over and shook his hand as he said, "You know I've been spending time with Miss Canterfield-Smyth. Weston, she's the most beautiful woman I've ever seen, and I've begun to have strong feelings for her. I'm going to visit her in Lincolnshire, after I've spent some time with my family."

Weston looked at Henry as he said, "I enjoyed meeting Miss Canterfield-Smyth at the ball the other week. She seemed to be quiet and shy. How in the world did you get her to talk to you? She is quite lovely to look at, and I'm sure that I'm not the only man who feels that way."

"She really isn't that shy, she's just somewhat reserved until you get to know her. Once I got her to open up, she was delightful, and she has a wonderful sense of humor. We actually have quite a bit in common, since we both love to read and we also enjoy riding."

Weston thoughtfully looked at Henry and replied, "Are you sure you want to go visit her at her home? That would definitely put you in a position where you have raised her expectations, and that's definitely how her parents will see it."

As they walked outside, Henry turned to Weston and said, "Weston, I'm going to ask her to marry me when I go see her, so I'm not troubled about raising her expectations. I just need her parents to like me, so they'll approve the match. I know it seems fast, but I just know that Melody is the one for me."

With an astounded look on his face, he said, "Well, Montgomery, I must say I'm surprised, since I know you have always said that you would not marry until you were at least thirty, if at all. I wish you all the best, but I'm glad it's you and not me that's getting leg shackled! When are you leaving town, old friend? Do you have time to give me a chance to get back at you? You trounced me at Gentleman Jackson's the last time we went a few rounds."

Henry shook his head and said, "I'm headed out right now. Sorry, old friend, it will just have to wait until spring. Well, I'll see you next year, and hopefully, I'll be a married man by then!"

Weston saluted Henry as he watched him ride away.

Henry made good time and arrived in Surrey that afternoon. As he came over the hill, he looked down and saw Sanderford Park for the first time in two years. How he had always loved it here! Everything was so peaceful and quiet. The park was so beautiful that he got a lump in his throat just seeing it again. Henry galloped down the hill, and when he arrived, a stable boy came running up to take his horse.

"Hello, Freddie! Please take Jupiter to the stables and give him plenty of oats. I've ridden him hard for several hours, and he deserves some special treatment. How have you been?" Henry asked.

"I'll take Jupiter right now, and I'll make sure he gets them oats. I been right good, milord. It's good t' see ye home!" Then Freddie led Jupiter away.

Henry dashed up the steps and opened the door. He ran into Simpson, the butler and said, "Simpson, it's so good to see you! Where is everyone?"

Simpson bowed and said, "The family is in the drawing room, my lord. It is very good to have you home. It has been quite some time since you have been here."

"I'll go right up so that I can see everyone." Henry took the steps, two at a time, and rushed into the drawing room. His mother was sitting on the settee with his sisters, Helen and Kathryn. Nelson was standing by the fireplace, and his father was in his favorite chair. Henry looked at everyone and said, "I'm home. How have all of you been? I've really missed you!"

Henry's father looked disgusted, and his eyes were as cold as ice. He stood up and said, "I see that you have still not learned to show respect. Why do you have to be in such a hurry all the time, Henry? It is not dignified to rush about so much!"

Henry looked at his father and said, "Sorry Father, but I'm so pleased to be home, I forgot myself for a moment. It's wonderful to see all of you again. I hope that all is well with you."

His mother looked at him with distain. "It is about time you came home. I know that you have been back in the country for quite some time, but you chose not to come home until now. I would have thought that you would come straight here. Instead, you stayed in town to be with your friends."

"Mother, I had to put in my request for time off from my regiment and that took awhile," he said. "I didn't mean for you to think that I didn't want to see all of you. I just wanted to get all my business handled before I came home."

"Well, I still think you are an inconsiderate son. What do all the neighbors think about you not bothering to come see your family and gallivanting all over London?" the duchess asked.

"I'm sorry, Mother, you are right. I should have come straight home, but now that I'm home, can we please just be happy to see each other?" He looked over at his sisters and said, "Do you have a hug for your brother? I've missed both of you so much." Helen and Kathryn rushed over to him and gave him a big hug. Then he looked over at Nelson and added, "Nelson, it's so good to see you. How are you doing?"

"I'm doing fine, Henry. It's good to see you made it home safely. I'm so proud of what you've accomplished. Our country is a much safer place because of your willingness to serve," Nelson replied as he smiled proudly at Henry.

"Thank you, Nelson. I'm just glad the war is finally over and our country is now at peace. I'm going up to my room, because I have had an exhausting and hard ride, so I need to freshen up." Henry turned to everyone else and said, "I look forward to seeing all of you at dinner."

Henry hurried up the stairs to his room. He entered and was so relieved to have that over with. It was just as he had expected; his parents could care less that he was back home. Even though his mother asked why he did not come right home, Henry knew it was not because she missed him. It was just something that she could find fault with! *Oh well, it was pleasant to see his brother and sisters again.* He was astonished at how much his sisters had changed in the last two years. Helen was a real beauty, and Kathryn was as pretty as ever. He could not wait to spend some time with Nelson. Henry knew that Nelson had missed him and would be grateful for any help that Henry was able to give him in managing the estates.

Henry rang for his valet and requested a bath so that he could wash all his travel dirt away. Mansfield prepared his bath and then started to get out his evening clothes. "Mansfield, how have you been? I'll have to get used to having someone to take care of me again. It's been a long time since I've had anyone do that for me."

"I look forward to serving you again, my lord. You have always been a pleasure to serve. It is very good to have you home!" Mansfield said.

Henry smiled as he said, "Well, thank you, Mansfield. I appreciate your help. I'll see you later this evening, and we can catch up, all right?"

"Very good, my lord, I look forward to it," he replied.

Dinner went about as well as he expected. His parents continued along the same path they had started when they first saw him. It was not pleasant. When the duke got him alone over port and cigars, he really let him have it, and he even brought up Lady Penelope again. Henry reiterated again that he was not going to marry her and that there was not a thing that he could do about it, so he might as well quit bringing it up. By the time Henry left him, he was quite exasperated and went straight to bed instead of joining his sisters in the drawing room.

The next day, Henry and Nelson toured the estate, and Henry was pleased to see how prosperous everything was. It was obvious that his brother was doing a superb job of managing the estate. He just wished he did not look so sad. Nelson was obviously not over losing Nora. Henry knew how much he had loved her, and it must have been so hard to not only lose his wife, but also his son. Henry had hoped that Nelson would be doing better by now. "Nelson, how are you doing? You look tired. Are you feeling all right? I can just imagine how hard it was on you to lose Nora. I wish I could have been here to help you deal with it all."

Nelson pulled back on the reins of his horse so that they could talk. "I'm doing all right. I just haven't been feeling well lately. I'm sure that I'll feel better soon. It's good to have you back home again. I know that you would have been here when I lost Nora, if it were possible. How long are you going to stay?"

As they allowed their horses to meander along, he said, "I'll be home for about a month, but then, I need to go to Lincolnshire. I've met someone. Her name is Melody, and . . . I'm in love with her. Nelson, I'm going to ask her to marry me."

When Nelson heard this, he stopped his horse altogether, looked at Henry with astonishment on his face and said, "Henry, am I hearing you correctly? Did you just say you were getting married? I thought you always said that you would not marry until you were at least thirty and maybe not even then. She must truly be a special lady for you to change your mind about marriage. This is astonishing news. How long have you known her?"

As Henry stopped his horse, he said, "Sometimes things just happen when you least expect them to, and Melody and I are just meant to be. She's so beautiful and sweet. I knew from the first moment that I had met someone very special. I met her shortly after I got back from the continent. I think I need someone now that I've returned from the war. I'm ready to settle down, and Melody is the one for me." Henry smiled as he thought about how much he loved his sweet Melody. The more he thought about her, the stronger his conviction became that he was doing the right thing by asking her to marry him.

"I'm happy for you, Henry. Are you going to tell Mother and Father about your plans?" he asked. "You know that they'll probably not be happy about you getting married. Father still wants you to marry Lady Penelope. He's definitely not going to be happy that you're leaving so soon. Father was planning on you helping out around here for a while, and then he wants you to take over the Doncaster Stables in Yorkshire."

Henry knew that Nelson was probably right about his parents, but they would just have to accept his decision in regards to his marriage. "I'm going to do that, but I just need to make sure that I get my life settled before I take up the management of Doncaster Stables. It's going to be at least six months before I can do that anyway, because I need to get my men settled first. I want to make Melody my wife, and I need to do this soon, before someone else comes along and tries to take her away from me. I'm not going to tell them I'm getting married. I'm going to just do it and then tell them. That way they can't try to do anything to sabotage my marriage, before it even gets started. You'll keep my plans to yourself, won't you, Nelson?"

"I won't say anything, but you know that they're not going to be happy about this. It's going to be very difficult for them to accept her, because they always planned on you coming home and marrying Lady Penelope. You know that they want to join our lands together, and since she's her father's only heir, she'll inherit everything."

Henry was so tired of hearing about Lady Penelope. He kept telling his father he was not interested, but he just did not want to believe him. He knew Nelson did not feel that he should marry Lady Penelope and that he was only pointing out how his father would feel, but he was beginning to get a little angry so he said, "The ducal holdings are already immense. They will survive without that property. I love Melody, and I'm going to marry her. I don't care about what she can bring to the marriage, and I don't need a dowry since our grandmother left me her estate. I deserve to have peace and contentment now that I've come back from the war. For God's sake, I'm giving up the military career that I love! He needs to just be happy about that! Melody will make me happy. I just know it."

Nelson held up his hand as he replied, "Wait a minute. I'm not the enemy here. Henry, I'm happy for you, and I want you to have a love match. I just want you to realize that this isn't going to make our parents happy. Father was counting on that property. I would marry Lady Penelope myself, but I don't feel that we would suit. She likes town life too much for me, and she's far too young. She's only a year older than Helen. She would never be content staying in the country, and besides, I'm just not ready yet. It's only been a year since I lost Nora."

Every time Nelson mentioned Nora, Henry could hear the pain in his voice. He wished there was something he could do to help ease his suffering. "Nelson, I know how much you miss Nora, but I do think that you have to consider marrying again soon. You need an heir. I never want to have to step into your shoes. I'm counting on you to take care of it so that I don't have to. But you're right about Lady Penelope. You would definitely not suit, because she's much too frivolous for you."

"You're right, Henry, about me needing to move past my grief. I just need a little more time. And I promise I won't leave you having to be my heir for long. I have already made up my mind that I'll go to London next year to find myself a wife, but not some young giddy debutant. That's why I'm so glad to have you back home. Now Father will start focusing on you instead of me. Well, it's past time to head back. We've been gone all day. If we don't hurry, we'll be late for dinner, and you know how angry Father gets if anyone is ever late." They turned their horses around and at a brisk trot, they headed back to the house.

Over the next few weeks, Henry and Nelson spent quite a bit of time together. Everyday they would ride out to all the different farms to make sure that all the tenants had everything they needed. It was rewarding to see all the folks from his youth and to see how well received he was by them. Henry also helped Nelson with the books. Nelson never did enjoy working inside, so Henry took some of that burden off his shoulders. His parents were very cold to him, but that was nothing new. He also spent time with Helen and Kathryn. They were such sweet-natured girls. It was hard to imagine that Helen was old enough to be going to town next season to make her come out.

Finally, it was time for Henry to leave for Lincolnshire. He told his father that he was going to visit one of his school friends that had been wounded in the war. To appease him, he promised to go to Doncaster and check on Doncaster Stables while he was up north. Needless to say, his father was not happy, but he knew that he could not keep Henry from going. It bothered Henry that he had to lie to his father, but if he wanted to avoid telling him about Melody, it was necessary. After hearing the duke go on about Lady Penelope, he knew he would be livid over his plans to marry her. Lying had never set well with Henry, but in this case it was the lesser of the evils.

Henry left Surrey in time to make it to Melody's by the third week of September. As much as he enjoyed spending time with his brother and sisters, he was anxious to get to Melody. He hoped he was reading her right and that she did return his regard. The trip was long, and it rained part of the way. No matter how long it took, or what kind of weather he had to ride through, it would be well worth it when he was able to finally see Melody's sweet face again. As he entered Lincolnshire, he noticed how beautiful the countryside was, with lots of verdant green pastures and rolling hills. He had not realized how lovely Lincolnshire was. The closer he got to Little Smythington, the more excited he became. Soon he would be seeing his darling Melody again.

CHAPTER 4

September 1814

MELODY WAS OVERJOYED to be at home with her parents. She had missed them a great deal. Her father was getting up in years, and his health was not as good as she would like. Melody knew she was very dear to them, and they were so pleased to have her home again. She told them more about Henry and that he was supposed to be arriving around the middle of September. Her parents were happy for her and hoped that it would all work out the way she wanted. They wanted her to have a love match, but they were not sure she was ready for marriage yet. She knew it was disconcerting to her parents to think of her getting married and moving away, as she was their only child. She also knew that they had always hoped she would find someone closer to them when it came time for her to marry. It was apparent that it bothered them because Henry lived in the south of England.

Everyday, Melody would think of Henry and look forward to his visit. She did receive one letter from him, and he told her he should be there around the third week of September, a little later than he had planned. Melody kept herself busy by helping her father with his sermons. She would write them for him, as his hands were crippled up with rheumatism. "Father, I have finished writing your sermon. Do you want to check it over and make sure that it's right?"

Her father looked over at Melody and smiled, then replied, "I'm sure the sermon is fine. It's such a joy to have you home again. Your mother and I missed you greatly while you were gone. We were so pleased when Miriam asked you to visit her in London and that she was willing to sponsor you for a season. However, we're glad that you're home. Now, why don't you tell me more about Henry?"

With a dreamy expression on her face, Melody said, "Oh, Father, he is so wonderful. I think that you'll like him a great deal. I already told you his father is the Duke of Sanderford. I don't think he gets on well with his parents. He made some comments about it when we were together. He has an elder brother, who will inherit the dukedom, and he also has two younger sisters. I gather that he hasn't spent much time at home in the last six years, due to the war. He's still in the army, and he hasn't made up his mind about when he will sell his commission. He seems to like the army and isn't sure he's ready to leave it yet. The duke wants him to sell his commission so that he can help with all the ducal holdings. I'm sure that he will do so, but not until he gets his men settled."

"You seem quite taken by this young man. It sounds as if he's still quite young and may not be ready to settle down. Four and twenty is still very young for a man to be thinking of marriage. I don't want to see you get hurt, so it might be smart to take it slow. Give yourself plenty of time, to make sure that you're truly in love with him and that he feels the same way. Your mother and I married for love, and that's what we want for you. We always hoped that when the time came for you to marry, you would find a nice local young man, so you would live close by. This young man lives so far away," he replied.

With determination in her voice, she said, "I don't need to think about it. I know that I'm in love with Henry, and I feel he loves me. He hasn't told me so, but all his actions tell me he does. I don't think he would spend the time to come all the way here if he weren't serious about his intentions. Father, please be happy for me and just listen to Henry when he comes. He'll be here in a few days, and I want you and Mother to give him a chance to prove that he really cares for me. That's all that I ask, all right?"

Her father patted her shoulder, and with love in his eyes, he said, "Of course, we will listen to your young man, and if he's as wonderful as you say he is, I'm sure that we'll like him."

Finally, the day had arrived, and Melody could not wait for Henry to get there. She was so eager and excited. When Henry arrived, he was riding his horse, Jupiter. He looked so handsome that he took her breath away. Melody felt so nervous about seeing him again. *What if she was wrong and had misjudged his intentions?* She would be so devastated, if that were the case. It would also be embarrassing, because she had led her parents to believe that he loved her. Henry dismounted from his horse, and when he looked at Melody, all her doubts melted away. The look in Henry's eyes said it all, because they were filled with love and tenderness. She was sure that he loved her! Melody's hands began to shake, and her heart began to beat rapidly as Henry walked over to her, took her hand, and raised it to his lips. He placed a kiss in the center of her palm, and shivers ran up and down her spine.

"Melody, it's wonderful to see you again. God, you are so beautiful! I've missed you so much. I came as soon as I could get away from my family. How have you been? Did you miss me?" he asked.

She looked at Henry's face and smiled happily at him as she replied, "I've missed you desperately, and I'm pleased that you have arrived. Let's go inside so I can introduce you to my parents. I've told them all about you, and they're looking forward to meeting you."

As they went into the house, they gazed lovingly into each other's eyes. They went into the parlor so that Melody could introduce him to her parents. She was very nervous and excited, and she just hoped that her parents would like him! "Mother . . . Father, this is Lord Henry Montgomery. Remember, I told you he would be coming for a visit."

Melody's father stepped forward and offered Henry his hand as he said, "It's a pleasure to meet you, my lord. Melody told us you were coming for a visit. How was the trip up here?

As Henry shook his hand, he said, "It was a pleasant trip, and for the most part, the weather cooperated. I only encountered rain one day, and it wasn't a hard rain."

"It was quite a long distance for you, wasn't it? You're from Surrey, correct?" Melody's father asked.

"I'm from Cranleigh, Surrey, which is about thirty miles south of London. I appreciate you allowing to come for a visit," he said.

Melody's father smiled jovially at Melody and Henry as he said, "Have you found a place to stay while you're in the area? We would be happy to offer you our hospitality, if you haven't already found a place. Oh, by the way, you can call me Magnus, as we aren't formal around here."

"If it wouldn't be too much trouble, I would very much enjoy accepting your kind offer of hospitality. This will give us all a chance to get to know each other," Henry answered.

"Good . . . Good!" Magnus replied. "Why don't you go get your things and Melody can show you to your room."

Henry had tied Jupiter up out front, so Melody showed him where he could put his horse. The stable was small, but clean. Henry put Jupiter in a stall and proceeded to take off his saddle, brush him down, and give him some oats. There was no one in the stable, but the two of them, so Henry took advantage of that. He pulled Melody into his arms and kissed her.

His blood began to boil, and his heart was pounding, because he was so excited to be kissing her again. It seemed as if it had been so long. Melody was kissing him back with fervor, and he felt his desire rise. He tentatively placed his hand on her breast. This was the first time he had touched her like this, and it felt incredibly titillating. She let out a sigh, so he knew she was enjoying it as well. As he deepened the kiss, he pulled her tightly against him. The stall was full of soft hay, and he pulled her down so that they were lying together facing each other; he continued to kiss her. He kneaded her breasts and felt her nipples grow taut through her dress. Her heart was pounding in her chest; he could feel it under his hand. He pulled up the skirt of her gown and felt her smooth calf; his hand traveled further up to her plump thigh. It felt incredible to be touching her like this, and she was so responsive. Melody was making little sounds as he stroked her pretty legs. Soon, he knew that if he did not stop, he would lose all control, and Melody was so innocent that he did not want to take advantage of her first feelings of passion. After all, he loved her and planned to marry her, so he gently pulled his hands back and ended their kiss. "Hello, sweetheart does that show you how much I've missed you? It feels as if it's been months, instead of weeks, since I held you in my arms!"

Melody blushed as she coyly looked at him and replied, "I couldn't wait for you to get here so you could kiss me. My dreams have been filled with visions of us kissing and being in each other's arms. I've been counting the days waiting for your arrival, Henry."

They stood up, and Henry brushed some hay off her and grinned. She looked at him and smiled back as he said, "We had better return to the house before someone comes looking for us. The last thing I would want is for us to be caught in a compromising situation." She led him back into the house and showed him where he would be staying.

Over the next few days, they spent every waking moment together. Whenever they were alone, they would kiss, but Henry was careful to not let things get out of hand. He liked Melody's parents, and her mother reminded him of Melody. She was just as sweet natured and kind as his darling Melody was. Henry knew he was ready to have a talk with her father. He was sure she was in love with him and would say yes when he asked her to marry him. The study door was open, so he knocked on the doorframe and asked, "Sir, could I have a few minutes of your time?"

Magnus gave Henry a knowing look, motioned him into the room as he replied, "What can I do for you?"

"Sir, I would like to ask you for Melody's hand in marriage. I love your daughter very much . . . and I believe that she feels the same way about me. I have the financial resources to take care of her and any children we may have. My maternal grandmother left me her estate, and I have an income of two thousand pounds a year, plus numerous investments to supplement my income. I promise that I'll take care of her and love her for the rest of her life. Do I have your permission to pay my addresses to your daughter?" Henry was concerned about the expression on Magnus's face. He hoped he was not going to tell him no. *Oh god, surely not.* He loved her desperately, and he knew Melody would never disobey her parents. He would just have to convince her father that he would always take care of her.

Magnus looked intently at him, as he said, "Henry, please take a seat. I appreciate you speaking with me regarding your intentions. I've been waiting for you to say something. I can see that you and Melody care about each other a great deal. My only concern is about your military career and that you live so far away. Melody told me you're on an extended leave, but that you haven't sold your commission. Do you plan to stay in the military? I'm not sure that Melody would do well following the drum, and I feel she wouldn't want to be left behind while you went away."

Henry looked determinedly at Magnus as he answered, "I do plan to sell my commission, sir, and soon. I just want to wait until most of my troops are settled and have decided what they want to do, now that the war is over. I have spent six years with many of my men, and I don't want to leave them until I've helped them get back to their lives. This shouldn't take more than six months. My regiment is close to my home in Surrey, and Melody can live with my family while I finish up with my men. But once I do that, we'll be coming back up here. The estate my grandmother left me is close to Doncaster, and of course, Doncaster Stables is in Yorkshire. I'll be managing the stables for my father, so we won't be too far away. I would like to marry Melody soon, sir."

Magnus sighed deeply and with resignation in his voice, he replied, "All right, Henry. You have my permission to ask Melody to marry you. You just make sure that you take good care of my little girl. She's all that her mother and I have, and we want her to be happy and safe."

What a relief! He had said yes. He could not wait to ask Melody. "Thank you, sir. I promise I'll take good care of her, and I'll keep her happy and safe. May I go speak with Melody now?"

"Go on," he said. "I'm sure that she's waiting for you to tell her why you wanted to talk to me."

Henry hurried from the room and headed out into the garden, where he knew Melody was. He walked outside and saw her sitting in the arbor. The sunlight cast a glow all around her, which formed a golden halo around her head. She glowed with innocence, and his heart swelled with love for her. She appeared lovelier to him than she ever had before. He walked up to her and sat down beside her. He knew she was waiting for him to tell her what he had talked to her father about. "Melody, I have just spoken with your father, and I have something to ask you." Henry got down on his knee and took Melody's hand in his. He looked into her face with love shining in his eyes. As he held her hand, he could feel her trembling, and he said, "Melody, I hold you in great esteem. In fact . . . , I have fallen in love with you . . . I hope that you feel the same way about me. Will you do me the great honor of becoming my wife? I'll always love you and take care of you. Please . . . say that you'll be my wife!"

With tears in her eyes, she answered, "Yes . . . oh yes . . . I'll marry you. I love you very much . . . It would be a great honor to be your wife."

Henry helped Melody to her feet and put his arms around her, pulled her close, and kissed her. He could hear Melody catch her breath, and he knew she was overcome because he could see the emotion in her lovely face. He had asked her to marry him, and it was the happiest moment of his life. Henry deepened their kiss and gently pulled her close. He did not want to scare her, so he concentrated on keeping his desires in check, but it was very difficult, because it felt so wonderful to have her in his arms. As he released her, he gave a slight groan. Melody opened her eyes and gave Henry one of her beautiful smiles. The joy was shining brightly in her lovely eyes.

"Your father gave me permission to marry you, and I hope we can marry soon. Please tell me you don't want a long engagement, because I don't think I can wait very long for you to be my wife!" Henry said as he gazed into her eyes.

With tears of joy rolling down her pretty face, she said, "I would marry you today, if that were possible. However, I think it will take at least three weeks, since it takes that long for the banns to be read. I don't care about a big wedding. I just want to be your wife!"

Melody and her mother hurriedly put together the plans for a small wedding. The wedding date was set for Saturday, October 22, which was only three weeks away.

While Henry and Melody were talking about whom to invite to the wedding, he said, "I just want you to be my wife as soon as possible. Whoever you want to be there is fine with me. Since my family will probably give us some kind of reception later, it isn't necessary for them to be here. I don't want anything to delay our marriage, and waiting for them to travel all the way up here would take too long. They would bring an entire entourage with them, so it would probably take them several weeks to even start the trip. The only person I want at our wedding is my friend Weston. He can travel fast and be here in plenty of time for our wedding."

Two days after Henry proposed, Melody took him around the village, introducing him to all her dear friends. As they walked and held hands, Melody's heart was bursting with pride and joy. Henry was so courteous to everyone, and all the villagers went out of their way to welcome him. When they arrived at Brandon's house, she said, "Remember when I told you about my friend Brandon? This is where he and his wife, Lily, live. I want you to meet them. I know you're going to like both of them tremendously."

Melody and Henry walked up the path and knocked on the door. A pretty young woman, who was obviously with child, answered the door, and when she saw Melody, she gave her a hug and said, "We were wondering when you would bring your friend for a visit." She looked back behind her and said, "Brandon, please come here. Melody and her friend have come for a visit."

A tall, thin young man with light brown hair and gray eyes came to the door, and when he saw Melody, he grinned and said, "It's about time you came over here! We understand that congratulations are in order. Please come in. We're happy you've stopped by. I'm Brandon, by the way, and this is my wife, Lily." Brandon opened the door wide, and they went into their parlor. "Please take a seat. Lily, why don't you get some tea for our guests?"

Melody laughed and said, "Brandon, wait! I haven't even introduced you to Henry. Brandon, Lily, this is my fiancé Lord Henry Montgomery. I've told Henry all about both of you. Lily, please don't go to any trouble for us. We just had luncheon, so we don't need any tea. Let's just sit here and talk."

Lily smiled, took a seat by Brandon, and said, "It wouldn't have been a bother, Melody. We're just glad you finally brought Lord Montgomery over to meet us." Lily looked over at Henry and said, "It's a pleasure to meet you, my lord. Melody has told us all about you. I know Brandon offered you congratulations, but I want to tell you how pleased we are that Melody has found you. I hope you'll be as blessed in your marriage as Brandon and I have been."

Henry gazed at Melody with joy in his bright blue eyes as he replied, "I know we'll be happy. I'm the most fortunate of men that Melody has agreed to marry me. I'm glad to finally meet both of you. Please, call me Henry. Any friend of Melody's is a friend of mine."

They stayed for about thirty minutes, and by the time they were ready to take their leave, Henry was laughing and joking with Brandon as if they had been friends for years. This pleased Melody so much since Brandon and Lily were so special to her.

As they walked back to the vicarage, Melody and Henry held hands, and she asked, "What did you think of Brandon and Lily? Aren't they wonderful?"

Henry pulled her close to his side and said, "I enjoyed meeting both of them. I can see why you like them. They're very friendly people. How long have they been married? They both seem very young, Melody."

As they continued down the path, Melody said, "They've only been married for eight months. Brandon is one and twenty, and Lily is nineteen. Brandon met Lily when she was sixteen and immediately fell in love with her. Of course, Brandon had to finish school before they could marry. He's the schoolmaster at the local village school. Brandon has always wanted to teach, for as long as I can remember. I'm so pleased you liked them."

"Darling, as much as I enjoyed meeting them, I'd rather take advantage of this time we have alone to kiss you!" Henry took her into his arms and kissed her passionately, and Melody ardently returned his kiss. Soon they were both breathing heavily, and Henry's hands were roaming down her back. He cupped her bottom and pulled her closer to him. Melody could feel his manhood against her belly, and she felt a fierce wash of pleasure stronger than she had ever felt before. Henry slipped his hand inside Melody's dress and gently squeezed her nipple. Desire wove its spell, and soon, Melody was trembling from excitement.

Henry released her lips and murmured, "Oh my darling, I want you so badly, but we must stop. I love you too much for your first time to be hurried. As much as it pains me, I want to wait for our wedding night."

Melody smiled up at Henry and said, "I love you Henry, I know that when we finally make love, it will be beyond my wildest imagination. I'm glad you stopped before we got too carried away. Anyone could have come along this path and seen us. We need to get back because it's almost time for tea."

CHAPTER 5

October 1814

THE DAYS STARTED to fly by, and before Melody realized it, her wedding day had arrived. Melody chose to wear an ecru gown with Belgian lace on the bodice and flounced around the bottom. Once she was dressed, she looked in her cheval mirror and admired how well the silk fabric gently draped her body. The style was very becoming to her and showed off her voluptuous figure. There were tears in her mother's eyes as Melody turned around and faced her. When Melody saw her tears, she said, "Oh, Mother, please don't cry on my wedding day. I truly love Henry, and I know we're going to have a wonderful life."

Melody's mother smiled as she replied, "I know you are, darling. I'm just a little overwhelmed seeing you all grown up and ready to start your new life. I promise they're happy tears. You have grown up to be a wonderful daughter. Your father and I are so very proud of the woman you have become. Now, we need to go downstairs. It's time to leave for the church."

The small church was simply gorgeous. Her mother had decorated the church with gold chrysanthemums and yellow mums. There must have been a hundred candles lit all around the church. White and gold tulle bows decorated the pews. As Melody stood at the entrance and listened to the music swell, she looked up at the altar and saw Henry standing there with her father and Lord Weston. As Melody walked up the aisle toward Henry, her knees were shaking, and her hands were trembling so badly that she could barely hold her flower bouquet.

The walk down the aisle seemed to take forever, but finally, she was standing by Henry, and her father started the Mass. They turned toward each other as they repeated their vows to love, honor, and cherish each other for the rest of their lives. Each word took on a new meaning for her. Henry's voice was strong and sure, and Melody's was soft but steady. As

Henry slid an incredibly beautiful emerald and diamond ring on her third finger, she was overcome by the love she felt for him. Then her father said, "In the name of the Father, the Son, and the Holy Ghost, I now pronounce that you are man and wife. What God hath joined together, let no man put asunder. You may now kiss your bride." Henry raised her veil and softly kissed her lips, with reverence. She placed her hand in the crook of his arm, and they walked back down the aisle to the rear of the church, where they signed the church registry. They were married at last.

They walked back to Melody's house, where the small wedding breakfast was being held for them. Lord Weston made the first toast, wishing Melody and Henry many years of happiness. Then Brandon offered his toast, wishing them all the happiness in the world and hoping that they would be as happy as he and Lily were. Melody's stomach was jumping with excitement, so she was not able to eat anything, but she did manage a bite of the incredibly beautiful wedding cake that her mother had made for them. The sugar roses were so lovely that it seemed a shame to eat them. Soon it was time for her to change into her traveling dress, and she went upstairs with her mother.

Her mother looked at her with love and pride shining in her eyes as she said, "Melody, you're a beautiful bride. I'm so happy you have found someone to love. Henry is a very nice young man, and I know he'll take good care of you. We'll miss you terribly, but your father and I won't be sad, because we know you'll be happy. Besides, you're going to eventually be living in Doncaster, which isn't too terribly far away. I probably should have asked you this earlier, but do you have any questions you would like to ask me about the wedding night before you go back downstairs?"

Melody hesitantly asked, "Mother what . . . will happen tonight? I don't know anything, and I'm a little . . . frightened. Please explain everything to me."

"Henry will be gentle, and he will take care of everything. You don't need to worry, because he'll know what to do. The physical side of love is so beautiful when shared between two people who genuinely love each other. Just let your husband guide you," she said.

"All right, Mother . . . I'll put my trust in Henry. I'm sure you're right. He'll know what to do." Then with fear in her voice, she said, "It's just that I've heard . . ." Then she hurriedly finished saying, "It's painful to lose your virginity."

"Melody, there will be some mild discomfort, but it will be very fleeting, and then everything will be fine, so stop worrying. I understand your concerns because I felt the same way when your father and I were married. It's perfectly normal to be apprehensive. I promise you'll be fine, and tomorrow you'll be so happy you won't even remember you were scared. It's time to go back downstairs to your handsome new husband. You have a long drive ahead of you, so you need to get started."

Melody came down the stairs, and her eyes met Henry's. He was looking at her with so much love that it brought tears to her eyes. He took her hand as she stepped down to the floor and said, "My love, it's time for us to go. We have a long drive before we stop for the night. Come, my darling."

As the carriage left Melody's home, she looked back and watched as her parents grew smaller and smaller, until she could no longer see them. She felt the tears silently slip down her cheeks. Henry had a concerned expression on his face when he asked, "What's wrong, my love? Why are you crying? Have I done anything to upset you?"

Melody was pleased by the concern he was showing, so she smiled through her tears and said, "No, Henry. I just realized that I'll never live with my parents again, and I love them so much. I shall miss them terribly. I know that I'll come back for visits, but it won't be the same. I promise I'm not sad to be leaving with you, and I'm sure we'll have a wonderful life together."

"Thank goodness! You had me worried when I saw your tears. I promise we'll have a happy life, and I'll always love and protect you. I'm thrilled that we're finally married . . . and that you're now my bride. Is there anything else bothering you?" he asked.

Melody thought for a minute and then replied, "There is one thing that I'm concerned about. Your father is such a powerful man, and your parents move in the highest echelon of society. I wonder if they will be willing to accept me as your wife. Do you think they'll like me?"

Henry looked uncomfortable as he answered, "Darling, it will take some time for them to adjust to the idea of our marriage, but I'm sure you can win them over with time. You're right about them being high in the instep. My parents have expressed the opinion that I should marry to bring more prestige to the family. A person's standing in life is more important to them than anything else. I need you to understand that my parents are cold and distant, but they're like that with everyone, so I don't want you to take anything they may say, personally. To be honest with you, they rarely like any of my friends, and you can't let it bother you. As I said, just give it time. I'm sure they'll come around eventually. Come over here and let me give you a hug. I need to hold you close to my heart. I'm so pleased to have you as my wife, and I'm the happiest of men."

Melody smiled up at him with such a look of trust as she said, "I'm sure you're right. I'm relieved you told me how they are, so I'll know what to expect. I was so excited last night that I barely slept at all, so I'm going to lay here in your arms and take a short nap, if that is all right with you."

Henry gazed at her with love glowing in his eyes and said reassuringly, "I'll be happy to hold you while you sleep. Just rest your pretty head on my shoulder. I'll wake you when we arrive at the inn." Melody sighed as she closed her eyes and drifted off to sleep.

They traveled until dusk. He saw the coaching inn up ahead, where he planned to stop, so Henry gently woke her up. She looked enchanting as she slowly opened her eyes. She looked around and asked, "Are we there yet?"

"We're arriving at the inn now. I've made arrangements for us to have a private dining parlor, and we'll have adjoining bedchambers. We should be quite comfortable. Weston recommended this coaching inn, and he usually knows where the best places are." When the carriage had stopped, Henry turned and helped Melody out of the carriage. He offered his arm, and they entered the inn. The innkeeper came forward and welcomed them to his inn, and then he led them to the private dining parlor. He assured them that dinner would be served shortly. Henry helped Melody remove her cloak and pulled out her chair; then he took his seat. The innkeeper returned with a serving girl, and they laid out the food on the table and then excused themselves. The food was excellent, but Melody was so nervous that she found it difficult to swallow. After they were through eating, he escorted her to her room. Henry told Melody that he would send up her maid, to help her get ready for bed, and he left her alone.

Melody looked around the room and was pleased to see how clean and inviting everything was. As she walked around the room, she noticed the lovely lace curtains at the window. There was a comfortable-looking bed with a pretty homemade quilt and lots of pillows on it. There was a fire burning in the hearth, and the room felt invitingly warm. There was a knock on the door, and Melody went to see who it was. Since it was her maid, Millie, she let her in.

"Your husband sent me up to help you get ready for bed, my lady." She immediately began pulling out Melody's nightclothes. There was a beautiful, fine, lawn night rail with a matching dressing gown for the night. Melody smiled as she remembered how her mother had worked on it each night, making sure she would have something pretty to wear tonight. Millie helped her remove her traveling dress and then brushed her long hair until it was tangle free and shining. Melody left it loose because she knew that would be how Henry would want it. Finally, she was ready for bed, so she sent Millie away for the night.

Her nerves were on edge, and she was not sure what she should do. *Should she go ahead and get into bed, or should she sit in the chair until Henry joined her?* Her heart was beating rapidly, and her breathing was shallow; her hands were trembling because she was so nervous. Soon Henry would be coming through the door, and she was terrified, because she was not sure what would happen. She thought about what her mother had told her and tried to take comfort from her words. *Oh, why couldn't her mother have been more forthcoming!* Melody decided she would go ahead and get into bed to wait for Henry. Soon, she heard a knock on the door from Henry's room. As he opened the door, he came into the room and stopped when he saw her in bed. He had on a long, dark blue, silk dressing gown tied at the waist, and Melody could see that he did not have anything on underneath his robe.

Henry just stood there and gazed over at Melody. *How lovely she looked with all her golden hair around her shoulders!* It was the first time he had ever seen Melody with her hair down. It fell almost to her waist, and he could just imagine losing himself in all that glorious hair. The scent of lemons filled the air, and Henry knew it was Melody's special essence. His nostrils flared, and he had to stifle his raging desire to make her his own. The very thought that Melody was all his, had his senses aroused, and he felt very possessive. It was a powerful aphrodisiac to know that she had never been touched by another man. Henry walked over to the bed and smiled down at her. "Melody, you look so beautiful. I knew you had beautiful hair, but I had no idea how lovely it truly was. I've dreamed of burying my face in all your gorgeous hair. Your hair always smells like lemons, and I have always loved that scent. May I join you in our marriage bed?"

Melody did not speak, but she nodded her head as Henry turned down the bedside lamp. He pulled back the covers and got into bed. As he looked over at Melody, he held his arms open, and Melody went to him. He gazed deeply into her eyes and gently stroked her cheek. Her skin felt as soft as silk, and he could stroke her lovely skin all night. She looked up at Henry and then laid her head on his shoulder. Henry pulled her close, lifted her chin, and slowly lowered his head to kiss her. Melody was trembling, and Henry knew she was terrified.

"Do you know what will happen here tonight, in our marriage bed?" he asked. "You have nothing to fear. I promise I won't do anything to hurt you. Just let me kiss and hold you, and if anything bothers you, let me know, all right?"

He kissed Melody again, and this time, he deepened the kiss as he pulled her closer to him. His desire was running hot, but he knew he had to control it so that he did not frighten her. As he kissed her, he nibbled at Melody's luscious lips, and soon she sighed and parted them. He slid his tongue into her mouth and tasted her sweet essence. She hesitantly followed his lead and used her tongue as he did. The kisses grew firmer, and their breathing became heavier. He started rubbing Melody's back and gently placed his other hand on her breast. He could feel her nipple grow taut as he lowered his head to kiss Melody on her slender neck. Then he nibbled his way down to the swell of her breasts. He could feel her quiver and knew she was experiencing her first real taste of passion, and he felt incredibly honored that he would be the first and only man to ever see her in the throes of passion.

"Let me help you remove your gown . . . I want to see your incredibly lovely breasts. I've been dreaming of them ever since I first met you. I love that you're so voluptuous. You look just as I always imagined you would."

Melody nodded her head and let Henry remove her gown. He took his robe off and tossed them both over the side of the bed. He began to kiss Melody again, but this time with more urgency. He pulled her up against him, and it felt marvelous to finally be skin to skin with her. He rained kisses all over her face and cheeks. Her skin was so soft and smooth, and he was aroused by her fresh, clean, womanly scent. He nibbled down her neck again and moved lower to take her nipple into his mouth. She gasped with pleasure, and soon he had her moaning and writhing. Her breasts grew heavy, and her nipples became rigid as he circled her areola with the tip of his finger and brushed his thumb across the tight little bud. Henry moved to her other breast, took the nipple into his mouth, and gently suckled. His other hand was roaming slowly downward, and soon he was at the apex of her pretty, plump thighs, where her lovely golden curls were. Melody quivered as Henry touched her there. Soon, she was panting as he moved his hand between her thighs and found her little nubbin. Henry began to circle it, and he felt how wet she was. It amazed him that she was so responsive to his touch. Melody looked embarrassed by what was happening to her body, but he could tell it was feeling so marvelous that she did not want him to stop. Henry took his finger and slowly and gently pushed it inside of her and she stiffened. So he said, "It's all right, love. I won't do anything to hurt you. I promise that you'll enjoy this, so try to relax." He gently stroked her with his finger and worked a second finger in to gently stretch her so she would be ready to receive him.

He parted her lovely thighs and moved in between. Her thighs were just the way he dreamed they would be—all plump, soft, pink skin. He felt Melody stiffen up when she felt his thick rod nestled against her belly, so he said, "Don't be afraid, Melody. God made my body in a unique way so that it will fit perfectly inside yours. What you're feeling is the part of me that will enter your body. If you want, you can call it my love tool. Your body is designed to accept me inside. That's why you're so wet. That way, when I enter you, it won't hurt."

He kissed her deeply, and he could feel Melody relaxing as she began to moan and toss her head back and forth on the pillow. He carefully placed his shaft at the entrance of her passage. He moved his thick shaft up and down her nether lips, to get it wet with her love juices. He gently entered her, and he could feel how tight she was. He had never felt anything as wonderful before. He knew he would need all the control, he could find, to keep from hurting her. He pushed further in, until he came to her maidenhead. He stopped to gather his strength, and as he kissed her; he pushed through and was buried all the way to the hilt. It was an incredible feeling to know that they were now joined and made one. Melody gave a little whimper and started to tense up, so he said, "I'm sorry. I know this hurts, but I promise that soon you won't feel any more pain."

He stayed very still, to give her a chance to get used to him being inside of her. It felt indescribably wonderful to finally be inside her tight sheath. As he felt her begin to relax, he started to move. Soon, Melody had picked up his rhythm and was moving with him. She was making sounds that let Henry know that she was starting to enjoy the friction of his movements. He picked up the pace, moving faster and faster. He could not hold back any longer, but he wanted to make sure Melody was there with him, so he reached down and rubbed her little bud of desire, and he felt Melody's muscles begin to tighten around his shaft. It was obvious she did not know what was happening; it felt so good to be the first man to bring her to fulfillment, and he knew she did not want him to stop. He watched her face as she went flying, and the waves of pleasure rolled through her delectable body. Her channel tightened around his thick shaft as she reached the heights of ecstasy, and the spasms kept coming. Henry stiffened; then his seed flowed into her, and it felt incredible. There were no words that could describe how wonderful it felt. He gently pulled out of her body, fell to the side, and pulled Melody into his arms and held her tight. "Are you all right?" he asked. "I didn't hurt you too much, did I? I know there was some pain, but I tried to be as gentle as possible."

Melody looked at Henry and gave him a soft smile, then said, "That was the most incredible thing I have ever felt. Is it always like that?"

"Oh my darling girl, it just keeps getting better and better." So . . . he showed her . . . all over again!

CHAPTER 6

October 1814

MELODY WOKE UP and looked around the room. It took her a moment to realize where she was. *She felt something hard against the back of her bottom, and she realized it was Henry's . . . , what did he call it? His love tool, and what a tool it was!* Melody had never imagined how wonderful lovemaking could be. It was so much more than she ever expected. As she lay there, she felt Henry begin to stretch and knew he was waking up. His hand found her breast, and he gently rubbed her nipple. Henry started kissing the nape of her neck. He pulled her close and whispered, "Good morning, did you sleep well? I hope you aren't too sore from our lovemaking."

"I slept better than I ever remember, and I feel marvelous." Melody closed her eyes in embarrassment and quietly said, "I'm not in any discomfort."

Henry growled as he said, "Roll over then, so I can give you a proper good morning kiss." He kissed her and slid his tongue into her mouth as he continued to run his hand over her breast and up and down her sides. Before long, he was slowly entering her sheath. She spread her thighs wider and welcomed him inside. He pulled her legs up and wrapped them around his hips, which deepened his thrusts. He was kissing her breasts and sucking on her nipples. She began to feel like she had the night before. The waves of pleasure started rolling over her. Henry was moving faster and faster, and Melody was meeting him stroke for stroke. Suddenly, she stiffened and went sailing over into the amazing sensations she had felt the night before. Henry threw back his head and shouted out her name as he emptied his essence inside her. She loved the way he looked as his seed filled her. He collapsed on top of her, and she felt such tenderness for him. Melody held him in her arms and kissed his shoulder. He rolled off, pulled her to him, and kissed her temple as she ran her fingers through his chest hair and purred with contentment.

"That was a marvelous way to greet the morning. Just think, we can do this everyday for the rest of our lives, but as splendid as this feels, we need to get up because I suspect that it's quite late in the morning and we have another long day of traveling before us. I'm going back to my room now, so you can get ready to leave. I'll send Millie up, and I'll have her bring you some hot water for your morning ablutions. Meet me in the dining parlor when you're ready, and we'll have some breakfast before we leave. See you soon, sweetheart."

Melody lay there and remembered all that had happened last night and again this morning. She decided she was really going to enjoy being married, even more than she had ever dreamed. She got out of bed, and suddenly she realized she was a little sore, but it just reminded her of all the wonderful things she had experienced! She went to the dressing table and began to brush her hair. It was quite tangled, but then again it was worth it because she knew how much Henry loved her hair. There was a knock on the door, and she got up to let Millie in. The steaming hot water helped to soothe the soreness. As she washed herself, there were traces of blood on her thighs, and when she noticed it, she blushed all over, from head to toe. Melody finished her morning ablutions while Millie pulled out a fresh traveling dress. As she dressed in her pale blue gown with light gray trim and matching pelisse, she hoped that Henry would think that she looked attractive. Soon, Melody was dressed and made her way down to the dining parlor. Henry was already seated, and he stood up as she entered and said, "Come in, my lovely one, and take a seat. You look very pretty this morning. Breakfast has arrived. I'm starving, and I'm sure you must be very hungry too. After all, you had a busy night and morning."

Melody blushed and gave a little laugh, then said, "Please, Henry, I'm embarrassed enough, without you talking about that!"

"I'm sorry, love, but you're just so much fun to tease. Let's eat, so we can get our day started. We have a full day of traveling ahead of us." After they finished their breakfast, they went out to their carriage, and he helped her get seated inside and said, "I'm going to ride Jupiter for a while, since I know he needs a good run. I'll join you in a few hours. Why don't you take a nap, since you didn't get much sleep last night?"

Melody watched him mount Jupiter and ride off. The wind was blowing his thick, red gold hair, and it made her long to run her fingers through all that marvelous hair. She admired how nice he looked in his dark green jacket, buff breeches, and glossy black Hessians. His breeches hugged his buttocks and well-developed thighs, and she felt a tingling sensation between her legs. Melody now knew that this was definitely a sign of desire. What a fortunate young woman she was to have such a handsome, virile, young husband. She settled back and pulled out the book she was reading, and soon, she was lost in the story and did not notice the time. The carriage slowed down and then stopped as they arrived at another coaching inn. Henry helped her out of the carriage, and they went inside. They had a delicious meat pie, a variety of cheeses, and dark bread with some ale for their luncheon. The food was delicious, and soon their appetites were appeased.

He joined her in the carriage after they got back on the road. He started telling her stories about his youth, and he soon had Melody laughing over all the mischief he used to get into. She shared more stories about her childhood, and again he wished he could have had parents like Melody's. No wonder, she felt sad at leaving them. While Henry was not close to his parents at all, Melody was obviously very close to hers. He promised himself that he would make sure that she was able to see her parents often. Even though they would not live close to them initially, they would be close to them in the not too distant future.

Over the next five days, Melody and Henry grew to know each other much better. The nights were glorious as they filled them with passion and tenderness. He was amazed at how adventurous Melody was in bed. She was more than willing to try whatever he suggested. Her untutored enthusiasm was quite arousing. They were nearing Henry's home, and the closer they got to Sanderford Park, the more nervous Henry became. He had sent word of his marriage, but he knew that the news would not have been well received by his parents. He felt sure they would feel that Melody was not good enough for him. He would just have to make it clear to them that he loved her and that they must treat her with the respect she deserved. After all, Melody's father was well born, being a younger son of the Earl of Wyldwood and her mother the daughter of Viscount Millings. Melody was just as highborn as he was. If his parents had not been so set on him marrying Lady Penelope, he was sure they would be more willing to accept her.

When they returned to the carriage after their last stop, it was apparent that something was bothering Henry because his face gave it away. He was always so open and honest that it was easy to see when he was upset about something. He had shared enough about his parents that she thought that could be what was bothering him. It seemed that the closer he got to his home, the tenser he became. She hoped he was not ashamed of her, as he had shared how high in the instep his parents were. Melody knew she did not bring a dowry to the marriage, and she was sure it would affect how they felt about her.

Finally, they turned onto a long drive, and Henry explained that they had been traveling on Sanderford Park for quite some time. As they approached the house, Melody became nervous when she saw how incredibly large the house was. It was truly magnificent to look at but very overwhelming. She could not imagine living here, but it was to be her new home, so she would have to adjust.

The carriage pulled up to the portico, and several footmen came out to help them out of the carriage. Henry offered her his arm as they walked up the steps and entered through the immense oak doors. The entrance hall had black-and-white marble floors with white marble statues on each side of the entrance. The room was at least three stories high with al fresco art painted on the ceiling. There was a magnificent staircase leading up to the next floor, and it looked as if it went on forever. It was an incredibly beautiful room but a little overwhelming for Melody. *If the entrance hall was this opulent, what would the rest of the house be like?* Simpson, the butler, was there and offered to take their outer garments. He called for the housekeeper, Mrs. Milton, and she asked if they would like to go to their rooms to freshen up before they joined the family. They told her they would like that, and she led them upstairs.

The suite of rooms was lovely. There were two bedchambers with dressing rooms attached, and a sitting room was situated between their bedchambers. There was even a bathing room, which Melody had never seen before. The chamber she would be using was decorated in shades of blue and yellow, and it had gilded white French furniture. The counterpane, on the bed, was a lovely shade of blue with ecru lace around the edge and a marching canopy. Melody thought of what it would be like to make love to Henry in that glorious bed and it caused a warm sensation to run throughout her body. There was a small French desk, which would be perfect for her correspondence. French doors led out to a balcony that overlooked a lovely rose garden, and she knew that next spring it would be truly glorious to behold with all the roses in full bloom.

The walls in Henry's chamber was painted a deep blue with pale gray accents with much heavier dark oak furniture, giving the room a masculine feel to it, and there was an enormous oak bed. It was the biggest bed she had ever seen—two people could easily get lost in it—of that she was sure. She thought she could be very comfortable living here, as long as Henry's parents accepted her. Before Henry left Melody in her chamber, he said, "Your maid should be up shortly. Why don't you take your time and rest a bit before you join the family. I'll return in an hour, and then we'll go down together to meet everyone."

Melody met Henry's eyes and said with trepidation, "Whatever you think is best Henry. I look forward to meeting your brother and your sisters, but I dread meeting your parents. I just know they're not going to like me."

Henry shrugged and said, "I don't want you to worry. Remember what I told you they're like and that they're the same way with almost everyone. Try to overlook their rudeness, and I'll be there to protect you. You'll love my sisters, and I know they'll love you. Nelson will be thrilled when he sees how happy you make me, so relax. I'll return shortly. See you in a bit, my love."

He rushed through, getting his travel dirt off and hurried down to speak with his parents. When he found his parents in his father's study, it was obvious, by the expressions on their faces, that they were not happy to see him at all. His father was sitting behind his big desk, and he motioned for Henry to take a seat. His mother was sitting on the couch by the window looking very haughty. Henry took a seat across from his father and said, "Good afternoon, I hope both of you are doing well. My bride and I have just arrived. Melody will be down shortly to meet both of you. I hope you'll welcome her into the family. I told you in my letter that she comes from a good family and that I love her very much, so please be kind to her. She's feeling a little overwhelmed by it all, so she needs to feel welcomed."

With distain on his face, his grace said, "Why should we welcome her? You know you were supposed to marry Lady Penelope. She would have enriched the ducal holdings. What does this little country mouse bring to us? Not a thing! Her father is a vicar with no consequence to speak of, and you did not even have the decency to let us know you were getting married. We did not have a chance to voice our opinion regarding this marriage. This is so like you, Henry. You have always been so impulsive and thoughtless. I guess we should have expected this type of behavior, as you have been this way all your life! Your mother and I are extremely disappointed in you."

"Regardless of how you feel about me, you'll treat Melody with respect. Any wrongdoing has been done by me, and I shan't allow you to punish her for what you see as my misguided decisions." It was just as he expected; they were going to give Melody a difficult time. At least he would be there to protect her for a few weeks as she settled in, and he would make sure that Nelson took over for him when he had to go back to his garrison. "Melody is the kindest and most tender-hearted young woman you could ever hope to meet, and she is very apprehensive about meeting you. Please keep your opinions to yourselves and be nice to her!"

The duke looked at Henry with disgust and said, "We will be polite, but we do not have to like her, nor like the fact that you have made her your wife. Keep in mind that you are only our second son, and we do not have to support you or your wife."

"I don't need you to support me or my wife because Grandmother left me her estate and enough income that I don't need assistance from you to support Melody. I have also done quite well with my investments." Thank God, he had been smart enough to invest some of his inheritance when he came into his majority. "I neither need nor do I want anything from you, other than a place for Melody to stay while I'm finishing up my military career. I'll be selling out my commission, just as soon as I get all my men settled back into civilian life. Melody will need to live here with you while I travel back and forth between here and my regiment in Kent. Can I at least count on you for this?"

His father nodded his head as he said, "We will allow her to stay here, but just know that we are not happy about this whole situation."

"Thank you, your grace. We'll try to stay out of your way as much as possible. Now if you will excuse me, I'll go get Melody and join you in the drawing room for tea." Henry then turned and left the study.

He returned to their suite to get Melody, and she could see that he was tense as soon as he entered the sitting room. She wondered if he had been speaking with his parents. He always seemed to tense up when he thought about his parents, and it was causing her to get quite anxious about meeting them. It was hard enough to even think about meeting a duke and duchess, but this was even more intimidating because they were her in-laws.

"Melody, my love, let me take you down to the drawing room. Tea is about to be served, and I want to introduce you to my family. You don't need to be apprehensive, for I'll be with you the entire time. You'll like my brother and my sisters, and they'll adore you, as I do. Come on, let's get this over with, and then we can relax." They went down the stairs and entered the drawing room. Henry's parents were sitting on the settee. There was a man standing by the fireplace that Melody thought must be Henry's brother. It was astonishing how much they looked like each other. His sisters were also there. Everyone looked up as they entered the room.

"Hello, everyone. This is Melody, my wife. Her father is the son of the Earl of Wyldwood, and her mother is the daughter of Viscount Millings. As I stated in my letter, Melody is from Little Smythington, Lincolnshire. I hope you'll make her feel welcome. She's very excited about meeting all of you." Henry smiled over at Melody and took her hand as they walked over to where his parents were seated.

"This is my father, the Duke of Sanderford . . . and my mother the Duchess of Sanderford," Henry said. Melody politely acknowledged the introduction and gave them an elegant curtsey, and then Henry introduced her to his brother, "Melody, this is my brother, Nelson."

Nelson walked over, bowed, and said, "It's such a pleasure to finally meet you. Henry told me all about you when he was here last month. I welcome you to our family."

Henry turned to his sisters and said, "These are my two sisters, Helen and Kathryn. I'm sure you'll all get along splendidly."

The older of the two girls said, "Hello, I'm Helen. I'm so pleased to meet you. Unlike Nelson, Henry didn't tell me anything about you, but I can't wait to get to know you. I'm sure we'll become fast friends in no time."

Kathryn timidly smiled at Melody and said, "I'm Kathryn, and I'm very excited to meet you. I wish you and Henry all the happiness in the world."

They all made Melody feel very welcomed except for his parents. They looked at her with a condescending expression on their faces. She guessed that it was to be expected, after all; she was sure they thought she was not worthy of their son. Henry seated her in a chair close to his sisters, and the duchess began to serve tea. Soon everyone began to relax and enjoy their tea and biscuits. Henry ate several sandwiches as usual. After tea was over, Henry escorted Melody back up to their suite.

"Well, that went well. What did you think of my brother and sisters? I told you they would like you and be happy for us. I know that my parents were a little cool, but they're like that with everyone. I'm just relieved that we've got that behind us. Come here, darling, you look as if you to could use a hug, and I know that I could." Melody went into his arms as he lifted up her face and tenderly kissed her. She responded, and he deepened the kiss and pulled her close to him. She felt desire begin to blossom and tentatively kissed him back as passion took over. Henry picked her up and carried her into his bedchamber, and he undressed her as he continued to kiss her passionately. Soon, they were both naked and laying on the bed. Melody decided to be bold and began to touch Henry on the chest. She rubbed his flat male nipples, and Henry gasped with pleasure as she continued to run her fingers through the hair that grew on the center of his chest. He lowered his head to Melody's breasts, took her dusky pink, engorged nipple into his mouth, and sucked gently. Then he started to kiss his way down her body and over her soft belly. He spread her thighs and began to lick her little bud of desire between her legs. Melody stiffened up with shock and embarrassment. Surely, this was too wicked, but then it started to feel so good that she just did not care if it were wicked or not. She began to tingle all over, and her nether region began to ache for fulfillment. Her breathing became shallow, and she was writhing trying to get as close to Henry's decadent mouth as possible. She started to shake, and then she exploded as her body shuddered in ecstasy. Henry lifted his head and grinned at Melody, and she grinned back. He crawled up her delectable body and surged inside her. She reached her peak again, just as Henry found his release. They clung to each other and fell asleep.

They barely made it down to dinner on time as they rushed laughing into the drawing room. Henry's parents looked disgusted, and they were obviously angry about something. His grace said, "Henry, you know what time we gather here for dinner, and you are five minutes late. You know how much I value punctuality. I do not expect to have to talk to you about this again."

Simpson came in to announce that dinner was served. Everyone was quiet, and it was one of the most uncomfortable meals she had ever had. The food was superb, but it might as well have been sawdust, for all that Melody could taste of it. Finally, the duchess rose and requested all the ladies come with her so that they could leave the men to their port and cigars.

When they arrived in the drawing room, the duchess indicated that she wanted Melody to sit beside her. This was not a good sign. She began to question Melody about her family. "Are your grandparents still living? I understand you are an only child. What are your prospects? Will you inherit anything from your grandparents? Speak up, gel, and answer my questions."

Melody hesitantly replied, "My mother's parents are still alive, but we don't see them often because they're in bad health. My father's parents have passed away. My father has one brother. He inherited everything, and his children will inherit from him. While my mother's parents are of the nobility, there is no money, so I don't have a dowry."

"Just as I suspected! You will not bring anything to the ducal coffers. I do not understand what Henry sees in you. You are not beautiful, and you are a little on the dumpy side. He will obviously grow tired of you quickly and do not expect anything from us. You are all on your own, and when he tires of you, which he most certainly will, you can just go back to where you came from. Do I make myself clear?"

"Yes, your grace, I shan't expect anything from you. I think it would be best if I went up to my room now. Please excuse me." Melody quietly turned around and left the room.

When the men joined them in the drawing room, Henry asked where his wife was, and the duchess told him that his scared little rabbit of a wife had scurried up to her rooms. Henry gave his mother an angry look and left. He found Melody in their rooms, and she was crying as if her heart were breaking. He went to her and gently put his arms around her.

"Don't listen to anything my mother said to you. You are the light of my life, and you don't need to even think for a minute that she speaks for me or my brother and sisters. She is a hateful, bitter old woman, and you are worth ten of her!" Henry said as he slowly rubbed her back.

"Oh Henry! She said you would get tired of me and cast me aside. I don't bring anything of value to the ducal coffers. I couldn't bear it, if you got tired of me," Melody cried.

"Shush, love, I'll never grow tired of you. I love you to distraction. Please believe me. I'll love you for all eternity!" Melody sniffed and began to calm down. Henry held her in his arms until she fell asleep.

Once she was asleep, he carried her to her bed and carefully undressed her so that he would not wake her up. He slipped on her night rail and tucked her into bed. *Why did his mother have to be so cruel?* There was no kinder or gentler person than his Melody. Henry went to his room and got undressed, and then he came back to Melody's room and got in bed with her. As he lay there, he worried about how Melody would handle his parents. He knew she was not used to being treated badly, and he was not sure how he could protect her from their distain, especially when he returned to his regiment. He would definitely need to speak with Nelson and ask him to watch out for Melody while he was away and protect her from his parents. With a plan in mind, he pulled her into his arms and held her as he drifted off to sleep.

When Melody woke up the next morning, Henry had already left her bed. The pillow on his side still had a dent in it, and she could still smell his clean masculine scent, so she knew he had slept there, and she was comforted by that knowledge. She thought about what his mother had said last night and what Henry said, and she decided she would believe Henry. It would be best if she stayed out of the duchess's way, as much as possible. Hopefully, she could avoid future unpleasantness. The drapes were open, the sun was shining in through the window, and it looked like a beautiful fall day. She hoped they could go riding because the weather was sure to turn colder soon. Her maid had been there, for there was a pitcher of steaming water for her to bathe in. She went about her morning ablutions and was soon ready to face her day. As she left her chamber, she realized she did not have any idea how to get to the breakfast room. She wondered how she had found her way back to her chamber last night. It was just by luck that she did not get lost last night, especially since she was so distraught over her conversation with the duchess. There was a maid coming toward her, and she asked, "Hello, could you please direct me to the breakfast room?"

The maid giggled and replied, "Of course, my lady. Just follow this hall to the end and then keep turning right until you get to the staircase. The stairs will take you to the right floor. At the bottom of the stairs, turn left, and it is the first door on the left. If you would like me to, I could take you there myself."

"No, that's all right. I believe I'll be able to find it. I appreciate your help." Melody proceeded down the hall, in the direction that the maid had pointed out to her, and soon, she was at the breakfast room. There was a sideboard filled with all kinds of breakfast foods. Melody took a plate and began to fill it with coddled eggs, bacon, and a muffin, as she was particularly hungry, for she had not eaten much the previous night.

As she went to the table to sit down, Nelson came into the room and started filling his plate. "Good morning. I hope you had a restful night," he said. "I'm pleased that Henry married you because I know you'll make him very happy. I want you to be happy here, so if there is anything I can do for you, just let me know."

"Thank you, my lord. I appreciate your offer, and I may take you up on it. In fact, do you know where Henry is this morning?" Melody asked as she placed her napkin in her lap.

Nelson smiled pleasantly as he replied, "I believe he went for a ride, but I imagine he should be back shortly. Oh, by the way, please call me Nelson. And may I call you Melody? After all, you're now my new sister."

Melody gave him a beatific smile. It pleased her greatly that Henry's brother wanted to be a brother to her. "I would be happy to Nelson, and certainly, call me Melody. I don't have a brother, but I've always wanted one." Once she finished her breakfast, she excused herself and went outside to find the stable. As she turned the corner, she ran into Henry.

"Good morning, my love. Where are you going in such a hurry?" Henry asked as he pulled her into his arms.

Melody gave him a sweet smile as she said, "Actually I was looking for you. I was hoping we could go for a ride, but Nelson told me you had already gone out today."

"I'm sorry, if I had known, I would have postponed my ride and come and gotten you. I tell you what, why don't we get the gig and I'll take you to town." Soon they were off to the village. As they drove through the countryside, Melody noticed how gorgeous it was with all the pretty fall colors on the trees. Once they arrived in the village, they got out of the gig and walked around. Cranleigh was a quaint little place, and surprisingly, it had quite a few shops. Melody was looking forward to exploring them, especially the bookseller. They talked and laughed as they walked along. They went into the confectionery and bought some candies. Then they got back in the gig and headed back to Sanderford Park. The drive back was pleasant, and Henry told her more stories about his youth.

Everyday they would either ride their horses or take long walks. Their love for each other deepened as each day passed. The more time they spent together, the closer they became.

CHAPTER 7

November 1814

A FORTNIGHT WENT by, and all was going well. Henry's parents kept their distance but were polite, if cool to her. She got to know his sisters, and she was growing to care for them. Helen was very pretty. She had hair the same shade as Henry's with his beautiful blue eyes. She was medium height and very slender, which was what Melody would have chosen, if one could choose something like that. Clearly, when Helen made her bow next spring, everything would go well for her since she was so pretty and vivacious. Kathryn was shy, but so sweet. She was all arms and legs, with bright red hair, and she looked just like a typical young lady, beginning her teen years.

Everyday, they would go riding. Henry found Melody a gentle, but spirited mare named Molly and she was thrilled to have her own horse for the first time. They took long walks and went on several picnics in the woods, where they found a secluded spot by the lake, so they could make love and let their passion soar. Every night, he introduced her to new delights of the flesh, and afterward, they would fall asleep in each other's arms. Melody was very happy and growing to love Henry more each day. He was a charming companion and was always making her laugh, so time just flew by.

The day finally came. It was time for Henry to go back to his regiment since his leave was up. On their last night together, Henry took Melody to heights of passion she had never imagined. As dawn was breaking, he woke her and gently kissed her, then said, "I need to leave if I'm going to get there in time, but I'll be back in a month. You'll be fine, and if you need anything, ask my brother. He'll take care of you for me. Try not to miss me too much, though God knows I'll miss you terribly! Remember me in your dreams as I'll remember you in mine." He tenderly picked Melody up and carried her back to her bed. Gently, he laid her down and kissed her one last time. Then he turned and quickly left her room.

Soon, he was on Jupiter, riding at a fast gallop, and as the wind was blowing in his hair, he felt wonderful. He hated to leave Melody, but he was looking forward to being back with his men. In a few months, he would put his military life behind him, and they would move to the estate his grandmother had left him in Yorkshire. Melody would love it there, and she would be much closer to her parents. It was a small estate, but it had a wonderful old manor house, and it was situated in a beautiful little valley, so the weather was better than in many of the other areas of the north. It would be a great place to raise their children, and in his mind's eye, he could see a beautiful little girl who looked just like Melody.

Henry just hoped his parents would continue to be civil to Melody. He had asked Nelson to watch over her for him and make sure that she was all right. He knew he would really miss her; in fact, he already did.

The trip went by quickly, and he was back at the garrison in no time. The first person he saw was his friend Captain Edward Hayden. When Hayden recognized Henry, he said, "Hello, Montgomery, I see you've finally decided to join us. How's married life treating you? I'm still having a hard time believing you're married."

Henry had a huge expression of satisfaction on his face as he replied, "It's good to see you, Hayden, and married life is much better than I ever expected. How are all our men doing? Have many of them left for civilian life yet?"

Hayden clapped him on the shoulder and said, "Come on, let's go find out, all right?"

Melody woke up later than usual. Her first thought was of Henry and that he had gone back to his regiment. *What was she going to do for an entire month without him?* She would miss him terribly. They had grown so much closer over the last few weeks. Melody was concerned about living with his family without him, especially his mother. After that incident, the first night they had arrived, she had stayed as far away as possible. At least, with Henry there, he formed a buffer between them. *Oh well, this was not getting her day started.* She got up and rang for her maid. She arrived, and soon Melody was ready to meet her day.

The breakfast room was empty when Melody arrived. She went to the sideboard and picked out her breakfast. The pastries looked delicious, but she passed them up, electing to have her usual toast and jam instead. She sat down to eat her breakfast and drink her hot chocolate. Nelson entered the room, went to the sideboard, and filled his plate; then he turned and asked, "May I join you?"

Melody took a sip of her hot chocolate, and then replied, "Of course, I would like some company. It looks like it will be a beautiful day even though we're well into the fall."

Nelson sympathetically asked, "How are you feeling this morning? I know Henry left for his regiment, so I expect you're already missing him, right?"

"I'll be fine. I just started a new book and that should keep me entertained for a few days, and I also have some letters I need to write. I've been neglecting my correspondence since my marriage. Of course, I hope to spend some time with you and your sisters, so we can get to know each other better, if that is all right?" Melody asked with a tentative smile on her face.

As Nelson took a seat across from her, he said, "Melody, I think I can speak for my sisters when I say that we already look upon you as part of our family. We know Henry loves you, and he asked me to take care of you while he's away. Please let me know if you need anything at all. I want you to feel at home here."

"Thank you, Nelson. You've already helped to make me feel welcome. Henry told me some stories about you and the mischief the two of you used to get into while you were growing up. I'm sure you have some interesting stories also. I would love to hear them, if you would share them with me?" she asked.

Nelson laughed, and then said, "All right, after you finish your breakfast, we can go for a walk in the garden, and I'll endeavor to entertain you with some stories about Henry that I'm sure he failed to mention to you."

"Yes, I would enjoy that very much. I'll go to my room and get a shawl," she replied.

"How about if we meet on the terrace, and we'll start our walk from there?" Nelson asked as he stood up, when Melody got up from her chair.

As Melody turned to leave the room, she said, "I'll be there. Just give me ten minutes to get my wrap."

Nelson was already waiting on the terrace when Melody arrived; she could not get used to how much he looked like Henry. "I'm ready for our walk. Henry told me there's a maze, but we never found the time to go through it. Can we go there today?"

"It would be my pleasure!" Nelson offered Melody his arm, and they headed toward the maze. As they walked along, he started to tell Melody about the time that Henry fell into the lake. "Henry had climbed up a tree, trying to hide from me, and all of a sudden, the tree limb gave way, and he fell into the lake. I had to go fetch him out, since at this point, Henry didn't know how to swim. The water was freezing that day, as it was early in the spring of the year. Henry was only six years old, and by the time I got him out of the water, he was shivering all over. That was when I decided to teach him how to swim. We spent that whole summer at the lake, and by summer's end, he could swim as well as I could. We also did quite a bit of fishing. The lake is stocked with plenty of fish, and Henry and I spent many happy moments fishing there through our adolescent years."

Soon, they arrived at the maze. Nelson told her that the third Duke of Sanderford built the maze many generations ago, back when Henry the eighth was king. They walked and made several turns and then arrived at the center. There was a fountain with the Greek god Apollo in the center amid dozens of rose bushes. Melody looked forward to seeing it in the spring, once all the roses were in full bloom. "My goodness, this is lovely," she said. "However, I'm glad I didn't try to come into the maze by myself. I'm sure I would have gotten lost and might never have found my way out again."

Nelson laughed and replied, "There's a secret: All you have to do is keep turning left, then right at each turn, and that will lead you to the center, and then you just reverse it to get back out."

"I still think I would get lost, so I think I'll stay out of this maze, unless you or Henry is with me." Melody walked around the walkway and looked at the various kinds of plants that decorated the maze and knew it would be spectacular next summer.

"We used to take girls into the maze when we were young, for a romantic interlude, so I'm sure Henry would be happy to bring you here anytime you want. He could show you the many delightful alcoves that are scattered throughout the maze. Then you'll really be confused about how to get out, so you'll have to let Henry lead the way!" Nelson offered Melody his arm and they strolled back through the maze, entered the gardens, and walked through the many varieties of rose bushes all along the walkway.

As they approached the terrace, Helen was there and hurried over to Melody. "I wondered where you were. I wanted to see if you would like to go into Cranleigh with me. I need to get some new hair ribbons to match my new day dress. Would you like to come?"

"Oh yes, that would be lovely. I need to pick some up for my pink day dress, and I need a new bonnet. Can we find one in the village?" she asked as she smiled brightly at Helen.

Helen returned Melody's smile and said, "Of course, we can. I'll order the gig and meet you in front of the house in ten minutes, all right?"

As Helen rushed off, Melody called after her, "I'll be there, and I look forward to going to the village again. I've wanted to explore more of the shops." Melody turned to Nelson and said, "Thank you for showing me the maze. It was an enjoyable morning. I hope we can do it again some time."

Melody hurried up to her bedchamber, got her new pelisse, and met Helen outside. Soon they were on their way to Cranleigh. She had already been to the village several times with Henry and knew there was a bookshop there. She hoped they would have time to go there while they were in the village. Melody enjoyed spending time with Helen because she was always so cheerful and full of life. She was already feeling much more relaxed about being at Sanderford Park without Henry.

They went to the dressmaker and then on to the bookshop. They decided to go to the confectionery also, and Melody picked out some delicious chocolate sweetmeats to have later while she was reading her book. By the time they returned, it was time for tea.

Simpson took their wraps and told them that the rest of the family was already in the drawing room, so they went there. When they entered, Melody saw the duke and duchess already seated and having their tea. The duke looked at Melody with distain and said, "You are late. Where have you been, gel? We have been waiting to have our tea. It is very inconsiderate of you to keep us waiting. I like everyone to be here sharply at four o'clock, not three minutes after the hour. Make sure you do not let this happen again!"

"I'm sorry, your grace. We went to the village and misjudged the time. I'll be much more careful in the future." Melody sat down in the chair, and the duchess handed her a cup of tea and some biscuits. It seemed as if she could not do anything right, in the eyes of Henry's parents. She tried to make herself as pleasant as possible to them, but they seemed to find fault with everything she did.

Nelson turned to Helen and asked, "Did you and Melody have fun in the village today? And did you find those hair ribbons you were looking for?"

Helen enthusiastically replied, "We had so much fun! Melody found a wonderful new novel, and we're both going to read it. Melody lent me some of her books, and now I just love Mrs. Radcliffe's novels. We also went to the confectionery and got some delicious-looking sweetmeats."

The duchess turned to Melody and looked her over with an expression of disgust on her face as she said, "It appears to me that you do not need any sweetmeats. You need to watch your figure, or you will turn to fat and let us see how Henry likes that!" Melody was mortified. She knew she was a little plump, but she had never had anyone infer that she was fat!

Helen looked over at Melody, rolled her eyes, and whispered, "Don't listen to Mother. She's critical of everyone."

Melody excused herself and went up to her rooms. She thought about what the duchess had said and wondered if Henry thought she was fat. He had never said anything, but he was so kind, he would not want to hurt her feelings, even if he did think she was too plump. Maybe she should try to refrain from eating so many sweets. She certainly did not want Henry to think she was fat. Melody sat down on the chaise, picked up her book, and began to read. Soon, she was lost in the story and forgot all about the cruel things the duchess had said to her.

That evening, she decided to have a tray sent to her room instead of joining everyone for dinner. She had a slight headache, so she would just spend a quiet evening alone. She wanted to finish her book, so she could start that new Radcliffe novel she had purchased in the village that day. She tucked her feet under her and began to read. Finally, she started to get sleepy and decided to go to bed. She rang for her maid so that Millie could help her undress. She crawled into bed and started to think about Henry, and she wondered what he was doing. *Did he miss her, or was he enjoying being with his men so much that he didn't even think about her?* As she thought of Henry, she began to cry. She knew he had to go, but she missed him so. She rolled over and hugged a pillow, wishing Henry were there to hold her. She could still smell the sandalwood scent Henry always wore, and it helped her feel closer to him. She would make sure no one washed the pillowcase because she wanted to be able to hug it each night so she could pretend that Henry was still with her. Then she slowly drifted off as she cried herself to sleep.

Over the next month, Melody had to endure quite a few negative comments from both the duke and the duchess. She believed they would never accept her or feel any affection for her, no matter what she did. Thank goodness for Helen and Kathryn! They helped to keep her busy and treated her with kindness. Nelson was always very thoughtful; he had taken her for several more walks, and they even went riding most mornings when the weather permitted. He always told her funny stories about Henry and some of the mischief that he got into while growing up. It sounded as if Nelson had been a very good brother to Henry and that must have helped him, since his parents had treated him so poorly. Melody wondered why the duke was so judgmental toward Henry. It was obvious they did not treat Nelson that way, and while the duke and duchess did not spend much time with his sisters, they were never cruel to them.

Melody wrote Henry everyday, and she had received several letters from him. He always told her how much he loved her and that he could not wait until they could be together again. She did not tell Henry how hateful his parents were being to her because she did not want him to worry about her. She kept her letters cheerful and told him about the fun she was having with his sisters, especially Helen.

The days passed slowly, and finally it was time for Henry to return. He was supposed to be home the next day. Melody had Millie prepare a bath for her so she could wash her hair because Henry always told her how much he loved the way her hair smelled. She used lemon juice whenever possible because it brought out the lighter streaks of blonde in her hair.

The next morning, Melody was so excited. She wondered what time Henry would arrive. She hoped it would be earlier in the day because she doubted she would be able to do anything until he got home; she was that excited. She spent time with Kathryn in the schoolroom. Kathryn was a marvelous artist, and she was painting Melody's portrait. So far, she had not let Melody see it, but she said she would be finished that day, so Melody could give it to Henry when he arrived.

Kathryn motioned to Melody to come over, and she showed her the portrait. Melody stood there looking at it in astonishment. Kathryn had made her look so beautiful! "Oh, Kathryn, it's beautiful. Is that the way I look to you? I can't believe this is me. You see me so differently than I see myself. I only wish I looked like that."

"Melody, you do look like that. You're very lovely, and I'm not sure this portrait does justice to your beauty. You have a certain quality about you that radiates an inner beauty that was very hard to portray. I'm pleased you like it," Kathryn said.

Melody smiled over at Kathryn and laughed, then said, "I hope Henry sees me this way, for you have made me look very beautiful!" Kathryn laughed with her and since it was time for luncheon, they went down to join the rest of the family.

Melody decided to take a walk to the lake, hoping it would help the time pass. As she stood there looking out over the lake, she remembered the time she and Henry had made love there. All those wonderful feelings came rushing back to her. Melody tried to avoid thinking about their lovemaking, as she became frustrated because they could not be together, and it was easier, if she did not think about it. Soon Henry would be there, and they could be together again. Melody blushed. Just thinking about making love with Henry brought a tingling sensation deep in her belly. She turned and headed back to the house, and as she walked up to the terrace, she saw him standing there.

He walked over to her and took her into his arms. It was like coming home. The wind had blown his hair, and he needed a shave, but he'd never looked more attractive to her. He looked down at Melody with tenderness in his eyes and said, "Oh my darling, I've missed you so much. This has been the longest month of my life. Did you miss me?"

"Of course, I missed you. I thought this month would never end, so I'm glad you're back. How are your men? Have many of them returned to civilian life?" she asked.

As he cradled her in his arms, he replied, "Some of them have, but many of them don't have jobs to return to, so they're still there. I've been trying to find work for them, but it's hard. There are so many of them and so few jobs to be found. Some of my men are very down, and morale isn't at its best right now. They're restless, and because of this, some altercations have broken out. I've had to discipline several of them, which is never pleasant for me. Let's change the subject to something more pleasant. I talk about these problems all the time with Hayden, so I just want to talk to you and tell you how much I adore you. Your letters were so cheerful. I appreciate you writing to me everyday, and I look forward to receiving them on such a regular basis. You're spoiling me dreadfully, and I love every minute of it. I do try to write you everyday, but my men keep me so busy that some nights, I'm just too tired to pick up my pen. I'm glad you seem to be getting along with my brother and sisters. You didn't mention much about my parents. Have they been treating you well?"

"They don't talk to me very much. I think they would rather pretend I don't exist," she replied. "I spend most of my time with Helen. She's been so nice to me, and we've become good friends. Kathryn has painted my portrait, and she just finished it today. She said she would give it to you. She flattered me greatly. I was pleased she wanted to paint me, and she's very good. I've seen some of her other works, and they're wonderful."

Henry grinned at her as he said, "I'm sure I'll love the portrait, and I'm sure she painted you in all your glory. Every time I see you after having been apart, your beauty astounds me. It's time for tea, so we had better go in. His grace gets very irritable if anyone is ever late for tea."

"Oh, I know about that! Helen and I were late coming back from the village, right after you left, and he let me know how displeased he was with me, so let's go right in." Melody and Henry went to the drawing room, and all the family was already there. The duke looked displeased again.

"So I see that you have returned, boy . . . How long will you be staying this time?" he asked. "Nelson needs your help with running the estate. When are you going to sell your commission? You're needed here."

"I'm sorry, your grace, but I feel I can't leave my men until they are settled. I have a commitment to them, and I need to fulfill that responsibility first," Henry politely replied to his father.

"That is ridiculous! Your family should come first. Those men do not need you to hold their hand. Let them find their own jobs!" he said.

Even though the duke looked as if he was ready to explode from anger, Henry did not let it intimidate him, so he said, "Nonetheless, I won't desert my men. I've told you this before. Nelson has assured me he's just fine. He told me to take as long as I need."

The duke's face turned a bright red as he said, "I can see there is no use talking about this. You are as stubborn as ever. Just take your wife and get out of my sight!"

Henry drew himself up to his full height. Melody could tell he was ready to lose control, but then he kept his temper and said, "Melody, come with me, and we'll have tea sent to our suite instead. I'll see the rest of you later. Excuse me, your graces, Nelson, Helen, Kathryn. Good day to you all."

Henry asked Simpson to have tea sent up to their suite, and they went upstairs. They entered their sitting room, and Henry pulled Melody into his arms. He kissed her hard and said, "I've wanted to do that ever since I saw you on the terrace. You look so pretty in that yellow dress. It brings out all the green flecks in your beautiful eyes." There was a knock on the door; he opened it, and a footman entered with their tea. "Just put it over there on the table, and you may go."

Melody sat down and poured their tea. She filled a plate with sandwiches and biscuits and handed it to Henry. She took her teacup and began to drink. She watched Henry finish off his food and reach for more. It was obvious that he was very hungry.

Soon he finished and noticed that she was not eating anything. "Melody, you haven't eaten anything. Are you all right?"

Melody sipped her tea and said, "I'm fine, Henry. I'm just trying to slim down a bit. I've decided that I'm a bit too plump, so I'm watching what I eat."

"What nonsense is this? You're beautiful just as you are. I love every luscious inch of you, and I don't want you to lose an ounce. Here, let me fill a plate for you. Eat up!" he said.

"You really like me the way I am?" she asked. "I've worried that you thought I was too plump. Your mother indicated that you like slender women and I'm far from that."

Henry looked directly into Melody's eyes as he said, "Don't listen to my mother. She doesn't know my tastes. Let me assure you, I love you just the way you are. You're round in all the right places, and I want you to stay that way! Come here . . . I need a hug."

Melody went to Henry, and he pulled her into his arms and began to kiss her passionately. He thrust his tongue into her mouth, and Melody tentatively used her tongue in a dance as old as time. He picked her up and carried her to his bed. As he approached the bed, he put her down and let his eyes roam up and down her body. She grew hot just seeing Henry look at her with so much desire in his eyes.

Henry's eyes sizzled as he looked at her and said, "Melody, take off your clothes for me. I want to see all of you. Every night, I've been dreaming of seeing your gorgeous naked body."

Melody blushed but turned around so he could unbutton her gown and loosen her corset and stays. Melody turned back around; he stood there watching her, and she could tell he was getting very aroused. She dropped her dress, removed her corset, stays, and chemise but left her stockings and garters on. It seemed different and much more embarrassing to be without her clothes in the daytime. As Henry kneeled down and began to roll her stocking down her leg, shivers ran down her spine, and she felt her desire for him rise. As he removed her stocking and garter, he bent down and kissed the back of her knee, which tickled and Melody giggled. Henry looked up at her with passion raging in his eyes, then he repeated it on the other leg, and then he stood up and took Melody in his arms. He gently pushed her down on the counterpane and said, "I don't think I can take it slow this time. I need you too badly, and I can't wait to have you. Lie back with your bottom at the edge of the bed." Melody felt so exposed, but she loved the way Henry was staring at her, and it made her feel hot all over.

Henry started tearing off his clothes, and soon he was completely naked. She looked down and saw how aroused he was. His shaft was huge and engorged. He pushed her thighs wide apart and thrust into her tight sheath as her inner muscles clinched around his shaft. He was so aroused that he was shaking with desire as he began to pump into Melody and ride her hard. She was tossing her head from side to side from the ecstasy of it all. Henry rubbed her core. She could feel moisture dripping from her body, and then she came apart; sensation after sensation rolled over her. Henry made his last thrust and shouted out her name with his release as his seed filled her. Then he collapsed on top of her; both were breathing heavily, and it took awhile for their breathing to slow down to normal. Henry gently pulled out and climbed into bed while gathering Melody in his arms. Shortly after, she opened her eyes, and he was watching her intently.

"Melody, I love to see your face all flushed with passion," he said. "That's when you are most beautiful to me. I can't get enough of you. I could make love to you every minute of the day, and it still would not be enough for me. I love you beyond my wildest imagination."

"I love you too, Henry. I'm overjoyed that you're home again. I've missed you dreadfully and counted each minute until you could return to me. How long can you stay?" she asked.

"I have to be back on Monday . . . I wish I could stay longer, but it's just not possible. I'll be back in plenty of time for Christmas. I know this is hard on you, but it will all be over within a few months. By spring, at the latest, we'll be able to go to my estate up north. That way you can be closer to your parents," he said. "I gather my parents haven't been pleasant. I was afraid of that. I'll speak to them and let them know I expect them to treat you better."

Melody looked at him and said, "Henry, don't say anything. It hasn't been that bad, and your brother and sisters keep me entertained most of the time. Nelson and I have been going riding, whenever the weather permits. Just as you said, it will only be for a few more months, and then we can go north. I do look forward to seeing my parents again. I received a letter from my mother, and she told me that my father has been feeling bad lately. Nothing to worry about, mainly it's his rheumatism acting up."

Henry stroked her pretty shoulders as he said, "Well, I won't say anything right now, but if they become more difficult, then you need to let me know, and I'll handle it. You're too important to me, and I won't let anyone mistreat you. I'm thinking about finding a house close by my garrison, and that way you won't have to live here. I just don't know how much time I'll be able to spend with you, and I hate to think of you being alone. At least here, you have my brother and sisters to keep you company."

"Henry, I would rather spend an hour with you than a month with anyone else. I would have Millie for company, and I can always read to fill my time. Do you really think you could find us a place to stay?" she asked, while running her fingers through his chest hair.

He kissed her on her temple and said, "It may be difficult, but I'll start looking for a place just as soon as I get back. Right now, I just want to make love to you again."

And he did.

CHAPTER 8

December 1814

OVER THE NEXT few days, Henry and Melody spent as much time together as possible. They went riding through the park and took the gig into the village. They made love everyday and Melody was becoming much more comfortable with her body. Henry made her feel so pretty, because he always complimented her on what she was wearing and how she looked. Before they realized it, Sunday had arrived, and they got up and went to Mass. After church, they had luncheon with the family, and then it was time for Henry to leave. They went out to the stables, and he pulled Melody into his arms and gave her a tender kiss. Then he led Jupiter out; he got on his horse and looked down at Melody.

"Take care of yourself and write me everyday. You don't know how much your letters mean to me. I'll write as often as I can and let me know if you need anything at all. If my parents become too unbearable, I'll find some way to get you out of here. I love you, my darling. See you soon." Melody stood there and watched Henry ride away; then she slowly turned and walked back to the house.

The next couple of weeks went by quickly, because they started getting ready for Christmas. The duchess had everyone helping with the party they held each year for all their family and neighbors. She looked forward to this, because so far, the only people she had met were at church.

It was getting too cold to go riding, and Melody missed it terribly. Nelson still spent time with her, and she had grown quite fond of him. Since Melody was an only child, she enjoyed having a brother and sisters. It was the best part about living here. She would miss them if Henry was able to find a place for them, but she would still much rather be with him.

Dinner was the hardest time of the day because there was no way to avoid spending time with their graces. They were so cold and unfriendly, that it made the meal very long. After dinner, the men would stay in the dining room and have their port, and her grace would gather the rest of them and go to the drawing room. Melody always hated this part of the day. Her grace would make little hurtful comments about the way Melody looked and how she acted. Nothing she did pleased Henry's mother. Helen tried to steer the conversation in another direction, but her grace would always find some way to focus the conversation back on her faults. Once the men joined them, Nelson would get Melody to play chess or cards, and then the evening would go better.

Thank goodness for Nelson, for he was such a peacemaker. Melody wished he could meet someone to love. She knew he still mourned his wife, but it was time for him to move on and find some happiness in his life. She wanted him to have the kind of relationship she and Henry had. Of course, Nelson did not seem to be interested in doing this. Helen had told Melody all about Nora, and she could understand why Nelson missed her so much. They had been very much in love and had been so excited about having the baby. When she died, it just devastated Nelson. It was hard enough losing their child, but when Nora died also, it was almost more than Nelson could bear. It did not help that their graces were putting pressure on him to remarry. They wanted him to marry Lady Penelope, now that Henry had married Melody. They really wanted to join their properties together. Lady Penelope was the only daughter of the Earl of Stanton, and the property was unentailed, so Lady Penelope would inherit it upon her father's death. Helen did not seem to like Lady Penelope very much, so Melody hoped Nelson would not feel compelled to marry her. After having been married to someone he loved, he would not want to enter into a marriage, solely for financial gain.

Finally, the evening ended, and Melody went up to her lonely bed. She usually read for a while, and that normally helped her go to sleep. However, that night, it did not seem to be working. She kept reading long into the night. She heard the clock strike three, so she decided she would go down to the kitchen and get a glass of warm milk. She lit a candle and headed down the hall. As she approached the stairs, she heard a noise. She went to investigate and found Kathryn walking down the hall. She went over to her and started to ask if she was all right, when she noticed Kathryn looking very strange. Melody realized Kathryn must have been sleepwalking, so she gently guided her back to her room. Suddenly, Kathryn stiffened and gave out a startled cry. She looked over and started crying upon seeing Melody.

Melody gathered Kathryn in her arms to comfort her as she said, "Shush, it's all right, sweetheart. You must have had a bad dream. I found you walking in the hall, but you didn't seem to recognize me. I think you may have been sleepwalking. Have you done that before?"

"Oh no, I did it again!" she said. "I haven't done that in years. I used to do it quite a bit, a few years ago, but then it stopped. I hope it's not going to start up again. My parents get so angry with me over it. They can't know I've done this again. Please don't tell them about this."

"Don't worry, I won't say a word. Why don't you get back into bed. I was on my way to the kitchen to get a glass of warm milk, so I'll get you some. Will you be all right if I leave you alone?" she asked.

Kathryn looked relieved as she said, "I'll be fine. A glass of warm milk does sound nice. Thank you, Melody, for being so understanding about this."

Melody went down to the kitchen, got two glasses of warm milk, and returned to Kathryn's room. "Here you go, Kathryn. Hopefully, this will help you get back to sleep. I'm going back to my rooms now. If you need anything or you ever want to talk, please let me know. Goodnight, my dear." Melody returned to her rooms and thought about what had happened. She wondered why Kathryn was so scared when she realized she had been sleepwalking. She was sure their graces were appalled that they had a child with this affliction. They probably made her feel as if it was her fault. *Poor child, she could not control this.* She wondered if Henry knew about the sleepwalking. When he returned, she would ask him. Thank goodness, he would be home in the next couple of days.

The next morning, Melody got up and called for her maid. Millie came and readied her bath. This was one luxury she really enjoyed. Melody had always enjoyed a bath, but at home, it was so difficult, because all the water had to be carried upstairs and they only had one maid. Here, all she had to do was have Millie fill the tub. *Imagine having running water in a house! What a modern convenience!* She took off her robe and night rail and sank down into the tub. Millie had used her special lemon scented bath oil. Henry had told her several times that he loved her scent, and relaxing in the bath felt wonderful. She put her head against the back of the tub and closed her eyes. Suddenly, she felt someone's arms around her. When she looked up, she saw Henry was there and said, "Henry, when did you get here? I thought you weren't going to be here until Saturday. My love, I'm so glad you've come home. What a pleasant surprise!"

"I was able to leave sooner than I expected. I left last night and rode through the night to get here this morning. I wanted to see you in your bath. You smell wonderful. Hand me that sponge, and I'll wash your back." Melody handed him the sponge, and he slowly slid the sponge down her back. Then he lathered both of her arms; only it was not the sponge he was using but his hands. He slid his hands around her shoulders and started stroking her breasts, and Melody felt desire rising in her. His hands moved down lower and lower, until he touched her feminine core, and then he leaned forward and kissed her. As he put his finger inside her, she shuttered, for it felt so sublime. Then he stood up and tore his clothes off. Once he was naked, he stepped into the tub with her. He pulled her to him, so she was straddling him. She could feel his manhood hard against her belly, and it excited her. He lifted her up and then lowered her down onto his shaft. He started slowly moving in and out, by lifting Melody's hips. Soon, she was writhing and twisting from the pleasure of it all. Henry touched her little nubbin, and she came apart as wave upon wave of pleasure rippled through her. Then Henry surged upward and groaned as he filled her with his essence. She slumped against his chest and sighed deeply. They lay there until the water grew cool. Henry stood up and pulled her to her feet, and they stepped out of the tub. There was a big fluffy towel lying beside the tub, so he picked it up and dried them both off; then she reached for him, pulled him down, and kissed him.

Henry asked, "Did you miss me? Now that was a wonderful way to be welcomed home."

"That was the best bath I've ever had! Anytime you want to help me take a bath, go right ahead!" Melody said.

"I agree that was the best bath I've ever had also! How have you been?" he asked. "Have my parents been giving you a hard time?"

"No more than usual. I'm getting used to it by now, and I just ignore them. I've developed the ability to not let it bother me. We better put some clothes on before we catch a cold!" she said.

"Why bother, we would just have to take them off again because I'm certainly not satisfied yet." Henry threw her over his shoulder and carried her to the bed, dropped her in the middle, and fell down beside her. Then he kissed her all over, and they made love again.

They did not come down for luncheon or tea. They did come down to dinner, and Henry's parents glared at them when they entered the drawing room.

"It is about time that you joined us," the duke said. "I understand that you got here at ten o'clock this morning, and you could not even be bothered to let us know you were here. Simpson mentioned that you had arrived. Henry, this is simply appalling behavior. This is not the kind of example you should be setting for your sisters."

"Sorry, your grace, I needed to speak with Melody about an important matter, and then since I traveled through the night, I decided to take a nap. Was there something you needed to see me about?" he asked.

"When are you going to sell your commission so you can start taking care of your responsibilities to this family?" he asked. "You promised you would take over the management of Doncaster Stables in Yorkshire, and you have not done so."

Henry sighed in exasperation as he replied, "I've explained to you on numerous occasions that I need to settle my men first. I'll have everything taken care of by late March, and then I'll be more than happy to meet my responsibilities to the family."

The duchess spoke up and disdainfully said, "It will not be a day too soon for me! Then you can take your wife and get out of here. I am so sick of her and her common ways!"

Melody knew he wanted to explode, but he controlled his anger as he said, "My wife is far from common! Don't worry, your grace, I'll be taking Melody with me when I return to my regiment. I've found a place for us to live while I finish up with the army. You don't have to be further bothered by either of us. Now, can we move ahead and go into dinner?"

Everyone went into the dining room. Conversation was very stiff throughout dinner. Henry knew he had not heard the last of this from his father. He was sure he would start in on him again, once the ladies left them alone with their port.

It was just as he suspected; his father had quite a bit more to say. He was being very stubborn about the issue of when Henry would leave the army. He did not want to hear about how his men needed him. He finally told his father that he did not want to discuss it any further and left him to go join the ladies.

The rest of the evening went better. He had a chance to talk with his brother about how he was doing. He was worried about Nelson because he looked tired, and there were lines of tension around his mouth. So he asked, "Nelson, are you all right? You look terrible, and you seem to be all tensed up. Is there anything that I can do to help you?"

Nelson sighed and shrugged his shoulder, then said, "I'm just a little tired. I haven't been sleeping well, that's all it is Henry. Father has been after me again about marrying Lady Penelope. Sometimes, I think it would just be easier if I went ahead and did it. I won't ever love anyone like I loved Nora, and I do need to have an heir. I guess, one female is as good as another. I just don't like the idea of giving into our father on this issue."

"I can understand how you feel, but don't give up," he said. "You know how selfish Lady Penelope is. She would make your life a living hell."

"You're right, Henry. I won't give in to him. As I told you, when you first got back, I'm planning on going to London for the season, this coming year, and I can find a wife then. I want someone of my own choosing . . . someone older than the average debutant. I want someone who may have lost her husband and is looking for companionship and not a love match." Poor Nelson looked so troubled by all this. Henry wished there was something more he could do to help.

"That's a very good idea. In fact, I know of someone just like that. Remember me mentioning Matthew Bronson. He has a sister who lost her husband about eighteen months ago. I met her, and she seemed quite pleasant. Her name is Mary. She was married to Captain Harrison, and he was killed in Portugal. She has a young son, and she has been struggling financially ever since he died. Why don't you look her up when you get to town?" he asked. "She may be just what you're looking for."

Nelson smiled when he heard this and said, "Maybe, I'll do that. It would save me from the marriage mart. I don't think I could handle all those giddy young debutants and their marriage-mad mamas."

Henry yawned as he said, "Excuse me. I really am tired. I think I'll get Melody and go upstairs. I haven't slept much in the last twenty-four hours. What with leaving late last night, so I could spend time with Melody this morning. I need some sleep. Good night, Nelson."

Henry went over to Melody and asked, "Are you ready to retire for the evening? I want to spend some time with my pretty wife, in private."

"Of course, I'm ready. I'm fairly tired myself, and I would enjoy spending time with my handsome husband." They went upstairs to their rooms; Melody sent Millie to bed, and Henry told Mansfield to go also. They undressed and got into bed. Henry pulled her close, and after they tenderly made love, they fell asleep in each other's arms.

The next few days went by swiftly. The duchess had everyone working on the arrangements for the party. Henry helped decorate the ballroom for the gala, and Melody helped with the menu. They were still able to break away, so they could spend time alone.

Melody asked Henry about Kathryn and the sleepwalking. He told her that Kathryn had been doing it since she was a small child. It made his parents angry, and they even locked her in her room to make sure she did not wonder the halls at night. He was surprised to hear that Kathryn was having problems with it again. "I'm just glad you found her. My parents would have found someway to punish her if they knew about it. I hope she doesn't start doing this again, as she used to. I'll talk with her and see if something is bothering her, but she may not want to confide in me. Why don't we talk with her together? She may be more willing to talk, if you're with me. She simply adores you. I'm so glad you have gotten to know my sisters and that you get along with them so well."

"We can go talk to her right now. I believe she's in the schoolroom, painting." They did indeed find Kathryn in the schoolroom, and she was painting. She asked them in and showed Henry some of her recent work. Henry was amazed at how much she had improved in the last two years.

"Kathryn, this work is astounding. I had no idea you were such a talented artist. Have you talked to our parents about getting some formal training?" he asked.

Kathryn woefully replied, "I mentioned it to Mother, but she told me it was fine for a hobby but not for anything else. She said I should stick to watercolors and leave the oils alone. Mother feels that type of painting is for men, and it would be unacceptable for me, especially after I get married. I tried to tell her I might not want to get married. I told her I wanted to be a serious artist, and she just laughed at me."

Glancing again at some of Kathryn's work, Henry said, "Well, Melody and I both feel you have a remarkable talent and that you should be able to pursue it. I'll tell you what, I'll hire someone to work with you, and I'll pay for it myself."

Kathryn threw her arms around Henry and gave him a hug. She was so happy that she was crying. "Oh, thank you, Henry. I know I can be a serious artist with the right instructor."

"Melody told me about the sleepwalking. I was wondering if you have been having any of those nightmares you used to have?" he asked. "I remember you used to have more trouble with sleepwalking when you had them before."

Kathryn looked down as she said, "Yes, I had a nightmare the night Melody found me. It's always the same nightmare, and I wake up finding myself somewhere other than my bed. That's the first one I've had in a very long time."

"Is there anything that has been bothering you lately? Henry thought if something was bothering you, it could cause the nightmares," Melody asked.

"I was very disappointed when Mother refused to take my desire to be an artist seriously, but nothing else that I can think of." Kathryn appeared to be unwilling to make eye contact, so Melody suspected there was more she was not telling them. They would just need to be patient and watch for anything that could be a clue to what was really troubling her.

"Henry, it's time for us to go and get ready for your mother's party. It's already five o'clock, and it will take me awhile, because I still need to bathe, and Millie is going to try a new hairstyle for tonight." Henry looked at her, and she could tell he was thinking of the bath he had interrupted the other day. It gave her chills just remembering what a sensual experience it had been. She loved the way Henry seemed to want her all the time, and of course, the feeling was mutual. She was astonished at what a wanton she was becoming!

Melody took her bath and was a little disappointed when Henry did not interrupt her again. However, it was a good thing he did not because it would have made them late. If they were late again, they would have had to listen to the duke make derogatory comments about it. She was so glad Henry had found them a place to live, close to the garrison. It would be nice to see Henry everyday, even if it were only for short periods of time. He had made it clear that he would be very busy and that she would need to find ways to keep herself busy. This was not a problem for Melody because as long as she had a good book to read, she would be fine. Millie returned and helped Melody finish getting ready for the gala. She was looking forward to meeting more of Henry's friends. He had mentioned that Captain Hayden was supposed to attend. He also said his lieutenant, Matthew Bronson and his sister, would be there. Henry had just heard they were at the garrison, and he wanted Nelson to meet the lieutenant's sister, Mary. He thought they would get along well since she was a widow, and Nelson had told him, she was the kind of woman he would like to meet. Melody hoped for Nelson's sake, Henry was right. Nelson deserved to find someone he could love again.

Henry came into the sitting room, and they went down to the party. The rest of the family was already in the drawing room. His mother seemed very pleased about the upcoming gala. It was the most animated that Melody had ever seen her since she had started living there. Their graces had even allowed Kathryn to participate in the party. That surprised

Melody, but Henry explained that some of the rest of the family would be there and that there would be other younger people attending. They went into the entrance hall to receive the guests.

Soon, the ballroom was full. Henry introduced her to all of his friends. Lord Weston was there along with Captain Hayden. The lieutenant and his sister had arrived, and Melody could see why Henry thought she might suit Nelson. As they were getting to know each other, Nelson came over to them.

Henry introduced everyone to Nelson, "Everyone, this is my brother, Nelson Montgomery, the Marquess of Wyndham. Nelson, this is Lieutenant Bronson and his sister, Mrs. Harrison. Remember, I mentioned them to you the other day. They've just arrived in Canterbury, at the garrison. I believe you have met everyone else."

Nelson bowed and took Mrs. Harrison's hand, brought it to his lips, and placed a soft whisper of a kiss on her fingers. "It's a pleasure to meet you." He looked over at Bronson and said, "Lieutenant, it's also nice to meet you. My brother has had good things to say in regards to your bravery while serving under him during the conflict with France. I hope both of you will have an enjoyable time this evening." Nelson bowed to Mrs. Harrison and asked, "Mrs. Harrison, would you care to take a walk around the room with me?"

Mary timidly looked at Nelson as she answered, "That would be lovely, my Lord. I would enjoy that."

Melody and Henry continued to speak with Henry's friends as Nelson and Mrs. Harrison left to stroll around the room. Soon, the dancing started, and Henry and Melody began to waltz. Henry noticed that Nelson had asked Mrs. Harrison to dance also and he whispered in Melody's ear, "I think Nelson likes Mrs. Harrison. I hope so, because he deserves to have someone in his life as wonderful as you are. By the way, have I told you how pretty you look tonight?"

Melody smiled up at him and said, "Why, thank you, husband! Let me return the compliment and tell you how handsome you look. Do you realize this is the first time we've danced together since our marriage?"

"Yes, and you dance as divinely as you did last summer. I love to hold you in my arms, but of course, I would rather have you naked than with all these clothes on you!" he said.

"Henry, be quiet. Someone might hear you," she said, then laughed up at him. Melody gazed up into Henry's eyes and saw the tenderness shining there for her. Just being in his arms, made her feel so loved and safe.

It turned out to be a splendid evening, and Melody enjoyed herself tremendously. She danced with all of Henry's friends, and then she danced with Nelson. While they danced, she asked, "I saw you dancing with Mrs. Harrison. What did you think of her? I think she's very nice, don't you?"

"Mrs. Harrison seems to be pleasant, and I enjoyed dancing with her. I asked her if I could see her again, and she said yes. I plan to go visit her while she's visiting her brother in Canterbury. She lives in London with her small son, and if all goes well, I plan on spending more time with her this coming spring, Miss. Nosey!" Nelson replied.

With a concerned look on her face, she said, "I just want you to meet someone and have the type of relationship Henry and I have. I'm sorry if I was prying."

"It's all right, Melody. I was just teasing you. Actually, I appreciate your concern. It's just hard to think of being with anyone after losing Nora, but I know it's time, and Mrs. Harrison just might be the answer. At least she's a little older and shouldn't be looking for a love match. After Nora, I don't think I'll ever fall in love again," he said.

Toward the end of the evening, Melody saw Henry across the room, talking with an older gentleman, and he motioned for her to come over. When she joined them, Henry said, "Melody, this is my uncle Theodore, Viscount Manningly. He is my mother's brother. He'll be staying with us for the holidays. Uncle, this is my wife, Melody."

Henry's uncle gave Melody a very disdainful look, so she knew this was not someone who would be a friend. He reminded her of the duchess in appearance and attitude. She politely said, "My lord, it's a pleasure to meet you. I hope we'll find time to get to know each other during the holidays."

With a supercilious expression on his face, he said, "My sister told me Henry had married. How did you meet each other?"

"Henry and I met this past summer. I was in London for the season, and soon after we met, he asked me to marry him, and of course I said yes!" Melody said.

"Well, we shall see how long this glow of new love lasts. I am sure Henry will become bored with you. After all, you are nothing like the other women he is usually attracted to," Henry's uncle disdainfully replied.

Melody stood there in shock at how rude Henry's uncle was. She could not imagine anyone saying something like that to another person.

Henry looked his uncle directly in the eyes and said, "Sir, if you were a few years younger, I would take you out to the garden and give you the thrashing you so richly deserve. You will apologize to my wife!"

"I will not apologize! I would remind you, young man that I am your uncle, and I can say whatever I believe to be true!" he said.

Melody touched Henry's arm and said, "It's all right. I'm not concerned by what he said. I know you love me, and that's all that matters. Let's join your friends. I think they are getting ready to leave."

They walked across the room, wished his friends a good night, and told them to be careful on the ride back tomorrow. All his friends were staying at the local inn since it was too far to the garrison for them to drive back at night. Henry would have liked to have them stay with him, but with so many family members already there, it was not possible. His friends called out, "Good night and happy holidays! We'll see you back at the garrison after the holidays are over."

Finally, all the guests left, and they could retire for the evening. Henry opened the door to their suite and followed Melody into the room. She went to her bedchamber, and Millie helped her get ready for bed. After she was in her night rail, she sent Millie away. Henry opened her door and came into her room. He had changed into his robe, and he had taken a quick wash. He had a lock of hair that always fell over his forehead, and it made him appear younger than his age.

"Come here!" Henry pulled her close and started kissing her. He nibbled on her earlobe, which sent shivers up her back; she was so sensitive there. He slipped his hand inside her robe and started unbuttoning her night rail. She untied the sash of his robe, pushed it off his shoulders, and let it fall to the floor. She then kissed her way down his chest. Henry's chest had a small patch of hair in the middle, and she gently pulled the hair. He gasped as Melody took his flat male nipple into her mouth and suckled it. Then she trailed kisses down his chest to his navel. Henry could not believe Melody was being so bold. She had never been this way before, and he found it quite arousing. His shaft grew even more swollen and pushed against Melody's breasts. She tentatively licked the tip of his shaft, slowly lowered her mouth, and started sucking. Henry was in shock, but it felt so incredible that he was not going to complain! He could feel his erection grow even larger and felt his ball sac draw up, and knew he had better stop Melody now, or she would get a big surprise.

"My love, stop. You will unman me if you continue." Henry pulled her back up into his arms and passionately kissed her. He drove his tongue into her sweet mouth. Melody was kissing him back, just as passionately. He pushed her down to the bed. He spread her thighs wide, and in one quick thrust, he was inside her. Melody tightened her inner muscles around him, and he almost lost control. It felt so incredible, but he wanted to make this last and make sure she reached her fulfillment first. He ran his finger down her belly and touched her core, and she was wet and ready. He started stroking her and then felt her inner muscles contract and knew Melody had found her release. He thrust into her over and over again. Harder and faster, he rode her. Then Henry exploded inside of her, pouring his hot seed deep into her hot, sweet sheath. He fell on Melody gasping for breath. She sighed softly and hugged him close to her. Never had he experienced such satisfaction. He gathered her into his arm, and then they both drifted off to sleep.

CHAPTER 9

Winter 1815

CHRISTMAS EVE ARRIVED, and everyone worked together to decorate the house. Holly and evergreen were brought in and placed around the doors and on the banister. They hung wreaths above the hearths in all the main rooms of the house, and mistletoe hung from the crystal chandeliers. There was a festive feeling about the house, and Melody was getting excited about all the celebrations planned. Henry and Nelson brought in the Yule log. It was enormous, and it barely fit in the fireplace. Right after they returned, it began to snow, so they were going to have a white Christmas after all. Everyone gathered in the drawing room before dinner. Henry and Melody spent most of their time with Helen and Kathryn before dinner. Again, Kathryn was allowed to dine with the adults, and Melody knew she was very excited. Henry's uncle kept staring at Kathryn, and Melody did not like the way he was watching her. So she turned to Henry and said, "Your uncle keeps watching Kathryn, and I don't feel comfortable with the way he is looking at her. Have you noticed this?"

"No, I haven't been paying attention. Where is Kathryn?" he asked. "She was here a minute ago."

Melody saw Kathryn over by the pianoforte, and Uncle Theodore had approached her. She looked over at Melody and indicated she wanted her to come over. So Melody said, "Henry, she's over by the pianoforte, and I think she wants us to come to her." They walked over as Kathryn moved toward them, and she had a scared expression on her face. Uncle Theodore put his hand on Kathryn's arm; she shrugged him off and quickly moved over and stood beside Henry.

Henry looked down at her and said, "Hello, sweetheart, are you all right? We thought you looked as if you needed us."

Kathryn held tightly onto Henry's arm as she said, "I'm just having a good time, but I'm getting a bit hungry. When will we go into dinner?"

Henry smiled at her and said, "I'm sure it should be soon. Are you getting bored with all this adult talk? Look, there's Simpson now coming to announce dinner."

Dinner was excellent; every course was delicious, and everyone was having a splendid time. Most of the guests were laughing and joking, and even the duke seemed to be having a good time. After the dessert course, the duchess stood up and asked all the ladies to join her in the drawing room, so they could leave the gentlemen to their port and cigars.

Melody walked over, sat down by Kathryn and asked, "What was really going on earlier when you motioned for us to come over to you? Something was going on. Is everything all right?"

Kathryn did not meet Melody's eyes as she said, "I don't like Uncle Theodore. He always wants to touch me, and it just doesn't feel right. I know he's my uncle, but I don't care for him at all. Every time he comes for a visit, he tries to corner me when I'm alone, and he gets an odd look in his eyes, and it scares me."

"I'll talk to Henry and let him know how uncomfortable he makes you feel. Why don't you stay here with me when the gentlemen join us, so Uncle Theodore will stay away," she said, just as the gentlemen came in, and joined them. The duke indicated that it was now time to hand out the presents. Henry gave Melody a beautifully wrapped gift. When she opened it, she found a gorgeous emerald necklace, bracelet, and earbobs to match. She looked up at Henry with tears in her eyes and said, "These are just beautiful. I have never had anything this lovely. Thank you, Henry."

"I decided to get you emeralds, because they'll bring out the green flecks in your lovely eyes, and they match your wedding rings." He picked up the gift Melody had given him and opened it. It was a handsome leather-bound book of Shakespeare plays. "Thank you. You remembered that I love to read and Shakespeare is one of my favorite authors."

Everyone admired Melody's jewelry, especially Helen and Kathryn. Their parents had given each of them a lovely strand of matched pearls. They loved the hand-stitched handkerchiefs Melody had given them and the book of poems from Henry. Melody gave Henry's parents hand-monogrammed handkerchiefs as well.

One of Henry's cousins, she thought it was Harold, began playing Christmas carols on the pianoforte, and everyone gathered around to sing along with the music. Someone suggested they roll up the carpets and dance. Soon, they were all dancing and having a marvelous time. Melody was surprised to see Henry's parents dancing, who otherwise were always so stiff and proper. Melody and Henry ended up under the mistletoe, and he gave her a kiss on the cheek. After midnight, everyone headed upstairs to their rooms, because they knew the next day would be a full day.

When Melody woke up on Christmas morning, Henry was still sleeping. She loved to watch him when he slept. He always looked so peaceful. As she started to get out of bed, she felt Henry's arm pull her back as he said, "Good morning, were you going somewhere? I hope not, because I have plans for you."

With delight in her voice, she said, "I was just going to look out the window to see if there's enough snow to cover the ground."

"That sounds like a great idea. Let's look together." They went to the window, and when they looked out, they did indeed have a lovely white Christmas. Henry kissed her, and soon they ended up back in bed, so it was much later before they made it outside to see the pretty snow. The snow lasted several days; everyone went on sleigh rides, and they even had a snowball fight with Helen and Kathryn.

It was sometimes difficult to find time for them to be alone, but they would usually find a way to be together. After the snow melted, they found other ways to entertain their guests. Each night, they would play either charades or cards, and one evening they took turns reading one of Shakespeare's plays, which everyone seemed to enjoy tremendously. Most of Henry's relatives stayed through the twelve days of Christmas. The majority of the family was very polite and seemed to genuinely like her. Kathryn stayed close to them, and she did not have any more contact with her uncle. Melody had told Henry about her conversation with Kathryn, and he told her he would handle it. Since Uncle Theodore stayed away from Kathryn, he must have taken care of the issue.

Melody and Henry planned to leave when the rest of the family left. Finally, that day arrived. Helen and Kathryn came down to see them off, told them they would miss them and that they would write everyday. Melody knew she would miss Henry's sisters, but she would not miss his parents. She was so pleased that Henry was able to find a house for them so they could be together.

The trip took all day, so they arrived well after dark. The house he had found was a small cottage, but it was certainly big enough for them. It was two stories with ivy climbing the walls. While the rooms were small, they were comfortable, and Melody was sure she would be very happy there. The cook, Mrs. Holden, had supper ready for them when they arrived.

After dinner, Henry stood up, stretched, and said, "Melody, I have to be at the garrison very early tomorrow, so I think I'll turn in. Are you ready to come to bed?"

"Yes, I'm ready. It's been a long day, and I feel as if I could sleep for a week. While the holidays were wonderful, they were very exhausting." Melody was thrilled that they would be sharing a bedroom. When they entered their room, the bed had been turned down and their nightclothes were lying on the end of the bed. He turned her around and unbuttoned her gown so she could put on her night rail. They both were so tired that they climbed into bed and fell asleep right away.

The next day, Henry was already gone by the time Melody woke up. After breakfast, she decided she would go out and explore the town with Millie. They walked down the main street and looked in many of the shops. Canterbury was a much larger town than she realized. It was a very old place, and there were several wonderful old medieval churches to explore. She looked forward to doing that in the near future. The shops were delightful, because many of them were in medieval structures on narrow winding streets. The bookshop had many works by her favorite authors, and they had the new Minerva Press novel she had been looking for. By the time they got back to the cottage, Mrs. Holden had luncheon prepared. The food was simple country fare but very delicious. Melody spent the rest of the day reading her new book. Henry got home at six o'clock, and they had a quiet meal and talked about his day.

"I had a very busy day. I was in meetings with my superior officers all day. We received some news that the Congress of Vienna wasn't going well. Talleyrand is giving the coalition some problems. I'll rest easier, once everything has been agreed upon. We don't want to punish the French people, but they need to accept King Louis the XVIII, for he is now the rightful ruler. It will take years to clean up the mess that Bonaparte left behind. How did your day go?" he asked.

While lying down her fork, she said, "I took a walk around town, and then I read this afternoon. I'm overjoyed we can be together like this. I love this sweet little cottage, and Mrs. Holden is very friendly. I just know we'll be happy here. Sanderford Park is beautiful, but this cottage is so much more comfortable. It reminds me of my parents' home."

"I'm pleased you like it here. Just remember I won't be able to be here very much. There will be some days that I may not be able to get away at all. I hope you won't get too lonely," Henry said as he leaned back in his chair and sighed with contentment, replete from his meal.

Melody smiled over at Henry and said, "You told me how it was going to be, and I'll be fine with that. I would rather have a little of your time than none at all. All I ask is that you let me know what is going on, so I won't worry about you. Last night, was the first time we just slept together, and it was nice, but I hope that tonight you won't be quite so tired. I know I've got my energy back."

"Never fear my dear . . . I'm more than ready to fulfill my husbandly duty. In fact, why don't we go upstairs and I'll show you." Henry slowly pulled her up the stairs, while gazing deeply into her eyes and once they were in bed, he tenderly made love to her, before they fell asleep.

The days went by slowly, but the evenings passed quickly. Their nights were filled with passion. Everyday, they learned more about each other and fell more in love. Henry was very considerate, and whenever he was not going to make it, he would send Mansfield to let her know when or if he would be home. She enjoyed their little cottage; she was making things so that it looked more like a home. She knew Henry loved the way she took care of him, and she could not think of a time when she was as content.

Shortly after they arrived in Canterbury, Melody received a letter from her parents, telling her that Lily had died while she was giving birth and that the babe had been stillborn. The tears ran down her cheeks as she thought of Brandon and Lily and how happy they had been about the baby. Melody was so distraught that she cried all afternoon. When Henry arrived home and saw her, he rushed over to her and pulled her in his arms as he asked, "My darling, what is wrong? For you to be this upset, something terrible must have happened. Are your parents all right?"

"Oh, Henry . . . it's so horrible." Melody trembled in his arms as she continued, "Lily . . . Lily died while trying . . . to have their baby . . . and the baby was stillborn!"

Henry patted her on the back, trying to comfort her. "Oh, Melody, I'm so sorry! I know how close you were to them. God, Brandon must be devastated by this. Please write to him and offer him our condolences. I know that if anything were to ever happen to you, I would not want to go on living." Melody sobbed, and she was shaking from emotion. As he cradled her in his arms, he said, "My love, please try to calm down. I fear you'll make yourself sick if you don't stop crying." Henry picked her up in his arms and carried her upstairs. He laid her down on their bed, then lay down beside her and gathered her in his arms. She cried for a long time, but eventually she fell asleep.

Henry just laid there and held her while she slept. His poor darling had worn herself out from all the crying. He felt terrible about Brandon's loss, and he knew he would not be able to survive if anything were to happen with Melody. While he wanted children, he would not want them at the cost of Melody's life. He prayed that Melody did not become pregnant anytime soon.

Time passed, and Melody let go of her grief. Henry was relieved that she seemed to be back to normal. She was eating again, and he had even gotten her to laugh at one of his jokes. He knew she still was deeply saddened about Brandon's loss, but she was making a valiant effort to be cheerful. The rest of January passed, and soon, it was almost February 10. Melody's birthday was in two days. He had ordered her a beautiful diamond pendant necklace, and he hoped she would like it. He knew she would be happy with whatever he gave her, but he wanted to give her something special, something that showed her how much he loved her. The morning of Melody's birthday, Henry told her he would probably be home early, and he hoped they could have a quiet evening alone. He made no mention of her birthday, because he wanted to surprise her that evening. He kissed her good-bye and left.

After he left the house, to go to the garrison, she wondered if he remembered it was her birthday. He did not say anything at all about it. She would be very disappointed if he had forgotten, and after all, she would be one and twenty and that seemed important to her. The mail came, and it was a package from her parents with a letter. She decided she would wait to open her present until Henry got home. She went to talk with Mrs. Holden about what she wanted her to fix for the evening meal, and then she decided to do some reading that afternoon.

At six o'clock, Melody began to worry. Henry had said that he thought he would be home early, and yet he was still not there. She went to the window and looked out, but she could see no sign of him. She was beginning to get a little concerned. Surely, he had not forgotten her birthday, but it was certainly beginning to appear that way. Melody was feeling chilled, so she went upstairs to get her shawl. As she was getting ready to go back downstairs, she heard the front door open. She hurried downstairs, knowing Henry had finally arrived. She went into the parlor, and there Henry stood with a big grin on his face and a dozen yellow roses.

"Happy birthday, darling! I would have been here sooner, but I had a hard time getting these yellow roses. Sorry, if I worried you. I bet you thought I had forgotten your birthday, didn't you? Shame on you!" Henry laughed.

"Well, I was beginning to wonder as you had said you would be home early. Thank you for the roses, they're so beautiful, but where did you find them at this time of the year?" she asked.

With a mischievous grin on his face, he said, "I had Mansfield search all of Canterbury until he found a greenhouse that had the roses. It took him a little longer than I expected. Come here, my lovely one, and give me a kiss."

Melody went to him and kissed him on the cheek. Henry grabbed her up, pulled her into his arms and gave her a real kiss. She felt all a flutter from his passionate kiss, and she knew he was as aroused as she was because she felt his manhood probing her belly. Since Mrs. Holden would be in to announce dinner at any time, she slipped out of his arms and said, "Henry, I received a present from my parents today, and I waited until you got home to open it. Here it is . . . I've been dying to see what they sent." Melody unwrapped the gift and opened the box. Inside was a lovely matched set of bed linens, monogrammed with their initials on them. Henry handed her his present, and her face lit up when she opened it. Melody was thrilled with the diamond pendant. "Henry, this is just beautiful. First, the gorgeous emeralds at Christmas, and now, diamonds. You're spoiling me terribly, and I love every minute of it! Here, help me put it on!"

"Turn around so I can fasten it around your neck." As he fastened it, he gave Melody a kiss on the nape of her neck. Then he pulled her close and started nibbling on her earlobe, which sent chills up her spine.

"Henry, stop! Mrs. Holden could walk in here any minute to announce dinner. Behave yourself." Melody laughed. Henry looked up as Mrs. Holden entered the parlor to tell them that dinner was served.

The meal was lovely: baked chicken in a fricassee sauce with parsley new potatoes and carrots. For dessert, Mrs. Holden had baked a cake and decorated it for Melody's birthday. Melody appreciated all the effort Mrs. Holden had gone to for her birthday meal, so she said, "Thank you, Mrs. Holden. Everything was delicious, and the cake is gorgeous. In fact, it's so pretty I hate to cut it."

"Oh Lord milady, go on with yourself. Go ahead and cut it. It has cherry filling inside, just the way you like it. I know how you love cherries!" Mrs. Holden said. Melody cut the cake and handed a piece to Henry, and then she cut a piece for Mrs. Holden and one for herself. The cake was scrumptious.

After dinner, they went upstairs to their room. Earlier that evening, Melody had told Millie that she would not need her. Henry turned her around, unbuttoned her gown, and pushed it past her hips, and then it fell to the floor. Then he loosened her corset and stays, and they fell to the floor too. Before long, Henry had removed all her clothes, and she was completely naked. As he gazed at her, her cheeks grew flushed as she noticed how his eyes glowed with passion. He stepped back and took off his clothes, and once he was naked, he picked Melody up and carried her to the bed. "Have I told you how much I love you lately?" he asked as he allowed his eyes to roam down her luscious body. "You're such a pretty woman. When I see you in all your naked glory, I know you're all I'll ever want in a woman. I love the way your luscious breasts fill my hands. Your delectable belly was made for kisses, and these lovely thighs are in my dreams when I'm away from you."

Melody loved it when Henry said things like this to her, because it made her feel as if she were the most beautiful woman in the world. He pulled her close and started kissing her passionately. He trailed kisses down her neck, lowered his head, and took her nipple in his mouth. As he suckled her, Melody felt her passion rise. Her breathing grew rapid, and the place between her legs began to pulse. Henry continued to kiss her all over, and then he lowered his body so he was between her thighs. He put her legs over his shoulders and began to lick her core. Melody went wild; her head was moving back and forth on the pillow as she felt her passions explode. She felt waves of glittering sensations roll over her. He moved up and kissed her deeply; she could taste herself in his kiss, and it excited her. He slid inside her tight sheath and began to stoke in and out, and his movements became faster and deeper. Melody felt her passion burgeoning and growing ever stronger, and then she was soaring higher than ever before, just as Henry threw his head back and groaned as he reached his release at the same time. He fell to the side and pulled Melody to him.

He sighed contentedly as he said, "I can never get enough of you, my love. You have started a fire in me that won't go out. I love you."

"Henry, I love you too. Is it always this wonderful?" she asked.

"I've never felt like this with anyone else," he said. "I think it's because with you, my emotions are engaged, where before, it was just physical lust. My love for you just keeps getting stronger everyday that we're with each other."

With love glowing in her eyes, she said, "I feel the same way, Henry. I never thought the marriage bed could be so fulfilling. I'm so fortunate to have found you, and I couldn't bear to lose you."

Henry pulled her close, and said, "Sweetheart, you'll never lose me. I'll always be here, forever and beyond." They just lay there holding each other and enjoying being together until they finally drifted off to sleep.

The next week, they decided to invite some of Henry's fellow officers over to the house. This would be Melody's first opportunity to be a hostess, and she was extremely nervous. Mrs. Holden was so helpful, and they soon had a delightful menu planned for the dinner. She also planned for them to have cards to entertain their guests. On the evening of the party, the guests began to arrive. Captain Hayden was the first to arrive, and he had Lieutenant Bronson with him and Bronson's sister, Mary.

Melody turned to Mary and said, "Good evening. I'm so pleased you were able to attend. Have you been enjoying your time here with your brother?"

"Oh yes. I was ever so pleased when I was able to come back for another visit. I enjoy Canterbury so much, and it's such a historic city. Is Lord Wyndham going to be attending tonight?" Mary asked as she shyly lowered her head.

"He was unable to take the time to come. Does this mean that you have been thinking about him, Mary?" Melody asked.

"He came to visit me here, shortly after the holidays, and I found him to be very good company," she said. "It's such a shame that he lost his wife. We have much in common, since both of us have lost someone we deeply loved. I would have enjoyed seeing him again."

The rest of their guests arrived, so Melody went to greet them. Soon Mrs. Worth announced dinner. The food was excellent, and everyone seemed to be having a good time. Melody led the ladies into the parlor so the men could enjoy their port.

Mrs. Cunningham, the wife of Henry's commanding officer, was a delightful woman, and soon they were talking as if they had been friends for a long time. When the men joined the ladies, they all sat down to play whist. This was the first time she had played cards with Henry and found out they played very well together. He was an excellent whist player, and they won the set. The evening turned out well, and Melody was glad they had decided to have the party.

After all their guests left, Henry gave Melody a hug and told her how proud he was of her. The party had been delightful, and everyone seemed to enjoy themselves, so it had been a success. She was relieved to know that everything had gone so well.

They went up to bed, and, after they tenderly made love, fell fast asleep.

CHAPTER 10

March 1815

HENRY ARRIVED AT the garrison, and obviously, something was going on. It was total chaos. He could not find any of his men and none of his officers. Finally, he saw Hayden up ahead, and he hurried over to him and asked, "What is going on? It's obvious that something momentous has happened. Where are all my men?"

Hayden shook his head and said, "Napoleon has escaped from Elba. We just got the dispatch from Wellington thirty minutes ago. We're meeting in an hour."

"When did Napoleon escape?" Henry asked with concern written all over his face. "How could this happen, and what are we going to do about it?"

"From what was in the dispatch, he escaped on February 26, and no one knows how it all went down. We should learn more in the meeting," Hayden said.

Henry went into the meeting to find out what was going to happen. Bonaparte had somehow made it past the British and arrived in France on March 1. He proceeded to gather his followers around him, and then he headed toward Paris. They were to be ready to leave at a moment's notice, just as soon as word arrived from Wellington. Wellington was leaving the Congress of Vienna and traveling to Brussels.

Henry arrived home at eight o'clock, and Melody could tell by his grave expression that something must have happened that had Henry very worried. "Henry, you're worrying me. You seem to be greatly concerned about something. What's going on?" she asked.

Henry looked at her and said, "Bonaparte has escaped from Elba, and I'll be receiving orders to join Wellington soon. I need to get you back to Sanderford Park, so I know you'll be safe. Can you be ready to leave tomorrow morning?"

Trying to hide the concern in her voice, she replied, "Of course, whatever you feel is best. I've enjoyed being here with you, but I know you'll be very preoccupied and don't need to be worried about me. I'll have Millie start packing right away."

Millie got everything packed that she would need to take back with her. Mansfield would pack up the rest and send the other part of their belongings later. She went back downstairs, and they had supper. Henry was very quiet all through dinner. She was so frightened because she knew Henry would eventually be going into combat again. She knew she had to be strong and not let Henry see how frightened she really was. They retired to bed, and Henry passionately made love to her, taking her to heights she had never reached before. They held each other until they fell asleep.

The next morning, they set off for Sanderford Park at dawn. Henry was still quiet, but he tried to talk about inconsequential things to reduce the tension in the carriage. When they arrived at Sanderford Park, Melody was exhausted. They had traveled practically nonstop to get there. Henry helped her out of the carriage, and they walked up the steps together. Simpson met them at the door.

"My lord, it is a pleasure to see you again, but we were not expecting you. However, your rooms are ready. Would you like to go and freshen up? Everyone is in the drawing room. Have you had dinner yet? I can have Cook prepare a light repast for you, if needed," Simpson said.

"Melody, why don't you go up to our rooms, while I bring his grace up to date on what is happening?" He turned to Simpson and said, "Food would be very much appreciated, because we have traveled practically nonstop to get here, so anything will be helpful."

Simpson told Henry that he would have Cook prepare the food and send it up to their suite.

Melody covered her mouth to hide her yawn, then said, "Since I'm so tired from the trip, I'll go up and rest until you can join me later."

Henry went to the drawing room, entered, and found all the family gathered there.

His grace stood up as Henry entered the room and asked, "Henry what are you doing here? Have you finally decided to sell your commission and take up your responsibilities to the family?"

Henry looked at them with great sadness in his eyes as he said, "I have some very grave news. Bonaparte has escaped from Elba, and I'll be going back to the continent to join the Duke of Wellington. I've brought Melody back, and I hope I can count on you to welcome her and treat her with respect. She's going to have a difficult time dealing with me leaving, so she'll need your support."

The duke stood up, began to pace, then said, "Well, I do not understand why you feel like you have to go. You have already given the army well over six years of your life. So, at this point, I think it is irresponsible of you, but that should not surprise me because you have been that way your entire life. You have been a disappointment to me since you were a young child. We will take your wife in, but we will not mollycoddle her. She will just have to adjust on her own. Maybe she could go back to her family, since you do not know how long it will be before you return, or if you will return. You have been lucky so far. However, this could be the death of you, Henry."

"I don't have the time to take Melody to her parents, because I've got to be back at the garrison tomorrow. Please just be polite. That's all I ask," Henry said.

The duke sighed and said, "Oh, all right. I guess we can put up with her again. She at least helps to keep your sisters entertained."

Henry turned to his mother and asked, "Your grace, I would appreciate your support. This will be a very trying time for my wife, and she'll need all the help she can get. Mother, can I count on you to be nice to Melody?"

"I will be polite, but I refuse to do more than that. Why do you not send her to her parents?" she asked. "She would probably be happier, and I would not have to see her."

Helen asked, "Where's Melody? You know you can count on us to be there for her. All she has to do is ask. We'll do our best to keep her from worrying about what you'll be doing, and taking care of Melody will help us also."

Henry looked at Helen, grateful for her kind words as he said, "Melody is in her room resting. We've had a tiring journey, so I told her to lie down until some food could be brought up."

Helen, in exasperation, said, "This is just awful. I can't believe that terrible man has escaped! What is going to happen? Are we going to be at war again?"

"We have no choice, for that lunatic has to be stopped and this time for good. Please help Melody adjust to me being gone. I would really appreciate it. Well, I'll take my leave now. I'll be leaving first thing in the morning, so I won't see you again. Please know that I love all of you and

I'll miss you tremendously. Just pray that we recapture Bonaparte quickly." Henry slowly turned and left the room.

Henry went up to their suite and found Melody asleep on the couch in the sitting room. She looked so sweet and incredibly lovely lying there. *How could he leave her? This time he would have so much more to lose, if something were to happen to him. God, he loved her so much. He wished that he could take her to her parents.* His mother was right about that: she would be much happier there. She stretched, opened her eyes, looked up, and smiled, then said, "My goodness, I fell fast asleep. I don't know why I'm so tired tonight. It must be all the changes, what with moving back here and you leaving. When do you have to be back?"

"I have to leave tomorrow morning . . . I wish I had more time; I would take you to your parents instead of leaving you here," he said. "I know my parents don't treat you well, but Helen is glad you're back, and I know I can count on Nelson to take care of you while I'm gone. I'll try to get back before I have to leave for the continent, but I can't promise I'll be able to make it back. Let's put all of this out of our minds and try to enjoy this evening. Dinner should be arriving shortly, and then we can go to bed after we eat."

The footman arrived with the food, and Henry had him leave it on the table. When dinner was over and everything cleared away, he sat down on the couch and motioned for Melody to join him. She sat down next to him and leaned her head on his shoulder, and they sat that way for a long time. Then Henry carried her to bed and made love to her with an intensity that had not been there before. He massaged her back and then had her roll over so that he could massage her front. He spent a long time just stroking her breasts and belly. When he took her, he made sure she reached her satisfaction before he took his own. They lay there in each other's arms, not talking, but not sleeping either. Before they were ready, it was time for Henry to leave.

Melody bravely smiled, then said, "I'll see you soon. Take care of yourself and return to me as soon as you can. I love you, and I'll miss you terribly. May God keep you in his loving arms while we're apart."

He bent down, softly kissed her, and left the room. He quietly closed the door . . . He was too overcome to say anything.

Henry made good time and was back at the garrison late that evening. There had been no more news while he was gone. When he walked into their cottage that night, it seemed so empty without Melody. He knew he could not stay there without her. There were just too many memories, so Henry told Mansfield to pack his things and make sure that everything was ready to leave in two days, and then he left to go back to the garrison.

Tension was high and morale low. Everyone was anxious to just get this over with. News came that Bonaparte had been declared an outlaw on March 13, and he had arrived back in Paris on the twentieth. The French peasants and the low class welcomed him, declared him Emperor again, and the French King fled.

Henry got his orders, and he was to leave for the continent on April 4. He got permission to go home for the weekend. He made the trip in eight hours and poor Jupiter was worn out when he arrived home. He told Freddie to give him plenty of oats and hurried into the house.

Henry rushed up the steps and threw open the door. "Simpson, where is my wife?"

Simpson said, "I believe she is at luncheon in the small dining room, my lord."

Henry ran up the stairs and did indeed find Melody and his sisters sitting down to luncheon. As he entered the room, he said, "Melody, I'm back, but I can only stay the weekend. I leave for the continent on Tuesday, but I was able to get away to see you before I go."

"Oh, Henry, I've been dreading this news for a while! Do you have any idea how long all this will take?" she asked, with concern written all over her sweet face.

Keeping his voice cheerful for Melody's sake, he said, "Darling, there's just no way to know, but most of us believe we'll have Bonaparte back into captivity quickly. I feel that this will be one large battle and that we will be victorious. Please, I don't want any of you worrying about this. England will prevail. Now, let's talk of something more pleasant. What did you have planned today?"

Melody bravely smiled and said, "Have you eaten yet? Please take a seat and join us. We were just talking about visiting some of the tenant farmers later today. The Morrison family is down with an ague, and we took them some of Cook's famous chicken broth. I'm so thankful they let you come, even if it is only for the weekend!"

Henry joined them, and soon they were talking and laughing over silly tales, which helped to take their minds off where Henry was going. After lunch, they decided to take a walk in the garden and go down to the maze, as it was such a nice day. They walked holding hands and just glad they were able to see each other one more time before Henry had to leave for the continent.

They spent every moment together. They took long rides, and they were even able to go on a picnic, since the weather was unseasonably warm. On Sunday, they went to Mass together. They tried to make this time as normal as possible and pretend that this was not the last time they would see each other, for God knows how long. Making love was so poignant and tender that it brought tears to Melody's eyes. They were able to avoid his parents so they did not have to deal with any conflicts. Melody told Henry they had treated her well and that he did not need to worry about her. She had Helen and Kathryn; she was helping Helen get ready to go to town for her first season, and Helen was very excited about it all. Nelson was already in town, getting the house ready for all of them, and they were planning on leaving around the middle of April. Melody had decided not to go but stay at the park with Kathryn instead. She told him that since he could not be there, she would not have an enjoyable time anyway.

After church, they went up to their rooms, and they made love until he had to go back to the garrison. They had agreed they would not have any tearful good-byes. As Henry was getting ready to leave, she kissed him and said, "I'll see you soon, my love. Now go get rid of that terrible Bonaparte so you can come back to me."

"I'm sure this will be over quickly, and this time, we'll be rid of him for good. Please write me, darling. Your letters mean the world to me. This will all be over with soon, and then we'll go up north and have a very happy life. I promise!" Henry pulled her close and kissed her one last time, and then he left the room.

When Melody woke up the next morning, she remembered that Henry was gone. She did not feel well, so she decided to stay in bed for the day. Helen came to check on her, but Melody just told her that she wanted to be alone. She promised she would be up and about tomorrow.

The next morning, she got up and was resolved to not be morose. She went downstairs to the breakfast room, and Helen and Kathryn were already there. Melody filled her plate and joined them at the table. As they ate their breakfast, Helen mentioned that she needed to go into the village that day and pick up some things from the dressmaker and Melody agreed to go with her. While they were in the village, they also went to the bookshop and the confectionery. Over all, it was a pleasant morning, and the time went swiftly by. That afternoon, Melody went to Helen's room so she could model all her new clothes she would be taking with her to London. Again, the afternoon went by quickly. Melody appreciated what Helen was doing. She knew she was trying to take Melody's mind off Henry. At four o'clock, they went down for tea. The duke and duchess were already in the drawing room when they arrived.

"I see you have finally chosen to join us, gel. You have been avoiding us, I do believe," stated her grace.

Melody smiled pleasantly and said, "I haven't intentionally been avoiding you. I just haven't been feeling well, but I'm feeling much better today. Are you looking forward to going to town next week?"

"I'm ready to leave the country. I enjoy the season every year, but this one will be particularly busy, what with Helen's come out and presentation at court. I just hope she will meet someone this season, and we can marry her off," she said.

In frustration, Helen said, "Mother, I told you that I don't want to get married yet. I want to just enjoy myself this year and not take anything too seriously."

Melody put her arm around Helen as she said, "Helen, you're going to have so much fun. I know you're going to be well received. You'll have dozens of beaus, and you may meet someone very special, just as I did when I met your brother. I didn't go to London with the expectation that I would meet someone and be married seven months later. Sometimes, it just works out that way. I want you to be happy, so just keep an open mind when you get there."

"I guess you're right, Melody. I wouldn't mind finding someone like you did. Someone that I could love and that would love me as Henry loves you." Helen looked over at Melody with determination in her eyes. "I wish you would change your mind and come with me. We would have so much fun, and you could help me navigate through the ton. Please change your mind and come with us. I think it would be better for you. It would help keep you from worrying so much about Henry. Please say you will come?"

Melody could tell this was important to Helen. So she said, "Well, maybe I'll go for a few weeks, just to help you adjust, if it's all right with your parents."

The duchess turned to her and said, "You can come with us. I know you would help entertain Helen and keep her busy, so I can enjoy myself with my friends. At least, until the season gets fully under way and Helen makes her curtsey at court. Yes, I think it would be a very good idea for you to come, so no more discussion."

They finished their tea and biscuits, and everyone went upstairs to rest before dinner. Melody thought Helen was probably right and that going to town would help take her mind off Henry, now that he had left for the continent. Once she got there, she might change her mind and stay for the entire season. They went to the schoolroom and told Kathryn that Melody was going to London after all.

"I'm glad that you decided to go, Melody. I think it will be good for you. It will take your mind off Henry, and I know he would want you to go and have a good time. He won't worry that you're sitting here alone feeling blue and worrying about him. You need to write him and let him know you're going." Kathryn wistfully hugged Melody and then said, "I wish I could go. Even if I'm too young to be out in society yet, I would love to be able to visit all the museums and go to some of the other attractions that are available in London. I've never been able to go there."

Melody wanted to help Kathryn feel better, so she said, "Helen and I will see if we can convince your mother to let you go and just stay while I'm there. I'll tell her that I'll help to keep you entertained and will chaperone you so she doesn't have to do it herself."

Kathryn hugged her tightly as she said, "Oh, thank you, Melody! I hope she'll say yes. Will you ask her tonight after dinner?"

"Yes, Helen and I will both do our best to persuade the duchess to let you come with us," she said. "Well, I need to go to my room, so I can read. I'm at a good spot in my book and want to finish it before dinner."

Melody sat down on the chaise in her room and was soon lost in her book. Before she realized, it was time to get ready for dinner. She called Millie and was soon ready to go down. She arrived in the drawing room, just as everyone was ready to go into dinner. The duke gave her a hard cold stare. It was obvious that he was not pleased that she was cutting it close and had almost been late again. Dinner went well, and soon the ladies left his grace to his port.

Melody and Helen approached the duchess and Melody said, "Your grace, we would like you to consider letting Kathryn come to town with us. Now that she will be left all alone, except for her governess, she'll be lonely. Remember that always before, she had Helen to help entertain her, but Helen won't be here, since she's going to town, and now I'll be going as well. She'll be all alone. Please let her come, just for the time while I'll be there."

Melody watched the duchess closely, hoping she would say yes, because she knew this was important to Kathryn. Then the duchess replied, "You make a very good argument for Kathryn. I agree she would probably get into mischief, if left on her own. She can come, as long as you take full responsibility and keep her entertained."

Melody was shocked but so happy for Kathryn. She could not believe she had actually convinced the duchess! "Thank you, your grace, I promise to watch over her. I know it's what Henry would want me to do, and besides, I love Kathryn very much and find her company delightful."

Helen and Melody went to the pianoforte so Helen could play and Melody could sing. This helped to pass the rest of the evening, and at ten o'clock, they went upstairs to bed.

The next morning, they told Kathryn that the duchess had agreed to allow her to go to London. Kathryn ran to Melody and Helen and hugged them. She was overjoyed that she was able to go and started talking about all the wonderful things she would be able to do. Melody was pleased that she had been successful in persuading the duchess to allow Kathryn to go. Maybe the duchess was starting to accept her, because she had been a little nicer to her lately. She knew she was making the right decision to go with everyone, because it would help keep her mind off what Henry would be doing.

CHAPTER 11

April 1815

THE NEXT WEEK went by quickly, what with getting everything ready to go to town. Before Melody knew it, they were off to London. The trip was pleasant, and soon they arrived at Sanderford House. Melody had never been there, so she was amazed at the size of it. It looked almost as large as Buckingham palace. There was a level of opulence she had never seen. It was somewhat overwhelming, and she was sure she would get lost before she learned her way around. Melody liked the library most of all, because it had floor-to-ceiling bookshelves, and she could just imagine spending many delightful hours curled up with a good book. After the housekeeper, Mrs. Stewart, finished the tour, she showed them to their rooms. The suite she would be using was beautiful. Melody could see herself spending many pleasant hours writing letters at the small delicate French desk in the sitting room. She loved the soft shades of mauve and cream in the sitting room, and the bedroom matched. Of course, what would have been Henry's room adjoined her room. His room was very masculine with another large bed with heavy dark mahogany furniture, and she thought of Henry and wished he was there so he could make love to her in that big bed. She liked the colors used to decorate his room. The shades of deep green with beige accents were very restful, and then she felt a sharp stab of pain, remembering what Henry was doing and where he was. They would have had such an enjoyable time, just like last year. *Oh well, there was no use dwelling on what could not be.* That would only cause her to become melancholy, and she knew that Henry was counting on her to be strong. She was still waiting on a letter from him. It had only been a fortnight since he had left for the continent. She probably would not hear from him for at least another week.

The first week went by quickly. They went to the modiste, Madame Devy and were having new gowns made up for the season. Melody was pleased to see that the duchess seemed to be more pleasant ever since they had arrived in town. It had been her idea for Melody to have a new wardrobe along with Helen. She told Melody that she needed new clothes because, after all, she was now part of the family and needed to dress accordingly. The duchess was very controlling about what she would wear and was constantly making comments about Melody's weight. She told Madame Devy to make sure that all Melody's gowns hid her plumpness. This was quite embarrassing to Melody, but there was nothing she could do about it except maintain her dignity. Just when she thought she was making progress with the duchess, she found out that she was wrong. She realized that the only reason the duchess was buying her new clothes was that she did not want Melody to embarrass her. She did compliment Melody on doing a fine job of entertaining Kathryn, but Melody knew this was because she did not want to have to do it herself. They had all their new clothes by the second week. Melody just wished Henry could see her in all her new finery. Madame Devy was brilliant, and she did have to admit that her new gowns were very slimming.

Finally, Melody received her first letter from Henry. He was very busy, and his men were impatient to get a chance at Boney. They landed on the continent and were making their way to Brussels. It would be a slow process, but they should be there by mid-May. The weather had been truly dreadful. Henry told her that it had been raining everyday since they landed. He seemed to be in a good frame of mind, and he reminded her that he loved her and missed her very much. She was relieved to hear from him and immediately wrote back. She let him know that she had been having a lovely time with Kathryn. They had gone to several museums so Kathryn could see art by some of the great masters. Kathryn enjoyed her art instruction and diligently worked on her lessons. The duchess had even consented to let her continue her instruction even though they were in London.

That evening, they were all going to the Duke of Ashurst's opening season ball. Melody had a beautiful, new ball gown to wear. Once she was dressed, she noticed how nice she looked in her gown, which was a deep rose satin with gold trim on the bodice. The gown was simple yet elegant, and it definitely enhanced all of Melody's best attributes. Millie did a remarkable job on dressing her hair in a new style, which was very flattering to her face. Nelson would be escorting them to the ball. It was so nice to see him again, and he looked happier than she had ever seen him. He had shared with her that he had been spending quite a bit of time with Mrs. Harrison, and they were getting to know each other very well.

Melody descended the stairs, and most of them were already in the entry hall. They turned to look at her, and she could tell that they were impressed with how well she looked. Nelson met her as she stepped down from the stairs. He bowed, raised her hand, and kissed her fingers as he said, "Melody, you look lovely. I may have to watch out for you. There will be quite a few men trying to get your attention this evening. I'll have my work cut out for me, protecting you from them."

Melody looked over at Nelson with astonishment in her eyes. Surely, he did not think she would want other men flirting with her. "Nelson, I would never give my attention to any other man. I only want Henry, you know that."

Nelson laughed as he gave her a quick hug and said, "I do. I was just teasing you. Henry would be very proud of you if he could see how elegant you appear tonight." Nelson turned to everyone and said, "Well, it's time to be off."

They all got in the carriage to travel to the Duke of Ashurst's residence It appeared that the ball would definitely be a crush as they waited in line with all the other guests. A red carpet was rolled out to protect everyone's evening attire, and finally, it was their turn. The footmen helped all of the ladies out of the carriage, and they went up the stairs. At the head of the stairs, the majordomo announced their arrival. Melody was slightly taken aback by all the heads that turned when her name was announced. They moved through the receiving line, and she made her curtsey to the Duke and the Duchess of Ashurst. The duchess was a lovely woman, only a few years older than Melody. She gave her a welcoming smile, told her she was glad she could come, and mentioned that Melody should come for a visit so they could have tea together and get to know one another. They eventually made it down the stairs, and Melody spied her friend Susan standing by Aunt Miriam. They greeted her warmly, gave her a hug, and kissed her on the cheek.

"My darling girl, you look marvelous, and where did you get that gown?" Aunt Miriam asked. "Obviously, marriage has agreed with you. I have never seen you look so happy. I was sorry to hear that Henry had to leave. I'm sure you miss him quite a bit. If you need anything, just let me know. Please come for tea tomorrow so you can catch me up on everything."

"Thank you, Aunt Miriam. The gown is part of my new wardrobe, and it's one of Madame Devy's designs. I would be happy to come for tea. I look forward to it. I have so much to tell you." Melody turned to Susan and said, "Susan, you look lovely tonight. How have you been?"

Susan looked over and giggled, then said, "I have so much to tell you! I've met someone. His name is Arthur Taylor, and his father is a viscount. He's very handsome and also very funny. He makes me laugh all the time, and I really like him. He should be here soon. I want to introduce him to you. Are you going to have time to help with the orphanage while you're in town?"

"Yes, Susan, I'm looking forward to seeing all the children again. I'm glad you've met someone. You deserve to be happy. I'm so happy with Henry, but I miss him terribly. I hope this conflict can be cleared up quickly, so he can come back to me. Here comes Nelson. He's my brother-in-law, the Marquess of Wyndham, and he has been so helpful to me since I joined the family." She smiled at Nelson as he joined them, and said, "Nelson, this is my best friend, Susan Wilton. Susan, this is Henry's brother, the Marquess of Wyndham."

Nelson made his bow and said, "It's lovely to meet you. Melody has mentioned you several times. I'm pleased she has a good friend to help occupy her time while she waits for Henry's return." He looked over at Melody and asked, "Melody, may I have this dance?"

Melody smiled and said, "Of course, I would be pleased to dance with you."

Then Nelson turned to Susan and asked, "Do you have room for me on your dance card, Miss Wilton?"

"Yes, my lord, I have a quadrille coming up. Would that do?" she asked.

Nelson smiled as he replied, "That would be perfect. I look forward to our dance, Miss Wilton." They talked a few more minutes, and then Nelson said, "I believe this is my dance, Melody."

They made their way to the dance floor and joined the line for the country-dance. As they danced, Melody asked, "Is Mrs. Harrison here tonight?"

"Yes, she's over there with her mother," he said. "I would like it if you would befriend Mary. She's a little shy and doesn't have many friends in town. She's missing her brother, and I know you could comfort each other."

Melody smiled up at Nelson, and said, "I found Mary delightful when I met her at Christmas and also when she came back to visit her brother in February, so I would be happy to make her acquaintance again."

Once the dance was over, Nelson led Melody over to where Mary was sitting, and he introduced her to Mrs. Bronson. Soon they were chatting as if they were old friends. Melody liked Mrs. Bronson, and she enjoyed seeing Mary again. While standing by Mary, she said, "I volunteer at an orphanage when I'm in London. Would you be interested in helping?"

Mary replied, "I would love to help out. There are so many children less fortunate than my son. I know I would enjoy helping out very much."

"I'll be going there tomorrow at ten o'clock. Would you be able to come with me?" she asked.

Mary turned to her mother and asked, "Mother would you mind watching Roderick while I go with Lady Montgomery?"

Mrs. Bronson said, "I would be happy to watch him." She turned to Melody and added, "I think it's a wonderful thing you are doing, Lady Montgomery. Not many young women are willing to donate their time to the less fortunate."

"Thank you, ma'am, I truly love working with all the children. It's so sad that so many of them are left without their parents. I want to help them out anyway that I can. Oh look, here's Susan Wilton. She also volunteers at the orphanage. Let me introduce you to her." As Melody welcomed Susan into their group, she said, "Susan, this is my friend Mary Harrison and her mother Mrs. Bronson. Mary has offered to help us at the orphanage. Isn't that wonderful?"

Susan enthusiastically replied, "I'm pleased to meet both of you. You'll enjoy all the children, and I'm glad you'll be joining us."

They all stood there and talked for a while. Helen came over, and Melody introduced her. Once Helen found out about the orphanage, she told them that she would like to help also, and they all agreed they would go together. Melody looked around and saw Lord Weston walking toward her.

She smiled at Lord Weston as she introduced him to everyone. "Lord Weston, let me introduce you to Mrs. Bronson. I believe you know her son, and of course, you met Mrs. Harrison at our home at Christmas."

"It's a pleasure to meet you, Mrs. Bronson. I think highly of your son. I'm sure you miss him, but he is one our brave heroes on their way to fight Bonaparte. I'm sure he'll return to you soon. From all the news, this conflict should be over shortly." Lord Weston turned to Melody and asked, "Lady Montgomery, would you care to dance this next set with me?"

"Certainly, my lord, I would be happy to dance with you." They walked to the dance floor and joined the other couples dancing. It was a waltz, and it made Melody think of the last time she and Henry had danced together.

"How are you, Lady Montgomery?" Lord Weston asked, "I'm sure you're missing Lord Montgomery. I was sorry to hear he had to leave for the continent to join Wellington. Have you heard from him since he left?"

Melody smiled and said, "Please call me Melody. After all, you're Henry's best friend. I received a letter from him yesterday, and he sounded in good spirits. He was complaining about all the rain they were having. He told me that his men were getting impatient waiting for something to happen. They're ready to see some action. I dread it when they do because I worry that Henry will be hurt or even killed. I don't know what I'll do if anything were to happen to him."

As he twirled her around the dance floor, he said, "Please try not to worry. Henry has been in the army for a long time, and he'll make sure that nothing keeps him from coming back to you. I know he cares a great deal about you and will make sure he's able to come home to you as soon as we defeat Bonaparte. If I'm to call you Melody, then you need to call me Weston. That's what all my friends call me. If there is anything I can do to help the time pass easier for you, just let me know. In fact, how would you like to go for a drive in the park tomorrow afternoon?"

"Thank you, Weston. I would love to go. I have plans for the morning, but I'll be free later in the day and thank you for offering to help me. Henry told me I could count on you to be there for me," she said.

"I'll come by to pick you up at four o'clock, and we'll take a drive through Hyde Park. Will that be convenient for you?" he asked.

Melody smiled as she said, "That's fine. I should be back from Lady Helton's by then."

Once the dance had ended, he returned her to her friends. Nelson was dancing with Mrs. Harrison, and they looked as if they were having a deep discussion. Melody hoped they would get together. Mary seemed just the right kind of woman for him. Of course, his parents would not be happy if anything were to come of this relationship. They were still pressuring him to marry Lady Penelope. Melody had met her at the Christmas party, and she really did not care for her at all and knew Nelson would be miserable if he were to marry her. Melody danced several more times with some of Henry's friends. She had a very pleasant evening, but she was glad when everyone decided to leave.

The next morning, she got up and hurried through her morning ablutions, because her day was full. She remembered that she had promised her aunt she would come by for a visit today. She was also supposed to go to the orphanage and then for a drive with Weston at four o'clock. She went down to breakfast and had her usual toast and jam with hot chocolate. Helen was there talking excitedly about the ball. She had had a marvelous time and was supposed to go driving with a nice young man she had met last night. His name was Andrew Hamilton, and he was the Earl of Everwood's heir.

Helen giggled and said, "Melody, he's so handsome, and he dances divinely. I liked his sense of humor, and he was so polite. He told me he thought I was beautiful!"

"Helen, you're very beautiful. I'm not surprised at all that he found you so. When is he picking you up?" Melody asked.

Helen sipped her tea, and then she said, "He's going to be here at three o'clock, and Mother even approves of me seeing him. She told me he was from a very good family. Will you be here this afternoon when he comes to pick me up?"

"I doubt that I'll be here. Remember we're going to the orphanage at ten o'clock this morning. I'm going to see my aunt Miriam at one o'clock, and then I'm also going for a drive with Henry's friend, Lord Weston, at four o'clock, so I have a very busy day ahead of me," she said.

"Well, maybe we'll run into each other at the park later this afternoon. If we're going to the orphanage at ten o'clock, I had better hurry and get ready," Helen said as rushed out of the room.

They went and picked up Mary and Susan and then went to the orphanage. Melody was so glad to see all the children again. Some of the children from last year had been adopted, and other children had arrived. While they were playing with the children, Melody pulled Susan to the side and asked, "How is Brandon? I felt so awful when my mother wrote and told me about Lily and the baby. I wish I could have been there to help console him. I'm sure he was devastated by it all."

"I saw him right before I left to come to London, and he's terribly morose and misses Lily desperately. I've tried to be there for him, but he doesn't want to talk about it," Susan said. "He's even talked about moving somewhere else because the memories are so painful. I'm sure a letter from you would help him tremendously. You've always been so close."

"I wrote to him right after I heard the news, but I haven't written since then. What with Henry leaving for the continent and all, I've just had too much on my mind. I'll write to him tomorrow. Well, if I'm going to get to my aunt's on time, I need to leave." As Melody left, she added, "Susan I'll see you in two days.

Melody had a pleasant visit with her aunt. They planned on meeting at the Milton Musicale that they were both attending that evening. She rushed home and got ready for her drive with Lord Weston. He picked her up on time, and they drove to Hyde Park. It was a lovely spring day, and the drive was very enjoyable. "Thank you for asking me to go driving with you. It's a lovely day, and all the flowers are so beautiful. I particularly enjoy the spring of the year. It's hard to be blue when everything is so pretty." Lord Weston was driving his phaeton, and it was obvious that he was a very good driver. She had never ridden in a high perch phaeton and was enjoying it tremendously.

"I'm pleased you could come for a drive today. Your husband has been my best friend since we were at Eton together as young boys. I wanted to go with him when his father bought Henry his commission, but since I'm an only child, my father refused. Of course, shortly after that, my father died, and then I inherited my title. I was so disappointed and a little envious of Montgomery. In some ways, I've lived vicariously through him, imagining that I was in the army with him. The army has been good for Montgomery, and he wasn't looking forward to civilian life until he met you. You make him very happy," Weston said as he pulled to the side to let an approaching carriage pass.

"He makes me deliriously happy, and I do miss him desperately. He has become my best friend, not just my husband." They continued to drive through the park and ran into Helen with her beau. They chatted for a while, but then it was time to leave. She had had a very pleasant afternoon with Lord Weston, and they planned to do it again soon.

When Melody got home, she went to her room to rest before dinner, as she knew it was going to be a long night. When she woke up, she barely had time to dress for the evening and just made it downstairs in time for dinner. They arrived at the Musicale at nine o'clock, and they stayed there for several hours. Melody was exhausted when she finally made it to bed, and she fell into a deep sleep.

She remembered to write Brandon the next day, and she hoped her letter would cheer him up. She wrote about Henry having to leave to go fight Bonaparte and told him she was in London for a few weeks, but then she would be going back to Sanderford Park.

The next month went by very quickly. They went to either a ball or some kind of entertainment every night. She especially enjoyed the opera. When they went there, *The Barber of Seville* was playing, and the soprano had a stupendous voice. Melody had always enjoyed singing, and she had a lovely light soprano voice herself.

She was very tired and was glad she would be leaving to go back to the country the next day. Nelson was going to take her and Kathryn, because he had some estate business he needed to take care of. She had no regrets about coming to town, but she was more than ready to go back to Sanderford Park.

They left the next day, early in the morning and were there by four o'clock that afternoon. Melody slept most of the way. She could not understand why she was so tired and sleepy all the time, and she had been nauseous lately. This was puzzling to Melody because she was rarely, if ever, ill. It only happened in the morning, and then she was fine for the rest of the day. Nelson had asked Melody to come to his study after she had freshened up. He had something he wanted to talk to her about, and she wondered what it was. She met Nelson, and he asked her to take a seat.

"I want to run something by you. I've decided that I'm going to ask Mary to marry me. We get along well, and her son is delightful. She's very peaceful to be with. You've been spending quite a bit of time with Mary. Do you think she'll want to marry me?" he asked.

"Nelson, I know she'll want to marry you. She's mentioned several times to me how much she has enjoyed your company. I think you'll suit each other very well. Henry just knew she would be the right woman for you, and I wish you every happiness. You deserve to have someone in your life that you can care about. I know you loved Nora very much, but I'm sure she would want you to move on with your life. Have you told your parents about your decision?" she asked.

"I've decided not to mention anything to them until after I find out if Mary accepts my proposal. If she says yes, then I'll tell them at that time," Nelson replied. "I'm glad you feel this is a good direction for me to take. Mary is so pleasant that I know we'll get along well. I don't love her as I loved Nora, but I admire her tremendously, and I feel I could grow to love her in the future. I'll be going back to London in a few days, and I'll ask her then."

"I hope you have a safe trip and please tell Helen to have fun. I just hope she can meet someone she can love and who will love her. I've grown so fond of all of you, and I appreciate all of you so much. Having you in my life has helped me deal with Henry leaving. I'll be so grateful when all this conflict with Bonaparte is behind us and we can get on with our lives," she said. "Well, I think I'll go upstairs and rest before dinner. I'll see you later."

The next day, Melody received a letter from Brandon. He thanked her for writing and told her he was sorry that Henry had to leave her to go fight. He also told her that he was looking for another teaching position because the memories of Lily were driving him mad. Melody's heart went out to him. She could only imagine how horrible it would be to lose your true love. Melody decided she would write Brandon occasionally, just to let him know she was thinking about him.

CHAPTER 12

Brussels, Belgium
May 1815

HENRY ARRIVED IN Brussels at the beginning of May. The passage over the English Channel was rough, and many of his men were seasick. It had been a grueling march ever since they had arrived in France. His men were very tired, and morale was extremely low. What was surprising was the amount of people that were arriving in Brussels. Many of the ton were setting up house, and there were balls, galas, and parties every night. The Duke of Wellington hosted many of them, himself. Henry did not feel like going to these events, but Wellington gave direct orders to all his officers, telling them they had to attend. During the day, they were scouting out possible battle sites and then dancing all night. Henry was missing Melody terribly. He almost wished he had brought her with him. He would have, had he known there were going to be so many of the ton here. Her letters were all that kept him sane. She must have been writing everyday, because he was receiving letters on a daily basis. They were always so cheerful, and he was pleased she had decided to go to London for the season, after all. Evidently, Helen and Melody had convinced his mother to let Kathryn come to London too. Henry was relieved that Melody was in London, because that way she would stay busy and would not miss him as much.

As May moved along, there were rumors flying everyday. Bonaparte was holding back and not taking the offensive. Wellington was waiting for Marshall Blucher to arrive. Henry wished they would just get this over with. The army was not holding the appeal that it once had. Everything was dependent on the seventh coalition. Bonaparte was trying to get some of the allied to change sides, and it looked as if he had been successful, because Marshall Ney had joined forces with him.

Henry was trying to write Melody everyday, but it was difficult to find the time, and he wanted to be positive in his letters; for the most part, he was. Sometimes, he did mention the morale problems and the level of boredom of his troops. After all, how many times could his troops practice drills without any action and without growing bored.

Thank goodness for Melody's letters. They were always so cheerful, and it sounded as if she were having a good time. Her last letter stated that she had returned to Sanderford Park. Kathryn had come with her, because that had been the arrangement she had made with the duchess. She said she was tired of all the parties anyway and wanted the peace and quiet that she would find there.

Sanderford Park
May 1815

Melody spent quite a bit of her time, over the next few days, just catching up on her sleep. She spent every morning walking through the lovely gardens. They were as beautiful as she had known they would be when she walked through them last fall. Writing letters to Henry was something she relished, because it helped her feel closer to him. She was missing him a great deal, and now that she was back at Sanderford Park, she was missing him even more than she had in London. Nelson left to go back to town, and she hoped all went well for him. Of course, Mary would say yes, and then he would have to deal with the anger from his parents. Melody also spent part of her day with Kathryn, and she really looked forward to their time together.

As the days went by, she spent more time thinking about Henry. It had been almost two months since he left, and she missed him more each day. It was peaceful at Sanderford Park, and she was glad she had elected to leave London instead of staying for the entire season. She received a letter from Henry, two or three times a week, and she wrote him everyday. He told her they were playing a waiting game, and the troops were getting very bored, waiting around for something to happen. In his most recent letter, he told her that Napoleon had been able to amass quite a large army, and was moving toward Brussels. He told her he expected something to happen within the next couple of weeks, and he would just be glad when this was over so he could come back to her. She was still sleeping quite a bit, and the nauseous feeling was still there. She was beginning to wonder if something was wrong with her. She was so rarely ill that this was troubling, and she wished she had someone to talk to about it.

Brussels, Belgium
June 1815

It finally looked as if something was getting ready to happen. Rumors were flying all over Brussels, and Wellington was having meetings on a daily basis. The Duchess of Richmond's ball was scheduled for June 15, and Wellington requested that all his officers attend. Late that evening, Wellington received a dispatch from the Prince of Orange, telling him that Napoleon was rapidly advancing. He quickly ordered his army to concentrate on Quatre Bras. Marshall Ney was advancing, and it was imperative that they hold this town. Henry and his troops were sent there in the early hours of the sixteenth. Henry knew they would finally see some action, and the morale of his troops would improve dramatically.

Napoleon attacked, and Blucher's Prussian army was defeated at the Battle of Ligny on June 16. Wellington's troops joined the Prince of Orange at Quatre Bras, and they successfully defeated the French troops there and secured the town by early evening, but it was too late to send help to Blucher. The Prussian's defeat made Wellington's position perilous, so he was not able to defend it against attack. The next day, he moved back his forces to the low ridge of Mont-Saint-Jean, south of a small village called Waterloo. Henry's men were in the thick of it, and he had already lost some good men at Quatre Bras. He was given orders to hold the line. Napoleon went after the allied forces, and there was a brief skirmish in Genappe, but then there were torrential rains, so they had to set up camp for the night. The Waterloo position was a strong one, and things were beginning to turn for the coalition. Henry's orders were to hold the ridge on Ohain road. The fighting broke out in the early hours of June 18. Henry and his men were back in the middle of the fighting again. He was fighting off several Frenchmen at one time and saw several of his men fall. A Frenchman with a bayonet came at him and plunged it into Jupiter's flank, and he went down. Henry managed to jump clear, but the Frenchman was upon him. He felt the bullet tear through him, and as he was falling, his last conscious thought was of Melody and how much he loved her. His head hit something as he fell to the ground, and then he knew . . . no more.

Sanderford Park
Late June 1815

The weather was very warm, now that summer was here. It was hard to imagine that it was nearing the later part of June. Henry's letters indicated that a battle was imminent. Each day, she hoped, brought her closer to the time when Henry could come back to her. It seemed as if it had been a long time since he went away.

On June 26, Nelson returned to Sanderford Park. He appeared very somber, and Melody wondered why. He asked her to step into his study with him and take a seat. She was getting very nervous, because he had a look in his eyes that did not make her feel at ease.

"Melody, you know how much I care about you. I've received some news from the continent, and I came here as quickly as possible. I wanted to be the first to tell you." Nelson hesitated, and then he continued, "There has been a great battle . . . in a little place called Waterloo . . . We won . . . but there were terrible losses."

"What's wrong? Has Henry been hurt? Tell me what . . . what's going on now!" she cried.

Nelson looked at Melody as he said, "There's been a letter from Henry's commanding officer and the Duke of Wellington . . . Henry . . . was shot down in this battle . . . Melody . . . Henry didn't make it."

Melody felt a ringing in her ears, and she lowered her head. There was an expression of total disbelief on her beautiful face. Nelson came over, sat down beside her, and took her in his arms. Melody was having trouble breathing, and she felt as if she were going to be ill. Tears were streaming down her face, and she was wailing in distress. She had never felt so much pain in her life. She cried, "No . . . No . . . this can't . . . it can't be true! There has to be some kind of mistake. I would feel it . . . I would know . . . here in my heart . . . if Henry were dead. I don't believe you. Please . . . please tell me . . . this is not true!"

Nelson rubbed her back gently as he said, "Melody . . . his friend, Captain Hayden . . . he saw him get shot down during battle, when it was over, he looked for him and found . . . Henry's horse dead and Henry's body was next to Jupiter. His face . . . was damaged beyond recognition . . . , but one of your letters was on the ground next to him. It was Henry . . . there's no doubt about it. I'm so sorry . . . so very sorry, just know . . . I'm here for you. Anything I can do for you . . . all you have to do is ask."

Melody continued to weep, but she did not cry out any more. After a time, Nelson carried her up to her bed and called for her maid, Millie, and had her sit with her. Melody was inconsolable, and there was nothing anyone could do to take her pain away. Only time would do that.

They held Henry's funeral on June 30. All his family and many of his friends were there. Melody was in a daze through it all. She was still having a hard time accepting that Henry was gone. Melody tried to keep the tears from falling, but it was impossible. She buried her head into Nelson's chest as she sobbed. When they slid his casket into the mausoleum, she fell apart, and Nelson had to hold her up to keep her from falling. She did not understand how he could be dead. Surely, she would feel it in her heart if it were so. She knew she would have to accept this as fact, because Captain Hayden had been the one to bring Henry's body back. He told Melody all that he had seen, and he was finally able to convince her that Henry was indeed dead.

Once the funeral and the wake were over, Melody cried constantly, and she was very distraught. That evening, Melody went to Nelson and said, "I want to go . . . to my parents. I can't stay here . . . now that Henry . . . is gone. I need to be with my parents. Please, I beg you . . . please take me to my mother!"

Nelson gathered her in his arms and said, "Melody, we love you. Please stay here. I'll take care of you. Henry would expect me to make sure you are all right. I won't be able to do that if you go to Lincolnshire."

As Melody sobbed, she cried out with extreme pain in her voice, "Please, I have to go to my mother now. It's too difficult to stay at Sanderford Park where there are so many memories of Henry. I know that you and your sisters love me, and I love you, but please don't ask me to stay."

Nelson patted her on the back and said, "All right, Melody. If that's what you truly want, I'll take you to your parents. I'll make the arrangements to leave in two days. Will that give you enough time to pack?"

"Oh, thank you! I'm sure Millie can have everything ready. Please understand, I do care about you and your sisters, but I have to go. I need my mother." Melody laid her head on Nelson's shoulder and sobbed because she felt as if her heart had been ripped from her chest; the pain was so excruciating. Eventually she calmed down enough to go back to her room.

Two days later, Nelson and Melody left for Lincolnshire. The trip was grueling because Melody was ill the entire trip and the weather was simply dreadful. Torrential rain fell everyday, so the trip took eight days instead of the usual five. Nelson could not get Melody to eat anything. On the third day, he said, "Melody, I'm very concerned about your health. You haven't eaten anything for three days, and I can tell you've already lost some weight. Henry would not want you to grieve so."

"Nelson, I just can't tolerate food right now. Every time I do try to eat, I become ill. Isn't there any way we can hurry this trip along? I . . . I . . . need my mother," Melody cried.

"I'm sorry, my dear, but the weather is so terrible that we can't push the horses; the roads are in horrible shape. Why don't you lie down on the other seat and try to rest. Millie can sit over here with me." Melody lay down and eventually cried herself to sleep. Each day was a repeat of the day before, and Melody felt as if she were living in hell and that she was never going to get home to her mother. Nelson was wonderful, but she had a terrible time being around him because he looked so much like Henry. Every time she looked over at him, she felt her heart break even more than it already was. *Oh god, when would this trip end?*

They arrived in Lincolnshire, on July 10. Her parents came out to greet them. Her mother took her into her arms, and Melody began to cry copiously. She could not stop crying, and she looked as if she were ready to pass out. Nelson carried her upstairs, and her mother showed him where Melody's room was. He gently laid her on her bed. She turned away from them and asked to be left alone.

Nelson and her parents went down to the parlor, and as they sat there together, he said, "She didn't want to believe Henry was dead. It was only after Captain Hayden told her what he had seen that she began to believe. Just as soon as the funeral was over, she immediately requested that I bring her to you. She has been very ill the entire trip. I'm sure it's from the strain she's been under, but you might want to watch her closely."

Mr. Canterfield-Smyth shook his head and sighed, then said, "Thank you so much for bringing her to us, my lord. We'll take good care of her. I'm glad you were the one to help her. She respects you tremendously, and she has mentioned this in many of her letters to us. I know this has to be a hard time for all of your family. Please accept our condolences on your loss. I understand you were very close to your brother. How are your parents handling Henry's death?"

Nelson replied, "They are their usual stoic selves. They don't show their emotions, so it's hard to know how they feel. Helen and Kathryn are of course devastated, and they were terribly upset that Melody wanted to leave. They had become very close to her."

Mr. Canterfield-Smyth asked, "When will you go back? You're welcome to stay here with us as long as you want."

"I plan to stay for a few days, just to make sure Melody's all right. I need to be back home by mid-July if possible," he said. "The weather was dreadful coming here, so it took us much longer to get here than it normally would have, but I hope to make better time on the way back. Thank you for allowing me to stay with you. I appreciate your hospitality."

Melody slept the rest of that day and most of the next day also. The only person she wanted around her was her mother. Nelson visited her each day, but she would cry every time she saw him. He just reminded her too much of Henry. She could not bear to see him. On the morning of the third day, Nelson left, because seeing him seemed to make things harder for Melody.

She got up on the fourth day, and she ate some food, but it immediately came back up. She could not keep anything down. Melody had lost quite a bit of weight. Her cheeks were sunken in, and she had dark circles under her eyes.

"I can't bear to see her like this. If we can't get her to eat, we need to call in the doctor. She can't keep going without food. It could seriously damage her health," her mother cried.

"Mary, if she's no better tomorrow, I'll get the doctor. My dear, I'm as worried about Melody as you are. There may be something else wrong with her, besides the grief." Magnus put his arm around Mary and said, "Darling, try not to worry. I'm sure Melody will be fine. This has been such a shock to her. It's just going to take her some time to get over Henry's death."

The next day, Melody was no better. Every time she tried to eat anything, she could not keep it down. Her father went to get the doctor. When the doctor arrived, he went straight up to Melody's room to examine her, and after his examination, he came down to talk to them.

"Lady Montgomery is severely dehydrated, and she is weak from not eating. Part of the reason she is so ill is because she is with child. I would estimate she is about three months along. I have left some medicine for her to take, and it should help with the nausea. I did not tell her about the babe. I thought you would want to tell her yourselves. Just give her the medicine three times a day, and if she is not any better in a couple of days, come and get me. I suspect that once she finds out she is with child, she will begin to feel better. I am sure she will want to take better care of herself for the child's sake," explained the doctor.

Melody's mother bowed her head as she said, "I'll go up to her so I can tell her about the baby. Surely, this will help her begin to subside from her grief over Henry's death. If this doesn't help her, then God knows what will."

When her mother entered, she sat down on the edge of Melody's bed and said, "Melody, the doctor talked with us and part of your illness is to be expected. Honey . . . you're with child . . . He said you're about three months along. Did you suspect this at all?"

She sat up, looked at her mother, and shook her head as she answered, "I never even thought about a baby. Oh my, just think I'll have a part of Henry to carry in my heart. I need to eat something. I must gain back my strength for the child's sake. Henry would have been so happy." Melody began to cry, but this time, the tears were cleansing.

Everyday, Melody grew a little stronger, and by the end of the week, she was even putting some of her weight back on. She spent her days in the garden, on the bench in the arbor, where she had been sitting when Henry proposed. She spent much of her time reliving their time together. The time in Canterbury was her fondest memory of all. She had loved that little cottage. She had received several letters from Helen and Kathryn; they were in deep mourning and told Melody they missed her terribly. They wanted her to come back to them. Melody knew . . . she would never go back to Sanderford Park. It would just be . . . too painful.

One thing that brought Melody some relief from her grief was spending time with Brandon. Since he had lost Lily, and now she had lost Henry, they could console each other. Brandon came over a couple of evenings a week, and she thanked God for his company.

A Franciscan Monastery
Brussels, Belgium
July 1815

Meanwhile, back in Brussels, some Franciscan monks found Henry on the battlefield and took him to their monastery. He had sustained a severe head injury, and he had been shot in the leg. He lay unconscious for almost a month, and the monks did not give him much chance to survive. Everyday, they force-fed him to keep him alive. The end of the third week, he took a turn for the worse, and it did not appear that he would make it through the night. The next morning, Henry was still alive, but just barely. The infection in his right thigh was getting worse, but one of the monks, Father Francis, mixed a different type of poultice, and it seemed to be draining out the poisons from his leg. Father Francis continued to get water and gruel down him. That night, his fever broke, and he woke up.

"Welcome back to the living. You have been unconscious for almost a month. You are in a Franciscan monastery outside of Brussels. We found you on the battlefield after the battle had ended, and we brought you here. I know you are feeling quite ill. However, we would like to contact your family. What is your name?" Father Francis asked.

Henry looked confused as he said, "My . . . my name is . . . I . . . I don't know! I can't remember anything. Oh my god! What's happened to me? What would cause this?"

"You must be suffering from amnesia. It is hard to say. Most of the time when the memory is gone, it returns in a few days, but I have seen cases where it never returns. Are you sure you don't remember anything at all?" he asked.

"No, I can't remember anything! What is this battle you speak of?" Henry asked. "When did it take place?"

Father Francis answered, "It was fought on June 18, and it was near a small village called Waterloo. Many men were wounded and many died. It is now the middle of July. Why don't you rest? Maybe things will start to come back to you after you sleep."

Father Francis left his room, and Henry fell back to sleep. He slept for the next sixteen hours, and when he woke up, he still could not remember anything, not even his name. Each day his leg continued to heal, and soon he was able to get around using crutches. He kept trying to remember, but he would get severe headaches, so Father Francis told him to quit trying so hard. Since he could not remember his name, he asked the monks to call him Joseph. Fortunately, he spoke French fluently, so at least, he was able to communicate with them. Father Francis could speak English so that was helpful. He knew he must be wellborn because of the way he spoke, but that did not help him figure out who he was.

Everyday, he grew stronger, and soon he did not need his crutches at all. After a few weeks, he was walking with only a slight limp. He kept trying to remember, but nothing changed; he had no idea who he was. Father Francis told him he was welcome to stay until he got his memory back. Since he had no idea where to go, he thanked him, and said he would stay for a while.

Lincolnshire
Fall 1815

The summer passed, and then fall was upon them. Melody was almost five months along when she felt the baby move. She did not tell Henry's family about the child. For some reason, she was fearful of them finding out. She was afraid they would make her come back to Sanderford Park. At the very least, she knew they would try to control her life, and their graces might even try to take her child away. The duke was such a powerful man that she decided she would not tell them about the baby. Melody was determined to have this child and give it all the love she had in her heart. She would make sure that her baby knew about Henry and how brave, kind, and wonderful he had been.

On the day of her first wedding anniversary, Melody spent the entire day out on the bench where Henry had proposed to her. She gazed down at her hand and rolled her wedding ring around her finger. She remembered the joy she had felt when Henry placed it on her finger. *Oh, why, why did he have to die? Why was life so unfair?* Henry was too young to die. She tried to let go of her grief, but it was just too hard. Melody was determined to never forget Henry, and she would make sure her child knew him. She lowered her head into her hands and softly wept for all she had lost. As evening fell, she finally got up and slowly went back into the house.

Melody spent much of her time with her parents and Brandon and told them all about her time with Henry. She found it calming to talk about him. The hardest times for her were the nights. That was when she missed him the most. Just thinking about never being in his arms again, tore her apart. Her mother was willing to listen to her whenever she wanted to talk, and she was so grateful that she had decided to come home. She missed Henry's brother and sisters, but she knew she had made the right decision about coming home to her parents. Nelson had written to her and told her that he was getting married to Mary. They were planning a Christmas wedding. He wanted Melody to come, but she wrote back and told him that she could not travel because she was still not feeling well.

Christmas was particularly difficult. It brought all the memories of last Christmas and how much fun she had had with Henry and his sisters. She wondered if that horrible Uncle Theodore had come for the holidays. If he did, she hoped Kathryn would let Nelson know if he bothered her.

By the first part of January, Melody was very heavy with child and knew that her time was near. She went into labor on the fifth. The labor was hard but fast, and her baby was born after only six hours of labor. The midwife told her this was highly unusual for a first child. Melody was astounded when she first laid eyes on her beautiful little girl; she was tiny, and she had Henry's red gold curls and his bright blue eyes. The tears poured from her beautiful eyes as she gazed at her daughter. Melody decided she would feed her daughter herself instead of using a wet nurse. She named her daughter Mary Elizabeth, after her mother. Everyday brought a new change. She found motherhood healing and began to feel the pain of losing Henry lessen.

She continued to spend time with Brandon. He was very good with Mary Elizabeth, and she was so thankful for his friendship. Brandon was still thinking about moving away, but she hoped he would not do that any time soon. Just having him there to talk to, helped so much. Since Lily had passed away last December, she and Brandon had that in common: Each of them had lost the love of their life.

CHAPTER 13

Spring 1816

IN THE SPRING, an influenza epidemic came to Little Smythington, and many people were dying from it. Melody was very concerned when both her parents came down with it. They were extremely ill. She kept Mary Elizabeth away from them, and as much as it pained her, she left the nursing of her parents to their maid Rosie, for fear of giving it to her daughter. Each day, her parents grew weaker, and their fevers climbed higher. A week after they became ill, Melody's father passed away. Her mother was so ill that she did not even realize that her husband had died. Melody prayed constantly for her mother, and her fever did finally break, but she did not improve. The doctor did not expect Mrs. Canterfield-Smyth to make it because of the damage to her heart. Two weeks after Melody's father died, her mother quietly passed away in her sleep.

Melody felt hollow inside; her grief was so awful that she could not even express it through tears. She buried both of her parents in the parish cemetery side by side. After her mother's funeral, the parishioners came to Melody and let her know that they would have to find a new vicar, but she could stay in her home until a new one was assigned. She was in a state of shock, for not only had she lost her parents, she was also going to lose her home.

Melody met with her parents' solicitor, and he read her their will. They left her all they had; however, it was just their personal belongings, some furniture, and five hundred pounds. She did not know what to do. There was no way they could live on that money for very long. She thought about contacting Nelson, but she still did not want to go back to Sanderford Park. Nelson was newly married and had been sick, so she did not want to bother him. She knew she would get no help from Henry's parents, and they just might try to take her child away from her. The new vicar was to arrive in two weeks, so she needed to find somewhere else to live quickly.

There was a little cottage on the outskirts of the village, and they were willing to rent it to her for ten pounds a month. Melody and Millie packed everything up for the move. Brandon told her he would be willing to help her move the furniture to her new home.

It was so sad to see her home empty of all her parents' belongings and furniture. As she got ready to leave, for the last time, she went out to the arbor, and all the memories of the day Henry proposed came flooding back. It almost crippled her; the grief was so intense. *Oh, why did Henry have to die?* She knew that she had to go on with her life, but sometimes the grief was more than she could bear. She held Mary Elizabeth in her arms and said, "My precious one, this is where your father proposed to me. He was the most wonderful man in the world. We're going to cling to his memory for the rest of our lives. I'll make sure you know what an incredible person he was. Now, my sweet one, let's go to our new lives."

Once she got everything moved, Brandon helped her get settled in and told her that if she needed anything at all, she should let him know. "I'll continue to check on you a couple of times a week. I know that it's going to be lonely for you out here."

Melody appreciated Brandon's concern, but she did not want to be a burden to him, so she said, "Brandon, I really appreciate all that you have done for me and for Mary Elizabeth, but I don't want to be a bother to you. I know that you have your own life to live."

"It's no problem, Melody. Spending time with you helps me deal with losing Lily, and you know I've become quite fond of Mary Elizabeth. She's like a daughter to me, and since I don't plan to ever marry again, I can shower her with my love and attention. Well, I'll leave you to get settled in." Then he squeezed her hand affectionately and left. This was the first time she had ever lived alone and it frightened her to death, but she knew she had to stay strong for her daughter. Her life . . . had to go on.

Brandon came around every Wednesday and Sunday, and Melody would share her meal with him on those days. Mary Elizabeth was growing more beautiful everyday. Her hair was so much like Henry's, and her eyes were as brilliantly blue as his; she definitely favored her father. She thanked God everyday for giving her Mary Elizabeth. Melody stopped answering Helen and Kathryn's letters. It was just too difficult to keep the fact that she had a child from them, and now that her parents were gone and she had moved, it was even more difficult. She was afraid she would accidentally say something that would give her away. Eventually, Helen and Kathryn's letters stopped coming.

The anniversary of Henry's death was extremely difficult for Melody, especially because the village had a celebration in honor of all the brave men who fought and died at Waterloo. She spent the day remembering all the wonderful times they had together. She knew in her heart that she had to stay strong for Mary Elizabeth's sake. Her life had to go on without Henry, no matter how difficult it was.

It was very expensive to live, and by the end of the summer, Melody knew she would have to find some work to help make ends meet. When Brandon arrived that day, Melody asked, "Do you know of anyone who might need some sewing done? I need to find some way to earn money."

"I do know of someone, but I have a better idea. I've been meaning to talk to you about something for a while now. I've been offered a new teaching position in Doncaster. It comes with a cottage and a decent salary. We've been good friends for a long time now. I know you'll never love anyone like you loved Henry, and I doubt that I'll ever get over Lily. However, we get along well, and I feel we are good companions and friends. Those are not small things, in which to build a marriage on. I think we should get married." As he saw Melody start to speak, he raised his hand and said, "Wait, I know what you're thinking, but you're wrong, Melody. Henry and Lily would want us to go on with our lives. You need to think about what is best for Mary Elizabeth. I can offer you both a safe comfortable place to live. Just think about it, at least for a few days, before you give me your answer. I have to be in Doncaster by the middle of September. I know that would not give you much time, but I really think this would be good for both of us."

"I don't know, Brandon. You know that I care about you, but you're right. I know I could never love you, because my heart will always belong to Henry. I do know this is probably what would be best for Mary Elizabeth, but I don't know if I could ever be your wife in anything but name only. I'm sure you would want to have children, and I just don't know that I could ever be a true wife to you. I need to think about this for a few days. I'll give you my answer on Wednesday," she said. Brandon nodded his head, came over to her, kissed her cheek, and then he left.

There were so many questions running through her mind. *What should she do? What would be best for Mary Elizabeth?* Her daughter was what was most important here. There was a need to give serious consideration to what Bandon had said, and it was important to decide what Henry would want for his daughter. She knew he would want her to be happy and safe. She hoped he would have understood why she did not want to go back to Sanderford Park. Nelson could be no protection now that he was sick, newly married, and expecting a child. That would mean their graces would control her life and her child's, and she did not want that. They would probably mistreat her daughter, just as they had Henry. *She would have financial security, if she married Brandon, and did she really want to live the rest of her life alone?* She did need to move on. Nothing was going to bring Henry back, no matter how much she might wish it were possible. The logical thing to do would be to marry Brandon. There was no way she could support both of them on the money her parents left. It would be gone in a couple of years at most, no matter how careful she was. She knew she had two choices, either marry Brandon or go back to Sanderford Park, and that was not a choice she was willing to make. Melody got down on her knees and prayed that God would help her make the best decision for her and Mary Elizabeth. She decided to sleep on it, and whatever felt right in the morning would be what she would do. The Lord would show her the right path she needed to take. She wished there was more time, but she understood that Brandon needed to be in Doncaster soon.

Melody woke up the next day and knew she needed to marry Brandon. That would be what was best for Mary Elizabeth. She felt at peace with her decision. She knew . . . that marrying Brandon would be what was best for both of them. It would be what Henry would want her to do and what God wanted her to do. When Brandon came over on Wednesday, she would tell him yes. As difficult as it would be, she knew Brandon deserved to have a wife in all ways, so she would just have to accept . . . that she would need to be his wife, in every way.

When Brandon arrived on Wednesday, he greeted her with his usual enthusiasm and asked, "Hello, Melody, how are you feeling today? Have you decided what you want to do? Will you marry me? If you do, I promise we'll take it slow. We don't have to be intimate until you're ready. I just want to take care of you and Mary Elizabeth. I promise I'll be a good father to her, if you'll let me."

Melody looked at Brandon, and she knew she was making the right decision. "I would be honored and proud to be your wife. I already care about you a great deal since you're been my best friend our entire lives, and I can think of no one, now that Henry is gone, that I would rather spend my life with, so yes . . . I will marry you."

He took Melody's hand, raised it to his lips and kissed it. "Thank you, I promise to be a good husband to you and a good father to Mary Elizabeth. I know you can never love me as you did Henry, and I'll always love Lily, but I believe there's enough love in our hearts to begin to love again, and I already do love you as my best friend. We'll need to do this quickly. I wish I could give you more time to adjust to the idea of marrying me, but I need to be in Doncaster by the middle of the month. The banns can be read over the next three weeks. I'll go to Doncaster and get everything ready for us. It will take me at least two weeks, and then I'll be back. This will give you enough time to get ready and say good-bye to your friends. Is that agreeable to you?"

"That will be fine, Brandon. I would like to take some of my parents' furniture with me. Will that be possible?" she asked.

"I'll make arrangements to have everything moved to Doncaster. I want you to have whatever will make you feel better about marrying me. Well, if I'm going to get all of this set in place, I need to leave. I'll see you in two weeks." He took her in his arms and gently kissed her temple.

Melody and Millie packed up all her belongings and readied the furniture for the move. She visited all her friends and told them she was marrying Brandon. Some of her friends were shocked by her decision, because they knew how much she had loved Henry, but they wished her well. Brandon returned, and they were married on September 10. They had a small ceremony, just the two of them, with Susan and her mother as their witnesses. After the ceremony, they went over to Susan's house, and her mother served them a light repast before they left for Doncaster.

Susan gave Melody a hug as she said, "I feel this is the right thing for you to do. I know how much you loved Henry, but you do need to move on with your life. I know you and Brandon will deal well with each other, because you have known each other since you were children. Sometimes, being friends is just as rewarding as a love match is. Please write me and let me know how you're doing, and I'll write you back."

"I'm at peace with this marriage. It's what will be best for both Mary Elizabeth and me. Brandon is an honorable, kind man, and I know we'll be well taken care of. I promise to write, and please keep me informed about Nelson, Helen, and Kathryn. I appreciate you not telling them about Mary Elizabeth. I'm sure that it's difficult, since you're such good friends with Helen and Mary. Thank you for keeping my confidence. Well, it's time for us to leave. Take care of yourself, and I hope everything works out for you with Arthur." Melody hugged Susan as she took her leave, promising to write often.

Brandon helped her into the carriage and handed her Mary Elizabeth, then got in. She looked out of her window and watched as she left her home for the last time. She knew in her heart that she would be content with Brandon. After all, he had been her best friend all her life.

They arrived at Doncaster late that same day. As Melody gazed at the pretty cottage with a small garden behind the house, she knew she would be very content here. The cottage had an upstairs where the bedrooms were, and it was beautifully decorated. Brandon had done an astonishing job when he moved in the furniture, and it made her feel as comfortable as if she were in her parents' home. He introduced her to the housekeeper, Mrs. Worth, and she told them that supper would be ready shortly. Millie went upstairs and unpacked for her and the baby. Mary Elizabeth was tired and started to cry, so Melody took her upstairs to feed her and put her to bed. Her daughter's room was pretty; it had pink walls and a homemade throw rug on the floor. Brandon had Mary Elizabeth's crib and dressing table all set up. Soon her daughter fell asleep in her arms, and she put her in her crib. Melody took a deep breath and went back downstairs.

Mrs. Worth had supper on the table in the little dining room and told them she would be back in the morning and left. They were alone, and Melody was suddenly nervous. She found it difficult to swallow her food and just pushed it around on her plate. Brandon was eating with gusto, and he was soon finished.

Brandon leaned back in his chair and said, "Well, that was a delicious meal. You didn't eat very much. Are you feeling well?"

As Melody stood up, she said, "I'm fine, just a little nervous. I think I'll go on up to bed. It's been a long tiring day."

"Yes, go on up to bed. I think I'll sit in the parlor and read my newspaper before I join you," he said, then seeing her face he added, "Don't worry, Melody, we're both tired from the journey, so all we'll do is sleep. I promised to give you time, and I meant it. You'll decide when you're ready to consummate this marriage. There is no hurry. We have the rest of our lives to be with each other, so relax, no need to be nervous, all right?"

"Thank you, Brandon. I'm tired, but I appreciate your kindness, and I promise I'll be ready to consummate our marriage soon. I just need a little more time to adjust. I'll see you in the morning." When Melody went to her room, Millie helped her get ready for bed, and then she left her alone. Melody looked around the room and saw the bed, which had a pretty blue counterpane with white ruffles and she appreciated the effort Brandon had made to make her feel at home. She hurried and got into bed, and since she was so tired, she fell asleep right away. She never heard Brandon come to bed. When she woke up the next morning, he was already gone, but he left her a note. He had gone to work and would be home around five o'clock. When she went downstairs, she found Mrs. Worth fixing breakfast in the kitchen.

Melody smiled as she said, "Hello, Mrs. Worth. When did you get here this morning? My husband didn't tell me your schedule."

Mrs. Worth curtsied and said, "I get here at seven o'clock in the morning. I stay until supper is finished and the kitchen is cleaned up. Is that acceptable to you?"

"That sounds fine to me. Oh, I hear my daughter, Mary Elizabeth, so I'll go up and get her. She likes oatmeal for breakfast. I usually put plenty of milk in it, to thin it down. Can you have that ready when I come back down with her?" she asked.

"Don't you worry about a thing. I know exactly how you want it fixed. I used to feed my little ones the same thing. Go on with yourself and get that precious little girl." Melody smiled pleasantly at Mrs. Worth, and then she left the kitchen to go get Mary Elizabeth.

Mary Elizabeth was standing up in her crib with a big smile on her face, and it almost brought her to her knees, because she looked so much like Henry. She could not get over how big she was getting. She quickly changed Mary Elizabeth and carried her back to the kitchen. Mrs. Worth had Mary Elizabeth's breakfast waiting for her. After she ate, Melody took her outside, as it was a nice day. They sat on a blanket and played for hours until she got sleepy.

She spent the rest of the afternoon helping Mrs. Worth tidy up the cottage. The unpacking was quickly finished. Thank goodness, Millie was so efficient and willing to help her. Melody really appreciated her dedication. It helped having Millie with her, because she had been with her through it all. The day passed fairly quickly, and before she realized it, it was nearly five o'clock. So Melody went upstairs to freshen up before Brandon got home.

He arrived home in an excellent mood, and he had a big smile on his face as he greeted her. "Hello, how did your day go? I had an excellent first day at work. My students seem very bright, and I look forward to teaching them. How was Mary Elizabeth today? Have you both settled in yet?"

"We're all settled in, and we had a splendid day. Mary Elizabeth enjoyed being outside. Since it was such a nice day, we played for hours, and then I helped Mrs. Worth tidy up the house. I'm pleased your day went well. How many students are in your class? And what ages are they?" she asked as she smiled at Brandon.

Brandon replied, "As you know, it's a boarding school for boys. I have fifteen students, and they're all eleven years of age. Most of the boys come from merchant families, and they're all very well behaved. I'm sure they'll respond well to my teaching. I think I'll go into the parlor now to read my newspaper. I'll see you at dinner."

"I'm going to get Mary Elizabeth up from her nap and go ahead and feed her. Then after we play a bit, I'll put her back to bed. She usually goes to sleep each night at seven o'clock, so we can have supper after that. See you in a bit. Enjoy reading your paper," Melody said as she left to go upstairs and get her daughter.

Melody fed Mary Elizabeth. They went back outside and played for a while. After that, she put her down to bed, and Mary Elizabeth was soon fast asleep. She went back to the parlor and told him that supper was ready. They ate a delicious stew with lots of fresh vegetables in it, and Melody was very hungry, so she ate more than she had the night before. Brandon had a hearty appetite so he again ate with gusto. They went back to the parlor, and he read while Melody did some sewing. At ten o'clock, she decided to go to bed.

Melody turned to Brandon and said, "Brandon I'm going upstairs now. I'll be ready for you to join me in thirty minutes. I've decided that I want to consummate our marriage. Waiting will only delay getting on with our lives. I appreciate your kindness, but I'm ready now. Will you join me?" she asked.

Brandon looked directly into Melody's eyes and said, "Whatever you want, Melody. I'll be happy to join you, so I'll come up in thirty minutes. See you then."

Millie helped Melody prepare for bed, and after she was in her night rail, she sent Millie away. Melody sat at her dressing table, brushed her hair, and then braided it. She was nervous about what was to come, but she trusted Brandon and knew he would be a gentle lover. Soon the door opened, and Brandon came into the room.

As Brandon entered the room, he asked, "Melody, are you sure about this? You know that I'm more than willing to give you more time, if you feel you need it."

She looked at him and stood up. She walked over to him and said, "You're my husband now, and I want to fully be your wife. I trust you. There is no reason to wait."

Brandon put his arms around her and gently kissed her lips. Melody found his kiss enjoyable and kissed him back. He deepened the kiss and started rubbing her back. He untied the sash of her dressing gown and slid it off her shoulders. Melody put her arms around his neck, and he pulled her closer. He picked her up, carried her to their bed, and gently laid her down. The night lamp was on the bedside table, so he turned it down, quickly removed his clothes, and got into bed. He pulled Melody into his arms and kissed her. He nibbled kisses down her neck, placed his hand on her breast, and he gently squeezed her nipple. She knew Brandon was trying very hard to control his passions, and Melody began to feel relaxed and kissed him back. He raised her gown to the waist and touched her core. It surprised Melody, but she began to feel pleasure, nothing as intense as she had felt before, but nonetheless, it was pleasure. It continued to build as Brandon gently parted her thighs and settled between them. He rubbed his shaft over her cleft and slowly entered her body. Melody felt his fullness as he began to move. She put her arms around him and started to move with him. Soon, he began to move faster, and she knew he was near his release. She closed her eyes as he spent himself inside her. It was a pleasant feeling, but nothing compared to what she had felt with Henry. She did not want to compare, but found that it was impossible not to. Brandon rolled over, pulled Melody into his arms, and fell asleep. She lay there, tried to stop the memories from coming, but she could not. Brandon had been as gentle and tender as a man could be, but he just was not Henry. Melody knew she would never feel the same level of passion with Brandon that she had felt with Henry. She was actually glad about this, because she did not want to have those feelings with someone else. She would welcome Brandon into her body, whenever he wanted, but she would probably never give him her passion. That she would keep in her heart for Henry. After a time, Melody rolled over and went to sleep.

CHAPTER 14

The Franciscan Monastery
Brussels, Belgium
Fall 1816

One day, while Henry was helping the monks clear their garden patch, he suddenly realized that his name was Henry. Nothing else came forth, but his name. He went to Father Francis and said, "Father, I've remembered my name! It's Henry. Don't you think that's a good sign?"

Father Francis smiled pleasantly as he replied, "It is a good sign, and it could mean that your memory is coming back to you. Do not try to force it. The memories will come back in bits and pieces. This could take several weeks or even months, but I do feel that your memory will be restored to you."

Henry ran his fingers through his hair in frustration, but he knew Father Francis was right, because every time he tried too hard to remember, he would get excruciating headaches. One thing he had learned about while living in the monastery was patience, so he just needed to apply some with this.

That night, Henry woke up fully aroused. He had been dreaming about a woman with long honey blonde hair, but he could not see her face. This woman was obviously important to him. *Why could he not see her face?* Eventually, he fell back to sleep. Next thing he knew, he was waking up with his heart pounding to the sound of cannon fire, and there were men dead and dying all around him. There was a horse, screaming from pain, and then his mind went blank again. *God, this was so frustrating. He would go out of his mind if he did not start putting all these pieces together.* He guessed that he was remembering part of the battle he must have been in. Maybe this meant that his memory was coming back. Father Francis did say that it would come back a little at a time. Tomorrow he would talk to him about these dreams. After a time, he slipped back to sleep.

Doncaster, Yorkshire
December 1816

The days became shorter as Christmas drew near. Melody enjoyed decorating the cottage with plenty of holly and evergreens. Mary Elizabeth had started walking, and it was such a pleasure to watch her grow. It was heartbreaking to know that Henry would never know this precious child. She was an adorable little girl, and Melody thanked God everyday for giving her this precious gift. She knew Henry would live on through his daughter. Melody suspected she was with child again. This time, she knew what signs to look for and they were all there. She decided she would tell Brandon after Christmas. They had grown closer, and she truly cared deeply for him. She was even able to enjoy the marriage bed. It was so different from what she had had with Henry, but enjoyable nonetheless. With Brandon, making love was like a warm bath: very relaxing and peaceful. Brandon was a good father to Mary Elizabeth, and he spent time each evening playing with her. She was glad that Mary Elizabeth would grow up with a father's love. She knew that was important, because her father had been wonderful, and she wanted that same kind of relationship for Mary Elizabeth. When the new child arrived, she hoped Brandon would still pay attention to Mary Elizabeth. It was so hard to believe that Henry had been gone for eighteen months. She just wished Henry had known about his daughter.

Christmas came and went, and Melody told Brandon about the baby. He was ecstatic and assured her that even though he would have a child of his own, he would always look on Mary Elizabeth as his daughter. Mary Elizabeth celebrated her first birthday, and she was already starting to run. She was a very active child and extremely bright. She already called Melody, Mama, and Brandon, Papa, and was adding new words to her vocabulary everyday. Life was good, and Melody had no regrets about marrying Brandon.

Melody received a letter from Susan, and she had married Arthur Taylor, who was now Viscount Hastings. His father had passed away six months ago, so he had inherited the title, and they were now living in Kent. She seemed to be very much in love with Arthur, and they were expecting their first child in November. Susan had written that Nelson was doing better and that he had a daughter now. Helen would be having her second season. They had missed last year because of mourning Henry's death. Melody wished she could communicate with them, but she knew it was not a good idea. She had already made that decision, and she would not change her mind, but she was always glad to hear of them from her friend Susan. Susan had become fast friends with Helen, because they both still volunteered at the orphanage along with Nelson's wife, Mary.

Spring came quickly that year. It went from deep snows to beautiful spring flowers in a matter of weeks. Her pregnancy was coming along nicely, and she was getting huge. She had experienced little difficulty and expected another easy delivery in July when the baby was due. Brandon really wanted a son, and Melody hoped for his sake that it was a boy. She would like a boy also, since she already had her daughter. Mary Elizabeth was getting so big, and it was hard to imagine that she was going to be eighteen months old when the new baby would be born. On the anniversary of Henry's death, Melody became very morose, but she tried not to show it. It had been two years since his death. She still could see his precious face in her mind as if he had just walked out of the room. She hoped that his memory would never fade, and she felt it would not.

The Monastery
Brussels, Belgium
Spring 1817

The weather was glorious in Brussels that spring. Henry enjoyed helping the monks put in their garden. He found that he liked the physical activity and suspected that he had been a very active man. He now remembered he could fence. The memory was just there one day when he was in town and saw someone with a sword. This memory had a man in it, and he was fencing with him, but he did not know who the man was—a name was not part of the memory. These pieces, that would suddenly come, would exasperate him, because he could not remember anyone's name. He continued to dream about the woman with the long honey blonde hair, and sometimes he would get a brief glimpse of her face, but nothing clear. He always woke up in an aroused state every time he dreamed of her, so Henry now believed that the woman was his wife. *God, he wished he could get his memory back.* Father Francis just kept telling him to be patient, but it was extremely difficult. He found that he did better when he did hard physical labor. He was still experiencing headaches if he tried to dwell on these memories too intensely. The days with the monks were very peaceful, but sometimes he yearned for more activity. *Oh well, enough daydreaming! Time to get back to the garden!*

Doncaster, Yorkshire
Summer 1817

July was very hot and dry, and Melody was miserable from her pregnancy. The baby was due any day now, and she just wished he would hurry up and come. She thought of the baby as a boy and felt very strongly that it would be. Brandon seemed quite nervous over the upcoming birth of the baby, but that was understandable, since he had lost Lily from childbirth. Brandon was such a thoughtful and caring husband, and she was so blessed to have him. When she thought about what her life would have been like, if she had not married him, she shuddered. On July 10, Melody went into labor. Brandon was at work, so Mrs. Worth sent a message to him, telling him that Melody was in labor. He went to the midwife's house and picked her up, then hurried home. The midwife examined Melody and said that everything was proceeding nicely. It would probably be another easy delivery for her.

Brandon was frantic when her labor went on into the night, and after twelve hours, she delivered a big boy. He had golden blond hair and hazel eyes. It had been a harder delivery than what she had experienced with Mary Elizabeth, and Melody was exhausted. The midwife cleaned her up, and Millie helped her put on a fresh gown, and then the midwife went to tell Brandon that he had a son.

Brandon glowed as he smiled lovingly at Melody and said, "Melody, he is so beautiful. He has your golden hair and your eyes. I'm so relieved that you and the baby are fine. I didn't want you to know, but I was so worried that something would go wrong. I didn't want to lose you like . . . I lost Lily. I . . . have fallen in love with you . . . I couldn't imagine my life without you. Don't worry. I know you don't return my love, and I'm fine with that. I just needed to tell you how I feel."

"You know I care deeply for you, and I'm happy that you love me. You're a wonderful husband, and while a part of my heart will always belong to Henry, I do love you. I'm very happy that we married. My love for you is peaceful and serene, and you make me feel very safe. I'm so grateful we married and that we have this beautiful child. He looks like me, doesn't he? Now what do you want to name our son?" she asked.

Brandon grinned at her as he said, "If it's all right with you, I would like to name him after me. All the firstborn sons in my family have been named Brandon Alton Foster."

Melody serenely smiled and said, "I have always loved your name, so please let's name him after you and your father. I think that it's a fine name."

Brandon picked up his son and cradled him in his arms. He looked at Melody and gave her a big grin. She smiled back at Brandon and then went to sleep.

The Monastery
Brussels, Belgium
Fall 1817

They were riding horses by a lake, and when they got off the horses, he pulled her into his arms and said, "Oh, Melody, I love you so much. Come, my darling, let's walk around the lake." Henry woke up and just realized that the woman in his dreams was named Melody. *What a pretty name! Why could he not remember more? Just these bits and pieces, it was driving him mad.* The other night he dreamed about a time when he was a child. He was playing in a tree by a lake, and he fell in, an older boy got him out of the water, because he could not swim. *Oh god, why could he not put these pieces together.* The dreams about the battle were the worst, because there were men dying all around him, and he could not do anything about it. A horse was screaming in pain, and he felt so helpless. *When would his memory come back?* Father Francis kept assuring him that it would, and he felt that it would happen soon. He was trying to be patient, but it was very difficult.

As the fall passed, he continued to have more dreams, but nothing in them told him what he needed to know about who he really was. His heart yearned for this woman called Melody. Surely, his memory would come back, and soon, because the dreams were becoming more detailed. Father Francis was very optimistic, which helped Henry feel more hopeful. *Soon, he thought, soon!*

Doncaster
Winter 1818

Little Brandon was a big baby and very strong. By Christmas, he was crawling. Mary Elizabeth loved her little brother and tried to help Melody take care of him. If she were really good, Melody would let her hold him, as long as Melody was right there with her. Over all, Melody was happy and content with her life. She still missed Henry everyday, but she knew she had made the right decision by marrying Brandon. It was a different kind of love, but, nonetheless, very fulfilling. The holidays went by quickly, and soon it was Mary Elizabeth's second birthday. Brandon held true to his word, and he showed just as much love to Mary Elizabeth as he did to Little Brandon. She was truly blessed in her marriage. As the days went by, she felt her love blossom for him, and she was at peace with this. She knew in her heart that Henry would have wanted her to be happy.

One day in March, someone came to the door and asked to speak with her. It was the director at Brandon's school, Mr. Worthington, and he looked very serious. Melody invited him in and asked if he would care for any refreshment.

Mr. Worthington shook his head and said, "No, thank you, Mrs. Foster. I came over to tell you that there has been an incident at the school. Your husband was teaching his students, and he passed out in the classroom. I have sent for the doctor, and they are bringing him here. Oh, I hear them coming now."

Melody ran out of the house and hurried over to the cart. Brandon was just lying there, not moving at all.

The doctor said, "We need to get him up to his bed, so I can examine him thoroughly. These men will carry him up, if you will lead the way." The men carried Brandon upstairs to their room, lay him on the bed, and left Melody alone with the doctor.

"Dr. Martin, what's wrong with him? He looks so pale . . . and he's not . . . moving. Please tell me . . . what's wrong with him?" Melody asked with terror in her voice.

"Mrs. Foster, I believe your husband has had some kind of seizure of the brain," he said. "I know that it is hard to believe with him being so young, but in rare cases, it has happened before. The next twenty-four hours will tell us what damage has been done. At this point, there is not much we can do for him, but wait and see if he comes out of it. I will come back tomorrow to check on him. Just keep him comfortable, and try to get some water in him."

Melody stayed by Brandon's side all night long, holding his hand and trying to get some water down him. She talked to him the entire time, hoping her voice would rouse him. She prayed that God would save him, because she did not want him to die. Brandon was such a good and kind person, and she did not want to lose him. Morning came, and there was still no change. He just lay there, growing paler, and his breathing shallower.

The doctor arrived and examined him again. He turned to Melody and said, "Mrs. Foster, I'm sorry, but Mr. Foster has gone into such a deep sleep, he may not come out of it. If he is going to survive, he will need to wake up soon. Just keep trying to get him to take water so he does not become dehydrated. I will come back tonight to check on him again. If anything happens, send for me at once."

Late that afternoon, Brandon . . . stopped breathing. Melody was all alone with him. The tears started running down her face, and she dropped her head down on her arms, on the bed beside him, and sobbed. Millie heard her and came into the room. She tried to console Melody and told her she would send for the doctor. Melody knew there was nothing the doctor could do for Brandon. He was gone, and nothing . . . would bring him back.

They held Brandon's funeral the next day. Most of the people at his funeral were his colleagues from the school. They did not know many people, so it was a small gathering. Melody felt so empty and sad. When they lowered Brandon's body into the grave, she felt as if she were coming apart. The pain she was feeling was overwhelming. She just kept saying in her mind, *Not Brandon, not Brandon too. How was she going to survive without her best friend? First, she had lost Henry, and now Brandon. Oh god, why . . . why?* It was so hard to understand how someone only five and twenty could die. After the funeral, she went back to the house and lay down on her bed. Millie took care of the children so that Melody could rest. The grief was almost more than she could handle. *How could God allow this to happen?* Brandon had been such a wonderful man and he was just too young to die. *What would she do now?* She was not even sure if she would have any money to take care of the children.

Two days later, she met with Brandon's solicitor. He told Melody that the cottage was part of Brandon's compensation, so she would need to move, but the school would give her two months to find somewhere else to live. Brandon had some investments, but they were not bringing in very much. There was one thousand pounds in his account, and Melody still had four hundred pounds left from her parents. She would survive some way.

She left and went home to be with her children. Mary Elizabeth kept asking for her father. Melody tried to explain to her that Brandon had died and that he had gone home to be with the angels. The poor child was just too young to understand that her father was gone and that he was not coming home again. It was heart wrenching to see her daughter so upset, especially when she was having such a dreadful time dealing with Brandon's death herself. Thank goodness for Mrs. Worth and Millie. She did not think she could handle it without their help.

Melody had no interest in food, and she had lost quite a bit of weight since Brandon had died. She had always wondered what it would feel like to be slender, now she knew, and she could care less. She was determined to get through this. She had survived Henry's death, and she would make it through losing Brandon. Her children needed her, and she would be strong for them. The first thing she needed to do was find some type of employment. She knew it would be difficult, but she was determined.

A few weeks later, while in the kitchen, Mrs. Worth said, "Millie, I'm very concerned about Mrs. Foster. She hardly eats anything, and I know she's lost quite a bit of weight. She's going to make herself ill if she doesn't start taking better care of herself. Does she have any family we could contact? Surely, there's someone."

Millie looked thoughtful for a minute and then said, "The only family Mrs. Foster has left, that I know of, is her aunt, Lady Helton, and from what I understand, she's on an extended trip to the continent and isn't expected back for several months. I guess we could write her and let her know about Mr. Foster's death. We could send the letter to Lady Helton's address in London and hope they forward it on to her."

"Little Brandon is only nine months old and now her milk is drying up. She needs a goat so he can be fed. That is the best milk to feed a baby. I'll talk to Mrs. Conrad and see if she'll let us have her goat's milk." Mrs. Worth went to see Mrs. Conrad, and she said that she would allow them to use her goat's milk.

"Mrs. Foster, I spoke with Mrs. Conrad, and she's willing to lend you her goat so we can feed the milk to Brandon, since you're no longer able to feed him yourself. Is that acceptable to you?" Mrs. Worth asked.

With a puzzled look on her face, she said, "Whatever you think is best, Mrs. Worth. I don't understand why my milk is drying up. That didn't happen with Mary Elizabeth."

"I suspect it's because you haven't been eating enough since your husband passed away. In fact, if you don't start eating more, you're going to get sick. Is there anything special you would like me to fix for you? I still have some of those cherries we put away last summer, and I could make you a cherry pie. That has always been one of your favorite foods. I'll make one for supper tonight." she said.

Mrs. Worth made a cherry pie, and Melody did her best to eat it. When dinner was over, Melody said, "Thank you Mrs. Worth. Your cherry pie was splendid. I'm sorry I couldn't eat more of it, but I have a headache. Do you think you could help Millie with the children? I need to go to bed. I'm sure I'll feel better in the morning." Mrs. Worth helped Millie get the children to bed, and then she left to go home.

The next morning, Melody was still in bed at ten o'clock, so Millie went to check on her. She was still sleeping, but she looked very flushed. Millie felt her forehead, and she was burning up with fever.

Millie rushed downstairs and cried, "Oh no, Mrs. Worth, Mrs. Foster is burning up with fever. Can you watch the children? I'm going to get Dr. Martin."

Mrs. Worth exclaimed, "Go get him right now. Hopefully he'll be in his office and can come over right away."

Millie went to Dr. Martin's office, but he was not there. His wife told her that he was out at the Miller's place, because Mrs. Miller was very ill with a high fever. Millie went to the Miller's and spoke with the doctor, "Dr. Martin, you need to come quick. Mrs. Foster is running a high fever, and we need you to help her."

Dr. Martin shook his head and replied, "I will be there just as soon as I can. There are already five cases of influenza, so I am sure that is what Mrs. Foster has. Go to her and bathe her in cool water and try to get her to drink plenty of water."

Millie went to the house and told Mrs. Worth what the doctor said. They took the children over to Mrs. Conrad's, and she said she would keep them. That way they could get them out of the house away from Melody. Millie gave Melody a cool sponge bath and got her to drink some water, but it did not seem to help. Her temperature seemed even higher than it had been earlier. Finally, the doctor came and examined Melody.

After Dr. Martin finished his examination, he turned to Millie and said, "She definitely has influenza, and she is very ill. Here is some medicine to give her. I hope that it will help to bring her fever down. Continue to bathe her with cool water and make her drink plenty of water. I will come back in the morning to check on her."

The next day the doctor came in the morning, but Melody was no better. She was delirious and calling for her husband; it was as if she did not realize he had died. They could not get her to keep down any water. The doctor left some additional medicine that should settle Melody's stomach, and he also told them there were three more cases of influenza in town.

Mrs. Conrad brought the children back, because her husband had come down with influenza. The children would not be any better off with her than they would in their own home; besides, they kept crying to come home.

CHAPTER 15

The Monastery
Brussels, Belgium
January 1818

HENRY HAD BEEN at the monastery for two and a half years, and he still did not have his memory back. He continued to have dreams about the beautiful woman named Melody. He now believed that this woman was definitely his wife. She was so beautiful with her long honey blonde hair and incredible sherry-colored eyes. The dreams were becoming very erotic, and he would wake up hard as steel. There was a huge sense of loss when he woke up after having dreamt of her. *Oh, god, if she were his wife, she must think he died. Would she have found someone else? Had he left children behind? "Please, Lord let my memory come back!"* He knew she was the key to getting his memory back. He was also experiencing even more flashbacks of the battle. Father Francis had told him that they had found him on the battlefield at Waterloo, so that must be what he was seeing in these flashbacks. Father Francis still told him that these were all good signs and that Henry's memory would come back to him soon. That was the most optimistic thing that Henry had heard so far.

One day, in late January, he was helping Father Francis repair a crumbling wall around the monastery. Henry climbed up to the top of the wall and leaned over for Father Francis to hand him up some bricks when he slipped and fell off. Henry hit his head hard on the side of the wall as he fell, and was knocked out. They carried him to his room, and he remained unconscious for several hours. Father Francis kept checking on him, but he still remained unconscious. Finally, during the night, he woke up.

He looked around and asked, "Where . . . where am I? Where is my wife? What is wrong with my head? Oh god, it hurts like hell!"

"My son, you fell off the wall yesterday and hit your head. What do you remember? Do you remember who you are?" Father Francis asked.

Henry struggled to sit up as he looked over at Father Francis and said, "Of course, I know who I am. My name is Henry Montgomery, and I'm a captain in his majesty's royal army. Now where is my wife, Melody? Who are you?"

Father Francis serenely replied, "I am Father Francis, Captain. You have been living here at this monastery for two and a half years, ever since the Battle of Waterloo. You did not remember anything at first, but then you did remember your first name, eventually. We knew you were English, but when we found you, your clothes were gone, so there was no way to identify who you were. You have been having dreams about a woman. Eventually, you remembered that her name was Melody, and you felt that she was probably your wife. You have had quite a few flashbacks of the battle. Evidently, when you hit your head yesterday, your memory has been restored. Do you remember me?"

Henry fell back against the pillow and groaned. The pain in his head was excruciating. Then he realized what Father Francis had told him and sat up as he said, "Oh my god, do you mean it's been that long since the battle? How could this happen?"

Father Francis calmly said, "Sometimes, when someone receives a blow to the head, the trauma can cause one to lose their memory. That is what happened to you, and when you hit your head yesterday, it restored your memory. But now it sounds as if you have no recollection of the past two and a half years. This time your recent memories should come back to you shortly. Where do you live? And can we contact your family?"

Cold chills ran down his spine. Melody must think he was dead! He had to get back to her immediately. "I need to leave at once. Do I have any money to get back home? I'll gladly reimburse you if you'll lend me the funds to get back to England. My father is the Duke of Sanderford, so paying you back shan't be a problem. I want to leave tomorrow."

Father Francis looked at him and said, "My son, we will surely lend you the money so you can get back to England, but I think it would be wise to wait a few days and see if your memory, of the time that you have spent here with us, comes back to you. Besides, you need to recover from hitting your head. I am sure you must have a terrible headache, at the very least."

"Father, I'll stay for a few days, but then I must leave even if I don't remember what has happened since the battle. I feel very tired, so I think I'll rest for a while. Thank you for all that you have done for me." Henry leaned back against his pillow, and then he closed his eyes and fell asleep.

Henry did regain his memory of the past two and a half years. He stayed at the monastery for three days, to get his strength back and for his head to stop hurting. Father Francis lent him enough money to get back to England. It took Henry almost a week to make it to the coast of France and find passage over the English Channel. The channel waters were rough, but nothing would hold Henry back from getting to Melody. When he arrived in England, he went to Sanderford House, but found out that the family was at Sanderford Park. Henry found some of his old clothes and took a bath. He gave himself a shave and cut off the long hair. Mansfield could tidy him up once he got back to Sanderford Park.

The next morning, Henry took one of the horses his father always kept in London and headed home. He made good time and was home by two o'clock. The first person he saw when he arrived was Freddie.

Freddie stood there with a look of utter amazement on his face and exclaimed, "Milord, how's this possible? Yer supposed t' have died at Waterloo!"

Henry looked at Freddie and said, "Well, that isn't true. As you can see, I'm very much alive. Take my horse and give him plenty of oats. He has been ridden hard this morning."

As he approached the front door, it opened, and Helen came out. She looked at Henry and fainted. Henry rushed to catch her before she fell to the steps.

Simpson came out and stared in shock. Then he found his voice and said, "My lord, we were told that you were dead. It is wonderful to know that this was not true. Everyone will be so shocked. Let me help you with Lady Helen."

Simpson opened the door so that Henry could carry Helen in. He took her into the morning room and laid her on the couch. Helen started to come around, and she just stared at Henry. She did not say anything at first, but then she called out, with astonishment in her voice, "Henry! Henry! You . . . You . . . are alive!"

Henry smiled at her and said, "Hello, sweetheart, I'm alive. I lost my memory when I was injured at the Battle of Waterloo. I had a head wound, and my leg was severely injured. Some monks found me and nursed me back to health. However, I couldn't remember who I was. In the beginning, I remembered nothing. Then about two years ago, I remembered my given name. Over the past two years or so, I've had bits and pieces of my memory come back to me. Then two weeks ago, I fell off a wall, hit my head again, and when I woke up, all my memory had been restored to me. Where's Melody?"

Helen burst into tears, and she hugged him tightly to her as she said, "Henry, everyone is going to be so shocked. You need to let me go tell them about you first. Nelson is dying. He has some kind of wasting disease, and he could die at any time. Father has been so distressed. First, you died, and then Nelson became so ill. I'm afraid that the shock of seeing you alive could be too much for him. Henry, Melody left after your funeral. She went to live with her parents. We corresponded for a while, and then she quit answering our letters. We haven't heard anything from her in a long time. We felt sure that the memories were too painful for her, and that's why she quit writing."

Henry looked in astonishment at Helen. He could not believe what she was telling him. "What, you just let her leave!"

Helen looked beseechingly at Henry and said, "Henry, she insisted that she wanted to go to her parents. We tried to talk her out of it, but to no avail. Nelson took her to her parents, but she couldn't bear to look at him, because you look so much alike. It was just too painful for her, so he left her with her parents. I don't know why she quit writing or answering our letters, but we felt she must have had a good reason."

In frustration, Henry ran his fingers through his hair as he said, "Well, at least I know where she is. I'll go get her, once we get everything sorted out with Nelson. Is he really that ill? Is there no hope that he'll recover?"

Helen shook her head as she replied, "Father has had a great many doctors examine him, and they all say the same thing that he'll die soon. Let me go to everyone and tell them you're alive."

Henry stayed in the morning room while Helen went to the family. It was hard to wait, but he trusted Helen's judgment. *God . . . why did Melody quit writing?* He knew that she had loved his sisters, so something was not right about this, and he would get to bottom of this immediately.

She found everyone in the dining room. As she entered, they all looked at her. Her father demanded to know where she had been. "Everyone, something has happened. It's wonderful news. It will be a shock . . . to all of you. I know that it has shocked me. Father . . . , sit down, this is important. Henry . . . is alive! It was all a mistake. He was hurt in that last battle, and when he woke up, he had lost his memory. He didn't even remember his name. As time went by, he started to remember bits and pieces, but nothing that told him who he truly was. Two weeks ago, he hit his head again, and his memory came back. He's downstairs in the morning room, waiting for me to tell him to come up here."

"Oh my god! How can this be? This is incredible. Are you sure that it is Henry?" her father asked.

With excitement in her voice, Helen said, "Come follow me, and I'll take you to him."

Everyone went down to the morning room and could not believe their eyes. It was indeed Henry come back from the dead. Kathryn was crying, and even his mother had tears in her eyes. His father bowed his head and then looked up and said, "Henry, I am so glad that you are alive. Did Helen tell you about Nelson? He is upstairs in his room, and he is too weak to leave his bed. I will go up to him and tell him you have returned to us. He will be so relieved. His wife is with him. You met her. He married Mrs. Harrison over two years ago, and they have a little girl. Come with me."

They went upstairs to Nelson's rooms. His father seemed changed. He looked very tired, and Henry could tell he had been under quite a bit of distress. The lines on his face were much deeper, and he looked twenty years older. The duke went into Nelson's room, and Henry waited outside to give his father a chance to tell Nelson he was alive. His father opened the door and motioned for him to come in. Henry was shocked when he saw Nelson. There was no doubt about it; Nelson was dying.

Nelson tried to sit up as he said, "Henry! Thank God, you're alive! Come here so I can see you better."

Henry walked over to the bed and said, "Hello, old friend, it's so good to see you again. I'm so sorry you're not feeling well. I understand congratulations are in order. I wish I could have been there when you got married. I told you that you would like her, did I not? Well, I don't want to tire you, so I'll come back and see you later this evening, all right?"

Nelson smiled, and he looked relieved; then he closed his eyes. Henry and his father left the room. He did not know what to say to his father. It was obvious he was in a great deal of pain over Nelson.

As they walked away from Nelson's room, his father said, "Henry, please come with me to my study so we can talk. We have a great deal that we need to discuss."

Henry was shocked. He could not remember a time when his father had ever said please. He followed his father to his study. It was always a room he had hated as a child. Probably because he was only there when he was being raked over the coals about something he had done wrong.

His father sighed and said, "Sit down, Henry. I am so thankful that you are alive. I thought all was lost, what with you dead and Nelson dying with no heir in sight. It would have been the end of our line when I died. Now I can rest easy, knowing that you will continue it on. I have much to make up for with you, Henry. I have not treated you well, and it was because you reminded me of myself when I was young. I thought I needed to be hard on you so you would grow up to be a strong man. I was wrong. Instead,

I alienated you. I want you to know that I was proud of you and of what you were able to accomplish in the army. When I found out you had been killed, I realized that I had never told you that. I am so sorry . . . I hope you can forgive me. I am not a well man, so I need you to take over running the ducal holdings. Things have been very difficult since Nelson became so ill. Can I count on you, Son?"

With poignancy in his voice, Henry replied, "All I have ever wanted from you was to know that you were proud of me. I never could understand why you were so hard on me. Now maybe we can start afresh. I'm more than willing to do whatever you need. I do need to ask you one thing. Why did you let Melody leave and then not keep track of her?"

"You do not understand how hard your death hit all of us. Your wife was devastated when we received the news of your death. Nelson tried to get her to stay, but she refused. She insisted that she be taken home to her parents," he said, as he sighed deeply and looked so distressed that Henry wanted to take his pain away, but he knew he could not. "I admit that I did not treat her well, because she was not my choice as a wife for you. Helen continued to write her for over a year even after your wife stopped writing back. We finally felt she had her reasons for breaking off communication, and we knew she was safe with her parents."

Henry sighed deeply, then he stood up and began to pace the room in agitation as he said, "Well, I need to go find her. She's my wife, and I want her back." Then, with a look of bewilderment, he continued, "I suppose I can understand why she wanted to be with her parents but to break off all communication baffles me."

Henry's father looked at him and said, "I understand that you want to go get her, but all I ask is that you wait a little while longer. Nelson will not make it much longer, and he needs you, Henry. You have always been so close. I also need to show you all that is involved with the ducal holdings. Please come here tomorrow morning, and I will start showing you everything."

"I know that I need to stay with Nelson, until the end, but then I'll go get my wife!" he said with exasperation in his voice.

His father looked at him with relief in his eyes as he said, "I appreciate your willingness to put off going to get your wife until after Nelson is gone. I know that it will be difficult to wait, but Nelson does need you."

Henry left his father in his study and went to his rooms. When he walked into the sitting room, all the memories of Melody came flooding back. In his mind, he could see her sitting on the couch reading a book.

How was he going to have the patience to put off going to her? Melody meant everything to him, but so did his brother. What a conundrum! Would Melody have moved on with her life? Could she have met someone else? Why would she have stopped writing to Helen? He knew how much she loved his sisters. Well, as hard as it would be to wait, he really could not leave Nelson.

That evening, dinner was the most pleasant meal he could ever remember having in this house. His father was so different, and it seemed as if his mother had softened up also. *Helen truly was a beauty, and my god, she was twenty years old.* She had had her first season back in 1815, but she obviously did not marry. Kathryn had changed so much, and she was so pretty. It was hard to imagine that she was sixteen now. After dinner, they elected to forgo their port and cigars and went with the ladies to the drawing room instead.

Henry glanced lovingly over at Kathryn and asked, "Kathryn, how have you been? Are you still painting? And did you enjoy your art lessons?"

Kathryn sat down beside him on the couch and reached for his hand. "I have been doing fine, and yes, I still paint, and take art lessons. I still want to do your portrait. Will you sit for me?"

As they sat there holding hands, Henry said, "I will. However, I'm going to be very busy, what with learning about all the responsibilities that are entailed with running the ducal holdings. I'll also be spending time with Nelson. Then I'll be going to get Melody and bringing her home."

Kathryn's face lit up when he said he was going to get Melody. "Oh, Henry, please bring her back. I have really missed her. I don't understand why she quit writing to us."

"I don't understand that either, but I'm sure there must have been a good reason." Henry turned to Helen and asked, "How have you enjoyed your seasons? Did you meet anyone special?"

Helen smiled as she answered, "I had a splendid time. And no, I didn't meet anyone special. I just wanted to have fun. I particularly enjoyed volunteering at the orphanage, and I've gotten to know Melody's friend Susan well, and we have become good friends. She's married to Viscount Hastings now, and they have a son. She was just as confused as I was when Melody stopped answering our letters."

Henry turned to his mother and said, "Mother, you look splendid. It's so good to see you again. I'm sure that with all that has been happening, you have had a difficult time."

The duchess sighed as she replied, "It has been very difficult. First, we thought you were lost to us, and now we are losing Nelson. We decided to forgo the season this year because of Nelson's illness."

Henry gazed over at his mother and said, "Well, that makes sense. In some ways, time has stood still for me because of losing my memory. In many ways, it's like waking up after a long sleep and finding out that life has gone on without you. It's going to take me a while to catch up on what has happened while I was gone."

Soon, everyone went upstairs to bed. Henry dreaded the nights. Since he had remembered everything, he did not get much sleep, because he kept remembering Melody. He burned to see her and make love to her again. When he did sleep, his dreams were filled with erotic images of the two of them making love. He woke up every morning hard as stone. Of course, it was not just making love he missed. It was just being with her and being able to talk to her. He remembered all the wonderful times they shared, especially the time they spent in Canterbury. They had been so close. Surely, she had not forgotten him. He certainly had not forgotten her. *It was such a puzzle: Why had she stopped writing to everyone?* Oh well, it would serve no useful purpose worrying over it, because he could not do anything about it until Nelson died. *Oh, the pain of it! Why did Nelson get this terrible disease?* He hoped that he had a satisfying relationship with Mary. He would find out more when they talked tomorrow. *God, he was tired; he hoped he could sleep that night without waking up thinking about Melody.* Henry went into his room and went to bed.

For the next fortnight, Henry spent his mornings with his father going over all the books regarding the ducal holdings. Each afternoon, he spent time with Nelson and the evenings with the rest of the family. He got to know Mary better, and it was obvious that she was deeply in love with Nelson and that he returned her love. His niece, Angela, was delightful and so adorable; she looked just like Mary—lots of dark brown curls and big brown eyes, and she was just beginning to walk. She was such a whirlwind that she was already trying to run. Her big brother, Roderick, watched over her, and he reminded Henry of Nelson when he was a child. Of course, not in looks, since Nelson was not his father, but in personality they were very alike.

About a week after he had returned home, he went for his usual visit with Nelson, and his mother was there, but she left so they could talk privately.

Nelson looked at Henry and said, "Henry, I'm sure you've seen the change in Father. It started when he found out about your supposed death. It really hit him hard, and I think it opened his eyes to the fact that he had been way too hard on you. I know he's thrilled that you've returned to us safely. I appreciate you staying here with me. I'm sure that it must be difficult having to wait to go get Melody."

Henry looked at Nelson and said, "I do want to go get her, but I would never leave you until you don't need me anymore. I know Melody would want me to stay."

"Poor Melody! She was so lost without you, and she couldn't stand to see me," he said. "When I took her to her parents, she cried the whole way there, and I couldn't get her to eat anything. She lost quite a bit of weight. I know it's hard to understand why she stopped writing, but I think it was because she found it too difficult emotionally. I know she hasn't forgotten you, so if you have been wondering about that, let me put your mind at ease."

Henry leaned forward in his chair and said, "I needed to hear you tell me that because I'm so afraid she may have moved on with her life and forgotten all about me. Melody means the world to me, and I can't wait to see her again."

"I owe you a huge debt of gratitude for introducing me to Mary. She is the light of my life, and I have truly been blessed to have her as my wife. I need you to promise me that you'll take care of her when I'm gone. I'm so thankful that we had Angela before I became so ill. She is the apple of my eye. I know that I can count on you to take care of my family. I'm glad we had this chance to talk. Go easy on Father, for he's having a struggle with all of this, and he's getting up in years. I think my illness has been particularly hard on him, and it has affected his health," he said as he tried to sit up.

Henry stood up and helped Nelson with his pillows so he could get more comfortable, and then he said, "Anything you need, Nelson. You know I'm willing to do it. I appreciate you taking care of Melody for me. I'm sure that going to her parents was what was best for her. I just wish she had continued to write to our sisters so I would know that she was all right. I told you that Mary would be right for you. I can tell that you love each other very much. Melody and I used to hope you would meet someone and fall in love again. You deserved to have someone in your life like Mary, and your daughter has stolen my heart. You don't need to worry. I'll take good care of your whole family when the time comes. Well, I can see you're getting tired, so I'll take my leave of you until tomorrow, old friend!"

Nelson took a turn for the worse the next day after their conversation. The doctors had to put him on a high dosage of laudanum for the pain, so he slept most of the time. Mary never left his side except to see the children. On March 10, Nelson passed away. In some ways, it was a relief to know that he was no longer in pain, but it did not make it any easier to lose him. Poor Mary was devastated by her loss, and Roderick was lost without him, because Nelson had been the only father that he had ever known. Little Angela was too young to understand what was happening.

On the day of his funeral, it rained, and the sky was dark. Mary silently wept throughout the entire service. He was entombed in the family mausoleum, and everyone in the village and all the tenant farmers came out to show their respects. Many of the members of the ton traveled down from London to attend, and it was obvious that Nelson had been loved and respected by everyone who knew him.

CHAPTER 16

March 1818

IT TOOK A fortnight, after Nelson's funeral, before Henry was finally able to leave to go get Melody. He decided to go to London and talk with Melody's aunt, Lady Helton, first. She would know what was going on with Melody. It rained the entire trip, so it took eight hours instead of the normal five, and he was drenched by the time he got to London. He went straight to Sanderford House when he got in town. He called for a bath and then got out of his wet clothes. The bath arrived, and he took a long soak. While he was soaking, he made the decision to go to his club and find some of his friends. After all, it was too late to visit Lady Helton today. He got out of the tub and dressed for the evening; he then headed for his club. He wondered if his membership would still be good, since he was supposed to be dead. He also wondered what type of reaction he would get from his friends, especially Weston and Hayden. He arrived at his club at seven o'clock and went inside. The majordomo questioned his membership, and the manager of the club verified that he had been a member, so they let him in. Henry walked into the main room and looked around.

He spied Weston over against the wall, walked over, and said, "Hello, Weston, how have you been?"

Weston looked up and nearly dropped his drink. "My god, I must be seeing things! I thought you were dead! Hayden told us that he saw you fall. He even brought your body back with him. How can this be?"

Henry smiled sardonically as he said, "I don't know whose body he brought back, but it wasn't mine, as you can see. I was injured after the battle and was left for dead. Some Franciscan monks found me and nursed me back to health, but unfortunately, I had no memory of who I was. Almost two months ago, I was hit on the head, and my memory was restored to me. I came home as fast as possible."

Weston grinned broadly at him as he said, "It's great to see you, Montgomery. What an amazing story! Who else have you seen? Oh by the way, I was sorry to hear about your brother. I missed the funeral, because I arrived back from the continent the same day."

"Thank you, Weston. Nelson will be greatly missed. As you know, we were very close. You're the first person I've seen other than family and servants. I've come to town to speak with Melody's aunt. Since she stopped communicating with the family, they aren't sure what she's doing." Then with a worried expression on his face, he added, "All they know is that she went to her parents after I was reported dead, and then after about a year, quit writing. Have you heard anything from her?"

Weston looked over at him and said, "I just know that she was completely undone when she found out you were supposedly dead and that Nelson took her to her family. I talked with Susan Wilton, who is now Lady Hastings, by the way. She indicated that Melody was at her parents and was very melancholy for a long time. Lady Hastings would just say that she was recovering and leave it at that. I got the impression that your wife wanted to cut all ties to anyone she had known here in London."

Henry sat down across from Weston and poured himself a glass of brandy as he said, "Well, I'm counting on Lady Helton to tell me how she's doing. Hastings' family seat is in Kent, is it not?"

As Weston sipped on his brandy, he replied, "Yes, but I think they've just arrived in town. So you might want to speak with her. I get the feeling that Lady Hastings knows what is happening with Melody, but, for some reason, isn't willing to talk about her."

Henry sat up straight when he heard this and wondered what Susan might know about Melody. This business of her breaking off all lines of communication with everyone was deeply troubling. "I appreciate the information, and I'll try to talk to Lady Hastings as well as Lady Helton. Do you want to go get some dinner? I haven't eaten since this morning and I'm famished."

As Weston adjusted his waistcoat, he said, "I was just getting ready to leave for Lady Millet's soiree, but I would much rather spend some time with you, unless you want to go with me to Lady Millet's."

Henry vehemently shook his head as he answered, "I'm not ready to face the ton yet, and anyway, as you can see I'm in mourning for my brother, so that wouldn't be a good idea."

"Well, let's go and get something to eat, and you can tell me what you've been doing for the last two and a half years!" Weston said, clapping Henry on the shoulder as they left their club.

The next morning, Henry went to Lady Helton's and found out that she was out of town and was not expected back for another two months. Her butler mentioned that she was on extended trip to the continent. He then went on to Lady Hastings, but she was not at home and would not be back for the rest of the day, but at least she was in town. After that, he then went to see his solicitor, because he needed to send funds to Father Francis so he could pay him back. His solicitor was in his office, so his clerk immediately showed him in. Mr. Cook looked up as Henry walked in and he said, "My lord! How can this be?"

Henry told him what had happened over the last three years, and then he said, "I need to send some money to Father Francis." Henry handed him a slip of paper with the pertinent information on it, then asked, "When was the last time you heard from my wife?"

Mr. Cook nervously replied, "I haven't heard from her at all, my lord. In fact, she never used any of her allowance since before you died. After you ah . . . supposedly died, I wrote to her at her parents' house, but I never received any answer. Things were quite confusing, since it appeared that you had died without a will. All your assets were frozen for several months. Once everything was cleared up, I wrote her again, but I never received a response then either. Now that you are back, it will take a few days to get your funds released back to you. Your investments have continued to grow and I know you'll be quite pleased, my lord."

Henry said, "Well, I'm pleased hear about my investments, but I'm extremely disappointed that you didn't try harder to contact my wife. I expect a full accounting of all my assets immediately."

Mr. Cook went to his filing cabinet, pulled out a file and handed it to Henry, and then he said, "Everything is in here, my lord. Again, I am so sorry that I did not get in touch with your wife."

All of this concerned Henry greatly, since he knew Melody's parents were not well off. *Why would she quit getting her allowance? Why did she not answer Mr. Cook's letters?* Well, hopefully Susan would be able to tell him what was going on with Melody. He would go to see her first thing in the morning.

When he arrived back at Sanderford House, there was a messenger from Sanderford Park. His father had had a heart attack! His mother needed him to come home immediately.

He thanked God; the weather was fair, and Henry made it to Sanderford Park in record time. He dashed up the stairs and rushed into the house. Simpson was at the door and informed Henry that her grace was upstairs with his father. He took the stairs, two at a time, and went to his father's chamber. He entered and found his mother beside his father's bed. His father was just lying there, not moving, and his eyes were closed. His mother stood up and motioned for Henry to step out of the room with her.

The duchess looked exhausted as she said, "Henry, your father's condition is very grave. His doctor says he is in danger of having another heart attack at any time. He has been calling for you, but he is resting right now, so please do not wake him. Go sit with him so you can talk when he wakes up. I need to go freshen up, since I have not left his side for the last twenty-four hours."

"Please, Mother, go and get some rest. You need to keep up your strength. You look very tired. Where are Helen and Kathryn?" Henry asked as he glanced back at his father through the crack in the door. His father looked diminished, much smaller than he usually looked and much older. He had deep lines all over his face with dark circles under his eyes. Henry was shocked to see the change in his father in just a few days.

His mother sighed deeply and replied, "I sent them to bed hours ago. They were exhausted. I will rest for a little while. Come and get me if there is any change with your father."

Henry went back to sit by his father, and all through the night, he prayed for him. He finally woke up the next morning, but he was too weak to talk. Henry told his father that he would be there whenever he was up to talking. His father fell back to sleep, and Henry continued to watch over him. His mother came in and told Henry to go get some rest and that she would sit with his father. Everyone took turns sitting with him, but he never woke up again. The seventh Duke of Sanderford passed away on April 5.

His funeral was held two days later. Many of the ton and all of the tenant farmers and villagers attended his funeral, and he was entombed in the family mausoleum beside his son. Henry was now the eighth Duke of Sanderford.

He spent the next fortnight going over everything to do with the ducal holdings with Stallings his father's secretary. Henry was relieved to find that all the holdings were in excellent condition. He was grateful for the time he had spent with his father when he first came home. He was much more aware of the magnitude of all the ducal holdings than he would have been if he had not had that time. Henry's mother and sisters were devastated over the loss of his father and Nelson. He did not have time to grieve because he had so much to do. He needed to travel to all the ducal holdings. Again, he was delayed in going to Melody.

It took Henry three weeks to visit all of his properties. He could not get used to being addressed as his grace. He never expected that he would have to take on the responsibilities of the dukedom. He finally made it to Doncaster, where he now owned Doncaster Stables. He saved it for last, since it was the property closest to Lincolnshire where Melody's home was.

It was now the middle of May, and finally he was able to go to Lincolnshire to get Melody. The rains made travel excruciatingly slow. It took him twelve hours to get to Little Smythington. It was much too late to go to Melody's house by the time he arrived there, so he spent the night at the local coaching inn. Henry had a difficult time sleeping even though he was exhausted. He kept replaying his reunion with Melody. He knew she would be shocked to see him alive. He could not wait to hold her in his arms. He finally fell asleep around three in the morning, but he dreamed that Melody did not want to see him, so needless to say, he was very anxious by morning. Henry arrived at her home the following morning, only to find out that Melody's parents had died in the spring of 1816. The new vicar did not know where Melody had gone. All he remembered was that she had moved to a small cottage on the edge of town. Henry remembered that Susan's family lived in the village, so he went there to see if they knew where Melody was living. Susan's mother was amazed when she saw Henry. She could not believe that he was alive. She was very guarded about Melody, but finally she gave him an address for her, and she was now living in Doncaster! *God, how frustrating! Now he had to go back to Doncaster, and he had just left there! Could his life get any more complicated!*

Henry headed back to Doncaster, but, at least, this time, the weather cooperated, and he made it back to the Doncaster Stables in eight hours. At this point, he would need to wait until morning to go see Melody, so he went to bed. Again, he had a hard time sleeping, for all of his dreams were very erotic, and he woke up fully aroused. It was so painful that he had to relieve himself, which was not very satisfying, but at least he was no longer in pain. After breakfast, he left to find Melody's house. Her house was on the edge of town, and it was a pretty cottage, but the yard was overgrown, and over all, it had an unkempt look about it. He went and knocked on the door. An older woman answered, and she had two small children with her: a beautiful little girl, who looked to be around two or three years old, and a boy child under a year.

Henry looked at her with trepidation and asked, "May I speak to Lady Montgomery, please."

The woman looked exasperated as she said, "There's no Lady Montgomery that lives here, only Mrs. Foster, and she's very ill. I don't have time to talk to you, so good day!" Then the older woman began to shut the door.

Henry put his foot in the door to keep it from closing as he yelled, "Wait, I know that Melody lives here, and I demand to see her at once!"

With a shocked expression on her face, she said, "Who are you to be demanding to see my mistress! She's extremely ill and can't see anyone. Who are you anyway?"

Henry folded his arms and said, "So Melody does live here. Take me to her at once! I'm the Duke of Sanderford, and Melody is my wife. You will not keep me from her!"

The woman immediately curtsied and replied, "I'm so sorry, your grace, please come in." The woman took him into the parlor, and she said, "Please take a seat. I'll be back in a moment." Then as she turned to leave the room she added, "I'm Mrs. Worth, by the way. It's an honor to meet you, your grace," and then she hurried away.

Henry started pacing and decided to follow Mrs. Worth. He went up the stairs and saw Millie coming out of a room at the end of the hall. Millie looked at him with an astonished look on her face, and then her face grew pale as Henry demanded, "Take me to Melody now! Mrs. Worth called her Mrs. Foster, and I want to know what is going on, right now!"

As Millie took a deep breath, she said, "My lord, we were told you were dead! Oh my goodness, how can this be? Your wife is very ill. I'll take you to her at once."

She opened the door to allow Henry to enter the room. He looked over at the bed and saw Melody lying there. She was so thin that he almost did not recognize her. Her beautiful hair was dull, and she had dark circles under her lovely eyes. He was extremely concerned when he saw her and he asked, "What's wrong with her?"

Millie hesitantly answered, "The doctor says she has influenza, and she has been like this for several days. I can't seem to get her fever down, and she can't keep anything in her stomach. She loses everything I try to give her. I'm frightened for her life!"

Henry rushed over to Melody's bedside and felt how hot she was. He immediately demanded some cool water and towels. He started bathing her in the cool water to try to bring her fever down. Millie told Henry that she had to go check on the children.

Henry was curious about these children, but he would worry about that later. Melody opened her eyes, looked at Henry, and started crying. Henry gathered her into his arms and told her that everything would be all right. She closed her eyes and fell back to sleep. He continued to bathe her with the cool water to get her fever to break. Millie entered the room, and he asked, "When was the last time the doctor came to examine my wife?"

"He should be here soon. He comes by every morning to check on her, and he leaves us some medicine for her. In fact, we thought you were the doctor when you knocked on the door." As Millie said this, there was a knock on the door downstairs, and shortly after, Mrs. Worth showed the doctor into the room.

Henry turned to the doctor and urgently said, "Do something for my wife. Surely, there's something that we can do, besides just bathe her with cool water. Help me here, Doctor. I can't lose her after having found her again."

"It is in God's hands now. All you can do is keep giving her the medicine and hope for the best. Who are you, by the way? And how are you married to Mrs. Foster?" the doctor asked.

"I'm Henry Montgomery, the Duke of Sanderford, and I've been her husband for almost four years. Why are you calling my wife Mrs. Foster?" demanded Henry, getting angry and wondering what was going on.

The doctor became very flustered as he bowed and said, "I am sorry, your grace, but I have known your wife for quite some time as Mrs. Foster. I treated her late husband when he passed away a couple of months ago. I . . . I do not understand. How is she your wife?"

Henry was stunned with what the doctor had just told him. He could not grasp the fact that Melody had remarried.

Millie entered the room and tried to explain to the doctor, "Mrs. Foster was married to this gentleman, but then she was told he had been killed at Waterloo. She moved back home with her parents. She found out she was with child after she got to her parents' house." Millie turned to Henry and continued, "My lord, she was devastated by your death. We were afraid that she would lose the baby. She was that upset. Her mother nursed her back to health, and she was able to keep the child. Your wife gave birth to your daughter on January 5, 1816, and then her parents died that spring from influenza."

Henry interrupted and asked, "But how did she become Mrs. Foster? Surely she didn't forget about me so quickly."

"After her parents died, she was left with no place to live and barely any money. She had no choice but to remarry or starve," Millie explained.

"That is simply not true! She could have contacted my parents! She would have inherited everything I owned, upon my death! My god, she was my wife, for Christ's sake. Why didn't she go to them or answer my solicitor's letters?" In an agitated state, Henry began to pace back and forth.

Millie fearfully replied, "I don't know the answer to that, my lord, but I'm sure that she had her reasons. She married Mr. Foster in the fall of 1816, and they moved here to Doncaster, where he had a teaching post. That little girl downstairs is your daughter, Mary Elizabeth, and she's two and a half years old."

Melody groaned, and they all looked over at her. Henry rushed to her bedside and felt her forehead. It was dampened with sweat and felt cool. Her fever had broken.

"Thank God, her fever has broken. Doctor, do you think she'll be all right?" he asked as he looked over at him.

"She should be fine now that the fever has broken. Just get her to take plenty of fluids, and give her some gruel. And whatever you do, make sure she stays calm. She is sleeping now and will probably sleep for quite some time. I recommend that you continue your discussion downstairs so that your wife can get her rest, your grace," the doctor replied.

Millie stayed with Melody while Henry escorted the doctor out. After the doctor left, he went to find Mrs. Worth. She was in the kitchen watching the children. He looked at the little girl and was amazed at how much she looked like Helen. There was no doubt that this was his child. Henry turned to Mrs. Worth and asked, "Could you go relieve Millie and ask her to come here? I'll watch the children while you're gone."

"Of course, your grace, I'll go get her for you right now." Mrs. Worth curtsied and left the room.

Henry kneeled down in front of his daughter and said, "Hello, sweetheart. I know you don't know me, but I'm your father, and you look just like your aunt Helen. May I give you a hug?"

Mary Elizabeth looked at him with her startling blue eyes and started to cry. "You not my papa! My papa go to angewls. Mama tolded me!"

Henry was at a loss; he did not know what to say to his daughter. Obviously, she had looked at Mr. Foster as her father. *Lord, what a tangle this was!*

Millie hesitantly entered the kitchen and curtsied as she asked, "I understand that you're now the Duke of Sanderford. If I may ask your grace, how did you become the duke?"

With irritation in his voice, he replied, "My brother passed away in March, and then my father died on April 5, so that's how I became the duke. When did Melody meet Mr. Foster?"

With great trepidation, she quietly said, "I believe that she had known Mr. Foster all her life. They were childhood friends, your grace."

Henry thought a minute and then asked, "What was Mr. Foster's full name?"

"Mr. Brandon Alton Foster III and she started seeing him the winter after your daughter was born, your grace. He helped her find a place to live when she had to move after her parents died. He would come by a couple times a week to check on Lady Montgomery. By the end of that summer, your wife was very concerned about finding money to make ends meet," Millie said, as she looked at him with fear in her eyes. "Mr. Foster had just accepted a position here in Doncaster. He asked her to marry him and come with him. I do know that she seemed relieved when he asked. I think she was afraid that she wouldn't be able to survive and raise Mary Elizabeth, so she married Mr. Foster."

Henry looked very angry, and, in frustration, ran his fingers through his hair. "That is just nonsense! She should have gone to my family. She had no reason to be afraid. They would have made sure she was well taken care of, her and my daughter. She never even wrote them and told them about the child. What could she have been thinking!"

In a trembling voice, Millie replied, "Your grace, as I said before, she must have had her reasons. I'm sure she'll share those with you, once she's feeling better."

"Well, I guess I'll have to wait to find out more. As you have said, she must have thought she had a good reason for not contacting my family. Thank you, for telling me all this, you have been very helpful. Can you watch the children, while I go up to my wife?" Henry tried to modulate his tone because he realized that he was scaring Millie and none of this was her fault. As difficult as it was, he would just have to wait for answers, until Melody was feeling better.

"Certainly, your grace," Millie replied. "It's time for them to take a nap anyway."

CHAPTER 17

May 1818

MELODY SLEPT THROUGH the night, and Henry stayed by her side. The next morning she woke up, and when she saw Henry, she looked at him and whispered, "I must have died and gone to heaven, because how can you be here with me any other way."

Henry looked at her and said, "Obviously the reports of my death were false. I'm very much alive. I'll explain it all later. We just need to concentrate on you getting well. You have been very ill, and you need to start eating, so you can gain your strength back. I've never seen you so thin. Let me get you something to eat. I'll be right back." Melody started to cry. Henry sat down beside her and put his arm around her. "It's all right, my love, please don't cry. You know I can't stand it when you cry. I'm back, and I'll take care of you. Sweetheart, I'm going to go get you some food now, but I'll be right back. Just rest until I return, all right?" Then Henry left the room. He returned in a few minutes, and Mrs. Worth was with him. She had some porridge, and Henry fed it to her. Melody kept looking at Henry as if she were seeing a ghost. *How could Henry be alive? Where had he been for the last three years? Oh, if only she were not so weak, she would make him tell her.*

Henry finished feeding her, and she ate the entire bowl. Mrs. Worth said that it was the most she had eaten, at one time, since Mr. Foster had died. Henry was glad he was able to get her to eat. It was obvious that she probably had not been taking care of herself. He was anxious to hear Melody's story, but he knew she was still too weak to get into it yet. He tried to conceal his anger and frustration, because he did not want to upset her, but it was very difficult, since there were so many unanswered questions in his mind. Mrs. Worth left the room and took the empty bowl with her.

Melody looked embarrassed and asked, "Henry, can you get Millie for me? I need her to help me get cleaned up. I feel as if I haven't bathed in days."

"Of course, my dear, I'll go get her now." Then he left the room.

Over the next week, Melody continued to improve, and she even seemed to put some weight back on, now that she eating again. Henry spent part of each day at her side. Their conversation was very stiff, and they were not comfortable with each other. He was trying to be patient and not show his anger, but he was failing badly.

Finally, Melody said, "Talk to me, Henry, I'm sure you have questions, because I know I do. Where have you been for the last three years!"

Henry was furious with Melody. *How could she question him about where he had been for three years! He wasn't the one that went and married someone else. How in God's name could she have done that? Surely their love meant more to her than sixteen months of grieving. If she had died, he would never have married again. Oh god, the pain of all this, it was killing him to know Melody had been with another man. That was not supposed to happen.* He knew he had to get his anger under control because Melody was still recovering from her illness.

Henry sat down in the chair, leaned back, and tried to relax. He took several deep breaths and began his story. "It's a long story, but I'll try to keep it short. I was injured at the Battle of Waterloo. I sustained a head wound and I was shot in the leg. I was found on the battlefield by some Franciscan monks. They carried me back to the monastery. There was no way to identify me because someone had taken my clothes, so I was completely naked. The monks took care of me, and I remained unconscious for almost a month. When I finally woke up and could talk, I had no memory of who I was. They nursed me back to health, but my memory didn't return. Since there was no way to know who I was, the monks let me stay with them. I became their bookkeeper of sorts. After a period of time, I started to have dreams . . . of you I now know, and then some flashbacks of the battle. In late January, I was helping the monks repair a wall that had fallen, and I fell and hit my head. When I woke up, I remembered who I was and immediately thought of you. Father Francis lent me the funds to return to England."

"But, Henry, that was months ago. What have you been doing since you came back to England?" she asked. "Surely, you wanted to see me. But . . . , maybe, you didn't. Maybe you found someone else and just don't want to tell me!"

Henry stood up with so much force that his chair tipped back and fell to the floor. He roared, "I'm not the one who forgot about you! You're the one who forgot about me. God Melody, how could you get married to someone else. If the tables were turned, I would have grieved for you for the rest of my life!"

Melody burst into tears as she said, "I never forgot about you. I did grieve for you this entire time you've been gone. I can't believe you could say anything like this to me." She rolled over on her side with her back to him, and he felt terrible about yelling at her.

Henry sat back down and said, "This is not getting us anywhere. I'm sorry, I yelled at you. Let me continue with my story, and then you'll understand why I didn't come to you right away. When I arrived back in England, I immediately went to Sanderford House but found out that the family was in the country. I then traveled to Sanderford Park. When I got there, I found out that Nelson was dying and that my father was ailing. Then they told me you had left after you found out about my death. Helen told me that Nelson had taken you to your parents and that after about a year, you quit writing to them. I didn't feel that I could leave because of Nelson. He died on March 10."

Melody rolled back over and said, "Oh, Henry, I knew Nelson had been ill, but I didn't realize it was that serious. I can just imagine how difficult losing him was. I thought the world of Nelson. I can't believe he's gone." Tears rolled down Melody's cheeks, and Henry sat down beside her on the bed and put his arm around her.

"I'm sure it's a shock to hear of his death, but you can understand why I wasn't able to come to you right away. After his funeral, I left to go to London and speak with your aunt Miriam. When I got there, I found out that she was out of the country. I then went to see your friend Susan, but she was unavailable. I received a message from my mother, telling me that my father had had a heart attack and that I needed to return home at once. Father died on April 5," he said.

Melody gasped as she exclaimed, "Oh no, not your father too! How awful it must have been for you to come home and find me gone, Nelson dying, and then to lose your father too! I'm so sorry, Henry. Oh goodness, that means you're now the duke! Oh lord, that means I'm . . . a duchess, doesn't it?" Melody started crying even harder, and Henry tried to comfort her, but he felt uncomfortable because his anger was still seething right under the surface. He had to stay calm so they could get through this.

He patted her on the shoulder and said, "It's going to be all right. We'll get through all of this somehow. It took me weeks to get everything settled so that I could come for you. When I arrived, I found out that, your parents had died and that you had moved to Doncaster. That's when I came here, found out that you had married again, and you were gravely ill. Melody, why didn't you contact my parents when yours passed away? You know they would have taken care of you. You didn't return any of my solicitor's letters. You had inherited everything that I owned. There was no reason you should have felt compelled to marry to survive. What were you thinking?" Henry stood up and began pacing the room as he continued, "I don't understand why you felt so desperate that you had to marry or starve as your maid so politely put it. Please explain to me what you were thinking because, for Christ's sake, I don't know!"

With tears rolling down her cheeks, she took a deep breath as she said, "I was devastated when I received the news of your death. After the funeral, I just wanted to go home to be with my parents. Nelson took me. He was so patient and kind to me, but I found it too difficult to be around him because he looked so much like you. I asked him to leave. I was exhausted because I had cried the whole way to my parents. They called in the doctor, and that is when I found out that I was with child. At first, I was so ill that I couldn't even think straight. Finally, I started feeling better physically. I was so pleased that I was going to have your child. I knew I would always have a small part of you through the baby. I was just going to wait a little while, and then I would write to your family and tell them about the baby. Each letter I received, I would answer, planning on telling them in my next letter, but then I started to get scared, so I didn't tell them. Henry, I never got any letters from your solicitor. God knows, I would have answered a letter like that, especially after my parents died. I was afraid that when your parents found out about the child, they would take her away from me. You have to understand, Henry. Your father was a very powerful man, and I knew he detested me. I became convinced that I could never tell them about our child. Several months after she was born, I quit answering their letters altogether because I was afraid I would say something accidentally, and then they would come and take my daughter. As you found out, my parents both died that spring. The house was owned by the church, so I couldn't continue to stay there. My parents left me five hundred pounds, and that was all I had to my name, aside from their personal belongings and some furniture."

Henry continued to pace furiously back and forth, as he interrupted, "You couldn't have been thinking! I would never leave you without resources!"

"That may be true, but at the time, that was what I thought. Now do you want to hear the rest of my story or not?" Melody asked.

"Yes, by all means, please continue!" Henry sat back down in the chair, folded his arms across his chest, and waited for her to continue. He tried to get his temper back under control because he knew Melody was still very weak from her illness and the last thing he wanted to do was upset her and make her sick again.

Melody leaned back on her pillow, looking so pale and weak that it made his heart ache. *Oh why did this have to happen?* Then she slowly continued, "I found a small cottage on the edge of town and moved there. My friend Brandon helped me move. As you already know, he had lost his wife, so we gained comfort from each other. He would come to check on me a couple of times a week. When he was offered the position in Doncaster, he didn't want to leave me alone, so he asked me to marry him. I didn't want to marry him because I knew that I could never love him. He told me he knew I would always love you but pointed out to me that you were gone, and nothing would bring you back to me. At least, we cared for each other, and there were worse reasons to marry than friendship. I considered writing to your brother, but I knew he was newly married, and I was afraid he wouldn't have time to protect me from your parents. I didn't want to have Mary Elizabeth grow up without a father. I tried to think of what would be best for her. That's why I married Brandon. It wasn't a love match, but I knew he would make a good father for Mary Elizabeth. My marriage to Brandon was comfortable; he was a wonderful father, a good husband, and he was my best friend. If I had had any idea that you weren't dead, I would have waited forever, but I have always been a very practical woman and knew I had to move on with my life. I hope you can understand why I married him."

Henry leaned forward, ran his fingers through his hair, and said, "I still don't understand why you were so afraid of my parents. Nelson would never have let them take your child. He would have protected you and Mary Elizabeth with his life. You should have had more faith in him than that. I'm very curious as to why you didn't get my solicitor's letters. Did you think that I would die and leave you without anything? I can't believe that you would be so slow-witted. You should have known better!"

Melody sat up straight and, with incredulity on her face, said, "I don't know why I didn't get those letters, and I am not slow-witted! I was so distraught when you died that I wasn't thinking clearly. We never discussed finances, so I had no idea what you owned or how much money you had. I didn't even know who your solicitor was! You should have made sure I was aware of all that before you went off to war! I'm not to blame here. I only did what I thought I must! I'm sorry, Henry, but I did what I felt was best for Mary Elizabeth and myself. I don't know what else to say. I'll understand if you don't want to stay married to me. I'm sure there must be some way that we can end our marriage without a scandal."

Now Henry really felt ready to explode, but he took some deep cleansing breaths, stood up, and started pacing the room again as he derisively said, "Melody, that is ridiculous! Of course, I don't want out of our marriage. Even though I'll probably never understand why you did what you did, you are still my wife, and you will be so until the day you die. So, I'll hear no more talk about ending our marriage. We'll get through this some way. You are right, though. I should never have gone off to war and not explained everything to you about our finances. I guess I was so concerned about what was happening that I didn't think of the future or what would happen if I were to die. I'm sorry for that, but you still should have realized that I wouldn't have left you without resources."

With sadness written all over her sweet face, she leaned back on her pillow again and sighed and then she said, "We aren't going to get anywhere like this, so we need to just try to move past what has happened. Neither of us can go back and change anything, so it serves no useful purpose to continue to argue about this. I need to concentrate on getting my strength back. Henry, you need to be very sure that you don't want out of this marriage. I'll make a very poor duchess. It's not something that I ever wanted."

Henry belligerently looked at her and said, "Well, I never expected to be the duke either, but here I am, and I have no choice but to meet my obligations head-on, and so will you. You have no choice either. I'm sure we will learn how to handle our new responsibilities as time goes on. The important thing now is to get you well. So you're right, we won't talk about this anymore. Later, after we get back to Sanderford Park, we can sort it all out."

CHAPTER 18

June 1818

HENRY KNEW THAT they could not end their marriage, and he did not want to anyway. He knew he would need to find someway to get past the fact that Melody had married, and worse than that, she had given her body to Brandon. He had liked Brandon, but that did not mean he wanted to share Melody with him. When he spoke with her the next day, he said, "Melody, we have to stay together. We are legally married, and the only way we could end our marriage would be for me to accuse you of adultery, and neither one of us would want to live through a scandal like that. Both of us need to put Mary Elizabeth's best interests first, and it would definitely not be beneficial to her if her parents went through a nasty divorce. There will be no further discussion about ending our marriage. I'd much rather talk about my beautiful daughter. I'm a bit overwhelmed by the thought of fatherhood, but I'm thrilled about Mary Elizabeth. I do hope she will warm up to me eventually, and I'm sure she will. We'll just take everything one day at a time. Once you're fully recovered, we'll return to Sanderford Park."

Melody gazed at Henry as she said, "Henry, I need time to get used to you being alive, and I need you to be patient with me while I adjust. I'm overjoyed you survived, but, nonetheless, it's all very overwhelming. However, my feelings for you are just as strong as they were before you left for the continent. I agree that we need to take things one day at a time, and I'm sure we'll be fine soon."

Leaning forward in his chair, he replied, "I understand that all of this is rather shocking. It's unusual for someone to come back from the dead. I just hope it doesn't take you long to adjust because I want you to fully be my wife again in every sense of the word."

They stayed in Doncaster for two weeks so that Melody could regain her strength again. Since Melody's house was so small, he stayed at Doncaster

Stables. He spent part of each day with her so they could get to know each other again. Mary Elizabeth did not want to have anything to do with him. Melody tried to talk to her, but she refused to believe that he was her father. She kept insisting that her papa was in heaven with the angels. Little Brandon was too small to understand, so he seemed to accept Henry without question. Henry found some coaches at Doncaster Stables, had them repaired, and made ready for the long journey.

Millie and Mrs. Worth packed up the cottage. Since Mrs. Worth's children were all grown and her husband was gone, she decided to come with them as the children's nurse, which pleased Melody immeasurably, since she had grown quite fond of her.

They left Doncaster the first part of June. Henry and Melody rode in the main carriage, and the children rode with Millie and Mrs. Worth in the second carriage. The trip was long and exhausting, mainly because of the children, and Melody still grew tired easily, so they could not travel very far each day. Henry suspected that the upheaval of it all was why Melody was recovering so slowly. At least, she was finally putting some of her weight back on, but she was still far too thin. He was still trying to move on from what he saw as a betrayal. *Henry knew he should not feel so resentful that she had moved on with her life, but dammed, if he could just forget it.* He could tell that Melody knew he had not forgiven her, and he knew that it bothered her. They tried to converse, but it was uncomfortable for both of them. Melody ended up reading or doing needlework, and he either read the newspaper or pretended to sleep. Every night, when they stopped at an inn, Melody would retire to her room and have a tray sent up. She would spend time with the children, and then she would go to bed. Henry would eat alone in the dining room, and then he would drink until he felt he could go to sleep. He had never really been much of a drinker, but it was the only way he could sleep without dreaming, and he was getting damned tired of living in a perpetual state of arousal.

By the time they were close to Sanderford Park, the children were inordinately irritable, and had been crying for days. Finally, they arrived. All the servants were lined up to greet them as Henry had sent word that he was bringing Melody home.

Once the children were in the nursery, Henry left Melody in their rooms and went to find his mother. As soon as he started talking to her, it was obvious she was back to her old vindictive self again. He should have known it was too good to last. She was not willing to accept Melody back into the fold. Henry tried to be patient as he said, "I need you to accept

Melody and treat her with the respect she deserves as my duchess and wife. You have a beautiful granddaughter named Mary Elizabeth. When Melody thought I was dead, she married her best friend, Brandon Foster. They had a child, and his name is Brandon. I expect you to treat him as if he were your grandchild in truth. He is not to blame for this situation."

His mother looked furious. She stood up, came over to him, and said vehemently, "You are entirely too accepting of what Melody has done. You need to be very careful that she does not wrap you around her little finger again. How can you be sure that this Mary Elizabeth is even your child? At least she is a girl, so she will not be able to inherit."

Henry looked directly into his mother's eyes and said, "There is no doubt about Mary Elizabeth's parentage. For one thing, the timing alone shows that she's my daughter, and besides, she looks just like Helen. So you can put that idea out of your mind."

The duchess returned his stare as she replied, "Well, I guess we will just have to make the best of a bad situation. I will treat her as you expect, but do not expect me to like it. I have never understood what you saw in her to begin with, but it is too late to do anything about it now."

As Henry turned to leave the room, he said, "You're right about that. Going forward, you will be pleasant to my wife, and let me say this, if I find out that you have said anything to hurt her, you will answer to me. I'm the head of this family now, and you need to remember that!"

He went to their rooms and found Melody already asleep in her bed. She looked so tired, yet so very lovely. He wanted to wake her up and kiss her all over, but he knew that he had promised to give her time to adjust to everything. Besides, it would not be right to make love until he could move beyond his feelings about her going on with her life. He went into his room to think about all that had gone on while he had been gone. He was feeling very overwhelmed and much older than his eight and twenty years. He truly found it amazing that he was a father. He never doubted that Mary Elizabeth was his child. She looked so much like Helen, when she was a young child. He knew there were bound to be difficult times ahead, but he still loved Melody very much. He would just have to try harder to get over his anger at what he irrationally saw as her betrayal.

He never expected to be the duke, nor had he ever wanted to be. He was just a soldier. He had never wanted to be anything other than that. At least, he had spent that short period of time going over everything with his father before Nelson had died. Henry went down to what had been his father's study; it was his study now. Stallings had left several reports on his desk for him to go over, but he was just too tired to peruse them that night. He poured himself a large snifter of brandy and proceeded to get royally drunk.

The next day, Melody woke up, and the room was full of sunshine. At first, she could not remember where she was, but then it all came back to her. She was back at Sanderford Park. She hastily dressed and went to find her children in the nursery. Mary Elizabeth came running to her, as soon as she saw her. Melody went down on her knees and gave her a big hug. Then she picked up Brandon and hugged him close. "How are you feeling this morning? I know that all of this must be a little strange to you, but this is your new home. Look at all the lovely toys for you to play with. These toys belonged to your father and his sisters when they were children. Mary Elizabeth, look at all these beautiful dolls. Won't you enjoy playing with them?"

Mary Elizabeth looked at her mother with her big blue eyes and nodded her head. "Yeth Mama, I tink I like it heyo."

The nursemaid came over and introduced herself. "I'm Suzie, and I have been taking care of Lady Wyndham's children, your grace." At first, Melody thought her mother-in-law must have walked into the room, and then she realized that Suzie was addressing her. *How strange it was to hear herself being addressed as her grace!* She was not sure she could get used to that.

Melody asked, "Have my children had breakfast yet? They usually eat porridge."

"Yes, your grace, and a fine breakfast it was! The children especially liked Cook's special oatmeal," Suzie replied.

"Well, good, I'm glad they enjoyed it." Melody then turned to her children and said, "I'm going to leave you with Suzie now, but I'll see you later after I go and talk to his grace, all right?" She looked over at Suzie and asked, "Where is Mrs. Worth? She's my children's nurse."

"She went to get something, but I'm sure she'll be back any minute. Do you want me to go find her for you, your grace?" Suzie asked.

"No, I'll speak with her the next time I come to the nursery." Then after giving Mary Elizabeth and Brandon a hug and a kiss, Melody turned and left the room. After she closed the door, she took a deep breath and thought to herself, *now it is time to find Henry.* She went downstairs and went to the study to see if Henry was there.

Melody knocked firmly and with purpose on the door. Henry said, "Come in." When he saw her he added, "Melody, don't you look refreshed. Did you sleep well?"

Melody looked at Henry and smiled, then said, "Yes, Henry, I feel much better after a good night's sleep. Did you sleep well yourself?"

Henry came around to the front of his desk and leaned back against it as he said, "It felt strange to be in my father's room, but I did sleep, and I feel much refreshed. Were your rooms acceptable? Please feel free to redecorate if you want."

"My rooms are fine. I may want to change them later, but for now, they will do. I'm sure your mother was not happy about moving out of them." Melody looked around the study, remembering the last time she had been in it and felt deep sadness roll over her. This was where Nelson had told her about Henry's death and that was one of the last times she had seen Nelson alive.

"I had Mother move out of the rooms before I left to bring you home, and while she's not happy, she'll adjust once some time has gone by." Henry looked up and saw Melody's face and asked, "Are you all right? You look incredibly sad."

Melody met his gaze and said, "I'm all right. I was just remembering the last time I was in this room. It made me think of Nelson and how horrible it is that he's gone."

Henry took her hand in his and gently said, "I miss him too. I also miss my father. I've been going through some of his papers. There's so much to learn, and I don't really know where to start. I never expected I would have to be responsible for all of this. I just hope I'm up to the challenge."

Melody wiped a tear from her eye, and then she smiled bravely as she said, "I'm sure you'll have it all well in hand in no time. You have always been very quick at everything, and I'm sure that once you get everything under control, you'll do splendidly."

Henry looked reassured and nodded his head. Then he asked, "How are the children this morning? Do they seem to be all right in the nursery? I'm sure that all of this must be very overwhelming for them."

"Children are quite resilient, and they adjust quickly to a new environment. As long as they have toys around them, they'll be fine. How did your mother take the news about Brandon?" she asked.

Henry sighed deeply and said, "Much as you would expect. She's back to her old vindictive self again. I knew it was too good to believe that she had mellowed. I told her she was to treat you with respect. Have you seen my sisters yet?"

As she watched Henry walk back around his desk, she replied, "No, I came to see you first. I haven't even eaten breakfast yet. How about you? Have you eaten?"

Henry shifted some papers around and said, "Yes, I ate an hour ago. I've been going over some reports Stallings left for me. I expect he'll be here soon, so we can go over them together. Why don't you go into the breakfast room? I'm sure you'll find my sisters there."

Melody nodded her head as she replied, "I think I'll do that. I'm very hungry, and I seem to be getting my appetite back. Before you know it, I'll be back to my old plump self again."

Henry laughed as he said, "Good, because I like you much better a little plump! Would you like to go riding this afternoon? I can probably break away around two o'clock. Would that work for you?"

"I would like that, Henry. Just be patient with me, for I haven't been on a horse for a long time. Well, I'll let you get back to your work, see you later." She turned and with a wave of her hand, she walked out of the study.

Henry watched as Melody left the room. *God, she was so lovely.* He wished they could go back to before Waterloo! Henry knew he had to find some way to forgive her. That was the most promising conversation they had had since they had found each other again. They just needed to take some time to get used to each other again. He knew that Melody was very uncomfortable about being a duchess, and he could not blame her. He was still getting used to being the duke, and he had had over two months to accept it.

Melody made her way to the breakfast room and both Henry's sisters were there. As she walked into the room, she was greeted enthusiastically. Helen and Kathryn both came over and gave her a hug, and then she hugged them back as she said, "It's so good to see you both. I've really missed both of you tremendously. I'm sorry I quit writing to you. I was so scared when I found out about the baby. I guess I wasn't thinking clearly. I hope you'll forgive me?"

Helen smiled reassuringly at Melody and said, "Henry told us about everything. Since I know how poorly you were treated by my parents, I can understand why you did it. But, Melody, surely you realized that Nelson would have protected you. He wouldn't have let them hurt you."

"I know that now, but at the time, I was still grieving the loss of your brother, and all I wanted to do was feel safe. I was just too afraid your parents would take my daughter away that I wasn't thinking rationally." It relieved Melody tremendously that Helen seemed to understand why she stopped writing to them.

"Well, I'm just glad you're back with us, and I don't want you to ever leave again," Kathryn said.

Melody turned to Kathryn and smiled, then said, "Just look at you! Kathryn, you're all grown up and so pretty. Are you still planning on being an artist?"

Kathryn smiled enthusiastically as she replied, "Yes, and Mother and Father let me continue with my art lessons. I'm much better than I was when I painted that portrait of you back in 1814, and I can't wait to paint your beautiful children. We peeked in on them this morning before we came down for breakfast and they're adorable."

"How is Mary taking the loss of Nelson?" Melody asked. "I was so pleased to hear that they had married. I'm sure they loved each other very much. I met her children this morning, and they both seem to be well-behaved children. Angela looks so much like Mary and so does Roderick. Where is she this morning?"

"Mary hasn't taken losing Nelson well at all. She rarely comes down for meals, and she doesn't even spend much time with the children. Hopefully, you can help her learn how to cope with her loss," Helen explained.

Helen and Kathryn sat back down, and Melody went to the sideboard and filled a plate. She made herself eat some coddled eggs with bacon and toast, and of course, she had cherry preserves with her toast. After they finished their breakfast, Helen and Kathryn decided to take a walk in the gardens and Melody went back upstairs to her children.

Melody met Henry at the stables at two o'clock so they could go riding. Her old riding habit was very loose on her, but at least, she could still wear it. After she returned from her ride, Millie would take it in so it would fit better in the future. They decided to ride down to the lake. When they got there, Henry helped her down from her horse. Melody felt a jolt of electricity shoot through her veins as Henry placed his hands around her waist to lift her down from her horse. He held out his arm for her to take, and they started walking around the lake. They soon came to the spot where they had spent many a happy moment together laughing and making love. It brought back so many wonderful memories.

Henry stopped and turned toward her, then said, "I remember this spot well. In fact, when I was getting my memory back, this is what I dreamed we were doing. We had many wonderful afternoons here, did we not?"

As Melody gazed up at him, she replied, "Yes, we did. I feel so strange being here. I never thought I would ever see this place again, much less be here with you. I never stopped loving you, Henry. Brandon understood that you would always have my heart."

Henry looked out at the lake, and then he answered, "I'm beginning to understand that, but it will take time for me to accept that you were with another man. I find it hard to believe there was no love between you. Melody, I know you couldn't have been with him if there had been no feelings."

Melody earnestly said, "It was different, Henry. Brandon was my best friend and I had known him all my life. Of course, I loved him, but I just wasn't in love with him, not in the same way I love you. It's hard to explain, but we did have a good marriage, and he was such an honorable man. I wish you had had a chance to know him better. When I first returned to my parents, Brandon helped me deal with my grief. Since he had recently lost Lily, we consoled each other."

"I'm relieved that you had someone whom you could depend on. I just wish you hadn't married him. I'm trying to move past this, but it's going to take a while. Well, enough about that. Did you enjoy spending time with my sisters?" he asked.

"Oh yes, Henry, and they're so beautiful. I always knew Helen was beautiful, but Kathryn has really grown into a lovely young lady. She still seems a little shy, but not as much as she used to be. I haven't seen Mary yet. They told me that she isn't handling Nelson's death well at all. I hope she can find it in herself to begin to move on. It does take a while, and it has only been a little more than three months. I was still grieving deeply, even a year after I thought I had lost you. The only thing that helped me was our daughter. Of course, when my parents died, I had to make some very difficult decisions as you are well aware of," Melody explained.

They turned around and started walking back to their horses. When they got to them, Henry pulled her into his arms and gave her a gentle kiss. Melody responded immediately and returned his kiss. It felt so good to have her in his arms again; he might not have forgiven her, but he definitely still wanted her very badly. Melody melted in his arms; he deepened their kiss, and she responded by putting her arms up around his neck and pulling him close. Soon their tongues were dueling as Henry took his hand and kneaded her breast. It was as if they could not get close enough. It was the best feeling that either of them had felt in three years. Melody's knees gave out, and Henry pulled her to the ground. He pulled up her habit and found her sweet spot. She was dripping wet and ready for him; he ripped open the buttons on his breeches and surged home. He was in heaven. He pumped into her forcefully, and Melody went wild; she grabbed his buttocks, pulled him tightly against her, and met him stroke for stroke. All of a sudden, she stiffened in his arms and went soaring, just as Henry made a final thrust and his seed spilled into her. They went limp and clung to each other as if they never wanted to let go. They both just lay there in shock. It had been such an electrifying experience. Gently, Henry pulled out of her and sat up. He looked at Melody and she blushed.

"Melody, I didn't hurt you, did I?" he asked. "I didn't mean for that to happen and certainly not so roughly."

Melody couldn't look at him, for she was so embarrassed. "No, Henry you didn't hurt me, far from it. I wanted you as much as you wanted me."

God, she was so beautiful with her cheeks flushed from the passion that had just taken them away from all their problems. "You're right. I did want you desperately, but I promised you that I would give you time to adjust, and what do I do? Ravish you the first time we're completely alone. I hope you can forgive me."

"There's nothing to forgive, Henry. I'm your wife, and as I told you earlier, I never stopped loving you. You're the one who can't forgive me." He felt a stab of pain when she said this. *God, why did this have to happen to them!*

"I know, Melody, but I just can't get the picture out of my head. I keep seeing you in Brandon's arms, and I just burn up. I have never thought of myself as a jealous man, but when it comes to you, I just don't like sharing." *Oh, why could he not let this go!*

Melody looked at Henry with sadness in her beautiful eyes, and it just about tore him apart. He had to move beyond this, if they were going to get back to the way, they were. He stood up and offered Melody his hand so he could pull her up. Melody straightened her clothes, and Henry tried to button up his breeches, but some of the buttons had come off. He did get them fastened, eventually. He helped her mount her horse, mounted his, and they headed back to the house. They didn't talk on the way back because they were both deep in their thoughts.

Once they got back to the stables, they both dismounted, and Henry turned to Melody. "I need to get back to my study. I told Stallings that I would be back by three o'clock, and it's after that now. Let me escort you to the house so that you can go freshen up and change your clothes. I'll see you this evening at dinner."

Melody went up to her room and had Millie draw her a bath. She got undressed and slipped into the tub. Millie left her to soak and took the riding habit with her so she could take it up for Melody. What an exhilarating experience. She had never felt so much passion, and she had definitely felt passion before, but nothing so intense. Melody thought about the afternoon with Henry and wished there was something she could do so he would forgive her. She guessed he was right. She just needed to give him time. She thought about the fact that she had not realized she would have inherited everything Henry had. She was amazed that she did not think of it at the time, but she realized she still did not regret marrying Brandon. She felt it had been the right thing to do for Mary Elizabeth. She just hoped that eventually, Henry would realize it. Melody finished her bath and dressed so she could go and visit her children.

The children had just gotten up from their naps. Mary Elizabeth came running over to her and cried, "Mama, I have fun. I have new fiend and hew name is . . . is An . . . ge . . . wa. Can I wealwy pway witf hew evee day? She live heyo too."

"Yes, darling, she's your cousin, and I'm glad to see that you like each other. Have you been playing with Brandon?" she asked.

Mary Elizabeth looked up at her and said, "Mama, he just wittle. He don't know how to pway. All he do is cwawl. He puw my dollhouse down."

"I know that he is little, but he is your brother, and you need to help Mama take care of him." Mary Elizabeth nodded her head, and then the little girls ran back to the dollhouse and started playing with it again. Melody picked up Brandon and turned to Mrs. Worth. "Have they been behaving themselves for you?"

Mrs. Worth curtsied and answered, "They're little angels, your grace. The girls have been playing together all day, and they're getting along well. Roderick was feeling a little left out because he doesn't have someone his own age to play with, but he's a good boy. His mother came and got him so she could spend some time with him."

Melody went over to where the girls were playing and kneeled down. They showed her the dollhouse and all their beautiful dolls. Then they went to the little table and chairs, and invited Melody to tea. She spent an hour, watching and playing with her children, and then she left to go back to her rooms.

Mary was in the drawing room, along with the others, when Melody joined them. She could tell that Mary was having a difficult time of it. Her eyes held so much sadness that Melody's heart went out to her. The duchess was sitting in her usual place and had a condescending expression on her face. It was clear that she did not think very much of either of her daughters-in-law. It seemed some things never changed. Henry came in, and then Simpson announced dinner, so he escorted his mother to the dining room, and the other ladies followed.

Dinner was pleasant, and the food was marvelous. Cook made all of Henry's favorite foods, and she even fixed cherry compote for dessert, which had always been Melody's favorite. When the meal had ended, the duchess stood up and indicated it was time to leave Henry to his port, so all the ladies went to the drawing room.

Mary sat alone, so Melody went over and sat beside her, then said, "It's good to see you again. The last time we saw each other was in London, shortly before I received the news about Henry's supposed death. I'm so sorry for your loss. I thought the world of Nelson and was very saddened when I heard he had passed away. I understand what you're going through, and if there is anything I can do for you, please let me know. When I thought Henry had died, I felt such incredible pain that I wasn't sure I could go on. The only thing that held me together, was knowing that I was going to have his child. You were visiting your brother, Lieutenant Bronson, when he was stationed in Canterbury. How is your brother, ma'am?"

With sadness in her eyes, Mary replied, "My brother is doing well. He came back from the war but lost his left arm. He is working as a secretary for the Earl of Overton. I appreciated you introducing me to Susan. We continued to work together at the orphanage. I thought you were so kind to me, and now we are sisters-in-law."

Helen came over and asked Mary if she would play the pianoforte. Mary went over and began to play; she was fabulous. She may well have been the best pianist Melody had ever heard. Henry joined them, and they all sat and listened to Mary. Even the duchess seemed to enjoy the music. When Mary finished playing, everyone decided it was time for bed. Henry escorted Melody to her room, kissed her cheek, and wished her a good night. Then he walked down the hall to his room and went inside to his lonely bed.

CHAPTER 19

July 1818

EVERYDAY, HENRY SPENT quite a bit of his time with his secretary. He also rode out to check on his tenants and got to know them better. Many he remembered from when he was a lad, but some were new to him. All of them needed something. They were having a hot, dry summer, and they feared that their crops would not be good this year. Henry assured them that if the crops were not good, he would waive or reduce their rents for the year. Henry thought about Melody constantly. He wanted to go to her, and yet he was still struggling with forgiving her. They spent very little time together, and Henry regretted this. There was no way they could get through this if they did not communicate. It was obviously his fault, because Melody had made several attempts to talk with him, but he always made up an excuse as to why he did not have the time. *God, why couldn't he just get over it and move on? After all, he was supposedly dead, and Melody had the right to get on with her life. So what, if she did not grieve for a long time! Would he have really wanted her to spend the rest of her life alone? Would he really be so selfish that he would deny his daughter a father's love?* All this made sense to Henry, but for some reason, he could not get over being jealous that Melody had been with another man.

Henry made up his mind that he would quit avoiding her and that he would start spending more time with her. He also needed to try to get to know his daughter. He had barely spent anytime with her since he had found out that she was his. Since it was such a beautiful day, he would go to the house and get Cook to fix a lunch and take Melody and the children out for a picnic. Henry turned his horse around and headed back to the house.

Melody was in the nursery, playing with the children when Henry found her. She looked so lovely sitting at the child's table, playing tea with the girls. Melody looked surprised when she saw him. It was the first time he had visited the nursery.

Henry walked over to the table, smiled at them, and said, "May I join you ladies for some tea?" Mary Elizabeth looked up at him with her gorgeous blue eyes and nodded her head. He kneeled down beside her, and his daughter pretended to pour him some tea, and then she handed him a tiny cup. Henry had a hard time holding the cup, but he managed somehow, and he pretended to drink. Mary Elizabeth started to giggle and got a big smile on her face.

"How would you lovely ladies like to go on a picnic with me today? I've just been outside and decided that it was too lovely of a day to spend it alone. What do you say? Will you come with me?" Henry asked as he smiled at his beautiful daughter.

Melody looked at Henry and smiled as she replied, "Thank you, kind sir. That would be delightful."

Mary Elizabeth turned to Henry and asked, "Can my fiend An . . . ge . . . wa come too?"

"Of course, she can. In fact, all of you can come. Roderick, would you like to come on our picnic?" Henry asked.

Roderick nodded his head, so they all headed out to the grounds for the picnic. Henry made arrangements for the pony cart to be brought around, and they all got in. When they arrived at the lake, Melody laid out the blanket. Brandon was fascinated with the grass and kept trying to pull it out of the ground and put it in his mouth. Every time she would get him back on the blanket, he would take off again; he was just too fast for her. Henry kept running and picking him up and carrying him back to the blanket. Roderick was skipping rocks and really doing it quite well. Mary Elizabeth and Angela were playing "Ring around the Rosie." Finally, Brandon fell asleep, and then Henry and Melody were able to relax a bit and talk. Henry found that he enjoyed being with her and the children. He realized that he had never been on a picnic with children before, and it was fun. Melody had a big smile on her beautiful face, and she was laughing at all the antics of the girls. Soon, it was time to eat, so she called the children over. Cook had packed roasted chicken, cheese, bread, and fresh fruit with a jug of apple cider to drink. Everyone enjoyed the meal, and Brandon woke up and ate his share too. Melody had to pull the chicken into little bite-size pieces for him. After everyone was finished eating, the girls laid down and fell asleep. Roderick went back to skipping rocks. Melody cradled Brandon in her lap. As Henry watched Melody, he could see what a good mother she was and she obviously loved her children very much.

As Melody rocked Brandon in her lap, she said, "I'm glad you thought of the picnic, Henry. This is the first picnic I've been on in several years. Remember the picnics we used to have in Hyde Park? We had so much fun that summer."

"I remember how much fun I had watching you enjoy yourself, just like you've done today. I realized something: if we don't spend time together, how can we possibly hope to overcome our difficulties? I have made up my mind that we should spend more time together. I need to get to know my daughter. Melody, she's so beautiful, and I'm so pleased that we had a child. I don't think that I've told you that. Can we start to get to know each other again?" he asked, while looking into her gorgeous sherry-colored eyes.

Brandon started fussing a bit so Melody picked him up and placed him on her shoulder, which seemed to calm him down again, and then she said, "I'm thrilled that you want to spend time with me. I've been very distressed and worried because I knew you were avoiding me. I agree that the only way to move on is to get to know each other again. What was it like when you were in Brussels?"

As Henry watched her with Brandon, he said, "It was very frustrating to not know who I was. The monks were dedicated men, and they lived together in such harmony. It was a very peaceful and fulfilling life, but I just knew there was something different for me. I could feel that I was used to a much more energetic life than the one I was living with them. I did their bookkeeping, so it helped me feel that I was contributing something, since they had taken me in. Father Francis and I would get into deep philosophical discussions, and I learned to be patient. I realized that I was not a very patient person by nature. When my memory returned, all I could think about was getting back to you."

With a sympathetic expression in her lovely eyes, Melody replied, "I can just imagine how frustrating it must have been to have no memory at all. I'm sure it was shocking when you did get your memory back to find out so much time had passed."

Glancing over at Roderick, making sure he was all right, he continued, "When Father Francis told me I had been with them for two and a half years, my first thought was of you. I knew you must have thought I was dead after so much time. Then when I found out they had even brought back a body when I got back, well, needless to say, I realized why you believed I was dead. All I wanted to do was get to you. It was so exasperating when I kept running into obstacles that kept me from coming to you. I knew I couldn't leave Nelson, but I was torn, because I wanted to come get you. I hated to see Nelson in so much pain. God, I wondered so many times, why him. Nelson was a wonderful brother to my sisters and me, and I felt it was so unfair that just when he had found someone to love, he became so ill. I spend time with him everyday before he died. He asked me to take care of his Mary, because he loved her very much, and it was clear that she loved him deeply. She would bring the children to see him in the morning when he was feeling his strongest."

Melody kept Brandon entertained while they talked, and then she said, "I'm still struggling with accepting that Nelson is gone. I don't know what I would have done without him. I just collapsed during your funeral, and he had to hold me to keep me from falling. I'm sure his death must have devastated your father."

With a look of utter sadness, Henry replied, "Father was a broken man. Melody, he apologized to me and said that the reason he had been so hard on me was because I reminded him of himself when he was young. He told me he was proud of the man I had become, and he spent every morning working on estate business with me. He wanted to try to prepare me for the role of duke, since I had never been involved in running this huge operation. Father knew he was going to die soon. He told me he had been having heart palpitations for quite some time. I felt terrible that I couldn't do more. He told me to go get you and bring you home, just as soon as we laid Nelson to rest. Of course, it took a fortnight after his death before I was able to leave."

Melody gazed at Henry and said, "I'm so glad your father made his peace with you before he died. I'm sure that meant the world to you. I can just imagine how awful it was when you received the news about his heart attack. At least you were able to see him before he died."

Henry felt his heart ache at the mention of his father as he said, "Thank God, I got here before he died. He woke up and tried to talk to me, but he was just too weak. He passed away a few days later while I was sitting with him. After the funeral, I had so many things to do. I had to visit all the properties spread out all across England. I left Doncaster Stables last, because I knew that Lincolnshire was close by. When I went to your parents' house, and found out they had both died, I panicked because the new vicar didn't know where you had gone. I remembered Susan was from there, so I went to see her mother. She was the one that gave me your address. When I got to your house, and found you so ill, I almost came apart at the thought of losing you, just when I had found you again. I felt as if I were living through hell here on earth, and wondered when it would all stop. Melody,

I know I have been very unfair to you about what happened. I guess I'm a very selfish man, because I can't stand the idea that you were with another man. I know we can get through this, as long as we both try. Now tell me how it was for you."

Melody looked over at the girls, making sure they were still asleep, and then she said, "I was at Sanderford Park. Kathryn and I had come back from London the middle of May. I had never intended to go for the season . . . I just went so that I could be there for Helen, and so Kathryn could go. The day Nelson came home unexpectedly, I sensed something was terribly wrong immediately. He asked to speak with me in the study. His face had such a serious expression, and his eyes were full of pain. I didn't want to believe him at first. I kept insisting that it was a mistake, because I didn't feel that you were dead. I just knew I should have felt it, if it were true. When he told me, what Captain Hayden had said and how he had brought your body back that was when I started to believe. He found one of my letters on the ground beside the body, and that is what finally convinced me. I just wish I had demanded to see the body, because then I would have known it wasn't you."

"Melody, I'm sure they wouldn't have let you see the body, even if you had asked. From what I understand, the fellow's face was completely destroyed. Nelson would never have wanted you to see something like that. I'm so sorry you had to go through all that." Henry reached over and gently touched her face, and Melody looked relieved that he seemed to understand what she went through.

Melody met his gaze as she said, "Once the funeral was over, all I could think about was getting to my parents. I just knew that I would be all right if I just got to them. Nelson was wonderful. I cried the whole way to Lincolnshire, and I kept throwing up every time I tried to eat anything. I couldn't even keep water down. By the time we got to my parents, I was very ill. My parents were afraid that I would lose the child, but once I found out about the baby, it was as if I willed myself to get well. I started eating and refused to be sick any longer. I would fight the nausea. Everyday, I felt a little bit better until I was recovered physically, but mentally, I was broken. I cried until there were no more tears to cry. As the months went by, and I began to see the baby growing inside me, it got a little better. When I felt the baby move for the first time, I felt such joy. I knew you would live on through our child. It helped tremendously to have Brandon to talk with. As he had lost his wife, he understood what I was going through. Without him, I don't know that I would have been able to survive the grief."

Henry looked anguished as he said, "God, why did this have to happen? Neither one of us deserved to have to go through this. I'm sure you gained comfort from talking with Brandon since he had recently lost Lily, but as I said before; I just wish you hadn't married him. I hope you didn't have too difficult of a time having Mary Elizabeth. I'm relieved that you had your mother with you for her birth."

Brandon tried to crawl away, but Melody stopped him, and then replied, "I had an easy delivery, only six hours, and when I saw her, I saw you in her face. She had your red gold curls and your penetrating blue eyes. I thanked God everyday for giving me such a precious gift. I began to feel the pain of losing you lessen, once I had our daughter. She became my reason for living."

Henry smiled over at her and said, "I'm glad you had her. I just wish I could have been there when she was born. It must have been extremely difficult to lose both your parents at once. I do realize you had quite a few terrible events happening close together."

"My parents got influenza, and they died two weeks apart. My father died first and then my mother. The only thing that kept me going was our daughter. That was when I truly got scared, because as I told you before, I found out that all I had was five hundred pounds and a few pieces of furniture. I know now that I wasn't thinking clearly. Of course, you wouldn't have left me without resources. I should have realized it then, but unfortunately, I didn't. When I moved into that cottage, I was very frightened because I had never lived alone before. Brandon was such a good friend to me. I hate to think what I would have done if I hadn't had his help. When he came to me and asked me to marry him, my first reaction was a resounding no, but then I thought of my choices, and there were only two in my mind at the time. Either contact your family or marry Brandon. I really did fear your parents. I never told you how bad it really was living with them. I prayed about it and asked God to help me make the right decision. When I woke up the next morning, I knew that marrying Brandon was the right thing to do. Mary Elizabeth needed a father, and I admit it, I didn't want to spend the rest of my life alone. We married quietly, and we immediately moved to Doncaster. Brandon left it up to me to tell him when I was ready to consummate the marriage. Truthfully, I never wanted to consummate the marriage, but I knew that it wouldn't be fair to him. I had taken vows and would stand behind them. Brandon made it easy for me, because he wasn't a very demanding man. Making love with him was pleasant, but nothing remotely like the passion we shared and still do, if the other day was an example. I found out I was with child shortly before Christmas. This time, I recognized the signs much faster. We had a good marriage. It was very peaceful, and I was content." Henry knew he had to be understanding, but it tore him up when she talked about her marriage to Brandon. *Oh god, why couldn't he move past this!*

Melody checked on the girls again, and they were still sleeping, so she continued, "When Brandon died, I found out again that I was in for hard financial times. All I had were some investments, and there was one thousand pounds in his account. I wondered again how I would make it. I didn't deal well with his death. At first, I was very melancholy, and I wasn't eating enough, but then I told myself that I had to go on for the sake of the children. It was shortly after that, that I became ill. Well, the rest you know, so that's my story."

"I'm glad we talked today. I don't know about you, but I feel lighter. I feel as if much has been lifted from my shoulders. This is a start toward healing from all this. Well, it's getting late, so we need to head back to the house." As they gathered up the children, Mary Elizabeth and Angela woke up, and Brandon had fallen asleep again. They all got in the cart and rode home. Melody took the children up to the nursery, and Henry took the cart to the stables.

After that day, things were better between them. It was as if they silently agreed to avoid discussing what had happened, but it hung there, right under the surface, so they still didn't grow as close as he knew Melody would have liked. He just was not ready to forgive her, and he knew she was incredibly sad over this.

CHAPTER 20

Late July 1818

AT THE END of July, Henry had to go to London. He was making his first appearance in the House of Lords. He was expected to make a speech, so he had been working on it daily with Stallings, for the last week. Henry told Melody he would be gone for at least a fortnight. He also needed to meet with his solicitor about issues with some of his investments.

He traveled by coach, since he was taking Stallings and Mansfield with him. This made the trip longer, but they still made good time, because the weather was clear. Of course, Henry almost wished it were raining, because it had been so dry this year. They really needed rain badly.

Once they arrived at Sanderford House, Henry went to his rooms and freshened up. After he was dressed, he headed to White's where he planned on meeting Weston and some of his other friends. When he arrived at his club, he immediately found Weston. "Have you been waiting long?"

Weston shook his head as he answered, "No, I just sat down a few minutes ago. How's everything going? I got your letter telling me about Melody. Are you reconciled to the situation yet?"

"It's been difficult. I'm overjoyed that I found her, but it's tearing me up inside when I think of her with another man. I never thought I was a jealous man, but evidently I am. She's being so accommodating that I almost wish she would get angry with me. I've been avoiding her and haven't even spent much time with my daughter. Weston, Mary Elizabeth is beautiful, and she looks so much like Helen did as a child. I made the decision to spend more time with her and my daughter, but then I had to come here to make this damned speech. I tell you, I'm really dreading it. I'm not a politician . . . I'm a soldier." Henry bowed his head in frustration.

Weston straightened his cravat and flicked an imaginary piece of lint from the shoulder of his dark blue superfine dress coat as he said,

"Everything will work out. You just need to give it time. After all, you have been apart for three years. From what you told me, Melody had to face quite a few challenges, and you told me that your parents treated her badly. I can understand why she didn't want to go to them. Melody was devastated over your death. I spoke with her at the funeral, and she could barely talk; she was so distraught. As far as the speech goes, you'll do fine. I remember when I had to deliver mine. It's tough on the nerves. When do you go in front of Parliament?"

With an expression of exasperation on his face, as he adjusted his blue embroidered waistcoat, he replied, "The day after tomorrow. Stallings has been invaluable. I see why my father thought so highly of him." Henry looked up and saw Hayden crossing the room. This was the first time that he had seen him since his return.

Hayden rushed over when he saw Henry and clapped him on the shoulder as he exclaimed, "God, it's good to see you! I still can't believe you're alive. I saw you fall, and when I was finally able to get back to you, I thought it was you. Of course, it was hard to tell, because the poor man's face was shot all the hell. He had the same color of hair and the same build as you. Old friend, if I had had any idea that it wasn't you, I would have said so. Did you ever find out who that poor bastard was?"

Henry shook his head, as he answered, "So far, we haven't had any luck. It turns out, there are quite a few men missing that fit the description. I'm glad to see that you made it back in one piece. Were you injured at all?"

Hayden grinned, and then laughed as he replied, "You know me; I've always been a lucky bastard. I didn't get a scratch on me. Can't say that for Bronson. You heard that he lost his arm, right?"

"Yes, remember his sister married my brother, Nelson. She's having a terrible time accepting Nelson's death. Walks around like a ghost, most of the time. I'm hoping that Melody can help her." Henry turned back to Weston and asked, "Are you ready to go to dinner?" He then looked over at Hayden and asked, "Hayden if you don't have any plans, can you join us?"

"I have to be at Lady Martin's ball at nine o'clock, so I can, as long as I get there in time. I promised my mother I would be there. Now that I'm my uncle's heir, she has is it in her head that it's time for me to get married! It's the last thing I want to do, but I thought I would humor her a bit and show up tonight to get her off my back. If she thinks I'm looking, she'll leave me alone," Hayden answered.

Weston spoke up and said, "I'm thinking about taking a wife and setting up my nursery. My sisters will be coming out this next season, so a wife would come in handy. I was planning to go to Lady Martin's ball, but I won't get there until ten o'clock. Henry, do you want to come along? It's time you got back into society."

Henry rolled his eyes, but then he said, "I know you're right, but I'm dreading all the stares and the questions. You have to admit, not many men come back from the dead! I guess this ball will be as good as any to face the ton."

They all went to dinner and then on to Lady Martin's. It was ten o'clock before they got there, so the receiving line had already dissolved. It was not as awful as he had expected. Now that he was a duke, most of the people were too busy acting as if he were someone special and offering him their condolences to ask many questions about where he had been for the last three years. After he made himself known to his host, he spent the rest of the evening in the card room and ended up winning several hundred pounds from Weston. Henry left to go home around midnight.

His speech went better than he expected. *Thank God for Stallings! That man was brilliant.* His meeting with his solicitor was another story. He partly blamed the man, because he should have made more of an attempt to get in touch with Melody when he supposedly died. His solicitor apologized profusely and agreed with Henry. He should have gone up north to see her personally instead of leaving it alone when he did not receive a response from his letters.

He fell into a pattern: mornings he would go to Gentlemen Jackson's and go a few rounds with Weston, and then they would take lunch at their club. He spent the afternoon at Parliament and then on to some kind of function in the evening.

Henry missed Melody. He knew they were never going to get back together if he stayed gone all the time. Only a few more days, then Parliament would rest, and he could leave for Sanderford Park. He was determined to get through the issue he had with Melody, and he could only do it if he was able to spend time with her. A little wooing might not be a bad idea. Even if he had not completely forgiven her, they could still resume sexual relations. After all, they were married, he did still love her, and he felt that she still loved him.

Once Parliament was over for the summer, Henry made one last stop before he left London. He went to his favorite jeweler Gerard's and picked out a beautiful strand of matched pearls for Melody. He could just see her wearing them. Of course, he'd rather see them on her when she was naked. He was still having dreams about making love to her, and he was damned tired of waking up with an erection as hard as stone almost every morning.

The trip was grueling, because they were finally getting some rain, but, of course, they did not need a torrential downpour either. This heavy of a rain could damage the crops. Henry made it home in time for tea and found everyone in the drawing room. He noticed that Mary was there and almost looked cheerful as she was having an animated conversation with Melody when he walked in.

Melody looked up and asked, "Henry, when did you get back? I wasn't expecting you for a few more days."

Henry went over to her, leaned down, and kissed her on the cheek. "I was able to get all my business handled faster than I had anticipated. How are the children? Have you been on anymore picnics?"

She looked pleased that he had asked about the children. Melody smiled as she answered, "The children are fine, and we went on one yesterday. Good thing, we didn't plan it for today. Isn't this rain horrible? I know that we needed it, but did we have to get it all in one day? I imagine that it made the trip miserable."

Henry sat down as his mother handed him his cup of tea. "The rain did cause the trip to take longer. I just hope it doesn't hurt the crops." Henry drank his tea and ate a full plate of sandwiches. Then he asked Melody to come with him to the nursery so that he could see the children.

When they arrived at the nursery, the children had just gotten up from their naps. Brandon was a little cranky, as he was cutting some new teeth. Henry went over and kneeled down in front of his daughter. She looked at him warily, and it was apparent that she was still not sure if she liked him.

Henry asked her what she was doing and she said, "An . . . ge . . . wa and me take cawe of ouw babies. Mine has cowld."

Henry took out his handkerchief and proceeded to wipe the doll's nose. Mary Elizabeth started to giggle. When she looked at Henry, she seemed more relaxed with him. The girls asked him if he would read to them, so Henry pulled a book of fairy tales out and read it to them. Mary Elizabeth came over and leaned against him so she could see the pictures in the book. This was the first time his daughter had voluntarily touched him, and it was an incredible feeling. He looked over at Melody, and she had tears in her lovely eyes.

After they left the nursery, they went to their sitting room and entered together, and then Henry said, "Now that we're alone, may I have a kiss?"

She went over to Henry, rose up on her tiptoes, and kissed him. He put his arms around her and pulled her tight against him. He did not try to deepen the kiss. He left it up to Melody to take the lead. She ran her tongue across his lips, so he parted them, and Melody slipped her tongue into his mouth. She tentatively stroked the roof of his mouth and ran her tongue over his teeth. Henry groaned and deepened the kiss. He was becoming highly aroused; his erection pressed hard against Melody's belly. She put her arms around his waist and pulled him closer.

Henry looked down at her and said, "Melody, you do realize where this is headed, don't you? Are you sure, you want to make love? If you don't want to, I'll understand, but we need to stop what we're doing right now, if you aren't ready."

Melody coyly replied, "Henry, I want us to make love. I've missed you very much, and I'm so glad that you have returned."

Henry went over, locked the door, and then he came back and turned Melody around so he could unbutton her gown. With every button he released, he kissed his way down her back. When he got all the buttons unfastened, he pushed her gown over her hips, and it fell to the floor. He removed her corset and chemise, so all she had on were her stockings, garters, and slippers. He kneeled down and removed her slippers. Slowly, he rolled down her stockings and slipped them off her feet. He stood up behind her and pulled her close. As he was kissing the nape of her neck, his hand kneaded her breast. He gently squeezed her nipple, and it immediately grew taut. He lazily drew a circle around the areola. Melody was breathing fast as he turned her around and went down on his knees. He placed kisses on her belly and dipped his tongue in her naval. Then he nibbled kisses all the way down to the apex of her thighs, where her beautiful golden curls lay. He gently nudged her thighs apart and started licking and suckling her core. He felt Melody tremble as he kept licking and suckling, and he could tell that her passions were spiraling out of control.

"Henry, my knees . . . are shaking, and I feel as if there is a spring . . . coiling tighter . . . and tighter. Oh god, I'm . . . flying! Ah . . . Ah . . ." she sighed. Melody's knees did give away, and Henry lowered her to the floor. He pulled her on top of him, and she straddled his hips. His shaft was jutting up against her belly. He raised her and then lowered her onto the bulging head of his erection. She started moving, and soon she picked up his rhythm. Henry surged up and started lifting Melody up by her hips as their movements became more frenzied. Henry touched Melody's sweet little bud of desire. She tightened around him, and as she reached her peak, he let go and filled her sweet passage with his hot seed. Melody collapsed on top of him, and he hugged her close. They lay there, not moving for quite some time as their breathing returned to normal and their heartbeat slowed. Melody sighed and said, "Do you realize that both times we've made love since your return, it hasn't been in a bed?"

As Henry gently drew circles on her back, he replied, "Both times we've made love, were spontaneous. I hadn't planned on making love today, but I'm thrilled it happened. If we can get close in the marriage bed, then that may help me move past you giving your body to Brandon."

Melody stood up, took a deep breath, and she got an extremely angry expression on her face. Her eyes were flashing; her cheeks were flushed, and she started pointing her finger, then cried, "I'm getting very tired of having to defend my actions. Henry, I thought you were dead. I felt I had to move on with my life. Did you want me to spend the rest of my life mourning you? Your daughter needed a father, and I'll admit it, I wanted a husband! I didn't like being alone. I thought I couldn't financially support our daughter and myself. I know you think I should have come back here when my parents died, but I knew what it would be like. Even if your parents had let me keep my daughter, they would have controlled my life. They would have made my life a living hell, and you know it. I would have always felt as if I wasn't good enough for this family. You have seen how your mother treats me now. She's barely said anything to me, and she has never visited her granddaughter. You know that I'm right. You're just being stubborn about it! I'm going to take a bath, so you need to leave!"

Henry just stared at Melody. He could not believe what she was saying. *By God, if she wanted him to leave, then so be it.* Henry stood up, grabbed up his clothes, and stalked to his room. When Henry entered his room, he quickly dressed in his riding clothes, and left. He ran down the stairs and called for his horse. He left the stables at a gallop and continued to ride hard for miles. Finally, he calmed down and slowed his horse to a walk.

Well, that went well, he thought. What started out so promising . . . had escalated into an argument. He realized they had just had their first real argument. He did not know how he felt about that. When they were together before he left for the continent, they never had a cross word between them. This he did know: Melody was magnificent when she was angry. Her eyes were flashing, and she was pointing her little finger at him. He was getting hard just thinking about it. He had planned on giving her the necklace, but when she got so mad, he forgot all about it. She finally admitted it. She had wanted to marry Brandon. Henry thought about what Melody said, and he realized she had asked the same questions he had asked of himself weeks ago. *Was he such a selfish bastard that he would rather have had Melody spend the rest of her life alone?* When Nelson lost Nora, he had encouraged Nelson to move on with his life and to find someone he could be happy with. That was exactly what Melody did. She had moved on with her life instead of crawling in the grave with him. She stood on her own two feet and made sure his daughter was taken care of and had a father's love. He should be ashamed of himself. If only he could just get the image out of his mind of Melody with Brandon! He wondered if it would have been easier if she had married a stranger. He remembered what Brandon looked like, and in his mind's eye, he could see them making love, and it was driving him mad. *What could he do to move beyond this?* Henry was very heart sore, because he knew he was hurting Melody with his jealousy, and she did not deserve this treatment. She was right to be angry with him. She had not done anything wrong by marrying again. *For God's sake, he was jealous of a dead man.*

Henry spent the rest of the evening aimlessly riding with no direction in mind. Finally, he turned his horse around and headed home. By the time he got there, he had missed dinner, and everyone had evidently gone to bed. He went into his study and poured himself a large glass of brandy; he then drank it down in three gulps. He sat down in his chair and proceeded to get extremely drunk. The clock in the hall struck three times before he staggered up to bed.

CHAPTER 21

August 1818

AS THE REST of August passed, they had rain almost everyday. It was miserable weather but good for the crops. His tenants were in a much better mood, because now it looked like they would have a plentiful harvest. Henry was back to avoiding Melody, and this time she was not trying to smooth things over. Something was going to have to give, or they would spend the rest of their lives apart. It all came back to him, and it was his fault; they were apart. This was not working, so he needed to try a different approach. They had to start spending time together. It was definitely time to do some serious wooing, if he was ever going to get Melody back into his life and his bed.

That evening, he asked Melody if she would like to play a game of chess. They had played when they were living in Canterbury, so maybe it was a good place to start. Melody set up the chessboard, and they started to play. She was surprisingly good at chess, and before he knew it, she had taken his queen. He still ended up winning, but it had been a close game. The others had already gone up to bed by the time they finished their game.

Henry gazed into Melody's lovely sherry eyes and said, "Melody, I need to apologize to you. I've been avoiding you again. I've been thinking a lot about what you said, and I want us to start over. I want a chance to win your heart again. I'm willing to put it all into the past and start afresh. We need to spend time together, as we used to, and I realize that just because we are compatible in bed, doesn't mean it will fix all our problems. Are you willing to meet me halfway?"

Melody returned his gaze, and with joy glowing on her pretty face, she said, "Henry, I'm more than willing. Whether you believe this or not, I love you, and I've never stopped loving you. Even when I thought you were dead, I still loved you. I agree, making love is not going to fix our problems, but maybe evenings like this will. I enjoyed myself tonight, and it brought back some good memories. It's become quite late, and I'm getting tired, so I'm going up to bed. Will I see you tomorrow?"

"Why don't we go riding? We haven't done that for a while. I would also like to take the children to the lake again. We had fun that day. Let's meet at the stables tomorrow at ten o'clock. Will that be agreeable to you?" he asked, as he walked with her to the stairs.

"That's fine, I'll be there." Then Melody kissed him on the cheek and went upstairs to bed.

Henry watched her and knew he had made the right decision. Tonight had been pleasant, and he would make sure they had more evenings like this one in the future.

They went for their ride, and they talked about many things. This was the way they could begin to mend the break in their relationship. Later in the afternoon, they took the children down to the maze and let them play in the center, by the fountain. Brandon did his best to climb in, and Henry kept running after him to keep him out of trouble. For a child that had just learned to walk, he certainly moved very fast. Melody had brought a blanket, so she spread it out under the oak tree. Roderick, Mary Elizabeth, and Angela started playing hide-and-seek. It was so cute to watch the two little girls try to count.

"One, fieu, two, fouw, six, thwee, weady or not heyo I come," yelled Mary Elizabeth.

She would run as fast as her little legs would carry her. When she caught up with Angela, she would giggle. Of course, the little girls were easy to find, since they would giggle and give themselves away. Roderick would find them every time, and Henry found that he enjoyed watching the children. His daughter was so beautiful, and she was getting so big; it was hard to imagine that she was already over two and a half years old. He had missed so much. He certainly planned to take an active role with any future children they had, and he did not want to miss a single minute.

Brandon was an adorable child, and he looked just like Melody, but it was extremely difficult for Henry to feel close to him, because he was a constant reminder of the life Melody had while he was gone. He knew that it was important to Melody that he accept Brandon and treat him as a son, so he was trying to get close to him. In some ways, he owed it to Brandon's father, because he had been a good father to his daughter. Henry had never looked at it that way before, so maybe he was beginning to accept what had happened. There was no way to change the past, so all they could do was move forward.

Henry walked over to Mary Elizabeth and kneeled down. "Are you having a good time, little one? If you're getting tired, I would be happy to have you sit in my lap under the tree?"

Mary Elizabeth looked at him, shook her head, and then she ran over to Melody. Melody hugged her, then Mary Elizabeth ran back to Angela, and they started playing again.

Henry walked over to where Melody was sitting. With a despondent expression on his handsome face, he said, "I can't get her to interact with me. Other than a few times in the nursery, she won't even smile at me. What am I doing wrong?"

Melody gazed up at him and answered, "You're trying too hard to get her to respond to you. The best thing you can do is make sure you spend time with her, everyday. She needs to get used to you, and that will only happen with daily contact."

In frustration, Henry ran his fingers through his thick hair, causing it to look tousled as he replied, "Brandon comes to me, and I haven't spent any more time with him than I have with Mary Elizabeth."

Melody said, "Brandon is too small to remember his father. I know it's hard for you to hear, but Mary Elizabeth thought Brandon was her father. It will take a while for her to accept you. She'll eventually warm up to you. Just be patient."

Henry thought about what Melody was saying, and he knew she was right. "I told you I learned patience while I was with the monks, but I guess I still need to have more. I'll start spending time with her each day. When would be the best time of the day?"

Melody leaned back on her hands, crossed her ankles, and she had never looked lovelier to Henry. She looked thoughtful, and then she replied, "Definitely mornings, right after she has had breakfast is when she is most receptive. She has a full tummy, and she's wide awake. She takes her nap in the afternoons around one o'clock, and she usually sleeps for an hour. After her nap would be all right, but mornings would still be best."

Henry continued to watch Melody, and he wanted her so badly that he thought he would die if he did not make love to her soon. He brought his thoughts back and asked, "What time does she eat breakfast? I can usually take a break from my work at ten o'clock."

She drew her knees up, put her arms around them and said, "That would be an excellent time. I think it would be better if you go to the nursery without me. If she sees me, she'll want to stay by my side, and she'll be less likely to interact with you."

"I'll start going to see her each day as you have suggested. It does make sense to spend more time with her. I just love her desperately and long for the day when she will call me Papa. Well, as much as I've enjoyed this afternoon, I need to return to my study for a brief meeting with Stallings. We need to take the children back to the nursery, because it's also close to teatime, and you know how upset my mother gets if anyone is late." Melody folded up the blanket and took the children back to the nursery while Henry went to his meeting with Stallings.

When she arrived in the drawing room for tea, everyone was already there. Mary was staring out of the window with a woebegone look on her face. Helen and Kathryn were discussing the new bonnets and ribbons they had just bought in the village, and the dowager duchess was sitting on the settee ready to pour.

Henry's mother looked at Melody with venom in her eyes as she said, "Where have you been? Your hair is hanging around your face, gel. You should have fixed it before you came to tea. I see that you have put on some weight. You were looking slimmer when you first came back, but now you are getting plump again."

Henry sternly stared directly into his mother's eyes and said, "Mother, I don't want you talking to Melody that way. If you don't have anything nice to say, then don't say anything at all. I will no longer tolerate you treating her like this. She is not a girl; she's my wife and you will address her in the manner she deserves. Now may I have my tea?" The dowager duchess poured Henry his tea and handed it to him. Everyone sat drinking in silence.

Melody walked over, stood by Mary, and asked, "How are you feeling today? We just came back from the maze. We took the children there to play, and they had a delightful time. Mary Elizabeth enjoys having Angela as a friend, and she likes Roderick also. Would you like to come with us the next time we take the children out?"

Mary sighed deeply, looked down at her hands, which she was twisting nervously, and said, "I know that I need to do more with the children, but I'm just too blue most of the time, and children need someone who can laugh and play with them."

"Mary, Nelson wouldn't want you to grieve so for him. You brought joy to his life when he had none. He would want you to be happy. You have two beautiful children to live for, and that's a blessing," Melody gently replied.

With tears in her deep brown eyes, Mary answered, "I know that you're right. I'll try to do better, and I'll come with you the next time you take the children out to play."

Everyone finished their tea. Kathryn and Helen decided to go for a walk, and they convinced Mary to come with them. Melody excused herself and went to her room.

Melody thought about the conversation she had had with Henry. She hoped he would follow through with his plans to spend more time with Mary Elizabeth. He did seem to be trying to forget about her marriage to Brandon, but only time would tell if he was ever going to forgive her. She did not want to live the rest of her life waiting for that to happen. If he was unable to forget, then after she gave him an heir, she would ask him for a legal separation. It was just too difficult to love him and not have her love returned.

The first two weeks of September went by quickly. Henry was very busy with the harvest, but he still found time to go to the nursery and visit his daughter. He asked Melody to organize the Harvest Feast, so she was extraordinarily busy. She went to the village and met with the innkeeper to make sure there would be enough ale and food for all the tenant farmers and villagers. Cook was very helpful, because she had participated in many Harvest Feasts. All the wheat and barley were harvested by the middle of September, so they held the feast on Saturday. All the women of the village brought baked goods, and Henry supplied the rest of the food. They held the feast in the evening, and there was a huge bonfire with musicians so there could be dancing. Melody was excited, because she remembered how much fun she had at Harvest Feasts when she was a child. They arrived just as the dancing started. Henry grabbed her around the waist and pulled her onto the dance area. It was so much more relaxed than the formal dancing at a ball. She and Henry danced every dance, and she loved every minute of it. By the end of the evening, many of the men of the village and tenant farmers were definitely feeling no pain from all the ale they were drinking. Henry had indulged with the men. There was a lot of backslapping and congratulations, because the harvest had turned out to be so bountiful. They would not have to worry about the upcoming winter.

At the end of the evening, they gathered up Helen and Kathryn and headed home. They were all tired, so they went straight upstairs to bed. Henry knocked on Melody's door, and she opened it so he could come in. As Henry entered, he asked, "Did you have a good time tonight? I'm feeling the effects of all the ale that I drank."

Melody gave him a brilliant smile as she said, "Oh, Henry, I had a marvelous time. Thank you for asking me to help. I used to love the Harvest Feasts we had at home, so this brought back fond memories."

"I'm glad you had such a good time. I appreciate what you have been trying to do for Mary. She seems a little bit better. I know you have encouraged her to join you when you take the children out to play. I believe I'm getting somewhere with Mary Elizabeth. She actually let me hug her today!" Henry said with a huge grin on his handsome face.

Melody was so pleased for him. She knew how much he wanted Mary Elizabeth to call him Papa. She looked lovingly at him as she said, "That's wonderful, Henry! I told you that if you were patient, it would all work out. I feel sure she'll accept you as her father soon. Before you know it, she'll be calling you Papa!"

"Melody, I would like to spend the night with you tonight. I'll understand if you don't want to, but I miss sleeping with you. Remember how it was in Canterbury?" he asked. "We shared a bed every night. We don't need to make love . . . I just want to hold you in my arms as we sleep."

Melody quietly said, "Henry, I've missed sleeping with you too. I would love to sleep in your arms, and I want to make love with you. I would never deny you my bed. I know that you need to have an heir, and that won't happen if we don't share a bed."

Henry looked deeply into her eyes as he said, "Melody, as much as I want to make love to you I don't want you doing it out of a sense of duty. I want you to desire me the way I desire you."

"Oh, Henry, I do desire you desperately." Henry walked over to Melody, pulled her into his arms, and kissed her passionately. She returned his kiss with all the love she had in her heart. He picked her up and carried her to the bed. Then he lay her down and got into bed with her. They started kissing each other, with their tongues entwined. Melody almost forgot to breathe, in the glory of his kiss. He pushed her nightgown off her shoulders and unbuttoned it down to her waist. He opened it up and gazed at her lovely breasts.

"Melody, I have always loved your delectable body, and you're getting those luscious curves back again! Don't ever think that you are too plump. I love every beautiful inch of your body. Your breasts have the prettiest nipples: all rosy and puckered up ready for my touch. They look like tight little rosebuds." And he bent down, took her nipple into his mouth, and suckled on it. His hand was gently twisting her other nipple. "I could feast on your breasts all night, and your sweet aroma of lemons arouses my desire to fever pitch. I've always loved the smell of lemons, and your own special essence just drives me insane!"

Henry caressed her belly, and soon his finger slid down to her golden curls. He touched her sweet spot, and Melody began to writhe. She pushed her pelvis against his hand as his fingers found her entrance and slid home. Melody could feel her passion escalating higher and higher, and soon she was falling off the edge into ecstasy. He pushed her thighs wide apart, moved in between them, and thrust into her hot sweet passage. "Oh my darling! It feels like heaven to be inside you like this! I . . . can't hold out . . . much longer. Oh god!" He began to move in and out, over and over again, and Melody felt her body responding. Before she knew it, wild sensations rolled over her as Henry thrust one more time and then let out a shout, "Melody, my sweet!" just as he emptied his seed into her. He rolled to his side, taking Melody with him, and they lay there in peaceful surrender as they fell fast asleep.

Melody woke up, just as dawn was breaking and looked at his face. He looked so young and peaceful. She knew then that she could never live without him. There would be no legal separation. She would make him love her again. Surely, if they could feel this level of passion, there must be some love left in his heart for her. All she needed was just a small piece, and she would make it grow.

As he opened his eyes, he smiled at her as he said, "Good morning. Did you sleep all right? This was the best night's sleep I've had in over three years. It's so nice waking up to your smiling face."

Melody stretched and sighed as she replied, "It was the best night's sleep for me also. I've missed waking up in your arms. Those first months after I thought you had died were excruciating. My sleep was constantly tormented with images of us making love. I burned for your touch, and most nights, I ended up crying myself to sleep."

"Well, going forward, we'll just have to make sure we do this, every night. As much as I would like to lie in bed all day, I have to meet with Stallings early this morning. We're going over the harvest figures, and the yields were much better than expected. God, I hate to get out of this bed." Henry leaned over and gave her a quick kiss, got out of bed, and left to go get ready to face his day. She noticed that he had a bigger smile on his face than he had had in a long time.

After that night, Henry came to her bed every night. After they would make love, they would sleep in each other's arms all night. He did not bring up her marriage to Brandon, so Melody left well enough alone. She sensed that he still struggled with the thought of her being with Brandon, and he had not accepted that she had done no wrong by marrying again after his reported death, but she hoped he would soon.

Throughout the fall, they settled into a pattern. They went riding whenever the weather permitted, and then Henry would spend an hour with Mary Elizabeth. She was finally warming up to Henry, and she had even allowed him to give her some hugs. They spent their evenings together either playing chess or cards in the drawing room. Some evenings they would read to each other in the library. Henry's mother kept to herself and made no more derogatory comments. Melody actually felt sorry for her, because she had to be a very lonely woman. She tried reaching out to the duchess, but she was always rebuffed. Melody spent quite a bit of time with Helen and Kathryn. They would go into the village a couple of times a week, and even got Mary to come occasionally. Mary was beginning to get over her intense grief. Every time they took the children out to play, Melody saw joy in Mary's eyes as she played with her children.

Melody was now overseeing the management of the household. Henry had insisted that his mother turn everything over to her. Henry and his mother got into a heated argument, but he persevered, and Melody got the keys. It would have been so much easier on her if the duchess had been willing to help, but the housekeeper Mrs. Milton had been invaluable to Melody. Everyday, she would meet with her and decide on the agenda for the day, along with reviewing the menus that Cook had suggested. Running the household was very enjoyable to Melody, and she found it much less daunting than she had expected. She was concerned about taking her place in society as the Duchess of Sanderford. Here in the country, she had not found it difficult, but she knew it would be quite different with the ton. She had been corresponding with Susan and looked forward to having at least one friend when they went to town in the spring. Aunt Miriam had returned from the continent, so she would be there to help Melody navigate through society. Overall, she was fairly content. If Henry would only show more emotion, then she would be much happier. He was still holding a piece of himself apart from her. Their lovemaking was incredible, but Melody needed his love, and she was beginning to feel that it was not going to happen.

CHAPTER 22

December 1818

DECEMBER WAS AN incredibly busy month, because they began preparing for the holiday season. They were going to have the annual Christmas party, but because they were still in mourning, none of the ton would be attending. All of Henry's family would come, and most of them would need accommodations, since they would be staying for the entire Christmas season. She met with Mrs. Milton and discussed which bedchambers should be used, and Mrs. Milton even knew who should be placed where. Melody had Mrs. Milton see to cleaning all the rooms, so they would be ready for their houseguests. All the housemaids were very busy getting all the public rooms prepared. Simpson had the footmen cleaning the silver, which took several days. Everything was ready by December 18, and then it was time for Henry and his workers to gather the greenery and the Yule log that would be needed to decorate the house. Helen, Kathryn, and Mary helped out, but the dowager duchess refused to participate. Melody was saddened over this, because she remembered how much Henry's mother had enjoyed the Christmas season. She tried to reach out to her, but again, she was rebuffed. By the day before the party was scheduled, the house was ready and it looked quite festive. Greenery and holly adorned all the mantles and the banisters. Wreaths hung above all the fireplaces, and mistletoe hung from the crystal chandeliers. Everyone had worked together decorating all the rooms, and it all looked splendid.

The houseguests began to arrive, and the first person to get there was Aunt Miriam. Melody was so pleased she was able to come that she started crying and rushed into her aunt's loving arms. "Oh my darling girl, I'm so happy to see you again. It's been far too long. My goodness, how slim you are! Have you been taking care of yourself?"

Melody was thrilled to see her aunt again. It had been far too long indeed. She smiled and said, "I lost quite a bit of weight when I was ill last spring, but believe me I've put enough of it back on again. I'm sure that by the time the Christmas holiday ends, I'll have gained it all back! I'm so happy you were able to come. We must make time to catch up on everything, and I want to hear all about your travels. Come with me, and I'll show you to your room, so you can freshen up."

Melody took her aunt to the rose bedchamber but could not linger and chat, because other guests would be arriving soon. By the time Melody made it back downstairs, some of the family was already arriving. Thank goodness for Helen and Kathryn. They helped Melody with the names of all the family, since she had only met most of them once at Christmas four years ago. She did surprise herself, for she remembered them better than she expected. Henry was gracious as always and was a tremendous help. By teatime, most of the family had arrived that would be staying in residence.

Everyone met in the drawing room at four o'clock for tea. Melody was extremely nervous about serving tea to so many people, and Henry's mother refused to help her. Once she got started, she was fine, and soon everyone was chatting and drinking their tea. The footmen were there to replenish the sandwiches and biscuits, so that they did not run out. Henry came over to her and kissed her on the cheek as he said, "My dear, I'm so proud of you. You're every bit as gracious of a hostess as I knew you would be. Let me know if there's anything you need me to do." This thrilled Melody and helped to boost her sense of self greatly. After tea ended, everyone adjourned to his or her room to get ready for dinner.

Melody took Aunt Miriam up to the nursery so she could meet the children. This was the first time her aunt had ever seen them. The children were shy, but soon they had warmed up to her aunt, and she had them giggling and smiling in no time. Then Melody and Aunt Miriam went to her sitting room so they could talk.

As they took a seat, Aunt Miriam said, "I've never been to Sanderford Park before, and it's simply beautiful. I'm sure you enjoy living here. I know that we've been writing to each other, but there's only so much one can put in a letter. How are you doing?"

Melody smiled over at her aunt as she replied, "I know what you really want to know about . . . How is my relationship with Henry? We're not as close as we were before he went away. Aunt Miriam, he was so hurt that I got married when I thought he was dead. I'm not sure he can ever get over it and completely move past it. He hasn't told me he loves me since we got back together. I feel so confused about it all, and I'm not sure how to get through to him. It's wretched to love and feel that your love is not returned."

Lady Helton looked at Melody as she said, "Melody, I think you're wrong. If you could see the way he looks at you when he thinks no one is watching, then you would know that he loves you very much. Have you asked him if he loves you?"

Melody shook her head and said, "No, I'm afraid of the answer. I couldn't bear to have him tell me no. I couldn't stay with him if I knew he didn't love me. I had thought about seeking a legal separation once I gave him an heir, but then I decided that I would fight for his love."

"Good for you. Don't give up on him. Just give him more time and make sure that he remembers all the reasons why he fell in love with you, to begin with," she said.

"I love him too much to quit trying to gain back his love. My goodness, look at the time. We need to get ready for dinner." Melody kissed her aunt's cheek and then Aunt Miriam left to go back to her room.

Dinner went well. Conversation flowed freely, and there was much laughing and joking. Every course was superb, and she would make sure she let Cook know how much everyone enjoyed the dinner. It seemed so strange to be sitting at the end of the table, but Henry had insisted that it was her right, because she was his duchess and deserved to be treated as such. Melody stood up and led all the ladies out of the dining room, so the men could enjoy their port and cigars.

The gentlemen did not spend very long over their port and cigars, because they soon entered the drawing room. Melody noticed that Mary was mingling with the family, and it pleased her. Finally, she seemed to be doing much better at handling her grief. After thirty minutes, Melody ordered tea, and soon everyone was drinking their tea and conversation continued.

Henry came over to her and said, "You've done a splendid job of organizing all of this. I always knew you would be an excellent duchess."

"I have to admit, it isn't as difficult as I had expected. Of course, this is only family, not the ton. We'll see how I handle all those stuffy matrons and the dragons of the ton that lord it over everyone, when we go to London in the spring." Then thinking of Kathryn, she asked, "Have you noticed how quiet Kathryn has been this evening? She seemed to be coming out of her shell, but she's withdrawn again. What do you think has changed?"

Henry looked frustrated, and she knew he was worried about Kathryn as he said, "I'll try to get her alone and ask her if something is bothering her. She's been so excited about getting to go to town in the spring for her come out, that I'm surprised she has crawled back into her shell. She appears to be watching the door as if she expects someone to arrive, but all the family is here in this room, so that can't be it . . . Wait a minute! Uncle Theodore didn't make it here today. He's due to arrive tomorrow. Do you think that could be what's causing her to be anxious? You know she's afraid of him."

"That could be it, Henry. She detests the man, and I don't blame her. He's a thoroughly unpleasant individual, and I wish we didn't have to invite him. I understand that he's your mother's brother, but, nonetheless, I still wish we could have excluded him," she said with a worried expression on her sweet face.

Several of the young people came over to Melody and asked if they could go to the ballroom and dance, and since Melody did not see a problem with it, they all moved to the ballroom. Mary offered to play so that everyone could dance. Soon, everyone was dancing and having a marvelous time. Before they knew it, it was time to end the evening, and everyone went upstairs to their rooms.

Uncle Theodore showed up the next afternoon, just as everyone was going to the drawing room for tea. Melody watched Kathryn, and it was obvious that she was extremely nervous. As soon as she saw her uncle, she immediately stiffened her body as if she were afraid of an attack. Melody looked for Henry and spied him over by the mantle in a discussion with his cousin Harold. She tried to get his attention, but was unsuccessful. Helen walked by, and Melody asked her to get Henry for her. Henry came over and asked, "You wanted me, my dear? Is there something that you need?"

"Kathryn is very anxious. As soon as your uncle walked into the room, she looked frightened to death. Henry, do you think he's continued to bother her?" she asked. "Neither one of us have been here to make sure he behaved himself. Do you think he might have hurt her in someway? I know she's been having nightmares recently, and I even found her sleepwalking again the other evening. I didn't say anything to you about it, because Kathryn begged me not to."

Henry looked over at Kathryn and said, "Last evening, I asked her what was wrong, but she wouldn't tell me. Maybe she'll talk to you. I certainly hope he hasn't done anything to her, because if he has hurt her in any way at all, he's a dead man!"

The next morning, Melody went to Kathryn's room to talk to her. "Are you all right, Kathryn? I noticed you became very anxious yesterday when Uncle Theodore arrived. Did he continue to bother you when Henry wasn't here to protect you?"

Kathryn hesitantly answered, "It's been difficult to be around him each year. The Christmas after Henry supposedly died, he started trying to bother me again. I was able to get away from him and I told Nelson what had transpired, so Nelson had it out with him, and he hasn't bothered me since. I'm just afraid he'll try something, so I'm constantly on my guard when he's around. I don't want you and Henry to worry about me. I'll come to you immediately if he so much as looks at me the wrong way. Thank you for being concerned, but I'll be fine. I'll just make sure that I'm never alone with him."

Melody found Henry in the library and told him what Kathryn had said. He wanted to confront his uncle, but Melody convinced him to leave well enough alone, since Kathryn said he hadn't bothered her since Nelson had handled it for her.

The party went off beautifully. Everyone danced, laughed, and had a good time. Helen practiced flirting with all her male cousins. She told Melody that she had to keep her skills sharp, since they would be going to town for the season in the spring. The next several days were exceptionally busy. There were games and activities everyday to entertain their guests. Everyone seemed to be having a wonderful time, but Melody found it all very taxing on her nerves. Christmas day was enjoyable. Henry finally gave Melody the pearls, and she was thrilled with them. Melody turned around so Henry could put them on her, and they looked lovely against her creamy white skin. They had agreed to have another small party for New Years, just inviting a few of the neighbors along with the family.

The New Year's party was a wonderful idea, and everyone was having a superb time as they all sang in the New Year together. Melody noticed that Kathryn was not in the room and went to look for her. She could not find her, so she asked Henry to look with her. They checked all the usual places downstairs, but she was not in any of those rooms. Melody had already checked to see if she had gone to her bedchamber, but she was not there either. They became very worried, especially when they realized that Uncle Theodore was also missing. They went upstairs to Theodore's room, and as they approached, they heard what sounded like a muffled scream, and it was coming from Theodore's room. Henry tried the door, but it was locked. He backed up and hit the door hard with all his weight and the door flew back. They rushed into the room and saw that Theodore had Kathryn pinned to the bed. Her gown was pushed up to her waist, and Theodore's breeches were down around his ankles. Kathryn was trying to fight him off, but he was just too big. Henry grabbed his uncle and threw him against the wall. Theodore hit his head and fell to the floor. Kathryn was crying hysterically and shaking all over. Melody went to her and tried to help her cover up. Her gown had been ripped, shoved down to her waist, and her breasts were exposed. Henry grabbed his uncle and turned him over. He started to pound his fists into his face. Melody was afraid that Henry was going to kill him, so she yelled, "Henry, please stop. He's not worth going to gaol over." Through a blind haze of anger, Henry heard her and stopped hitting the bastard. Melody wrapped a blanket around Kathryn. Henry checked his uncle and found that he was still breathing. He walked out of the room, found a footman, and had him go get his cousin Harold, and then he walked back into the room. Harold arrived and could immediately see what had happened. He looked shocked, but agreed to make sure that Theodore did not try to leave. Henry gathered Kathryn in his arms and took her to her room. Melody went ahead and opened the door for him. He went into the room and lay Kathryn on her bed.

He turned to Melody and whispered, "Can you take care of Kathryn? I need to go back and make sure that bastard doesn't get away."

She nodded her head, and Henry left the room. Melody went over to the bed and sat down on the edge. Kathryn was sobbing, but she was no longer shaking. She placed her hand on Kathryn's shoulder and asked, "Are you up to telling me what happened? How did he hurt you, Kathryn?"

Kathryn sat up and cried, "He . . . he . . . tried to rape me I think, but I kept kicking my legs, so I think . . . I kept him from doing it."

Melody checked her for bruises, and she was mottled with them. They were all over her thighs, her breasts, and there were bruises on her arms, where it looked like he had grabbed her. Her nails were broken from where she had scratched at Theodore. There was no blood, so he had not penetrated her. She helped Kathryn take off her gown, found her night rail, and put it on her. She got Kathryn to lie down, and soon she cried herself to asleep. Henry returned, and Melody told him that his uncle had not finished the rape, because they had gotten there just in time.

"Thank God, I wanted to kill the bastard, but I knew I couldn't do it. I'm so thankful that you noticed Kathryn was missing. I've tied him up so he can't get away, and Harold is still guarding him. He assured me that he wouldn't say anything, and I put the fear of God in the footman. He won't be telling the maids or anyone else for that matter. He knows that not only would he lose his employment, but I would rip him apart. I don't know how we're going to keep this quiet, but we'll manage some way."

Henry lowered his head and looked as if there was a thousand pounds resting on his shoulders. Melody wished there was something she could do to take some of this burden away, but she knew that only time would do that. Henry looked back up and said, "I need to go find Mother and tell her what has happened. I don't know how she will react, because she has always thought Theodore was such an upstanding gentleman and could do no wrong. She may refuse to believe that he tried to rape Kathryn. Will you stay with her, in case she wakes up? I'll go back down to the party, and if anyone asks where you or Kathryn are, I'll tell them that Kathryn was feeling ill and you went to help. Then I'll get Mother alone and tell her about this."

Henry found his mother in the drawing room. She immediately started questioning him, wanting to know where they had gone. "Mother, we need to talk, but it can't be here. We'll go to my study so we can talk privately." Henry found Helen and asked that she cover for them and that he would explain to her later what was going on. His mother followed him to his study. Henry asked her to sit down, and as he went and sat behind his desk, he said, "Mother, there has been an incident. I don't know how to tell you this gently, but your brother just tried to rape Kathryn!"

The duchess looked furious as she said, "What do you mean? There is no way that he would ever do something like that. You must be mistaken. The silly gel is probably exaggerating."

Henry looked at his mother with disgust on his face as he replied, "First of all, Kathryn is the most levelheaded young woman in the world. You know as well as I do, she doesn't behave like a silly girl! There is no mistake. I had to break down the door to get into the room as he was trying to rape her. I pulled him off her, just before he could do it. Your daughter was hysterical. Her gown was in shreds, and she was covered with bruises. Melody was able to calm her down and get her to go to sleep. She's still with her now."

The duchess folded her arms and irately said, "I will not believe it. You are lying. You have never liked Theodore, and you are just trying to cause trouble!"

Henry jumped up out of his chair, sending it back a few feet, as he answered, "If you don't believe me, go to Kathryn's room and look at her arms and legs. I promise you it happened, and your daughter needs to have your support. This is going to be very difficult for her to deal with. I know that you love your brother, but you have never been able to see him realistically. Everyone knows he's a ravaging old rogue. He's had a terrible reputation for years, and the only reason he's accepted anywhere is because he's your brother. Now I strongly recommend you accept that this has indeed happened and help me figure out how to keep this from becoming a scandal. The only ones that know what he tried to do are Harold, your brother, Melody, and me . . . oh and the footman, Melvin. I've made sure that none of them will say anything, and we've come up with a story to cover up why your brother has to leave before the holidays are over. I've convinced him that he needs to go abroad and stay gone for a very long time. He'll be leaving for the coast at daybreak."

Henry's mother sat down and just stared out the window. It was clear that she was in a state of shock. He went to her and tried to put his arm around her shoulders, but she shrugged him off. Henry left her where she was and returned to the party. Helen wanted to know what was going on, but Henry told her he would tell her after everyone went to bed. Finally, the party broke up, and they all retired for the evening.

He found Helen curled up on the couch in the library. She looked up at him as he entered the room and asked, "What's going on? Why did you, Melody, and Kathryn disappear, and then only you showed back up?"

Henry glanced over at her with sadness in his eyes as he answered, "Sweetheart, your uncle assaulted your sister's person tonight. She's all right, because Melody and I found them before he could hurt her."

"What do you mean when you say . . . he assaulted her? Are you saying that he . . . he . . . raped her?" she cried. "How can you say she's all right?"

Henry sadly shook his head as he ran his fingers through his hair and looked at Helen. "We got to him before he could complete the job. He didn't rape her, but it was a near miss. If we had arrived a minute later, we would have been too late. Your sister has some bruises, and of course, she's very distraught, but other than that, she will be fine. She'll need your help while she recovers from this ordeal."

Helen had tears running down her face as she looked at Henry and cried, "I should have done something about it . . . I knew that Kathryn was scared of him . . . and that she detested being around him. I should have made her tell me why she felt that way. I knew Uncle Theodore was a dastardly old rogue, but I never dreamed he would accost my sister in such a horrible way. Oh, Henry, does Mother know about this?"

Henry kneeled down beside her and put his arm around her as he quietly said, "Honey, I know you feel terrible about this, but Kathryn wouldn't have told you anything. Melody and I tried to get her to tell us why she hated him so, but all she would tell us is that he made her feel uncomfortable. I told Mother, but at first, she didn't want to believe it, then I finally convinced her that he had done it. I think I have diverted a scandal, because I convinced our uncle he needs to move to the continent and not return any time soon. Cousin Harold is the only one who knows what happened and you know he won't say anything. Why don't you go on up to bed? You can see Kathryn in the morning. Melody is spending the night with her so that if she wakes up, she won't be alone."

Helen left to go to bed, and after he drank a glass of Brandy, Henry headed upstairs. *What a hell of a night!* He should have pressed Kathryn more about what that bastard was trying to do to her. If he had known to what extent his uncle was bothering Kathryn, he would have done more than just talk to him; he would have banned him from the house, regardless of what his mother had to say. Henry felt terrible because he should have convinced Kathryn to tell him what was really going on.

Once he entered Kathryn's room, he walked over, checked on Melody, and found her sleeping in the chair. He carried her over to the chaise and laid her there, and then he loosened her gown and corset so she would sleep more comfortably. He covered her up with a throw, kissed her on the temple, and left the room.

The next morning, he got his uncle out of the house without anyone seeing him. Theodore's face was covered in bruises, and he had a black eye, but Henry felt he had gotten off lightly. If Melody had not been there, he probably would have killed him. He had never felt such rage before in his entire life. Every instinct told him to kill the enemy, and that was exactly what his uncle was. Henry would make damned sure that his uncle never showed his face in England again!

They made it through the rest of the holidays without anyone suspecting a thing. If anyone asked, they were told that Kathryn was ill with a putrid throat. Melody and Helen took turns spending time with Kathryn. Little by little, Kathryn began to recover from the ordeal. When everyone left, it was a relief to have it behind them. Of course, it would take a while before Kathryn would feel safe again.

By February, Kathryn was almost her old self again. In fact, Melody planned a party to celebrate her birthday, and then she remembered that it was her birthday as well. It was hard to believe that she was turning five and twenty years old. The party was an excellent idea, and everyone had a wonderful time; even Mary seemed to enjoy herself. She was definitely doing much better, and Melody was so happy for her.

CHAPTER 23

March 1819

THEY LEFT FOR London in the middle of March, because all the ladies needed new wardrobes. Since they would be out of mourning in April, they would no longer need to wear black. The trip went by quickly, and they were at Sanderford House by four o'clock. Everyone went to their rooms to freshen up and rest. Melody found her new room lovely. As she looked around, she noticed all the different shades of lavender with white accents and the delicate white French furniture, which she always loved. The counterpane, on the bed, was also lavender with white Belgian lace around the edge and mounds of pillows to match. She could just imagine curling up on all those pillows with a good book. This was the first time she had seen the ducal suite and knew she would be very comfortable in these rooms. Of course, Henry had told her she could change anything she wanted to, but the rooms were so lovely that she knew she would leave them alone. Besides, they usually ended up in Henry's bed anyway. She wondered what his rooms looked like and decided to go explore. The sitting room adjoined her room, and it was just as lovely. She could see herself sitting by the fireplace with Henry having a quiet evening reading to each other or playing chess. The door across the room must lead to Henry's room, so she went over, opened the door, and entered. The room was empty. As she glanced around looking at the massive furniture and an enormous bed on a raised dais in the center of the room, she felt a tingling sensation run through her body when she thought of making love with Henry in that bed.

The door opened, and Henry walked in and asked, "Hello, sweetheart. This is a lovely surprise. Are you here to work your feminine wiles on me? I certainly hope so!"

Melody laughed as she replied, "I'll wait to do that until tonight. I just wanted to see where we'll spend many enjoyable nights. I love my room, by the way. I won't be changing a thing. This room suits you, even if it is a bit opulent. I feel a bit sorry for your mother. She's not going to like staying in the dowager suite I'm sure. I wish she would warm up to me, but I guess that's not going to happen. At least, she's finally stopped making all those negative comments to me. I appreciate you speaking with her, and I'm sure it wasn't a pleasant conversation. What with so much happening and worrying about Kathryn, this was the first chance I've had to tell you that." Melody walked over to Henry, gave him a kiss, and said, "Well, it will soon be time to go down to dinner, so I need to return to my room so I can get ready. I'll see you in a bit."

The dinner that evening was amazing. Each course was magnificently prepared, and Melody would make sure Chef Michelle knew how much everyone enjoyed the food. Henry's mother chose to have her dinner in her room, so everyone's spirits were high. Helen was excited about the upcoming season and could not wait for all the balls, soirees, and garden parties to start. Kathryn joined in on the discussion, but Melody knew her heart was not in it. After dinner, Henry chose to bypass his port and joined the ladies in the drawing room where Mary entertained them by playing the pianoforte and Melody sang. Since everyone was exhausted from the trip, they all retired early.

The next morning, after breakfast, all the ladies went to see the modiste, Madame Devy. They ordered day dresses, morning gowns, dinner dresses, and evening gowns, plus all the chemises, corsets and stays to go with them. Melody and Helen also ordered new riding habits. After they left Madame Devy's, they went to the millinery shop and picked out new bonnets, and then, of course, they needed gloves to match all their gowns and new slippers. Once they were through, they went to Gunter's for sandwiches and ices. It was a very pleasant afternoon. Even Henry's mother seemed to have an enjoyable time. Mary was not sure if she was ready to give up her mourning clothes, but Melody was able to convince her that it was time.

The invitations were coming in everyday, but they would not accept any of them, until after April 5. In the meantime, it would give them a chance to see some of the other amusements that London had to offer. They went to Astley's Amphitheatre, and Melody took Kathryn to the art museums. They went to Drury Lane to see a play and also to the Royal Opera House in Covent Gardens, which Melody thoroughly enjoyed. Henry was very busy with his responsibilities to the House of Lords. He would spend the morning at Gentleman Jackson's gym, have lunch with his friends, and after that, he would spend the afternoon in Parliament. He was always available to escort the ladies in the evening and took dinner with them.

Their new wardrobes arrived by the end of March, and Kathryn's presentation gown was magnificent. Melody was also being presented at court as the new Duchess of Sanderford. She was very busy because they were holding Kathryn's Presentation Ball on April 15, the same day they were to be presented at court. Everyone helped make out the invitations, and they were delivered by the end of the month. Melody was feeling a bit overwhelmed, but her aunt had assured her she would be fine. She visited her aunt almost everyday, and she had gotten in touch with Susan about volunteering at the orphanage again. Needless to say, her days were full, and they had not even gone to their first party.

The presentation at court went exceedingly well. Kathryn was breathtaking in her presentation gown. She looked so elegant and graceful when she made her curtsey. Melody was nervous, but since her focus was more on Kathryn than herself, she made it through without any mishaps. When they arrived back at the house, she went and checked on everything for the ball that night. The ballroom looked gorgeous. She stood there as she breathed in the scent of all the hothouse yellow roses that were placed around the room. Gold silk gently draped the walls in between the large mirrors and windows and it truly looked lovely. She could just imagine how it would look with everyone dancing tonight in a myriad of color from all the gorgeous ball gowns and the crystal chandeliers ablaze with hundreds of beeswax candles. Everything was ready, so all she had to do was get dressed. Henry came to her rooms and presented her with the family heirloom yellow diamonds. There was a tiara, necklace, bracelet, and earbobs to match. They were absolutely glorious, and they would match her ball gown perfectly. He kissed her neck as he fastened the necklace around her, and she felt chills run up her spine. It always astonished her that the slightest touch could affect her so.

"Darling, you are breathtakingly beautiful. You'll dazzle everyone, and I'm so proud of you. I know this has been so much for you to take care of, but you have handled it as well as any duchess could. You don't need to be worried. Your charm and grace will carry you through. Let's go down and welcome our guests."

The family gathered in the drawing room and then went into dinner. They chose not to invite anyone to dinner other than the immediate family so that it would keep Melody from becoming over taxed. After dinner, they went to the receiving room and waited for their guests to arrive. Susan and her husband, Viscount Hastings, were the first to arrive, followed by Henry's friend the Earl of Weston and Lady Helton. For the next two hours, Melody greeted one lord and lady after another. It seemed as if every single person they had invited decided to come. At ten o'clock, they dissolved the receiving line and went into the ballroom to open the dance. Henry led Melody out to the floor and Lord Weston led Kathryn. The first dance was a quadrille, and everyone looked so elegant. It was as lovely as she had imagined it would be. Melody began to relax, and Henry even had her laughing before the dance ended.

They strolled around the room, stopping to talk to some of Henry's friends and many of their other guests. They approached Susan and her husband and stopped to chat.

Susan gave her a quick hug and said, "Melody, you look radiant tonight, and the ballroom is magnificent. We've been looking forward to your ball ever since we received the invitation. Kathryn is so pretty. I'm sure she's going to do fine, and Helen is as vivacious as ever. How did everything go at your presentation this afternoon?"

With a relieved expression on her face, Melody answered, "I was very nervous, but I think that I was so concerned about Kathryn doing well that I didn't think about mine as much. Kathryn is very pretty, and when she opens up, she can really sparkle. Helen I don't worry about, for she's an accomplished flirt. Are we still going to the orphanage tomorrow at eleven o'clock?"

Susan smiled as she replied, "Oh yes, that's still a good time for me. Are Helen, Mary, and Kathryn coming with us? Helen and Mary usually go as often as possible, whenever they're in town."

"Yes, they're coming. At first, Mary wasn't sure she would go, but I was able to convince her to come with us. I think it would be good for her to get out more. Well, I need to go check on Kathryn, so we'll talk more tomorrow," Melody answered.

Henry asked Susan to dance, and Melody went to find Kathryn. She was sitting over against the wall, and she looked so despondent. Melody had hoped she would cheer up, but obviously, she was still having trouble putting the incident with her uncle behind her. She was so shy that she was probably going to have trouble attracting a possible husband. Of course, she still said she was not interested in marriage, but she could always change her mind. She would get Henry to introduce her to some nice young men.

Melody smiled down at Kathryn and said, "Sweetheart, why are you sitting over here by yourself? Where is Helen? I haven't seen her for a while."

Kathryn perked up and replied, "She went to dance with the Duke of Somerset. I think she likes him. Of course, he's a little old, but that doesn't seem to bother Helen. I was speaking with your aunt, but she just left to go to the card room. I really don't mind sitting by myself. I appreciate all the effort you have put into this lovely ball. I've always dreamed of the day that I could go to a ball, and now the day has finally arrived."

Melody was relieved to see Kathryn more animated and hoped she would come out of her shell now that she was officially out. "You'll get tired of all the balls before the season is over. Have you met anyone that you found interesting?"

"If you're referring to men, then the answer is a resounding no. I'm really not interested in getting married. I still want to be an artist. By the way, when are you and Henry going to sit for me?" she asked. "I want to do your formal portrait, but neither one of you will commit to sitting for me."

"I think that it will be hard to find the time now that we're in London for the season. I'll definitely get Henry to commit to sitting for you once the season ends. I see my aunt across the room, and I've been trying to talk to her all evening. Let me know if you need anything." Melody strolled around the room until she came to her aunt. Before she had a chance to talk to her, Lord Weston asked her to dance. Melody ended up dancing quite a few times before she got a chance to speak with her aunt. Henry came over, and it was time for the supper dance. It was a waltz, and she did so love to dance with Henry.

As they swayed to the music, Melody said, "Henry, you need to introduce some nice young men to Kathryn. She has been sitting by herself far too often, and I want her to have a good time. She says she is, but I worry. She has grown even shyer since the incident with your horrid uncle. I know she says that she's not interested in marriage, but she can still have fun getting to know other young people."

Henry gazed into Melody's eyes as he replied, "I introduced her to several of my friends, and all of them requested a dance, so that should help. The effort you put into this ball is much appreciated. I knew you would be an excellent hostess because you did such an exceptional job hosting all the activities at Christmas. Helen is certainly having a good time. I believe she has danced every set this evening."

"Helen is so vivacious she attracts hordes of admirers. I do feel that the Duke of Somerset is too old for her, and I don't care for him very much at all, but Helen seems to be very attracted to him. I just hope he doesn't end up hurting her. There's something about him that just doesn't sit well with me. Henry, the dance is ending. Let's go find Kathryn and go into supper," she said.

As he escorted her off the dance floor, he replied, "I don't know very much about the Duke of Somerset, but if Helen is interested in him, I will definitely find out more about him."

They found Kathryn and went into supper. The food was delicious. There were lobster patties, oysters, finger sandwiches, and several different kinds of fruit and cheeses to choose from, and the ice sculptures were incredible. Melody knew that she needed to tell Chef Michelle how wonderful everything turned out. After supper, Melody was finally able to talk to her aunt at last. She was having a superb time, and she said that several of her friends had commented on how beautifully decorated the ballroom was. Melody was ecstatic that everyone seemed to be having such a splendid time, and so far, the evening had come off extremely well. She even noticed that Mary was having an enjoyable time. Melody had danced with Mary's brother, Mr. Bronson. It was such a shame that he had lost his arm at Waterloo, but he seemed to be adjusting well to civilian life. As the ball was winding down, Melody's aunt was one of the last to leave.

"Darling, you really did have a wonderful turn out tonight. This could very well be the most talked about ball of the season. You should be very proud of your accomplishments. I'll see you tomorrow afternoon, as usual." Then her aunt kissed her cheek and left.

Melody was exhausted by the time everyone left. Helen was glowing and said she had had a sensational time. She talked all the way up the stairs about the evening. Kathryn thanked Melody and went to her room.

Henry was waiting for her when she came into her bedchamber. He was already undressed and in bed. She went into her dressing room, and Millie unfastened her gown and helped with her night rail, then Melody sent her to bed. As she crawled into bed, Henry pulled her close, gave her a kiss, and she fell fast asleep. He laid there and just watched her sleep. She was so lovely, and he knew, at that moment, that he was no longer resentful over Melody going on with her life. He felt a lifting of his spirits. He wanted to wake her up and tell her that he loved her, but he did not want to disturb her, because he knew how much time she had spent on getting everything ready for the ball. He just realized that he had not told her he loved her since he had found her again. Henry told himself that he would make sure that he found time tomorrow to tell her that he was sorry he had been such a horse's ass. *He could not believe that he had not told her that he loved her. He really was a selfish and self-centered bastard sometimes.* He just hoped that Melody would forgive him and that she still loved him. He would do whatever was necessary to win his way back into her affections. He gently kissed her forehead, closed his eyes, and drifted off to sleep.

Henry did not get a chance to talk to Melody the next day, other than briefly, to let her know that he had to go to Doncaster. There had been a fire and several of his racehorses had been lost. He took Stallings and Mansfield with him so they took the ducal coach. He knew they would not be able to travel as speedily, but he had no choice, because Stallings had to come with him. He was right in the middle of putting together a bill for Parliament, and he could not afford to wait until he got back to work on it. Melody wanted to come with him, but he convinced her to stay, because he did not trust his mother to watch over his sisters. They were just at the start of the season, and he did not want any of them to miss any of the entertainments. The children did not need to be taken on such a long trip either, so she agreed he was right and stayed behind.

They traveled nonstop, only stopping to eat and change the horses, so they made the trip in three days. Once Henry arrived, he saw that the damage was quite extensive and would require more time to repair than he expected. His main concern was for his horses. He had lost one of his best racing horses, and he had been planning to start using him for stud next year because of his outstanding bloodlines. The Doncaster Stables was known for producing some of the fastest racing horses in England, and he brought in quite a bit of revenue from his stud fees. Henry sent Melody a message to let her know it would be several weeks before he would be able to return.

Melody was very disappointed that Henry had to leave and that she could not go with him, but she knew Henry was right, especially about the children. It would have been too hard on them, since they did not travel well. It also would have been unfair to Helen and Kathryn. Henry was right about his mother; she would not have made sure that they continued to have an enjoyable season. The days went by swiftly, because they had a ball, soiree, or garden party everyday, and when they did not, they usually went to a play or the opera instead. Melody enjoyed the opera tremendously, and the ducal box was magnificent; it gave her the best view in the house.

Melody was becoming very worried about Kathryn as she continued to withdraw from the family, and she had even stopped painting. She had cancelled several of her art lessons, so this was serious. Melody had attempted to talk to her, but Kathryn would always say she was fine. Helen had also tried to talk to her, but to no avail. She grew paler and thinner by the day. By the end of the week, she felt so poorly that she did not leave her room. Melody knew something had to be done. She and Helen decided to approach her together.

They went to her room and knocked on the door, but there was no answer. Melody tried the door, but it was locked, and Kathryn did not answer when they called her name. It was disconcerting, and Melody decided to use her key to get into the room. As they entered, Melody noticed that all the drapes were pulled, so no sunlight could enter the room. She approached the bed and knew immediately something was very wrong. Kathryn was asleep, but it did not look to be a natural sleep. She had deep circles under her eyes, and her skin tone was ashen. Helen tried to wake her up, but there was no response. Melody shook her hard and still she slept on. By this time, she had grown quite alarmed. Melody called for one of the footman and sent him to get the doctor.

When the doctor arrived, Simpson showed him to Kathryn's room. Melody let him into the room so that he could examine her. He asked that they step out while he examined Kathryn. After about fifteen minutes, the doctor came out of the room.

Melody asked with great trepidation in her voice, "Dr. Holland, what is wrong with Kathryn? She wouldn't wake up, no matter what we did. Were you able to get her to wake up?"

Dr. Holland looked at her and shook his head as he replied, "She has been taking laudanum, I suspect, and I would say quite often and in large doses. Has she suffered weight loss and a need to sleep more than usual?"

"We've been worried about her for quite some time. She recently experienced something very traumatic, and ever since then, she has withdrawn from everyone. She hasn't shown her usual enthusiasm for any of her normal activities, but I wasn't aware she was taking laudanum. She has lost some weight recently and has been sleeping more. What does this mean doctor? What is wrong with her?" Melody asked with worry showing on her pretty face.

"I believe that all the symptoms are there to indicate opium poisoning, and she has become addicted to the substance. I will need to wean her off the drug. I must tell you that it is a very painful process, and she will become very ill and angry to the point of violence when she is no longer able to get any of the drug. She will need constant supervision to ensure she does not get her hands on any more laudanum. Do you have any idea where she has been getting it?" Dr. Holland asked.

Melody looked at Helen in astonishment as she asked, "Were you aware that she had been taking laudanum?"

With a worried expression on her face, Helen replied, "She's been complaining about headaches, so I did know she was taking it occasionally, but I had no idea to what extent she must have been using it. We should talk to her maid and see if she knows where she's been getting the laudanum from."

Melody rang for Kathryn's maid, Sarah. While they waited for the maid, she asked, "Dr. Holland, "I'm not sure I understand what you're talking about when you say addiction. Can you please explain this to me?

"Addiction happens when the body starts to physically crave the drug. It can be physically painful for her to go too long without the laudanum. There would be acute stomach cramping, her muscles would ache, and she would experience acute nausea. Over time, she would become extremely overwrought, believing that everyone was out to hurt her. Have you observed any of these symptoms?" he asked.

Before they could answer, Sarah entered the room. Melody immediately asked, "Did you know that Kathryn was taking laudanum?"

Sarah curtsied and said, "Yes, your grace, and I've been so worried because she kept wanting more and more of it. She was sending me to the apothecary everyday to get her more, and she kept getting nauseated all the time, but after she would take the laudanum, she would seem to feel better."

Dr. Holland nodded his head in satisfaction and said, "That explains how she was getting the drug and that she was definitely experiencing major symptoms of addiction. I will try to stay close at hand, because the next three to four days will be the most excruciating time for her. After that, she will still need to be watched constantly, because even after her body quits craving the laudanum, her mind will continue to demand the drug. I have to let you know that many people do not have the determination to leave the drug alone. Your sister-in-law is going to have to want to stay away from the laudanum, if she is going to recover from this addiction."

Dr Holland returned to the room. It was decided that Sarah would take the first round of duty to assist the doctor in caring for Kathryn. Melody knew that Kathryn might not want to quit taking laudanum, but it was hard to imagine sweet gentle Kathryn ever becoming violent. Helen had started to cry, so Melody went over to her and put her arm around her to comfort her.

The next four days were indeed every bit as horrible as the doctor had predicted. They took turns helping the doctor care for Kathryn. She could not hold anything in her stomach. They had to change her night rail and the bed linens several times a day, because she was sweating profusely. Toward the end of the fourth day, Kathryn fell into a more natural sleep, and she stopped the vomiting and sweating. The doctor said that the worst part of the physical addiction was over, but now came the time for her to start dealing with the mental cravings.

The doctor, before he departed, said, "Please call me if she starts to exhibit any more symptoms. I wish you luck on keeping Lady Kathryn away from the laudanum. I cannot stress enough how important it is that Lady Kathryn not take any more laudanum. I would recommend that someone stay with her constantly for a while."

Sarah became Kathryn's constant companion. She made sure that Kathryn ate and did not take any laudanum. Sarah said, "I feel responsible for Lady Kathryn, because I should have come to you, your grace, and told you what was happening to her."

Melody replied, "Sarah, you aren't to blame for this. All of us failed to realize how troubled Kathryn has been, so we too were at fault."

The first few days, after the doctor left, Kathryn was quiet and very biddable, because she was so weak from the aftermath of withdrawing from laudanum. Once she started to get her strength back, she became very irritable and at times alarmingly angry. She would shout at Sarah, and then she would start crying, pleading with them to give her some laudanum. She constantly complained of the headache and believed that only the laudanum would make it go away. Melody became increasingly concerned that Kathryn would somehow find a way to get some laudanum. If they could not convince her that she must not take any, Melody knew Kathryn would find someway to get it. It was very devastating when Kathryn would beg and cry. Then when she did not get the laudanum, she would shout out ugly things, which was not like Kathryn at all.

One day, while Melody was reading to Kathryn, she finally broke down and started to talk about what had happened to her, and how she had felt about what her uncle had tried to do to her. Kathryn had been blaming herself, because she had not told Melody and Henry the complete truth.

Kathryn began to cry and said, "Uncle Theodore has been bothering me for years. It started when I was around six years old. At first, I didn't understand what he was doing to me, but as I grew older, he began to make me do disgusting things. He told me that I was bad and that he had to teach me the error of my ways. The only way I kept my sanity was to lose myself in my art. Every time my uncle came to visit, I would become nauseated, just thinking about what he would make me do. Once he would leave, then the nightmares and the sleepwalking would start."

As Kathryn told her story, Melody became so angry over what that bastard had done that she began to cry. She went to sit by Kathryn and held her as they both cried together. From that day onward, Kathryn started to get better. She began painting again and wanting to spend time with her sister. Kathryn had Melody and her children sit for her so she could do their portrait. The children could not sit for very long without becoming irritable and restless, so they would do two short sessions each day.

Melody received a message from Henry telling her that he would be home by the end of the week. He had been gone for four weeks. She had written to him about what had happened to Kathryn, and he was so angry that he was talking about going to the continent to find his uncle and kill him! Melody knew it was very frustrating for him that he was not able to be there with Kathryn.

The dowager duchess, throughout the whole crisis, acted as if nothing was wrong and that they had just exaggerated the entire situation. She refused to believe that her brother had hurt Kathryn. She went to her parties and made her social calls as if everything was all right. Melody could not understand how a woman could be so callous toward her own child. If there was ever a time when Kathryn could use a mother's love, it was now.

Kathryn really started coming out of her shell. She embraced all the entertainments that were available. It was as if she had been asleep and had just awakened. She became animated at all the balls, and she sought out other young women, and befriended them, especially the shy ones. She was still wary of men, but she did dance whenever any of the gentlemen asked, and she even seemed to enjoy it. It was truly a miracle, and Melody was so happy for her. Henry would be so pleased when he got home and saw the change in his little sister.

CHAPTER 24

May 1819

HENRY RETURNED ON Sunday, and Melody was overjoyed to see him. It had been a very long four weeks. Henry had calmed down by the time he got home and was no longer ranting about killing his uncle, but he vowed that if his uncle ever returned from the continent, he would kill him.

The first time he saw Kathryn, he pulled her into his arms and said, "I'm so proud of you. I had men in my regiment who became addicted to laudanum, and I saw how difficult it was to overcome. Many of them weren't able to do it. Kathryn, you are a much stronger person for having gone through this and come out whole. Hopefully, now you'll no longer suffer from the nightmares and sleepwalking. I feel sure that what you were going through, at the hands of our uncle, was the cause of the nightmares and the sleepwalking, and they should stop now."

Henry was thrilled by all the changes in Kathryn. He had never seen her so vibrant and alive. He had always known that Kathryn would come out of her shell, but now he was going to have other worries on his hands. How to make sure she attracted the right kind of men, since all of them seemed to be vying for her attention. Both Helen and Kathryn were heiresses, and there would be fortune hunters trying to get their attention. He never thought he would have to be the one to protect them. Of course, Kathryn still proclaimed vehemently that she was not interested in any man. She told them that she was going to dedicate her life to her art and that she would never marry.

Kathryn finished the portrait of Melody and the children, and it was the best work she had ever done. She had caught the expression of love in Melody's eyes as she gazed at her children. Henry thought it was such a beautiful portrait that he had it hung in the drawing room above the mantle.

He stayed so busy the first two weeks that he was back that he had not found the right moment to tell Melody how sorry he was for the way he had been treating her. He decided he would take her to Vauxhall Gardens the next evening as a surprise. He knew she had never been there, and he wanted to make the night as special as possible. He told her to be ready at seven o'clock, but he did not tell her where they were going. He knew Melody was very curious about where he was taking her, but no matter how many times she asked him, he would not tell. All he would tell her was that she would need a mask and a domino.

Melody decided to have plans of her own. She made up her mind that she would seduce Henry. He had not come to her bed since he had returned from Doncaster, and besides, she was tired of him always being the one to initiate their lovemaking. She was determined to get Henry to admit that he loved her. That afternoon, after she had visited the children, she had Millie draw her a bath. She had some new lemon-scented bathing salts that she knew would drive Henry wild. She washed her long honey blonde hair and rinsed it in lemon juice to make it shine and bring out the lighter blonde streaks. After she had finished washing her hair, she luxuriated in the tub until the water cooled. She planned out her seduction and knew she would be successful in getting Henry to tell her he loved her. She refused to accept that he did not love her, and her aunt had helped to convince her that he did. After she finished her bath, she rubbed herself down with her verbena-scented lotion. She decided to take a short nap and told Millie to make sure she was up in an hour.

Melody woke up refreshed and got ready for the evening. Henry had sent her the family heirloom sapphires, which would match her new gown that had just been delivered. As she gazed at her reflection in the cheval mirror, she smoothed down the skirt of her deep royal blue taffeta evening gown with silver trim. She noticed how well the very low décolletage showed off her bosom. She had put some weight back on, but it was in all the right places. Her figure was much more curvaceous than when she had first met Henry, and she knew Henry loved that. She felt she had never looked lovelier and Henry was going to be astounded when he saw her. Millie had swept her hair up to the top of her head, with ringlets cascading to her shoulders. She had used the sapphire and diamond studs to accent her hair, and they sparkled as she turned her head. They looked stunning next to her golden tresses. She dabbed perfume behind her ears and between her breasts, where she knew Henry would kiss her later that night. Finally, she was ready, and she went downstairs. Henry looked up at her as she descended the stairs, and his mouth fell open when he saw her. He held out his hand, and she placed hers in his. Then he raised it to his lips and kissed her fingers. Chills ran up and down her spine in anticipation of what she had planned for the night. She boldly looked Henry over, noticing how attractive he was in his black tailcoat and sparkling white linen. His royal blue embroidered waistcoat matched her dress perfectly. They made an extremely handsome couple.

He placed the dark blue domino around her shoulders and kissed the side of her neck just below her ear, which always caused a tingling sensation in her belly. Henry turned her around as he said, "You look radiant this evening. All the other men will be green with envy when they see you on my arm. Come my dear, let's depart."

The ducal carriage was waiting for them. He helped her inside and sat across from her with his back to the horses. She noticed he kept staring at her with desire, causing the blue of his eyes to deepen almost to sapphire. "Henry, where are you taking me? You have kept me in suspense for two days, so can you finally tell me?"

Henry smiled at her and with a knowing look, he said, "We'll be there shortly, just relax and have a little patience. I promise, you'll enjoy yourself."

Soon the carriage slowed down and then stopped so they could get out. As they got out, Melody exclaimed, "Vauxhall Gardens! Oh, Henry, I've always wanted to come here." They got into the boat that would take them across the Thames to the gardens. Melody looked up and noticed what a beautiful night it was: the sky was crystal clear, and the stars shone brightly against the midnight sky. Henry helped her out of the boat and led her to their private box. There were lanterns hanging from all the trees, and people from all walks of life were moving about. He ordered dinner and champagne for them with strawberries and clotted cream for dessert. As they ate their dinner, Melody looked around at the gardens and was fascinated by all the people laughing and having a marvelous time. Henry dipped a strawberry in the clotted cream and fed it to her. Her knees trembled because she was so excited. She suspected Henry had also planned a seduction, but she was going to surprise him when he saw what she had planned for him. Melody looked seductively at Henry, and his eyes darkened with desire.

Henry had never seen Melody like this . . . She was acting so alluring tonight. He knew that his plan must be working. He was hard as a rock just thinking of the night to come. He knew exactly what he wanted to say to her and also what he was going to do to her. Her breasts looked luscious and the décolletage of her gown was so low that he could almost see the brownish pink areola around her nipple. *God, he had to stop thinking about ravishing her before he embarrassed himself.* Melody drank her champagne, and he could tell she was beginning to get a little tipsy. He had better make sure she did not drink too much. He wanted her relaxed, not intoxicated.

The fireworks started at midnight, and they lit up the sky. It was so fascinating to watch Melody as she looked up at the sky with awe in her beautiful eyes. Henry suggested that they take a walk, so he helped her out of their box. He headed toward the dark walk, which was known for its trysting spots. Melody held tightly on to his arm as they made their way through the crowd, and as they walked, she said, "Where are we going, Henry? I can't see the fireworks from here, because we've moved out of the light."

Henry took the path to the right, and soon they were surrounded by large trees. He pulled her behind a tree and then said, "This is where we're going." And he kissed her ravenously, and Melody gasped as his tongue slid into her mouth. Henry pulled her tightly against him, and she could feel the thick rod of his desire pressing against her belly. She clung to him as her passion began to spiral out of control. He placed his hand on her breast and squeezed her nipple, and it immediately pebbled and grew taut. He slipped his other hand inside her bodice, and her breast popped out as he lowered his head and sucked her taut nipple into his mouth. He sucked furiously on one nipple while he rolled her other one between his thumb and finger. She felt a jolt of desire shoot down to her nether region, and she could feel moisture pooling between her thighs. Her breasts were swollen and heavy, and Henry was panting as he continued to suckle. Melody remembered her plan of seduction and boldly grasped his thick shaft with her small hand.

Henry moaned from the sheer pleasure of it all, "Sweetheart, we must stop before I end up ravishing you up against this tree. As exciting as it would be, I don't think you're ready for anything like that. I find your behavior tonight incredibly titillating, and I'm loving every moment of it. I think it's time to leave so that we can finish what we have started, so come with me, my darling."

Henry helped her straighten the neckline of her gown, and they headed back to the boat landing so they could leave. They were going in a different direction from the rest of the crowd, and Melody's hand slipped out of his. He looked behind him, but all he could see was a crowd of people. Melody was so tiny that the crowd immediately swallowed her up. He pushed his way through the people, and he thought he saw the back of her head about fifty feet ahead. He followed as quickly as he could, but the crowds kept pushing him backward, and he lost sight of her again. He finally broke through and rushed to where he had last seen her head. There was a path that led to the right, and in the distance, he thought he saw her hair shimmering in the moonlight. He hurried in the direction where he had last seen a glimpse of her hair. He came to a dead end, and Melody was nowhere to be seen. He began to panic! Anything could happen to her. This was a public garden, and all kinds of rogues were lurking about. He hurried back the way he had come, and about halfway there, he spied a turn off that he had missed before, and he went down the path. He heard a whimper up ahead and ran toward the sound. He saw Melody struggling to get away from a very large man dressed all in black. Henry pulled him away from her and pushed the man out of the way. He was obviously very intoxicated, because he was staggering as he came back at Henry. Henry blocked the man's punch and hit him hard in the face, and the man collapsed at his feet. He did not check to see if the man was conscious; he just grabbed Melody's hand, and they ran back to where the lights were. Melody was having trouble keeping up, so Henry slowed down once they were close to the crowds.

With a relieved expression on her pretty face, she said, "Thank goodness you showed up when you did. That disgusting man was about to kiss me! I was ready to let out a big scream even if it did cause a scandal."

"Are you all right?" he asked. "Are you sure he didn't hurt you? I'm so sorry I let go of your hand."

"You didn't let go, we were pulled apart. I'm fine, Henry. I was a little scared, but I knew you would find me. But after so much excitement, I'm ready to leave. Can we go home now?" she asked.

Henry turned back toward the main path, and soon they were back at the boats. He helped her in, sat down beside her, and pulled her close to his side as they made the trip back across the Thames to their carriage.

Once they were back inside their carriage, he pulled her close to him and said, "Oh god, I was so scared that I had lost you and that something awful would happen to you. You were very brave. Most women would have been hysterical, but you stayed cool under pressure. You're truly an extraordinary woman."

Henry held her gently in his arms all the way back to the house. When they arrived home, it was dark, and Henry had to use his key to get in. He had told Simpson not to wait up for them, because he knew that they would be late. He scooped her up into his arms and carried her up the stairs.

"Henry, you don't need to carry me. I can walk. I'm too heavy for you to carry me all the way up to our rooms," she said.

He gazed down at her and said, "You're as light as a feather. Besides, I don't want to let you go. I almost lost you tonight, and I'm never letting you go again." Once they were in her room, he put her down. "Turn around so I can unbutton your gown and loosen your corset and stays for you."

Soon he had her gown loosened, and it slipped to the floor. Melody turned to Henry and said, "Sit down over there by the fire while I finish undressing." Henry sat down as Melody walked over to her dressing table.

"Are you sure you don't want any help?" he asked.

Melody boldly stared at him, as she said, "No, I just want you to sit there and watch me."

Henry looked shocked but pleased by her assertiveness. He leaned back in the chair to watch her. Melody slowly removed her stays and corset, and dropped them beside her on the floor. Then she gathered up her chemise and lifted it up her body revealing her creamy white thighs an inch at a time. *God, her skin glowed in the candlelight, and he felt his shaft pushing against his pantaloons.* Henry held his breath as he watched her seductively glance over at him. The chemise was now at her hips and her sweet golden curls were peeking out. It was almost more than Henry could stand, but for some reason Melody wanted to play the wanton, and he was more than willing to let her. She pulled the chemise up, and her breasts came into view; her nipples were drawn up into tight little buds. She slowly pulled her chemise off and tossed it in the corner of the room. She stood there in just her stockings, garters, and slippers, boldly meeting Henry's eyes. Melody put her leg up on her dressing table chair and slowly rolled down the first stocking as she ravished Henry with her eyes. Henry sat there in amazement. His erection was so hard that it was almost painful.

After Melody finished taking off her other stocking and slipper, she slowly walked over to where Henry was sitting, and she kneeled down at his feet. She huskily said, "You have on too many clothes, so let me see what we can do about that." She reached up, began to untie his cravat, and dropped it to the floor beside her, and then she pushed off his tailcoat. After she had removed it, she unbuttoned his waistcoat. She took it off and dropped it on the mounting pile of Henry's clothes. Slowly, she unbuttoned his shirt and pulled it over his head. She leaned back to admire his muscular chest. She loved the way his chest hair grew right in the middle between his nipples, which were standing at attention. She could not resist them; she leaned over and licked his right nipple. Henry gasped for breath.

"Are you feeling warm, Henry? Let me see if I can cool you off." She unbuttoned the flap of his pantaloons, and as it fell down, his huge erection sprang up. Melody wrapped her little hand around his thick shaft and firmly squeezed. Henry held his breath, wondering what she would do next. She lowered her head and kissed the bulbous head of his shaft. Henry felt as if he had died and gone to heaven. Melody slid her luscious lips down his shaft and began to suck as she slid her lips up and down his shaft. *Oh god!* Henry thought, *He did not know how much more of this he could handle; he felt ready to explode, but it felt too incredible to tell her to stop.* Melody reached her other hand into his pantaloons and gently cupped his ball sac, and then he really came undone.

"Stop, I can't take it anymore! I'll spill my seed right now, if you continue!" He pulled her up as he stood . . . He picked her up and threw her on the bed, pulled off his pantaloons, and fell on top of her. He started kissing her neck, running his tongue down to her breast, and he took her taut nipple into his mouth and sucked furiously. He squeezed her other nipple, and Melody felt a rush of sharply glittering pleasure. Henry licked and kissed his way down her belly and buried his face between her sweet thighs as he breathed in her fresh womanly scent. He licked and sucked on her little love bud and it sent her spinning over the edge into bliss. Henry crawled back up her delectable body, spread her thighs wide, and thrust deeply inside her tight passage. He was shaking all over, trying to gain control, but he could not; he moved powerfully into her undulating hips. Harder and faster, he rode her until together they crested and flung themselves high over the precipice and into the void. Just as he released his seed into her sweet little passage, he shouted out, "Melody, I love you," as he fell on top of her. He tried to hold himself up by his arms, but he could not. She wrapped him in her arms and stroked his hair. He slowly pulled out of her body, rolled over, and pulled her into his arms. They lay there for a long time, breathing in and out, as they slowly came back down to earth.

"Melody, I love you so much . . . I've been such a selfish bastard about you marrying when you thought I was dead. I've realized you were right to go on with your life. I've watched Mary, and I know she needs to do that. Nelson would not want her to be so morose all the time. I would not have wanted you to be like that. I should never have seen your marrying again as a betrayal. You were just doing what you needed to do to survive and take care of our daughter. Can you ever forgive me? I need your love. Please . . . let us love again."

"I never stopped loving you, not for a minute. Every waking hour you were in my mind and in my dreams as I slept. I could never love another like I love you. I did care about Brandon, and I loved him as my friend, but never as my lover. I'm overjoyed that you have finally let go of your resentment . . . of course, I forgive you. As long as we love each other, we can overcome anything." Henry gently kissed her on the temple, and they both closed their eyes and fell asleep in each other's arms.

When Melody opened her eyes the next morning, she saw Henry lying beside her fast asleep. He was still such a beautiful man. Her heart swelled with love for him. At last, they had found their way back to each other. Melody knew there would be struggles ahead, but as long as they faced them together, they would make it. Henry opened his eyes and gave her a big grin. He looked like an overgrown schoolboy, and she laughed.

He looked over at her and asked, "What are you laughing at, my love? By the way, do you know that you look ravishing this morning?"

"Why, thank you, husband, you don't look bad yourself. I was laughing at how young you look lying there sleeping. All your little lines around your eyes relax and disappear when you are sleeping. Not that you have many wrinkles, but after all, you're only nine and twenty today. Happy birthday!" she said.

Henry grinned at her and replied, "You're right. It is my birthday. I had forgotten all about it. Let's do something special with the children today. I want to spend the entire day together, Parliament be damned!"

And they did just that. They took the children to the park and had a picnic, and then they went for a drive in Henry's new barouche. The children had a wonderful time. He kept making funny faces at Mary Elizabeth, and the peels of laughter rang out, for all to hear. After the drive in the park, they went back and played tea with the children. Henry fell over as he tried to sit on one of the little chairs, and Mary Elizabeth cried, "Papa, you so funny!"

Henry froze . . . and looked up at Melody. He got a tight knot in his throat and had to fight to keep the tears from falling. His little girl . . . had just called him "Papa," for the first time. It was the most amazing feeling in the world. As they looked at each other, they knew . . . their lost pleasures had been found!

EPILOGUE

ALL THE DAYS of the rest of that season were filled with laughter and joy. Kathryn had quite a few beaus, but she still refused to show any interest in them. The Duke of Somerset was playing serious court to Helen, and she seemed very pleased about it. He seemed a little old for her, but she said that she liked mature men. Melody was concerned about this because she did not care for the duke at all, but Henry had checked him out and could not find any reason to discourage him. Mary had gotten very involved at the orphanage, and it was giving purpose to her life. The children were thriving, and Henry found that there was no boundary to his love for both Mary Elizabeth and Brandon. The highlight of his day was the time he spent with them, and the highlight of his nights were spent in his wife's loving embrace. Life was at its best. Henry had adjusted well to being a member of Parliament, and he told Melody he actually found it quite challenging. He told her that he felt he could help all the soldiers that had returned and were in such drastic situations now.

In August, they traveled back to the country. His mother decided she would go live in Bath, since many of her friends were there. Henry bought her a townhouse on the Royal Crescent, which was the most exclusive part of Bath. It had never been so peaceful at Sanderford Park that fall. They had another bountiful harvest, which meant plenty of bounty for all of his tenants.

Late one night, as they lay in their bed, after they had finished making love, Melody turned to Henry with the most incredibly lovely smile on her face as she said, "I have some wonderful news. We'll be adding an addition to our family in May. I'm with child!"

Tears filled Henry's startlingly blue eyes, and he dashed them away with his hand as he lovingly replied, "That is the most wonderful news I've ever received! Come here and give me a kiss." He pulled her into his arms and kissed her passionately as they let passion take them away to that special place where only lovers can go.

Christmas came, and everyone enjoyed the holiday season, especially without Uncle Theodore. Kathryn seemed to have truly put all that behind her. Henry was so proud of the young woman she had become. She had finished the formal portrait of him and Melody, and it now hung in the main drawing room, where it could be seen by all. The portrait was absolutely magnificent and by far the best work Kathryn had ever done. She had caught the love shining in both their eyes as they gazed at each other. She still wanted to be an artist, so Henry pulled some strings, and she had been accepted at the London Art Institute. She would be going there in the spring, but because of the child Melody was carrying, she was going to live with Melody's aunt, Lady Helton.

The winter passed, and then spring came. The gardens were in full bloom, and Melody and Henry spent many happy afternoons there with the children. Kathryn and Helen left for London: Kathryn to study art and Helen to enjoy the season with Lady Helton. Helen told Melody that she was looking forward to seeing the Duke of Somerset, and she had high hopes he would propose to her this year. Melody was trying to come to terms with Helen's choice because it would probably soon be a reality. There was just something about the duke that made her very uneasy. For Helen's sake, she hoped she was wrong about him.

Everything settled down after they left. Melody complained that she was as big as a house, and Henry had to admit that her belly was quite large, but he was enjoying every moment of her pregnancy. He loved to place his ear on her belly and try to hear the baby's heartbeat, and he loved it when the baby would move. Since he had missed her other ones, he wanted to savor everything about this pregnancy. As May rolled around, Melody became very irritable. They were having an unseasonably warm May, and she was extremely uncomfortable. In the middle of the night on May 12, Melody woke up moaning. Her labor had started. She woke up Henry and told him.

He jumped out of bed, started throwing on his clothes, and dashed out of the door, but then he ran back in and gave Melody a quick kiss and said, "Don't go anywhere, I'll be right back." Then he ran from the room.

Henry was back in record time with the midwife, and it was a good thing, because Melody's labor was progressing at an alarming pace. The midwife kicked Henry out of the room, and he did not like that at all. He paced back and forth, right outside their bedroom door. After an hour, he was ready to pull out his hair. He heard the door open and out walked Millie carrying a little tiny bundle in her arms. Henry approached and looked at the baby with wonder and amazement in his eyes.

As Millie put the baby in Henry's arms, she said, "Your grace, you are the proud father of a beautiful baby . . . boy." This time there was no holding the tears back as he felt his small son's body in his arms for the first time. Henry carefully held his son close to his heart as he walked into the room. Melody was laying there, her face glowing with happiness. He went over to her, leaned down, and kissed her on the cheek, then said, "Words can't express how I'm feeling right now. Thank you, for our beautiful son. I couldn't be happier. He has your blond hair, and I do believe he'll have your sherry-colored eyes. Are you sure about the name we picked out?"

Melody smiled as she replied, "Yes, Henry Elliston Magnus Montgomery has a distinguished sound, don't you think? I know my father would be proud of his namesake, and I'm sure our son will be a marvelous Marquess, because he'll have you to teach him to be an honorable man."

The next morning, after Melody had had a chance to sleep, Henry brought the children in to see their new brother. Mary Elizabeth looked up at Henry and said, "Papa, I'm a big guwl now. Aftew all, I'm almoth five yeaws old . . . so I want to howd my new baby bwothew." Her parents looked at each other, smiled, and with love shining in their eyes, agreed with their precious daughter.

They knew . . . that their love would always . . . see them through whatever life . . . sent their way.

The End

Love Sneaked In coming soon . . .

CHAPTER 1

Spring 1820

As Helen took her morning ride, and looked out over Sanderford Park, she felt an inner peace come over her. Every morning she would ride her dappled gray mare, Ginny to the lake and it recalled to mind all the wonderful summers that she had spent there with her brothers. Sanderford Park was such a wonderful place and she enjoyed spending time here because it was always so peaceful and serene. However, even though she loved her home, she was looking forward to the upcoming season. Helen had been afraid she was not going to get to go to London, because her brother, Henry, the Duke of Sanderford and his wife, Melody were expecting a child in May. Fortunately, Melody's aunt, Lady Helton was willing to sponsor her and her sister Kathryn for the season. Helen had missed several seasons over the past five years. Her first season in 1815, was cut short in June of that year, because her brother Henry was reported to have died at the Battle of Waterloo. She missed the follow season because she was in mourning for him. Of course, her brother had not died after all. He had had amnesia because of a head injury and it took almost three years before his memory came back. That was in 1818, which was the year she lost her father and elder brother Nelson, so again she missed another season. Even though Helen would be turning three and twenty in June, she had only had two full seasons.

Last year was the best season she had had so far, because she had met Hanford Preston, the Duke of Somerset and he had paid serious court to her at the end of last year. Hanford was so handsome and debonair. He was in his late thirties, so he was more mature than most of the men she had been interested in, in the past. She thought he was so attractive with his dark sable brown hair with touches of gray at his temples. There was a dimple in the center of his strong chin and he had pale gray eyes, which she had seen darken with emotion on several occasions. Hanford was medium height, but very well built. You could tell he was a physically active man, because he was very muscular with broad shoulders, and a trim waist. Each time she had spent time with Hanford, she admired how well dressed he was and he was always impeccably groomed. She was hoping he would continue to pay court to her this coming season. *Well, enough woolgathering, she needed to get back to the house, because it was time for tea.*

Once she returned to the house she changed into an afternoon gown and went downstairs to tea. When she entered the drawing room, her sister Kathryn and Melody, her sister-in-law were already there, along with her other sister-in-law Mary, her brother Nelson's widow. Soon after, Henry entered hurrying as usual. Henry always seemed to be in a hurry these days. Helen knew he had huge responsibilities and took them very seriously. Melody served tea and passed the plate of sandwiches around. Henry ate several as usual.

Henry turned to Helen and asked, "Did you enjoy your ride? At least the weather has warmed up.

As Helen sipped her tea, she replied, "I had a lovely ride today so many of the flowers are starting to bloom that I get excited because I know spring is definitely on its way.

"Are you getting excited about your upcoming season?" Henry asked. "It's so nice of Melody's aunt to sponsor you and Kathryn this year. Oh by the way, I've set up an account for you and Kathryn to draw on, while you're in London, so you don't have to worry about using any of your allowance for new clothes and such."

"Oh thank you Henry, we're very fortunate you're such a generous brother. I can think of quite a few things that I need this season and my allowance would not have covered everything," she said. "I'm definitely looking forward to this season and as much as I'll miss you, Melody and the children, I can't wait to go to London. I know you aren't able to come for the season, but I'll miss both of you dreadfully. Please promise to send word immediately when the baby comes. We'll come home right away because we'll want to see the baby and make sure Melody's all right."

"I promise to let you know as soon as the baby comes." Henry looked over at Kathryn and said, "Kathryn, I know you're excited about attending the Art Institute, but I do hope you'll participate in the season. I want you to have some fun this year."

"I'm sure I'll find time to enjoy the season. I only go to classes in the daytime, so my evenings will be free. I look forward to all the other entertainments that London has to offer. I love the ballet and the opera and

I'm sure we'll be attending both this season." Turning away from Henry, Kathryn gazed fondly over at Melody and asked, "Melody, how are you feeling today?"

"I'm having a very good day. Thank you for asking. I spent most of the afternoon with Mary Elizabeth and Brandon. They were playing knight and damsel in distress and it was so cute." Melody shifted in her seat, trying to find a more comfortable position, and then she added, "Brandon kept taking his little wooden sword and slaying the dragon so he could save his sister. I just love to watch the children play. They're going to miss both of you when you go to London." As Helen watched Melody, she realized that since Melody was such a tiny woman; she was already getting uncomfortable from her pregnancy, even though she still had more than two months before the baby would be born.

After tea, Helen and Kathryn went upstairs to visit their nieces and nephews. Helen loved all four children equally, even though her nephews were not blood related. Helen and Kathryn played with them until it was time to get ready for dinner.

After dinner that night, Mary played the pianoforte, which everyone enjoyed tremendously, since Mary was an extremely gifted pianist. Helen had a pleasant evening and retired to bed at ten o'clock.

As each day passed, Helen grew more excited about the upcoming season and looked forward to it with great anticipation. Thankfully, the next fortnight went by quickly and soon they were on their way to London. It was raining so the trip took longer than usual, but Helen used the time to read her new Minerva Press novel. Helen and her sister arrived at Lady Helton's, at three o'clock on the afternoon, of March 15. When they arrived at Lady Helton's house, Bradford, Lady Helton's butler was there to direct them to their rooms. Helen was impressed with she saw her room. The walls were a lovely soft blue with cream crown molding adorning the ceiling. She found the entire room restful and knew she would enjoy her time here. The counterpane on the bed was soft yellow with pale blue piping around the edge and there were mounds of lovely soft pillows. She could just imagine lying on the bed reading a good book. After she freshened up, she went back downstairs to the drawing room.

As she entered the room, Lady Helton came over to her, gave her a hug and a kiss on the cheek, and said, "I'm so pleased you could stay with me for the season. We're going to have a wonderful time. I have a great many activities planned for us. How is my dear Melody?"

Helen returned Lady Helton's hug then sat down on the sofa and said, "Melody sends her regards and she's doing well. Both Melody and Henry are so excited about the baby and they're impatient for its arrival. You would think it's their first child. Of course, in some ways it is for Henry, since he missed Mary Elizabeth's birth."

Lady Helton sat down next to Helen, smoothing down the skirt of her pale pink day dress, she replied, "I'm so happy for both of them. They've gone through so much and now deserve to have some happiness in their lives. Oh by the way, I've made an appointment for us at Madame Devy's tomorrow, so we can all freshen up our wardrobes for the season. I do hope Kathryn can find time to participate in the season this year. I know how important her art is to her, but she still needs to have fun! Ah, here she is now." Lady Helton went over, embraced Kathryn, gave her a kiss and said, "Hello my dear, don't you look lovely. Are you all settled? I hope your room suits you?"

Kathryn shyly returned her hug and kiss, then quietly replied, "Oh yes, Lady Helton my room is lovely and I know I'll be very comfortable here. I hope I didn't keep you waiting long?"

"Oh no my dear, we were just chatting as you came in. I'll just call for our tea." Lady Helton rang the bell and Bradford came in with the tea tray. Then Lady Helton continued, "As I just explained to Helen, I've made an appointment for us tomorrow with Madame Devy so we can add to our wardrobes for the season. When do you start your classes at the Art Institute?" she asked. "I do hope you'll be able to join us. After all, you'll still need to freshen up your wardrobe, even if most of your time is spent at the Institute."

"I don't start my instruction until next Monday, so I'll be happy to go with you." As Kathryn took her seat, she straightened the skirt of her pale lilac tea gown and added, "I do need a few new dresses and various other accessories so I look forward to it. I just love Madame Devy's designs."

Once they finished their tea, they went to their rooms to rest before dinner. Dinner was quite enjoyable that evening and Lady Helton shared with them all the latest gossip. Helen had never been much of a gossip, but it was nice to hear about what was going on in town. The season was just getting started, so they had not missed any of the balls or parties.

The next morning they went to Bond Street to do their shopping. Helen ordered quite a few new dresses and evening gowns and so did Kathryn. Helen picked out a particularly fetching silvery blue silk evening gown. As she held the fabric up to her creamy white complexion, she knew it complimented her brilliant blue eyes and would look marvelous when it was finished. Once they were through with their shopping, they went to Gunter's to have their famous shaved ham sandwiches and ices. Gunter's was an extremely popular place to go. Many members of the ton went there on a regular basis during the season, and of course, their ices were superb. If you wanted to see who had already arrived for the season, Gunter's was the place to go. After they had lunch, they took a drive through Hyde Park and again saw several people they knew. After their drive, they returned to the house to get ready for the evening's entertainment. Lady Helton was taking them to a play in Drury Lane. The play they were to see was *As You like It*, which was one of Helen's favorite Shakespeare plays.

This season was particularly important to Helen because she just knew she was going to bring Hanford, the Duke of Somerset up to scratch. She had been dreaming of him ever since the end of last season. If she were able to get him to propose, it would be amazing, because he had never shown any signs of being interested in marriage in past seasons. While she had never wanted for beaus, Hanford was the first man that had ever truly interested her. Helen was also looking forward to seeing her friends again. She was very popular with all the other young people because she was such a friendly, fun loving young woman.

The next morning, Helen was up early; she hastily completed her morning ablutions and went down to breakfast. As she enjoyed her morning meal, she thought about the upcoming evening with anticipation. They were going to Lady Crawford's Ball and she was excited about seeing Hanford again. She could not wait to dance with him because he danced so divinely. Helen wondered if he had missed her and if he would try to kiss her again. They had kissed at the end of last season and she had found it to be quite titillating. *Oh, she needed to stop woolgathering, because she had quite a few things planned for the day, and she wanted to give herself plenty of time to get ready for the ball.* This was so unlike her, but of course, she had never felt this way about someone before. *Oh, she hoped Hanford would be there tonight.*

Lady Crawford's Ball was one of the first of the season. Most of the ton must have decided to attend because the ballroom was extremely crowded. Lady Crawford should be pleased, because her ball was definitely a crush. Helen surreptitiously glanced around the ballroom looking for Hanford. At first she did not see him, but then she saw him dancing, with of all people, Lady Penelope. They appeared to be in a deep conversation and she wondered what they could be talking about so intently. Lady Penelope was the daughter of the Earl of Stanton and she was supposed to have married Henry at one time, because their estates bordered each other and Helen's father had greatly desired the match. Of course, Henry had fallen in love with Melody, so the match never happened. Lady Penelope was a witch and Helen had never cared for her at all. She wondered how well Hanford knew her.

She turned to Kathryn and asked, "Do you see his grace dancing with Lady Penelope? I didn't know they even knew each other. I wonder how well they know each other. Oh, I hope he sees me and he asks me to dance. I'm just dying to dance with him again, because he's such a wonderful dancer."

After the Duke of Somerset finished dancing with Lady Penelope, he came over to her and said, "Good evening Lady Helen. It's a pleasure to see you again. How was your time in the country this past winter?"

Helen gazed at him with delight in her startling blue eyes and replied, "I always enjoy my time at Sanderford Park, but I'm looking forward to having a wonderful time, now that I'm here in London for the season. Since my brother and his wife are expecting a blessed event in May, I'm staying with Lady Helton and she has quite a few entertainments planned for my sister Kathryn and I. Did you enjoy your time in the country?"

"Yes, but it was not as enjoyable as your time was, I am sure. I stayed very busy, what with running all my estates. I spent quite a bit of my time traveling from one holding to another. I will actually find the season relaxing compared to what I have been doing. By the way, you look lovely tonight. Do you have a waltz available for me?"

Helen coyly glanced at him and said, "The supper dance is open would you like that one?"

Hanford looked deeply into her eyes and Helen felt little flutters deep in the pit of her stomach as he replied, "That would be lovely. I would like to take you driving with me tomorrow at four o'clock, would you be available?"

With a questioning, tone in her voice, she said, "Yes, that would be splendid. I noticed you dancing with Lady Penelope. She's a neighbor of mine and I was wondering . . . if you have known her for a long time?"

Hanford arrogantly raised his eyebrow and replied, "One of my smaller estates is close to her home and I know her father quite well, so I have known her for years. Well, if you will excuse me I am going to the card room. I look forward to our dance later."

Helen watched him as he left the ballroom and worried that she may have made a mistake asking him about Lady Penelope. He had cooled slightly after she had asked him about her. Trying to put these thoughts out of her mind, she turned and joined the conversation that Lady Helton was having with her friends.

Helen danced several sets with some of her beaus from last season and was having a pleasant evening. She was impatient for the supper dance, so she could dance with Hanford. She had spoken with Susan, Lady Hastings and they were going to St. Mark's Orphanage tomorrow morning. She had been volunteering there ever since Melody got her involved with it several years before. In fact, it was due to Melody that she had become such good friends with Susan. Finally, the supper dance arrived and Hanford came to get her.

When Hanford approached her for their dance, she could tell by his expression he was glad to see her, so maybe she had been wrong to think it had bothered him when she asked him about Lady Penelope. The supper dance was the most important one of the evening, not only did you get to dance with your partner: you had supper with him also. As the strains of the waltz concluded, she realized she had enjoyed dancing with him just as much as last year. They went into the supper room where they sat at one of the small white linen draped tables. Hanford returned from the buffet table with plates filled with shaved ham sandwiches, lobster patties and finger sandwiches. After they finished eating, Hanford asked, "Would you like to take a stroll on the terrace? It has grown quite stuffy in here."

Helen smiled as she said, "Yes, I would enjoy that. It is quite warm this evening." As they strolled around the terrace, Helen looked up at the sky and said, "It's a lovely evening tonight and look at all the stars. Don't they seem to be brighter than usual? I always love the night sky and if I see a shooting star I make a wish."

Hanford looked directly into Helen's beautiful blue eyes and said, "I agree; it is a beautiful evening. I was hoping I would see you here tonight. I enjoyed spending time with you last year and hope we can do that again this year. You look so lovely in the moonlight . . . it illuminates your radiant skin and I just have to touch you."

Hanford pulled her into his arms, touched her face and then he kissed her. Helen felt her heartbeat accelerate, as he deepened his kiss. She gasped and he slid his tongue into her mouth. No one had ever kissed her like this and her knees grew weak from all the sensations that were running through her. He took his hand and gently cupped her breast, and then squeezed her nipple through the bodice of her gown. She felt as if she would swoon from the excitement of it all. Just as he started to slide his hand into the décolletage of her dress, she heard a noise. She felt him begin to pull back and she was disappointed that he was ending their embrace, but of course, it was just as well that he stopped. Helen would die if she ended up compromised. As much as she wanted to marry Hanford, she would not want it forced on them.

Hanford stepped back and asked, "Did you hear something? We need to return to the ballroom before anyone notices how long we have been gone. Come my dear; let me escort you back to Lady Helton."

Lady Helton was sitting with her friends when they returned to the ballroom and Hanford took his leave, once she was back with Lady Helton. Helen watched him as he left the ballroom. Surely, he must return her regard, because that kiss had been simply marvelous and she was just sorry he had ended it, when they heard that noise. At least she knew she would be seeing him tomorrow, when he came to pick her up for their drive.

When they returned to the house, she told Lady Helton goodnight and went up to bed. Once Sally, her maid, helped her into her night rail, she told her to go on to bed. She sat down at her dressing table and began to brush her thick red gold hair until it shone. She had cut it short this past winter and while sometimes she missed her long hair, most of the time she enjoyed the freedom her short hair gave her. As she climbed into bed, she thought about the evening and she knew her feelings had grown much stronger for Hanford. She wondered where that kiss would have led, if they had not heard that noise. She probably should have protested when he touched her breast, but it felt so exciting, she had not wanted him to stop. Of course, she was not sure what would have come next, because he was the first man she had ever allowed to take such liberties. As she heard the clock strike two, she closed her eyes, and drifted off to sleep.

The next morning, she went about her morning ablutions and Sally laid out her new day dress, which was a soft pale blue with white trim. She was pleased with how nice the dress looked on her and it certainly brought out the color of her eyes. She was due to meet Susan so she hurriedly finished getting ready. They had arranged to go to the orphanage and Helen enjoyed playing with all the children. Whenever she spent time with them, she remembered how much she enjoyed playing with her nieces and nephews.

When she entered the breakfast room, Kathryn was already there. Helen went to the sideboard and filled her plate with sausages, coddled eggs and a muffin, then took a seat across from Kathryn. "Where were you most of the evening, last night? I never saw you at all last evening, from the time we arrived, until we left the ball. Have you met someone interesting?"

As Kathryn toyed with her eggs, she replied, "I spend most of the evening talking to Lord Walling. He's an art connoisseur and has quite a collection. He's offered to let me see his collection and Lady Helton said we could go to his home this morning. I can't wait to see it. I also danced quite a bit and I actually had a very pleasant evening. What about you, what did you do most of the evening?"

Helen took a bite of her muffin, then wiped her mouth with her napkin and said, "I danced the supper dance with the Duke of Somerset and we took a stroll on the terrace. I think he returns my regard, because he kissed me and asked me to go driving with him this afternoon."

With a wary expression on her face, Kathryn replied, "Helen you need to be careful. I don't know that you should have let him kiss you. If anyone had seen you kissing, you would have ended up compromised. I know you care about him a great deal, but I don't trust him. Something just doesn't seem right with him."

"Oh Kathryn you're wrong. The duke is a very kind and sincere person. He would never do anything to hurt me. You just wait and see. He'll be asking me to marry him very soon, because I'm sure he returns my regard." Helen had finished her breakfast by this time so she stood up and said, "Well, I need to leave, because I'm meeting Susan at the orphanage at ten o'clock. Are you interested in coming with me?"

Kathryn rolled her eyes and with an exasperated tone, she replied, "Remember . . . I'm going to Lord Walling's house this morning with Lady Helton. I'll go with you next time. Enjoy your drive with the duke, but . . . be careful."

Helen hurried up to her room to get her pelisse, and then she left for St. Mark's. She took Sally and the footman, Charles with her for propriety's sake. Since it was such a lovely day, she decided to walk. Susan was already waiting for her when she arrived at the orphanage and Helen rushed over to her as she said, "Sorry if I'm a little late. I misjudged the time. Since the weather was so pleasant today, I decided to walk. I hope you haven't been waiting long. Did you have a nice evening last night?

With her usual enthusiasm, Susan replied, "I just got here, so no, I haven't been waiting long. I had an excellent time last night. I enjoyed seeing several of my friends and the food was excellent. I saw you dancing with the Duke of Somerset last night and the supper dance at that! It's not often that he dances the supper dance. What's going on between the two of you?"

"Oh Susan it was so exciting. He's such a wonderful dancer and I think I'm falling in love with him. We went for a walk on the terrace after supper and I . . . let him kiss me," Helen answered with a dreamy look in her eyes.

Shocked, Susan asked, "My goodness, Helen where were you when he kissed you? That was certainly very bold of him. Is that the first time he has kissed you or did he kiss you last year too?"

Helen hesitated, but then she said, "Well, he did kiss me once last year at the end of the season, but this kiss was quite different, much more exciting! It made me feel tingly all over and I can't wait for him to do it again!"

"Helen, you need to be very careful. I don't want to see you get hurt. The duke has avoided marriage for many years, so he could be toying with you. Please protect yourself; I would hate it if you got your hopes up only to have them dashed," she replied, with a worried look on her face.

Helen did not want to hear anymore talk like this, so she firmly replied, "Well, I believe he's serious in his intentions towards me. He would never toy with my affections, because he just isn't that type of man. I don't understand why you and Kathryn can't just be happy for me!" Helen looked up, saw the children coming out and said, "I don't want to talk about this anymore and the children are coming anyway."

They had a pleasant time playing with the children and as they were leaving, they agreed to meet again in three days. After a pleasurable walk back, Helen arrived home just in time for luncheon. Lady Helton and Kathryn had returned from Lord Walling's and Kathryn was raving about all the incredible objets d' art in his collection. She was also getting very excited about starting the Art Institute on Monday. Helen was happy for her, because she knew her art meant a great deal to her. It did seem that Kathryn was quite obsessed with her art, but Helen hoped she would still take time to enjoy the season. After luncheon, Bradford handed her a letter and it was from Melody. She wrote that she missed them, but that she hoped they were having a wonderful time in London. The children were all healthy and growing like weeds. Henry was getting nervous about the baby. The waiting was extremely difficult for him and there were still almost two months before the child was due to make its appearance.

The duke arrived promptly at four o'clock for their drive. Hanford looked so handsome today in his deep gray dress coat and light gray embroidered waistcoat, which made his unusual silver eyes sparkle. His snowy white cravat was tied in an intricate pattern and he had on black breeches and black tasseled Hessian boots. As usual, Hanford was dressed in the height of fashion, which was one of the things she liked best about him. As he drove his high perch phaeton through Hyde Park, they talked and laughed the entire time. Helen could not help noticing all the gorgeous flowers scattered around the park. The scent from all these flowers was intoxicating.

Hanford pulled back on the reins to slow the horses down, then said, "Lady Helen I'm enjoying our drive and I hope we can do this quite often this season. You look very pretty today. The sun is shining so brightly, it brings out the gold in your beautiful hair. How are you enjoying the season so far?"

"Why thank you, your grace." Helen was so pleased he had noticed her appearance and awarded him a brilliant smile as she continued, "The season has been quite enjoyable so far. We went to Drury Lane the other night and saw the Shakespeare play *As You like it*, and it was wonderful. We have also gone to the opera. I have always loved music ever since I was a small child. I play the pianoforte, but I don't sing. I leave the singing to my sister-in-law the duchess; she has an amazing voice. I always think of angels when I hear her sing."

"I must hear the duchess some time," he said. "I play the pianoforte as well. I find it very relaxing after a difficult day in Parliament. I have been working on getting a bill passed and I'm getting quite a bit of opposition from the Whigs. I don't want to bore you so enough about that. Let's just enjoy the rest of our drive."

The only problem with the drive was that it was over much too quickly for Helen. When they returned to Lady Helton's house, he helped her down out of the phaeton and he held her longer than was necessary. Every time Hanford touched her, she felt such a strong connection to him. She knew . . . she was falling in love with him.

Edwards Brothers Malloy
Thorofare, NJ USA
August 29, 2014